FOR THE PRICE

Love In Vancouver
Book Three

JEN-LEA MERCY

Author's Note

Each book I write is special in some way, but never have I been through so much whilst writing one. Over the course of the year that it took to craft Frankie and Evan's love story, I have hit hurdle after hurdle. I've had numerous heartbreaking moments in my personal life, and because of this, my mental health suffered. There were two or three months where I worried I wouldn't make it through. My writing—my favorite thing in the world, my passion, my coping mechanism at the best and worst of times—suffered for it. Days turned into weeks of staring at a blank page, or of not even opening my laptop at all.

Frankie and Evan were less helpful than you might think of getting me back in the saddle, so to speak. They are two of the most stubborn characters I've ever had the pleasure of getting to know. There were moments where I felt like Noah in *The Notebook*, screaming, "What do you want?"

Thankfully, a few things helped me not give up. My fellow sprinting authors (thank you Lisa and Katie), the wonderful class I looked forward to each Saturday with Tammy, Finn, and the rest of the students in the GCLS writing academy, and my sweet book-loving friends Amber and Dianna. THANK YOU.

Let me say one thing more. Frankie and Evan haven't had an easy life, and they don't fall in love over candlelight and serenades. They go hard, but, if I did my job, you'll be cheering them on every step of the way. Expect a slower burn with a satisfying amount of spice and kink. Expect angst and difficult story themes. Don't forget to hop over to my website and check the trigger warnings if you're at all concerned.

I hope you enjoy the ride and fall in love with Daddy Frankie and her little thief as much as I have.

Peace and Love,

Jen-Lea

You can find *For The Price's* music playlist inside the back-matter.

FOREWORD

The sex scenes in *For The Price* include on page BDSM kink, such as restraints, toys, spanking, bondage frames, and a femme Daddy who likes to strap up.

For The Price also touches on some sensitive, off-page topics and on-page fight scenes. If this concerns you, please check the trigger warnings before continuing. These can be found on my website @ https://jenleamercy.com

***If you're struggling with thoughts of self-harm or suicide, or are a survivor of SA and struggling, please reach out to someone who can help.*

DEDICATION

This one is for all of us who have learned to trust someone's
touch again.
It takes time and healing to leave the past where it belongs.
This is **your** moment. Keep up the good work.

CHAPTER 1

Frankie

DRUNK MEN PISSED HER off.

Okay, plenty of things pissed Frankie O'Rourke off, but drunk, belligerent, homophobic men were top tier on her list.

"I'm just saying, why do the gays get a whole month? Isn't it enough that we let them get married?" The man jerked his thumb over his shoulder, gesturing to her off-shift bar manager, Sloane, and her group of friends sitting in the back corner. Sloane and Taunya had pulled out all the stops, decorating the friends' table and surrounding area with engagement banners and pictures of the couple, Abi and Tess. "Why do they need to wave it in everyone's face with a parade?"

Frankie narrowed her gaze at the man. The pub was busy and loud, but clearly not loud enough if she could still hear him where she sat at the edge of the bar. He was seated several stools down from her, drinking a tumbler of Frankie's best whiskey. He had an open brown suede jacket over a restrictive black shirt that covered his rounded belly, and for the last hour, Frankie had watched his mustache dip into his drink more than once. His chubby, whiskered cheeks were flushed, and not for the first time, Frankie imagined him in a police lineup. She had little tolerance for people like him.

Closing her laptop, she slid off the stool and rounded the bar counter, coming to a stop in front of where he was still running his mouth to her staff. She placed a hand on Andy's shoulder, leaning in so she wouldn't be overheard. "Let me handle this asshole."

Andy nodded and stepped aside. Frankie skipped her three-strike rule—the one she typically used for customers stepping out of line—and snatched the man's tumbler out of his grasp mid-drink.

"Hey, gimmie that back, bitch!"

Frankie curled her lip at him, the pulse in her throat thumping like a jackrabbit on the hunt. Heat coiled in her veins, and it took every ounce of willpower she had not to throw the drink—glass and all—into his reddening face. Instead, she calmly handed it off to Andy without taking her eyes off the stranger. "The only bitch here is you. Now get the fuck out of my pub."

"You can't throw me out. I'm a paying customer. I paid for that drink!"

Frankie reached into her blazer for the thin bundle of folded bills she'd placed there earlier, pulling a twenty off the top before returning the rest to her pocket. She slapped the money on the bar counter in front of him. "Now leave and don't bother coming back."

"You've got some nerve, bitch. Someone oughta teach you some manners," the man spat, pointing his finger at her. Patrons occupying seats around him perked up at the idle threat. A young woman, close to Andy's age, slipped off the stool and backed away, clearly afraid. But not Frankie.

Nothing can scare me. Not anymore.

To her surprise, the man listened. She and Andy watched as he took the money and slid off the stool, tossing them one last scowl before retreating out the front door. Letting a soft sigh escape, Frankie relaxed her shoulders until another notion popped into her head. Her gaze flew to the round table in the corner again, squinting to see who was there.

Where is McCoy?

She and her girlfriend, Sawyer, should have been there by now. Frankie's chest tightened, and she eyed the front of the pub again. What if they met the drunk out on the street and the situation escalated?

Ugh, she was being ridiculous. She would have picked up on the man's intentions if they had been more than just loose-lipped and ignorant.

"I feel bad for people like him," Andy said, moving away to pour the man's drink—Frankie's *expensive*, top-shelf whiskey—in the sink before putting the glass in the dirty dishpan.

"Don't waste your empathy," Frankie replied, returning to her portable workstation. As she reopened the laptop, her gaze flitted around the pub once more. McCoy's arrival was part of the reason she was reviewing her liquor order here instead of in her office. Not that she would admit that to anyone. Since she'd fallen in love with Sawyer, McCoy came to the pub less and less. Frankie was happy for her, truly, but it didn't stop the burst of nostalgia she felt anytime they were in the same room together.

It had been months since she'd had reason to take her flogger off the hook in her playroom. Or felt the rush she got taking her lover from behind with a spreader bar fastened to their ankles, and their hands tied behind their back while their face pressed into the mattress. A week was a long time, let alone months, when Frankie was used to having a sub at her beck and call. Or rather, having *McCoy* at her beck and call. Frankie clenched her teeth.

Why did she continue to torture herself?

Andy appeared in front of her, sliding a mug of Irish coffee Frankie's way. He bent over, resting his elbows on the counter and peering at her. "Seriously, boss, imagine how stupid he'd have felt if he'd known he was talking to a trans man that whole time?" Andy shook his head, his black curls dancing with the movement, and laughed. "I mean, that's assuming he was generalizing the entire alphabet mafia."

"Let me know if he shows up here again." Frankie picked up her drink, the whipped cream on top coating her upper lip as she sipped the whiskey coffee. It was the only drink she allowed herself while on the clock. "This is perfect, Andy. Thank you."

"I will, and you're welcome." Andy rapped his knuckles on the counter once and left her to contemplate. The pub was getting busier, and Frankie knew she'd need to jump in and help sooner rather than later. She had two servers behind the bar, two on the floor, and Dakota and Rain cooking in the kitchen, but an extra hand was always welcome. It wasn't as if she had anything more pressing to do with her night, except wallow in her sour jealousy and steal glances at the table in the back. She loved love, she really did. It just had never been for her. The whole 'opening yourself up for more hurt later on' had never appealed to her.

Once Frankie's drink was finished, she carried her laptop past the right side of the bar and down the hallway toward her office. A lone figure was leaning against the doorjamb outside her office as she approached, their clumsy fingers jiggling the handle. They were on the shorter side, lean, and at first sight, nothing about them felt threatening to Frankie.

"Can I help you?"

"Yeah, why's this bathroom locked? I gotta piss."

Understanding dawned on Frankie, and she let out a faint laugh. "You wouldn't believe how many times this happens. Washrooms are down the hall a bit more on the right."

The man, whom she could see clearer now, swayed on his feet as he pushed off her doorjamb. "Shit location," he said before sauntering off.

"You're telling me," Frankie said, watching him a moment longer. Then she unlocked her office door, stepping inside to put her laptop on the desk. Then, as an afterthought, she transferred the bundle of bills from her jacket to her safe on the floor. She set the cash next to her business ownership papers and her 9mm SIG Sauer handgun before locking the safe again.

With any luck, the rest of her night would go smoother.

Business had picked up when Frankie returned to the bar. She quickly jumped into the thick of things, sending Lian out to the floor to take table orders while she and Andy manned the drink orders. For early December, it was unusually warm inside the pub—a problem that was exaggerated by the white and grey striped blazer she wore.

"Who turned the heat on this late in the year?" she groused. Hints of grapefruit, lime, and butterscotch wafted over Frankie as she poured her specialty draft ale into a chilled glass. She tapped the keg, unable to stop the smile when she noticed it was almost empty. Nothing lifted Frankie's spirits more than seeing her personalized take on an old favorite Irish pale ale repeatedly sold out. Creating a microbrewery in the basement was the first thing she'd done when she'd taken over O'Rourke's seven years ago.

"Couldn't tell you, boss," Andy replied, nudging Frankie as he went to the cooler. "By the way, Cash said the band's setting up by eight."

"Okay, great." Friday and Saturday nights were Frankie's busiest nights, and she usually tried to bring in live music on one of the days. She handed off the drinks to Lian before turning to Andy once more. "How's Claire enjoying all the late nights?"

"Loves it," Andy laughed, cracking two cans of beer open for a waiting patron. "She's only part-time actually, but still stoked about getting to play bass somewhere besides our living room."

"I can imagine." Frankie had known Andy's girlfriend long enough to know she had a real talent for music. It was good that she was finally getting stage time, even if she considered it a mere hobby.

The conversation came to a natural halt once more, and Frankie approached a petite butch patiently waiting in the same spot she'd been sitting earlier. "Hey, are you waiting for a table, or is here fine?"

"Here's good. Can I get a whiskey? Straight and on the rocks."

"Depends." Frankie sized the stranger up, trying to gauge how old they might be. They were small and thin, which was obvious even underneath the faded black leather jacket they wore. Their nose was crooked, like it had been broken a time or two, and they had a small face tattoo of a sword close to one ear. When she caught sight of them head-on, Frankie did a double-take, her mouth falling open a little. Unbelievably gorgeous mismatched eyes stared up at her. They were set behind an older pair of frameless glasses. Clearing her throat, it took a moment before Frankie found her voice. "You, umm, you have ID?"

"For real?" The stranger looked taken aback, a frown in place as they reached into their back pocket to retrieve their wallet for Frankie. "I'm twenty-four next week."

"Anyone who looks under thirty, I'm afraid. Thanks." Frankie accepted the card, sneaking another peek at the stranger before examining the Toronto driver's license of an ... Evan Landry, who had a birthday the following Tuesday. Frankie smiled at the "DIC" label under eye color, noting once again Evan's one brown and one blue eye. *Fascinating.* She returned the ID and clasped her hands together. "Now, what's your poison?"

"Poison?" Evan echoed, reaching up to scratch the back of their straw-blonde buzz cut.

"Yes, what's your go-to brand, Evan, or is this your first time trying whiskey?" Something about Evan had Frankie leaning in closer, not wanting to miss their response due to the clamor of ice and dishes clanging and patrons laughing. Evan intrigued her, and the shy way they cut their gaze from Frankie's to seek out the drinks menu on the wall behind her tugged low in Frankie's belly.

Despite wearing glasses, Evan squinted at the menu board. Seconds passed, possibly a minute, and a slow blush crept along Evan's exposed throat and cheeks the longer Frankie watched them. If Frankie had to guess, Evan either couldn't handle the pressure of an audience, or they simply had never drunk whiskey before. Why come into a pub, alone, without at least doing a little research first?

Had the ID been fake?

Frankie scrutinized Evan closer, noting the minor buildup of perspiration above the cupid's bow of their upper lip. A small scar, almost indistinguishable under the dimmed lights, sat an inch or so from the center of their lip.

"Want to know what my favorite is?" Satisfaction bloomed inside Frankie as Evan's stunning gaze fell to the generous cleavage straining against the buttons of her blouse. She'd known there was a reason she'd put on this outfit that morning. And despite the surrounding chatter, there was no mistaking Evan's sharp intake of breath. She wasn't sure yet what Evan identified as, but they were far from straight. The belief brought out a smug smile. This is what she'd needed in her life—a little harmless flirting to take her attention off ... other things.

"Sure, shoot."

Frankie stilled, Evan's final word catching her off guard. It wasn't one she was used to hearing, not anymore. Not since ...

Stop.

Nothing about that life was hers anymore, memories be damned. She forced out a chuckle, one that was low and breathy and had Evan's gaze lowering to her parted lips. "I love the fruit and spice sensation on my tongue from the sherry inside the Bushmills Irish Whiskey. It goes down smooth and is perfect for wintertime or, in your case," Frankie winked, "almost birthdays." She'd named off an affordable yet respectable brand, as she had a feeling it would be more in Evan's price range.

"Sure, yeah, that one sounds good." Evan gave her a small grin, just wide enough that one canine peeked out past their sensual upper lip.

Frankie wanted to moan. Had anything as simple as a twitch of someone's lips captivated her so thoroughly before?

"Be right back," she said, and pulled out of what felt like their private bubble amidst the bustle of her usual Saturday night. The moment the trance broke, Frankie bumped into Andy who was walking past with a tray of drinks. "Oh!" Frankie grabbed his arm in one hand and steadied the tray with the other.

Andy laughed. "Speedy moves, boss."

"Sorry for the almost tackle," Frankie replied, disengaging from her employee to get a start on Evan's drink. There was a hum of awareness tingling over her as she reached for the bottle of Irish whiskey on the top shelf. Evan was watching her. Evan was, well, looks wise, certainly no McCoy, but try telling that to Frankie's starving libido. It had been months since she'd topped someone, watched them come apart on her fingers, and something about Evan called to her in a way no one else had in a long time.

"I'm Frankie," she offered, setting the drink in front of Evan. Reconsidering, she added, "She/her pronouns." It was another thing she'd been meaning to do up for her staff after McCoy had suggested it. Considering she pulled in at least 50 percent queer clientele, and a good part of the other fifty being allies, it made sense to establish name tags with individual pronouns so that everyone could be as comfortable as possible.

"Evan, they/them pronouns. And thanks."

Frankie wasn't certain if Evan was thanking her for the drink or the added respect, but when they grinned wider this time, she no longer cared. The canine she'd seen earlier was noticeably longer than the other, and one of Evan's bottom teeth was crooked. Frankie wanted to test that sharp edge on her tongue.

You're thirty-eight years old, for god's sake. Fucking act like it, she reprimanded herself.

They chatted for a little longer before work pulled Frankie away. She helped her servers plate trays of appetizers and drinks and took a few orders when she relieved Lian for a break. Excitement over meeting Evan had put distractions of McCoy to rest, or at least until Frankie finally caught sight of her about ten feet away. She was on her knees before her girlfriend in the middle of the pub. Shock permeated Frankie, and she snapped her gaping mouth shut as she watched the scene unfold before her. Witnessed Sawyer cupping McCoy's cheek like she was the most precious woman in the world. No matter that she couldn't hear the conversation, Frankie knew it wasn't a simple declaration of love happening between them. No, McCoy never did anything simply. That was her way of submitting to Sawyer, right out in the open for anyone and everyone to see.

Tightness enveloped Frankie's chest, like fine pinpricks pressing into a pincushion. She reached up to rub the ache, swallowed down the burn in her throat, and strode away.

CHAPTER 2

Evan

HOW CAN SOMEONE ACT so nice and be so fucking evil underneath?

Frankie O'Rourke, the owner of O'Rourke's Pub, was not at all how Evan had imagined these past seven years. Hunched down on their stool, Evan's half-mast gaze trailed Frankie across the room. She was about a hundred times more attractive too. The fading picture Evan had stuck to their prison cell wall, and then in their wallet, hadn't done the evil bitch justice. Nor had the week of surveillance Evan had done before moving onto phase two of their plan. Seeing her up close and personal was an entirely different feeling from watching at a safe distance.

Sitting there while Frankie shamelessly flirted with them had Evan wanting to jump up and throttle the woman. What kind of professional leaned all over the counter with their cleavage on display? That had been unexpected—both the distracting visual and Evan's traitorous body.

Does she seriously not recognize me?

It had been what Evan was banking on all along. Really, they should be relieved they hadn't been found out, but the realization of Frankie's utter self-involvement was a bitter pill to swallow. Did she have no remorse for what she'd done?

"Hey, you want another?"

Evan blinked out of their daze, sat straighter in the seat, and took in the guy waiting expectantly behind the bar. *Andy Chaffey, twenty-six years of age, originally from Newfoundland, lives with his girlfriend Claire across town, and began transitioning as soon as he was of age.* Evan held back the sly grin itching to break free. Social media was a fountain of information if you knew how to dig for it.

"Erm." Evan was already thinking about how they could stretch the allotted funds while in Vancouver. But there was a price to surveillance. They couldn't very well loiter without spending more. Hopefully, their work wouldn't last longer than a couple of weeks, and then their contact back home would send them a plane ticket to get the fuck out of Dodge. Evan gave Andy a slight nod. "One more won't hurt."

"For sure. I'll whip you up another." Andy's smile was friendly enough, and from what Evan had seen in the last week, he seemed too good to be working for the likes of Frankie. That went for the rest of her staff. Frankie's bar manager, Sloane Miller, was one of the sweetest women Evan had ever met. They had spoken to her a hand-ful of times in the last week, always when Frankie wasn't around, and Evan genuinely liked her. If they weren't there for revenge, Evan might have been tempted to stick around and get to know Sloane on a deeper level.

Andy returned with Evan's drink, and they thanked him before casually glancing around the pub again. Sloane was at a table with her friends, drinks and food all around, and looking so happy that a pang of jealousy hit Evan. It had always been that way for them, even as a kid chasing after their older brother and his friends. Evan had never fit in the way most people did. They'd always been on the outside looking in, desperately wishing they could turn on the charm like their stepfather and brother were able to. Conning someone took a social intuition Evan lacked.

And yet Cecil expected them to do exactly that with Frankie. Con her, and then ...

Fuck. Evan swallowed hard, tilted their glass back, and finished the drink in one gulp.

Pulling out the wallet that their brother had given them for their fifteenth birthday, Evan traced a chapped thumbnail over the worn leather. It was old and frayed, much like Caleb's jacket Evan now wore. It didn't fit them as well as it had Caleb at twenty-three. Years ago, Caleb would joke about Evan hitting a growth spurt one day, but besides their chest enlarging in a way that gave them dysphoria more times than not, and their hips widening slightly, not much else had changed on their body. Well, except for the hair.

Maybe that's why Frankie didn't recognize me.

If shaving their head was all it took to throw a bloodthirsty hound off their trail, it was probably a good thing Frankie had fallen out of her previous line of work.

"Where can I find the washrooms?" Evan asked, placing a twenty-dollar bill on the counter for Andy when he walked past once more.

The bartender swiped the bill up and jerked a thumb over his shoulder. "Thanks, b'y," he said, and Evan grinned as his Newfoundlander accent became more evident as he said the slang word. It was pronounced like "bye", but as far as Evan could tell from their time eavesdropping, it meant the same thing as "friend" or "mate". "Washroom's 'round the corner and down the hall a bit."

"Thanks, man."

Evan slipped off the bar stool and past Frankie, circling the pub without her noticing. Watching the confident way she interacted with customers set Evan on edge. Frankie O'Rourke was a wolf in sheep's clothing.

And that meant no one was safe.

CHAPTER 3

Frankie

"HAPPY BIRTHDAY, EM." FRANKIE swallowed, staring down at the tombstone before her. The previous flower arrangement she'd placed over the headstone had disappeared, but thankfully, the hook was still secure. She took two steps and set the artificial flowers inside the clasp. They weren't as pretty as the ones Frankie brought in the warmer months, but she knew Emily wouldn't mind. The site was recently groomed, she noticed, with its grave blanket now in place to add some comfort during the winter months. A new photograph of Emily had replaced the old one.

"Auntie B must have stopped in," Frankie continued, studying the picture for a moment. Emily's youthful features smiled up at her, cheeks spattered with freckles and ginger hair in a ponytail. She was lovely, just as Frankie remembered all those years ago. Except now, the blinding pain of everything she'd lost had faded into a dull, persistent ache.

Squatting down, Frankie used her glove to brush the fresh snow off Emily's gravestone. "One day at a time, Em, I promise," she whispered, remembering the vow she'd taken the last day they'd seen each other. "No fear, not anymore."

The sound of boots crunching on wet gravel behind her stilled Frankie. When she turned around, her Aunt Belinda stood a few feet away, tears glistening in her eyes and her hands clutching the lapels of her button-down jacket. "Frankie. It's so good to see you, honey."

Regret gnawed at Frankie as she stood. It had been months since they'd spoken last, longer since they'd seen one another. Frankie was awful at keeping in touch on the best of days, but it was even harder with the wedge she'd thrown into their little family. "Hey, Auntie B."

"You don't have to look ready to run the moment you see me." Auntie B came to stand beside her, reaching for Frankie. Frankie tensed when she felt the gentle caress on her back.

"I'm not," Frankie lied, turning back to Emily's resting place. Their visit today wouldn't be as long after all. She cleared her throat. "I just can't stay. I've got a lot on the go. I'm busy, I can't just drop everything and—"

"When will you stop running, Frankie?" Auntie B placed her hand on Frankie's arm, a pleading look on her face as she searched Frankie's eyes. For what, Frankie never could tell. Maybe that one day she would magically forget and put it all behind her? "She would have wanted you to be happy."

"How would you know?" Frankie wrenched out of her aunt's grip, her throat swelling as the seconds ticked by. A flurry started around them, and Frankie watched as flakes of snow landed on the older woman's hat. A snowflake hit her cheek, melting almost immediately. She swiped the wetness away, swallowing hard. "Emily's dead. She hasn't been able to say what she wants in a very long time."

And it's my fault.

It didn't matter what tale her aunt spun, or how many years went by. A piece of Frankie had broken away that day. She didn't think she could ever get it back, or if she even deserved the chance.

When she arrived at work hours later, it looked as if her staff had slipped into full-on crisis mode hours before, and someone had forgotten to notify her.

"What the hell is going on?"

"Lian called in sick, and Dakota started puking his guts up in the kitchen sink," Sloane announced as she raced past Frankie with a tray of appetizers. At 4 p.m., the tables were filling up fast, Frankie noticed as she glanced around. It was too close to the supper rush for it to be just Rain cooking in the kitchen.

"Can you cook?" she asked and followed Sloane to a table full of college-aged guys.

Sloane scoffed, casting Frankie a stink eye over her shoulder. "Do I look like my sister?" Then she blew out a breath and rolled her eyes, muttering, "Don't answer that."

"Actually, no, not really." In her figure-hugging black long-sleeve shirt, the kind with built-in thumb holes, with a black leather skirt and edgy, punk-style leather boots that went up mid-thigh, it was sometimes hard to fathom that Sloane was McCoy's identical twin. McCoy, who was an irresistible cross between soft butch and masc lesbian, with a 100 percent golden retriever personality.

Realization dawned on her then, and she trailed after Sloane as she led the way to the bar. "You're here. On your day off." Sloane never worked on Sundays. It was actually one of her stipulations when she took the job, one Frankie had respected. "Why didn't anyone call me, for fuck's sake?"

Andy, busily throwing together drink orders, pointed to the waiting tray of beers. "Hey, boss."

Sloane picked up the tray, looked Frankie in the eye, and had the audacity to sigh. "I was gonna call you, but Coy told me not to. She was here too for a while, helping in the kitchen, at least 'til the old ball and chain pulled her away."

Frankie frowned, choosing not to reply to that remark. Apparently, Sloane still wasn't a fan of Sawyer. It wasn't until she was entering the kitchen that the rest of Sloane's words sank in. McCoy hadn't wanted anyone to disturb Frankie, but why?

Surely she doesn't know about Emily. They had been lovers for what seemed like forever some days, but Frankie had never opened up about her past. She'd tried, so many times, but with every attempt came the voice in the back of her head screaming not to.

"Ugh, what a mess." Frankie scanned the mountain of dishes waiting to be washed, with more that had already gone through waiting on the other side. Rain was sweating over the fryer and slinging burgers onto the grill. Quesadillas were burning on the flattop. Frankie quickly washed her hands and pulled on an apron before jumping in to help. Tossing the quesadillas in the garbage, she started anew. She wasn't the best cook. Taking over the pub hadn't been about the kitchen work. It had been about having something to call her own, about building a community who felt safe to let loose. She had purposely hired cooks so that she didn't need to do this part of the job.

"Jesus, how do I flip the fucking thing?" Frankie growled, seconds away from tossing the quesadilla against the wall.

Rain appeared, her deep brown eyes sparkling as she chuckled. She gently nudged Frankie aside. "Quit being so aggressive. Cooking is a delicate process at times."

"I'm calling in reinforcements. Is Nathan back from vacation yet?" Her third cook had requested two weeks off for personal reasons out of province. Frankie knew he wasn't due back until the following week, but damn, a girl could hope.

"Not that I'm aware of. Can you grab the fries? Just lift the—yep, you got it."

Frankie grimaced as the oil splatter came close to ruining her suit. Had she known *this* was what her night would look like, maybe, *just* maybe, she'd have foregone her usual fashion for functionality.

"Great. Now how do you feel about dishing some up onto the plates there?" Rain asked, pointing to the lineup semi-assembled on the nearby counter. "Fries and burger to each one."

Frankie did as instructed, knowing she'd need to dry-clean her suit by the end of this nightmare. One burger slipped off the spatula, shooting toward the dirty floor like a rocket, but at the last minute, Frankie scooped an empty plate under it.

"Probably work better if you take the plate to the burger, not the other way around." Rain giggled. Frankie snapped her tongs at the young woman like they were pincers, which only made the fit of giggles worse.

"I'm taking these out. I need air. And possibly a stiff drink." Frankie didn't wait for Rain to rebuke her, not that she would, and filled the serving tray with the three plates. The moment she left the sweltering kitchen, a gust of cool air hit her rosy cheeks.

"Here, take these," Frankie said as soon as Sloane got close enough. She heaved a sigh, relieved to be rid of the tray even temporarily, and slid behind the bar. Greeting a couple of Sunday regulars who came in for the appetizer special, Frankie's gaze landed on Evan, who stood a few feet away. They were wearing the same jacket and identical jeans as the night before but now held a piece of paper in their hand.

"You're back," Frankie said in a way of greeting, although she didn't stop on her way to the bar sink. She grabbed a glass and filled it with ice and water before guzzling half of it. She sighed, enjoying the cold liquid hydrating her parched throat.

Evan watched her drink, and Frankie had to squelch the flutter in her stomach at the sight of them. After seeing McCoy on her knees for Sawyer the night before, all Frankie had wanted to do was fuck away the deep-seated ache inside her. She was glad Evan was already gone when Frankie sought them out. Had Evan been there and willing, Frankie would have taken them back to her office and had them on their back on her desk in no time.

And I'd be dying with regret right now.

Frankie didn't *do* strangers. She never had. It took a lot to trust someone enough to show them her darker desires or learn that they too had the same longing for scene play and kink. Not to mention, there were sit-down discussions before anything took place, talks of soft and hard limits, needs, wants, and safe words. Just because Evan's entire persona screamed submissive, didn't mean they were aware of it.

"I'm back," Evan said, their voice coming out rather tentative in the loudness of the pub. "I, uh, wanted to drop this off." They held out the paper for Frankie to take.

Frankie scanned the paper, her eyes widening a little in surprise before she darted a glance back to Evan. "A resume?" Damn if this wasn't the best example of what good fortune meant. A laugh bubbled from her chest. "You want to work here?"

Evan shrugged. "I saw the ad in the window. I'm new to town."

Frankie set the resume under the cash register, side-stepping Andy as she got herself a bourbon. It was far too busy to sit and enjoy an Irish coffee right then. "How about a trial run? Starting now. I'm short-staffed and could use the help."

"Erm, okay. I guess, so long as it comes with cash at the end of the night." Evan folded their arms together, looking awkward as hell as Frankie poured a second shot.

"Well, what can you do? Any kitchen experience?"

"I got a few years in the kitchen. Dishwashing mainly, but I can manage my way around the stove okay."

Frankie smiled, lightness filling her chest for the first time all day. "If you'll accept a check, then you've got a deal."

CHAPTER 4

Evan

WHAT AN INTERESTING TURN of events.

Evan couldn't stop grinning. Well, on the inside at least. Considering their resume had next to nothing on it since their incarceration at seventeen—just a few bullshit jobs they'd made up so something was on the page—Evan had doubted Frankie would hire them. The longer they considered it, the more they appreciated the utter stroke of luck this afternoon turned out to be. It was almost a shame they couldn't take credit for Frankie's staff being out sick.

They rinsed off the rack of dirty plates before sliding it into the dishwasher and closing the lid. Despite the apron Evan wore, they were quite damp from the water spray of the last two hours. With Frankie and her cook also in the kitchen, the place bustled with activity. Evan had seen more of the pub and staff tonight than they'd managed to achieve in the last week, not to mention overhearing snippets of conversation as servers came and went.

Too bad none of it's useful in ruining Frankie.

"How you holding up, Evan?"

Evan glanced up from where they were loading the glasses onto the dish rack to see Sloane standing there, an empty platter tray dangling from one hand. She was athletic and sexy. A total femme, all the way to the pink tips she kept in her hair, yet she dressed down on her days off and hit the trails during mountain bike season. The research Evan had done on Frankie's bar manager had been highly entertaining. It appeared that serving drinks and taking orders was just a minuscule fraction of the woman's life.

"Hey, yeah. Good, I mean, this is pretty basic shit." Evan lifted the door open to the dishwasher and pushed in another rack of dirty dishes. In the process, it pushed the clean rack out onto the other side. "Glad to help out."

"Mm-hmm, Frankie met you just in the nick of time. Gotta run." Sloane flashed Evan an appreciative smile, and then she was gone again.

Fuck, she's hot, Evan thought, rolling their lips inward as they watched Sloane disappear through the swing doors, and then corrected themself. *In the most respectful, non-objectifying way, of course.*

When they turned back to the dish pit, Evan caught Frankie staring at them. Her jaw seemed clenched, even from across the kitchen, and when their eyes met, a mask slipped over Frankie's face. The reaction was stifling, and Evan couldn't help but feel completely affronted by it. They bowed their head and got back to work. The dishes were nonstop, which said a lot about how popular O'Rourke's Pub was. Taking Frankie's business down was going to be a challenge.

"Evan, come jump on the fryer so that Rain can go on break," Frankie told them half an hour later.

"Sure thing." Evan stopped at the sink to wash their hands first and then came to stand next to Frankie. It was hard to be around Frankie, knowing what she'd done and what Evan would soon do in retaliation. Their stomach was in knots, but it wasn't due to the flu.

"I don't care how she's taken care of so long as it's not traced back to me. Make her pay, Evan. Kill the bitch. And only then can you see your mother."

Evan bit the inside of their cheek, Cecil's words haunting them at every turn. It had been a long time since they'd seen Leah Landry. Evan knew something was wrong when she'd stopped visiting them in prison, but they only discovered what it was a month and a half ago, after their release.

"Total breakdown … you ruined this family. Your mother tried to kill herself because of you …"

Evan shook themself from the memory. They were prepared to do whatever it took to gain back Cecil's trust and see Leah again, sacrificing anything it took to avenge Caleb.

But murder? And today when Cecil called, he'd pressured Evan to hurry the timeline up. What was he thinking—that Evan was the type to shoot and not plan? *Idiot.*

"Thanks again for the help tonight. I guess it's good that we close at nine on Sundays," Frankie explained as she spread chopped vegetables over a tray of thinly cut fried potatoes. "You okay to work the fryer?"

"Should be." Evan didn't elaborate. Cooking in a prison was significantly different, but seriously, how difficult could lifting and loading a fry basket be? They worked in silence for a time, which Evan was grateful for. They didn't mind the quiet, and it gave them plenty of opportunity to study the femme out of the corner of their eye. Just like last night, she was wearing a suit. They ranged in style and color but always accented her curves perfectly. As a boss, Frankie was direct, fair, and hardworking. She wasn't afraid to smile and treated her staff with respect. But it was all a ruse. It *had* to be.

And it was up to Evan to uncover it.

"So, ah, what made you become a pub owner?" they started, shaking the fry basket before lowering it into the oil again. "You dress like a corporate businesswoman." Or at least from what Evan had seen on TV. Even the prison warden hadn't dressed as well as Frankie. It was as if she had something to prove.

"Do I? So not a drug dealer then?" Frankie bent to pop nachos in the oven, which happened to give Evan a bird's eye view of her exceptionally plump backside. Their gaze narrowed, at once wanting to kick themself for noticing. Frankie turned to them with a smirk. "That's the usual assumption I get from people."

"That didn't cross my mind," Evan said truthfully, but her being a drug dealer would have made sense, especially since her problem-solving skills involved gunplay.

"That's plus one for you then." Frankie's grin lightened the brown in her eyes to a milk chocolate. Evan's breath caught, and they cleared their throat, looking away. "To answer your question, I sort of came into it. My cousin wanted out of the business, and I was looking for a fresh start."

Adoptive cousin.

Evan wanted to puff out their chest at knowing such a personal fact about Frankie. It was kind of a bummer that Cecil had dug up her family history before they could.

When nine o'clock rolled around, Evan was glad. They'd spent as much time as they could safely handle near Frankie, so much that they were trembling to leave.

"Let me pay you, then you can head out."

The sound of Frankie's voice so close behind them made them jump a little. When Frankie reached out to steady Evan, they couldn't hold back their recoil. "Fuck, I'm sorry."

"No, I'm sorry. I didn't mean to scare you." Frankie frowned down at them, genuine concern showing in her eyes. Evan's stomach lurched. "Evan? You look like you've seen a ghost."

"I'm fine." Evan exhaled through their nose and grabbed their jacket. They shrugged it on, not waiting for Frankie, and left the kitchen. They had meant to stop at the bar and wait for payment, but their feet took them out of the pub altogether. Then Evan was running, their work boots slipping now and then on the icy sidewalks. Several people eyed Evan warily as they rushed past, the December chill and a mixture of snow and rain seeping into the open collar of their jacket.

Tears blinded Evan's vision by the time they came across a park a few blocks from Frankie's pub. There was an uncomfortable weight in their chest, and with each swallow, Evan winced at the ball lodged in their throat.

How were they going to manage taking Frankie down? Sometimes it was too much to even be within *touching* distance of her.

"Fuck."

It was closing in on eleven before Evan trudged up the path to the hostel they were staying at while in Vancouver. They'd steered clear of the place as long as possible, knowing they wouldn't have been able to think in the room they were sharing with three women. Their bunk buddies were loud, and for a loner like Evan, to say it sucked was an understatement. *But it sure beats sharing it with three dudes.* And it was a helluva upgrade compared to the tiny, smelly prison cell they'd shared with Rhonda. Not to mention the hostel had delicious hot cooked breakfasts and a patio garden Evan had taken advantage of in the last week. It'd been nice to relax with their sketchbook without anyone bothering them.

When they heard their name being called as they passed the front desk, Evan turned to see the manager waiting with a uniformed security guard.

They frowned. "Yes?"

"I'm sorry to have to do this, but your credit card was declined—"

"The fuck—?"

"—and an anonymous tip called in. Even if you could provide cash or debit at this point, with your criminal background, allowing you to stay would put others at risk. You can no longer be on premises."

"But my stuff—"

"It's all right here for you." The manager pointed to the lone black duffel bag at his feet. "And don't worry, Carson here watched me retrieve it."

"The fuck is going on," Evan muttered, closing the distance between them. They snatched up their bag, slinging it onto their shoulder along with their backpack. To add insult to injury, the manager actually looked apologetic as he handed Evan a blanket and pillow.

"Keep these. It's too late at night to get into the shelter, but if you go early tomorrow, you might get lucky."

Evan scoffed but took the linens anyway. "I dunno what Cecil said to you, but my stepfather's a lying sack of shit. Thanks for nothing."

As Evan strode from the hostel, head held high, they had one thought running tirelessly through their mind.

Cecil can try to rush the schedule all he wants. I'll take Frankie out when I'm good and ready. Fucking asshole.

Chapter 5

Frankie

"Fuck," Frankie groaned, tweaking her pierced nipple. Through her mirror, she watched the bronze bud grow tighter with the attention. Her other nipple still had the clamp over it, restricting circulation around the area. Pain pulsed at each of Frankie's pleasure points, yet she needed more. Her thighs were wet with arousal and lube, but watching in the mirror as she fucked herself wasn't the same high as bringing a sub to orgasm.

Frankie closed her eyes, a trembling sigh escaping as her thumb strummed her swollen sex. She tried to conjure up her usual image while getting herself off, knowing it would help. McCoy's chiseled jaw, lush green eyes, and septum ring over a wide smile appeared. "Fuck, yes. McCoy." *My pet.* Memories of them together filled Frankie. McCoy sitting exactly how Frankie was now, legs spread wide at the edge of the bed, the mirror's reflection capturing every cry of pleasure, every stroke of the dildo into McCoy's sopping wet pussy. At times, there had even been a gag in her mouth, and with each stroke, Frankie had used the crop on McCoy's inner thighs for added stimulation.

"Fuck, yesss." Raking her nails up her thigh, Frankie imagined doing the same to McCoy. The higher she crested, the harder she focused on one singular memory of McCoy. The utter affection and attraction that had been transparent in her green gaze as she knelt on her knees before Frankie.

"Ah, u-ugh, fuuuck." With shaking hands, Frankie released the nipple clamp, and the immediate pain as blood rushed back caused a loud moan to fall from her lips as she climaxed. She fell back onto the bed with a sigh, thighs trembling and pussy still spasming. For several minutes, Frankie lay there, catching her breath. Something had felt different with her lately, and she couldn't pinpoint what exactly. One thing *was* clear; fucking herself into oblivion no longer satiated her. She needed the rush of teasing a sub to climax, of hearing them plead to her to come, or the sweet urgency on their tongue as they cried out to their mistress.

You had that and ruined it, or did you forget, Mistress?

If only she had asked McCoy to be exclusive. If only she had trusted McCoy enough not to hurt her if she opened up; or trusted herself not to break. Holding people at arm's length was Frankie's specialty, though. Not just lovers, but everyone, including her aunt Belinda.

"How come you never let me touch you?"

Frankie swallowed, the memory of McCoy's question echoing in the recesses of her mind. Months ago, the answer had been so simple, and yet, one Frankie couldn't begin to stomach, no matter how often she tried. If only speaking the words didn't make her want to break out in hives, then maybe, just maybe, McCoy would still be with her.

Frankie reached for her cell phone, scrolling through her contacts until she found her mentor's name. Since she'd left Toronto, their contact had been sporadic at best, but if anyone could help Frankie find a new sub, it was her.

The call rang twice before Frankie heard a low, sultry greeting come through the phone. "Frankie, your ears must have been burning, darling. I was just thinking of you."

Smiling, Frankie pulled herself up and leaned against her headboard. She drew the blankets over to cover herself. "Hi, Natasha."

At ten to ten, Frankie left her apartment, alight with newfound possibilities. Her talk with Natasha had been enlightening, and they'd ended the call with Natasha confirming she'd get in contact with an old friend in Vancouver's BDSM community. Hopefully soon she'd have news for Frankie of finding a perfect sub looking for a new Domme. One who clicked with Frankie the moment they met, and she could finally put her unfortunate longing for McCoy to rest. It was unhealthy, not to mention humiliating, to be pining after McCoy the way she had been.

She descended the stairs to the main level where the pub was located, the never-ending list of things she needed to do that day already rolling through her mind. With two of her staff out sick, the day would be busy as ever. Not to mention, she still didn't have a clue what had happened with Evan the night before. *Did they no longer want the job?* Frankie had been set to pay them for their hard work when Evan had bolted from the pub so fast it was as if a firecracker had been lit under their ass.

If by some stroke of luck they showed up again, perhaps Frankie wouldn't have to cancel her class at the gym that evening. She'd been teaching self-defense to women and other vulnerable groups—such as the 2SLGBTQ+ community—since she'd returned to Vancouver. Feeling like she was contributing to someone's well-being did wonders for her own mental health and recovery.

"Lian is still out sick," Sloane announced the moment Frankie entered the dining area. She was stocking the fridge but must have heard the click of Frankie's heels as she came in. "So is Jessie. Dakota's here with Rain and Donnie in the kitchen but looks like death warmed over. Ted and Jon punched in, but you know, they're not much help up here."

"Greaaat." Frankie inwardly groaned at the news, heading for the coffee pot. "It's too early for this." She made herself a Classic Irish, knowing she'd need the extra indulgence of Jameson and Honey Jack to help get her through the day. No, the staff who worked solely in the brewery making beer wouldn't be much help in this crisis. It'd defeat the purpose of pulling them on a mill and mash day. Not when her on-tap beer brought in most of the pub's monthly income. It was crucial they got new batches started sooner rather than later.

"Coy's got a slow day at the shop, so I was gonna see if she could help out so Dakota can go home." Sloane worked as she talked, which Frankie was grateful for because she couldn't guarantee her facial expressions were under control.

She shook her head slowly. "No. Thank you, but no. I'll send Dakota home, but we can manage without McCoy."

"Is that your business savvy talking, or your ego?" Sloane griped, irritation sparking in her green gaze when she finally looked up.

"Careful, Sloane," Frankie warned. She took a sip of her coffee, adding quietly, "Don't be a brat today, okay? We're short-staffed as is, and I'm not in the mood."

"Too long since you spanked my sister?" Sloane volleyed back, and then visibly cringed as she must have realized her error.

Sloane's impulsiveness no longer surprised Frankie, and she found herself smirking. "Yes, actually, and if you don't fuck off, I'll have *you* bent over my knee instead. Except I'll make sure you don't get an orgasm out of it."

Sloane laughed, and just like that, the tension lessened between them. Frankie headed to the kitchen to greet her other staff. Rain and Donnie, the old man who had worked for Frankie's cousin before Frankie took over, were busy with food prep. Rain was a spunky young woman who could talk someone's ear off. Donnie was the opposite, quiet as a mouse. He was the only one of her staff who arrived even earlier than Sloane each day, eager to get ahead on battering the haddock and slicing the potatoes for apps and home-cut fries. He was pushing seventy and refused to work past four, stating his wife's supper was better than anything he could get at the pub. Frankie couldn't argue that. If she had someone at home waiting for her, living and breathing work would be the last thing on her mind.

You couldn't even open up to McCoy. Face it, there'll never be anyone waiting.

Frankie frowned. Her brain could fuck off too with the constant backseat-driver commentary. A long day awaited her, and she *so* didn't have time for a "glass half-empty" attitude.

"Where's Dakota?"

"Bathroom, boss," Rain replied, looking up from the onion she was slicing with a squeamish expression. "He's been in and out since he got there."

"Lovely," Frankie muttered, then spoke louder. "Send him home for me, will you? I'll be in the office for a bit but will be back to help with the dinner rush."

"Will do."

Once Frankie was in her office, the first thing she did was check this week's schedule tacked to the bulletin board. Since her dishwasher, Jessie, was out sick, she'd have to get George to float between cleaning tables and the dish pit. He was only fifteen and couldn't work past nine, but at least he could help cover the supper rush when he arrived after school. Andy would be in at two until close. Frankie tapped her nails against her desk, thinking. They would be short in the kitchen again that night without Nathan and Dakota.

I could really use an Evan right about now. Frankie smirked. For more than one reason.

CHAPTER 6

Evan

Cecil: Update.

Evan chewed their lip, gaze flickering around the pub before landing on the phone screen again. Their shoulders slumped a little, unsure how to reply with anything but a "fuck you, old man." Did Cecil not care at all that Evan had to sleep under the bridge the night before? He would never have pulled that stunt with his beloved Caleb. It'd taken every ounce of inner strength Evan had today to walk across the street and through the doors of O'Rourke's. It was like the first time all over again, the spike of adrenaline and fear making their legs rubbery and their stomach cramp so hard Evan worried they'd lose the bagel they'd eaten earlier.

But their stepfather didn't care about that.

Evan: Several staff out sick. I'm working on a plan to get me on the inside

Or I was, until I ran out like a fucking chickenshit. Would Frankie even hire them now?

Cecil: Good work. Did you do the salt trick?

Evan's jaw went slack. *Is he serious right now?* Did Cecil really think Evan was capable of playing around with salt measurements in filtered water? Their aim was to bring Frankie down, not kill her innocent staff.

Evan: I didn't get out of prison just to go back in. So far shit has been by the book.

Evan: Mostly.

Cecil: You said you'd get the job done. Don't let your mother down, kid. Again.

Evan gripped the phone tighter in their hand, jaw clenching just as hard. *Fucking crazy old man.* Evan's entire life had been like this. Them chasing after Caleb and Cecil, trying like hell to make Cecil love them as much as he did Caleb. It never did work, and when Caleb died, the pedestal had already been too steep for Evan to climb.

"Evan, heyyy."

Sloane's voice startled Evan out of the self-loathing trip down memory lane, and they blinked, quickly placing their cell phone face down on the booth table they occupied. Despite the emotional turbulence that swooshed around in the pit of their stomach, Evan managed a small smile. "Hey."

Sloane flopped down across from Evan, her easy grin relaxing them slightly. "With the way you tore out of here last night, I didn't think I'd see you again. Happy to see I was wrong."

Was she flirting with Evan? Their cheeks warmed, and they fought the desire to fidget by squeezing their hands together on the table. It was doubtful. The idea that Sloane was attracted to them was almost obscene. Sloane was fun and pretty and surely an intelligent woman. It would only take one look to realize how different their worlds were.

"Yeah, I"—Evan blew out a breath—"forgot I had to take care of somethin'."

"I like the way you talk." Sloane propped her chin in her hand, elbow resting on the table. Her green gaze was bright with interest. "Like you've got attitude, but you're almost too shy to show it. There's an edge to your words."

"Trying to suss out deets on my background, Sloane?" Evan cocked their head, arching one eyebrow in an unimpressed look.

"Oooh, defensive too." Sloane laughed, and Evan got a pleasant view of her straight white teeth as her full lips pulled back. The stud piercing in her nostril and long eyelashes only added to her appeal.

Evan looked away and reluctantly caught Frankie's gaze on them from behind the bar. She wore a plum-colored suit today with a black top underneath, once again open at the collar. Strands of her long hair had escaped its clip, and now tendrils of blonde, espresso, and strawberry teased Frankie's cheek. Evan gritted their teeth, forcing their attention back to Sloane to stammer, "S-shouldn't you be taking my order or somethin'?"

Sloane turned in her seat to look where Evan had, sighing dramatically. "Yeah, I better, or Frankie's claws will come out." She chuckled again before sliding out of the booth to take position next to Evan. Pulling a tablet out of her apron pocket, she leaned her hip against Evan's table. "So, what'll it be, cutie?"

Evan tried like hell not to blush at the flirty endearment but felt the burst of heat rise to their cheeks, nonetheless. They adjusted their glasses and pulled the menu closer. The words and letters danced on the page, blending into one another and pulling apart again, but not slow enough for Evan to catch them. Their ears began to ring loudly, Sloane's presence no doubt exaggerating Evan's condition. Swallowing down bile, they slammed the menu closed.

"I-I'll have a burger and fries, hold the mustard." They were sweating and couldn't quite meet Sloane's gaze as they held the menu up for her to take. "Thanks."

"Sure thing, Evan."

Evan breathed a relieved sigh the moment Sloane left. *Fuck, some spy I'm turning out to be.* They'd worked one shift in the kitchen and hadn't remembered anything on the menu but the burger.

They eyed the video surveillance secured to the wall over the bar, then casually took in the one by the entrance. There was enough surveillance in the main part of the pub that Evan was confident it would be too risky to sabotage Frankie's front house. Whatever concrete plan they came up with would have to be behind closed doors. Frankie's office would be a good start. If Evan could uncover financial records, then perhaps they could bring the bitch down that way before the grand finale.

They started when a white letter envelope landed on the table in front of them. Evan blinked out of their daze, staring up at none other than Frankie. "Your check from last night."

"Oh, uh, thanks, I guess." Evan's stomach clenched and then did a strange flip-flop. She was so close that Evan worried they'd suffocate with every inhale of the enticing perfume she wore.

"You guess?" Frankie echoed, giving them an odd look. Evan held their breath, hoping Frankie wouldn't take it upon herself to sit down like Sloane had. They stared at Frankie's hands resting confidently on her hips. *You can take the woman out of the uniform, but at the end of the day, she's still the same pig.*

Evan swallowed, unable to tear their gaze away. They tried to imagine Frankie holding a gun. What had it taken for her to pull the trigger? Two hands on the grip, or just the one? Had they shaken at all? Were there seconds before the trigger was pulled where Frankie had reconsidered?

"Anyway, I wanted to thank you again for the help last night. The flu appears to be hitting everyone at once." Frankie sighed. "Lian is back, and now Jessie's out sick."

"Jessie is ... another server?" Evan already knew at least five facts about the part-time employee, but playing along was key to this game.

"Dishwasher, actually." The tip of Frankie's tongue darted out to moisten her lips, and Evan zeroed in on the small, indecisive movement. "... the job."

"Hmm?" Evan shook their head, tearing their gaze from Frankie's mouth to look at her eyes.

Frankie took the seat Sloane had vacated and clasped her hands together. "Did you still want the job? I could use another person to float between the kitchen and bussing tables. The pay is fair, and the tips are divided amongst the staff, myself excluded. I don't ask for much, but no stealing or selling liquor to minors is a must. I require honesty and hard work while you're here. Each eight-hour shift allows for a half-hour unpaid dinner break and two fifteen-minute paid breaks. Thoughts?"

Evan was slow to respond. In fact, in the lengthy silence, Sloane returned with their cheeseburger platter, shooting Evan a wide smile as she placed the plate down in front of them before leaving again. If Evan took the job and later Frankie became suspicious of them, they risked Frankie looking into their past. Cecil always said it was better to stick to the truth as much as possible when lying. If Evan gave Frankie something juicy about them, she might not bother looking into anything further.

Picking up their burger, Evan met Frankie's eyes briefly, took a deep breath, and said quietly, "I've got a criminal record."

Frankie's eyes widened marginally, and she cocked her head to the side. "Did you serve time?"

Evan nodded, biting into their burger. A groan slipped out at the burst of flavors on their tongue. The bagel they'd had hours earlier hadn't been substantial enough to hold them. And damn, they were much too appreciative at the moment to think about being guilty over the pockets they'd picked to land them a bit of cash for a meal. Cards were much riskier to use, so Evan preferred cash whenever possible.

"What were you in for?" Frankie glanced around the pub, likely eager to get back to work. There was an afternoon lull with only three tables occupied now, but Evan was sure it could change in a heartbeat.

"Breaking and entering," Evan said between bites. They squirted a dollop of ketchup on the side of their plate, then picked up a fry to wave in Frankie's direction. "Served five years, one in juvie before they moved me."

"No early parole?"

Evan shook their head. Keeping eyes downcast, they murmured, "You know how parole works?"

Since Frankie's past in Toronto seemed to have stayed there, Evan expected her to evade the question. It was personal, and as far as Frankie was concerned, she and Evan were virtually strangers.

"I should. I was a cop once."

The fry Evan had been mid-chew on slid down the wrong way, and they choked.

CHAPTER 7

Frankie

WHY'D I JUST SAY that?

For several tense seconds that felt like minutes, they stared silently at one another. Evan looked as shocked as Frankie felt over the confession. She couldn't blame them. Frankie had made a point over the years to *not* talk about her past, let alone blurt that she'd been a cop to an ex-*convict* of all people.

Dozens of questions filled Frankie about Evan's history with the law. Where had the break-in taken place? Why, and with whom? And then came more personal questions she was dying to ask. What was it like for them behind bars? Evan was small and lean and looked like a punching bag more than anything else. Was prison where they'd broken their nose?

"I'm assuming since it wasn't a longer sentence, the break-in wasn't residential?" Frankie heard herself say instead, searching Evan's eyes for any hint of deceit. "Was anyone hurt?"

Evan shook their head. Their gaze darkened slightly, and the next bite of their burger bordered on anger. "It was a store, and no. Listen, Frankie, hire me or not, b-but I can't talk about it anymore."

Frankie studied them, noting how their shoulders had bowed over during their conversation, as if Evan was bracing for the worst. But Frankie wasn't like that. She preferred to give the benefit of the doubt, and for some offenders, she believed rehabilitation and change were possible. She just hoped Evan fell into that category.

"That's fair." Frankie got to her feet, brushing her hands over her suit. "Why don't you finish your meal and then come see me in my office? You can fill out a new employee form and start immediately if that works for you."

She didn't wait for a response. It was already later in the afternoon than she would have liked, with so much still to do before she could take off for her class. Frankie accepted a coffee from Andy on the way to her office, giving him her thanks.

"Perfection," she said after taking the first sip. She heaved a contented sigh and drifted into the office, thoughts of Evan lingering as she pulled out the proper employee forms. Evan had been on her mind a lot the past few days. There was something about them, a haunting darkness that reeled Frankie in. With that realization, she should avoid them like the plague, but it was proving the opposite. She wanted more.

Darkness feeds darkness.

Frankie understood that on a profound level. She kept her demons locked up, subduing them each time she restrained a lover. She'd discovered her power through kink, and with it, Frankie healed a little more each day.

How did Evan cope?

Frankie's cell phone vibrated at the same moment there was a knock at her door. Evan was standing over the threshold with one hand tucked into their jeans, watching her.

A shiver of awareness went through Frankie. She cleared her throat, waving them inside. "Come in. Have a seat. I'll be right with you, Evan." Frankie unlocked her cell phone to see a new message from Natasha.

Natasha: I may have found someone for you. An old friend of mine, Kelsey, lives in your city and is willing to meet you. She'd be familiar with any subs in the area.

Frankie nodded, quickly typing out a reply.

Frankie: I appreciate it, thank you.

"Sorry about that." She flashed Evan a quick smile as she slipped her phone into her desk drawer. They were staring at something beyond Frankie, and when she turned to look, she noticed the tablecloth disguising her safe had caught on her spare knee-high boots and ridden up. "Don't get excited. I'm still not a drug dealer," Frankie joked, but it sounded strained even to her own ears. Reaching to fix the cloth over the safe again, she didn't miss the way Evan watched her every move.

"It's got nothin' to do with me if you were," Evan deadpanned, as if nothing in life could surprise them anymore.

"I was a cop." Frankie huffed. There was absolutely no way she'd be into anything illegal.

Evan's gaze darkened, and the look they sent Frankie seconds before they got hold of themself caused the hairs on Frankie's arm and the back of her neck to stand up.

"Was a cop," Evan echoed, slumping into their seat more. They crossed their legs, ankle over the knee, and stared up at Frankie, boredom clear on their face. "And I was a robber. Now I'm gonna work for you. Interesting, isn't it?"

This is an act. It must be. Two seconds ago, it looked like Evan wanted to kill her for suggesting cops could do nothing but walk the straight and narrow life. *Someone hurt you, Evan, and I'm going to find out who.*

Evan was still on her mind as Frankie walked into her self-defense class that evening. During only a few encounters, the jaded butch had somehow crawled their way under her skin and snuck past her defenses. Frankie wanted to uncover all Evan's secrets and vow to protect each and every one. Something integral in Evan's makeup screamed out to Frankie, sparking her need to protect and possess. The weariness in Evan's mismatched eyes as they sat slouched in her office toyed at her memory as she dropped her duffel bag on the locker room bench.

"You look ready to go a few rounds," Courtney, an acquaintance of Frankie and frequent sparring partner, commented. She swiped a hand over her damp forehead, pushing loose tendrils of auburn hair away from her flushed cheeks. It looked as if the younger woman had gone a few rounds of her own already.

A wry chuckle left Frankie. "I've got tension, yes." *Nothing a good sparring match or sex won't alleviate.*

"What do you say we give your students something to talk about?"

Frankie smirked as she unbuttoned her winter coat and blazer, hanging them carefully in her locker. "I don't think either of your lovers will appreciate it if you come home with another broken finger or chipped tooth."

Courtney balled up her damp towel and threw it at Frankie with a laugh. "Fuck you. It was a sprain, one, and two, the tooth was fixed the next morning. You get one lucky kick, and I never hear the end of it."

"Luck would be me only winning once in the two years I've known you." Frankie's lips curled in a satisfied grin. "Sounds like a lot of lucky kicks if you ask me."

"Whatever. Guess I'll need to stop going soft on your old ass then," Courtney said as Frankie picked up her bag to head to the washroom. She never changed with an audience.

"Old? We'll see who's old after I'm through with you. You talk a big game, Ms. Cairns," Frankie called out, closing the door behind her. She was smiling as she stripped off her business attire in place of a pair of loose-fitting joggers, sports bra, and ribbed tank top. She headed barefoot into the studio, tying her hair back as she went. Several of her students were already there and waiting. Courtney was off to the side on the floor, stretching out her hamstrings and chatting with Rachel and Maria, a couple of Frankie's longtime students.

"How is everyone tonight? Toni, it's great to see you. We missed you the last few classes," Frankie greeted the small, withdrawn woman waiting quietly on the floor. Her head perked up at her name being called, and a tentative, brief smile graced her lips. Then it was gone. Frankie eyed the bruising on her cheek, Toni's piece of shit husband already in her mind's eye. "He do that to you?"

"Oh, no." Toni averted her gaze and swallowed. "I-I slipped on ice."

"I see." Frankie clenched her teeth, turning away before she pushed a conversation she knew Toni wasn't ready to have. There was always an excuse. Frankie could teach her students how to defend themselves until there was nothing left to learn, but it didn't mean a thing if they wouldn't use their newfound skills in the real world. It was hard to take back your power, Frankie knew that. Hell, she understood that better than anyone.

"Courtney has so helpfully volunteered to spar with us," she explained to the class, and headed to where the thick gym mats were stacked up. Dragging one back to the front of the dojo, Frankie opened it up and continued. "I thought it'd be fun this class if we just practiced using the force of our bodies to take our opponent down. Whoever takes Courtney down first, I'll gift them a hundred-dollar grocery card. And the kicker? Courtney won't fight back."

"That is so not what we agreed on," Courtney muttered, standing a few feet away. In just a sports bra and tights, her hair in two braids, and tattoo sleeves, no one would have ever guessed she was *the* Courtney Cairns, heir to the Cairns investment corporation. Frankie would bet, too, that not many knew she'd disappeared for a year and competed in illegal underground fights.

Frankie shrugged, smirking over her shoulder at Courtney. The younger woman had her arms crossed, but she didn't look upset at the idea. Frankie assumed she wouldn't; after all, allowing a group of vulnerable women to strike her would quell some of her masochist tendencies constantly brimming to the surface.

"Do you consent? I think a few of the students could really use an escape in this class." Toni certainly did. Just being able to lash out without fear of repercussion would act as therapy to some. Frankie hoped it worked on Toni.

"Hell yeah. You know I'll get pampered when I get home."

Courtney's two lovers came to mind, and Frankie nodded. One of them, Lexi, was a friend of McCoy's and a switch in the kink community. She knew as well as Frankie how hard it was at times to scratch desires someone like Courtney often had—like the need for pain.

Frankie stood aside, watching as her students lined up to face off with Courtney. Doing things this way wouldn't relieve much of her own stress over Evan, but if it helped Toni realize she had more power than she believed, it would be worth it. The Evan mystery could wait. With any luck, they wouldn't leave the city anytime soon.

CHAPTER 8

Evan

It was hard to concentrate on anything when they were so pissed off.

Frankie had sat across from Evan and all but said cops were perfect. So, she wasn't just a vigilante, she was also a fucking liar. That was okay, though. It was. If anything, knowing Frankie lied—likely every time she opened that gloriously sinful mouth of hers—would just make taking her down all the sweeter.

Evan was going to *crush* Frankie. They'd expose every facet of her life, starting with sabotaging O'Rourke's Pub.

"How're you getting along?" Rain called over the noise of the exhaust fans. She was two years older than Evan, with long dark hair she braided down her back, wide brown eyes, and an angular jawline beneath a set of chubby cheeks. Rain was the type of girl who was dying to tell everyone her life story. In the three hours Evan had been there, they'd already learned way more about Rain than they wished to, from her blood sugar problem to the long list of racial slurs she'd been called over the years. "No filter" really *was* a personality trait. But damn, if Evan didn't secretly find her fun to be around.

"Just peachy. You?" Evan returned, stacking clean plates from the dish pit. They carried them across the kitchen to Rain's station, noting the lineup of plates prepped for the main course. The kitchen was small yet clean, and Evan had seen at least two bait boxes for rodents. Most likely, there were a handful more around the pub. If they could find and dispose of them, then ... but no, that wouldn't work. Frankie would know they'd been tampered with.

I could make calls complaining about a rat problem. Surely, a health inspector would shut the pub down if the complaints were ongoing. It was one angle Evan wanted to explore, and a big one at that. They were aware of the microbrewery located in the basement, as well as at least two, possibly three, staff employed for that part of Frankie's business. From what Evan had seen so far, they clocked out each day by five p.m. That left a good window for them to get in and out of the basement.

"Fucking fantastic, bro. I live for this rush. No smelly dudes breathing down my neck while I'm cooking." Rain laughed, then let out a whoop like she was cheering them on for a job well done. "The only one I don't mind being shoulder to shoulder with in here is Frankie, know what I'm saying? That woman smells like sex appeal and—"

Evan's feet chose that moment to lose control, slipping on the slick floor on the way back to the sink. "Whoa!" There was an awkward, figure-skate-type dance seconds before Evan was careening backwards into a fall. All the air rushed out of them, and just when they knew they'd be sporting a bruise later, strong hands grabbed hold of them.

"Easy, kid. Think you need better shoes."

Evan's eyes flew open, only to scowl at their savior. "Don't call me a kid. I'm only a few years younger than you."

McCoy Miller, Sloane's identical twin, stared back at Evan with one brow arched up so far it almost hit her hairline. She wasn't pretty or feminine like Sloane. Handsome, maybe, but not pretty. Coy was all muscles and stockiness and tattoos that covered the better part of both arms. "And how would you know how old I am, newbie? Didn't you just start today?"

Shit. *Shit*. Evan raced through possible excuses, anything that didn't include blurting out that they'd done homework on every one of the staff. Not only was Coy still on the payroll as a casual, but she and Sloane were pretty big influencers on YouTube. Yeah ... Evan definitely couldn't let all *that* slip out. "I ... I, well, I'm almost twenty-four. You tellin' me you're not in your twenties?"

Coy let out a whistle before giving Evan a closer once-over. "That so? You look barely able to shave."

Evan chose not to correct Coy as the assumption didn't bother them. With a binder securing their chest in place and their small stature, being referenced to as a teenaged boy was at least a weekly occurrence.

"My bad, Ev, didn't think you'd get all flustered hearing me talk about the boss." Rain winked in their direction. "We've all crushed on Frankie at some point. Coy here used to have a thing with her."

"Rain, enough," Coy warned.

They had a thing? What kind of thing? Evan's frown deepened at the admittance. In all their research, Coy and Frankie being lovers hadn't come up. Evan watched Coy grab a platter of food and disappear out of the kitchen, but they still didn't move. Frankie and McCoy ... What did Coy see in her? Coy and Sloane, and the rest of their friends, seemed so normal and nice. What could Frankie possibly have hidden in her armory of deceit and violence that a softhearted person like McCoy Miller would have wanted?

"Don't mind Coy. She's always been shy talking about her and Frankie," Rain said, pulling Evan out of their thoughts. Mischief gleamed in her eyes. "I think it was supposed to be on the down-low, but it really wasn't. On the plus side, now that they're over, Frankie might be single again. I might never have a chance, but *you*, Evan, you are all-the-way her type."

Evan's eyes widened. The memory of the first time Frankie saw them came to mind, how she'd openly flirted with Evan. The pit of their stomach slid down to their toes. "Oh, no. Nope. That'll never happen. Frankie's not my type. Not at all. I mean, have you seen Coy? We're polar opposites."

"You're both cute and soft butches. Like I said, the boss's type."

Ignoring Rain's chuckle, Evan got back to work. They spent the remainder of the night brainstorming ways to get dirt on Frankie from Coy. The answer came as they were clearing off tables in the dining room area. Evan spotted the friend group in the corner, like they often were through the week, with McCoy the center of attention.

I need them to like me. If they think I'm their friend, they'll confide in me more.

It didn't bother Evan that they were openly spying on Sloane and Coy's friend group, affectionately referred to as the Fab Five. Sketchbook and charcoal pencil in hand, it was a relatively acceptable part of the job as an artist. And one the Fab Five likely wouldn't mind, if they were aware. Although it was common courtesy to ask permission, Evan preferred to dish out apologies rather than interrupt an authentic interaction among friends. People often stiffened up or developed disgustingly fake smiles once they knew they were being drawn. Evan didn't want that. They had also researched the Fab Five, but mostly out of curiosity. Sloane's friends, and Sloane specifically, fascinated Evan.

They paused to sip the soda Lian had dropped off at their table, scanned the sketch, and glanced back at the friend group. Out of the five women, Coy and Sloane fidgeted the most, so it was hard for Evan to settle on an exact location for their hands or how far away from the booth table they should sit in the picture. The twins and their friend Abi all talked a lot with their hands. It was distracting and comical, and not at all easy for Evan. They bit into a french fry, chewing absently, before using their finger to carefully smudge the line of Krystal's jaw. She appeared to be the quiet one in the group, and she had a slightly rounder face. Shading the lines would create a nice, realistic effect.

Evan was so focused they didn't realize they had company until a hand landed on their shoulder. They flinched, just enough to jerk the pencil where they'd been drawing in Taunya's eyebrows. "Fuck," Evan said, eyes narrowing on their newcomer. Frankie stood, nosily peering over Evan's shoulder at the sketch. Open appreciation shone on her face.

"I didn't know you were an artist. It's very good, Evan."

"Um, thanks. I guess." Evan turned back to the sketch, spotting the slip-up their pencil had made almost immediately. Their frown deepened. *Who just interrupts someone clearly mid-stroke? Fucking entitled bitch.*

"I just came to remind you of the time. Shift starts in ten minutes."

Really? Evan checked their phone, realizing Frankie was right. They'd completely zoned out while sketching the Fab Five. An hour had passed without them being aware. Studying the picture again, Evan noticed it was almost complete. "Thank you." Continuing the drawing where their pencil had left off, Evan didn't glance at Frankie again. They were only vaguely aware of her walking away.

Five minutes later, the sketch was complete, turning out a lot better than Evan had expected, considering their ever-restless subjects. They gathered their belongings and headed to where the Fab Five were sitting in their usual corner booth.

"Evan, hey," Sloane greeted when Evan approached the table. Evan liked how she turned her full gaze on them, as if they were someone worth pausing a conversation for. It wasn't something that happened often, if ever.

"Hey. My shift's about to start, but, um, here." Evan handed her the sketch, turning to leave, but Sloane caught their arm.

"Shit, Evan. This is so good!"

"Thanks."

Heat crept up Evan's cheeks, and their embarrassment only grew as Sloane passed the sketch around the table. The Fab Five oohed and aahed, looking at Evan with newfound respect.

Taunya held her hand out. "I don't think we've met. I'm Tauni."

This is it, Evan thought, standing as tall as their five feet, one inch would take them before latching onto Tauni's hand. *This is my way in.*

CHAPTER 9

Frankie

"It's nice we were able to connect so soon." Kelsey's smile was kind as she took in Frankie sitting across from her in the spacious living room. When Kelsey had invited her to her private residence, Frankie hadn't known what to think. If the roles were reversed, she doubted very much she'd allow a virtual stranger into her private space. Mind you, Frankie's entire apartment could have easily fit inside Kelsey's living and kitchen area.

"It is. I wasn't sure it would work out with our jobs interfering. You must keep busy as a lawyer. Corporate, right?"

"Good memory." Kelsey nodded, leaning forward for the glass of water on the coffee table. As she took a drink, Frankie's gaze flitted to the younger woman kneeling beside Kelsey on the floor. Katie had her hands folded loosely in her lap, and although she'd watched Frankie with keen interest since her arrival, she hadn't spoken. "Don't worry, I've given my kitten permission to have her eyes up while you're here."

Frankie bowed her head in understanding, settling into the armchair more. "What's that like? Being a corporate lawyer?" she asked, crossing one leg over the other. Satisfaction warmed her as Katie's gaze followed the movement. She was a cute girl, blonde, ample in all the right places, and knew how to be a good, cooperative sub.

"A pain. I tell myself at least twice a year that I'll go back to family law." Kelsey chuckled, shaking her head. "The lies we tell ourselves." She glanced between Frankie and Katie, who hadn't taken her eyes off Frankie, and addressed the younger woman. "Kitten, do you like what you see?"

At once, the blonde head bobbed up and down with enthusiasm. Shyness brought a blush to Katie's cheeks. "Yes, very much, Miss."

"What do you like about Frankie, kitten?" Kelsey's voice dropped lower, almost to a purr. She winked at Frankie.

Katie's attention darted to her Domme before returning to Frankie. The tip of her pink tongue poked out to lick her lips. "She's very pretty."

"Mm-hmm. I agree. Prettier than me?"

Frankie watched the exchange in silence. She was out of practice with BDSM customs, but she knew not to interrupt them. Kelsey remained kind to Katie, which was the main focus for Frankie. She wouldn't tolerate anything less between a Domme and sub.

"Umm, no one is prettier than you, Miss." Katie batted her eyelashes up at Kelsey even as a placating smile appeared.

Kelsey lovingly stroked Katie's hair, and Katie's eyes fluttered closed. A contented sigh escaped her at the contact. Frankie studied the couple, knowing they were the reason for the ache building in her chest. She'd never come close to having that with McCoy. With anyone, ever. The love she'd had for Emily had been all-consuming at sixteen, or so Frankie believed at the time. Looking back now and witnessing the tight-knit longing between Katie and Kelsey, she had a feeling that what she'd felt for Emily hadn't even scratched the surface.

Frankie cleared her throat, shifting in her seat to reach for her own water. "Natasha mentioned you might know of a sub who was interested in part-time play?"

"I thought I had, yes. Jane, a cute butch who enjoys restraints, spanking, and doing household chores." Kelsey shrugged, looking apologetic. "Unfortunately for you, Jane paired up with someone since I last touched base with her."

"Oh." Frankie held in her disappointment, not wanting to seem unappreciative of the effort Kelsey put in, but why bother with the invite today if there was no news?

"But," Kelsey added, her blue eyes lighting up. Her hand paused mid-stroke on Katie's head. "I might have another, equally alluring, alternative for you."

"Oh?" Frankie repeated, this time in a question. She tilted her head to the side. "Such as?"

"Katie has expressed interest in trying a new Domme. Not to get rid of me," Kelsey quickly corrected. She resumed petting her lover, smiling across the room at Frankie as she continued, "but to explore her submissive needs and test her limits. I agreed so long as I got to vet any potential partners. We saw your picture and instantly wanted to meet you."

"You want to ... what? Loan your sub out to me?" Frankie had heard of this before in the kink community, but she'd never been propositioned herself. "Katie? Is that what you want?"

Katie remained silent, but the obvious excitement on her face gave her away. "Answer Frankie, kitten," Kelsey murmured, her fingers now trailing over Katie's neck and bare shoulders. The only thing Katie wore was a royal blue teddy, just enough material to cover her breasts and pussy. Frankie had considered it a bold choice when she first arrived, but now she understood why.

"I'd love to serve you, Frankie. I'm good at taking orders." Katie tugged her bottom lip between her teeth and batted blonde eyelashes up at Frankie.

"Jesus." Frankie blew out a breath. She shifted in her seat again, squeezing her thighs to alleviate some of the pressure building in her core. How many nights had she lain awake fantasizing about a sub saying exactly that to her? "Maybe Natasha didn't tell you, Kelsey, but I'm not merely looking for a sub to serve me. Or even just to restrain and spank, although that would be ideal as well. What I need is ... a sub I can tease for hours and then fuck them for just as long."

"We know." Kelsey smirked. "Are you saying you wouldn't jump at the chance to use Katie exactly how you described? We've invited others to our playroom before, but passing kitten off to someone else for their own pleasure is a first. This is what kitten wants, and I'd be lying if I said I don't get off on the idea of you fucking what's mine."

"I ... wow." Frankie swallowed. If she were halfway normal, she'd jump at the opportunity being handed to her on a silver platter. But something kept her glued to her seat. She was desperate for a sub, but did she want to share one? She'd agreed to an open relationship with McCoy, and how had that served her? Frankie didn't think she could share again. She wanted a sub that was just hers, one who would willingly commit their body and soul to her. Katie was objectively pretty, but femmes had never really appealed to Frankie. She wanted boyish, rugged features and sharp edges underneath her. She wanted to witness a tough protector type on the street become putty in the sheets.

Evan's blue and brown gaze, set behind those wireless frames, came to mind. Frankie frowned. *Not McCoy?* Her brain must be playing tricks on her, that had to be it. Working in close proximity to Evan for the last two weeks, as well as hardly seeing McCoy, must have been taking a toll on her.

"Kelsey, how about ..." Frankie tapped her finger on her chin, a slow smile spreading. "You and Katie give me a show today, and later tonight, I'll think about the other matter? I'm in the mood for a little voyeurism."

The next morning, Frankie was in the basement of O'Rourke's, conducting temperature readings on the current ale inside the fermentation tanks. Since she'd taken over from her cousin seven years ago, Frankie had branched out beyond the basic on-tap commercial ales and ciders. The tastes and creation of alcohol had always been something that intrigued her growing up, so the first thing she'd done as owner of O'Rourke's was create a microbrewery. Kink and martial arts might have brought the rush Frankie so often craved, but it was beer-making that brought peace to her life. Her brewery staff, Ted and Jon, kept the place running these days, but Frankie still made a point to inspect everything each morning.

As she worked, Evan popped in and out of her head at random. There was just something about them, but Frankie couldn't pinpoint what. She wanted to know them on a deeper level than a boss/employee dynamic. Frankie wanted their smile directed at her, wanted to know the reason they'd moved to Vancouver. And since

Kelsey's proposition the day before, she'd thought of little else than how it'd look to have Evan kneeling before her. Serving her, as Katie served Kelsey.

Why them though? It doesn't seem like they even like me half the time, Frankie considered, bringing the sample she'd taken from the batch of stout to her nose. At least thinking about Evan was taking her mind off McCoy.

"What the—" she said, sniffing the glass's contents. The stout smelled off, sour almost. And the taste ... "Ugh, god, that's awful." She grimaced after another sip. Whereas her stout beer usually had a smokey, coffee flavor that overjoyed the palate, this one tasted bitter. It gave a papery, cardboard feel on the tongue. Sampling the barley malt inside the two other tanks, a quick rise of panic seized the air in Frankie's lungs. *This can't be.* In the years since Frankie had begun making beer, she'd only had to toss a batch twice. And now she had three at the same time? She couldn't serve shit like this to her customers.

"Fucking hell." Panicking would *not* serve her well. Taking a deep breath, Frankie exhaled slowly and whipped out her phone to call Ted. He and Jon had better have a good explanation.

She made her way upstairs a little later, still fuming. Ted and Jon had no idea how the batches could have been ruined. They'd done everything exactly as they'd always done, but Frankie wasn't an idiot. Something got into her beer. She planned to pore over research in her office to see if there was any way she could salvage it. *Just as soon as I pee.*

Pushing the washroom door open, the ruined batches fled her mind as Frankie noticed Evan standing in front of the sink. They were completely naked save for a pair of black boxers around their lean waist. An open toiletry kit rested on the counter, and a used towel was balled up over it. But it was the faint bruising on Evan's back and legs that captured and held Frankie's widening gaze.

"What happened to you?" she demanded, startling Evan so much they flinched and almost dropped the mid-waist sport-like chest binder they were lifting over their head.

"W-what're you doing in here? I could've sworn I'd locked the door," Evan stammered, a deep blush flushing their fair skin. They yanked the fabric down over their chest and whirled around to face Frankie. In the process, Frankie got an unobstructed view of the muscled definition on their flat stomach. *Someone took up core workouts while in prison.*

Frankie's nostrils flared, but she didn't allow the tantalizing view to steer her off course. "If it was locked, then I wouldn't be in here staring at ..." She trailed off, shaking her head. "Evan, why the hell are you having a sponge bath in my washroom, and what happened to your back?"

"It's nothing." Evan wouldn't meet her gaze, only turned away from Frankie again, and continued to cover themself with the binder. The conversation was nowhere near finished for Frankie, and she locked the restroom door so no one else could barge in.

"It's not 'nothing.' Someone hurt you." Anger made her voice harder than she meant it, which was a complete contradiction to whatever shit-show of panic was welling in her chest at the idea of Evan being harmed.

Evan shrank away from her even more, actual fear flashing in their eyes as they grabbed a white T-shirt from their backpack. Frankie grimaced, backing off slightly, and tried to soften her tone. "Where are you staying? Are you renting a room, an apartment, or something?"

"Or something." Evan hurriedly pulled on a pair of jeans, one of the two pairs Frankie recalled seeing over the last two weeks. Now that she thought about it, there hadn't been a time when Evan didn't have a backpack with them. As a police officer, she'd met and dealt with many of Toronto's homeless, and she knew well how varied homelessness looked on different people. There was a chance she was wrong now, but she didn't think so.

"You're living on the street, aren't you?"

Surprise crossed Evan's face before their eyes narrowed. "Your skill of deduction is wasting away at the pub, Officer O'Rourke."

Frankie ignored the blatant dig, following Evan's jerky movements as they gathered up their belongings. Frankie's pulse was beating incessantly against her throat, and when she pressed her hand over her heart, it raced beneath her palm. Evan was defensive, perhaps even ashamed that Frankie had called them out, but something like this couldn't go unaddressed. "Why didn't you tell me you were homeless?"

"Why, so you wouldn't have to hire me?" Evan's voice broke, as if their predicament had finally sunk in. Now that she was more aware, Frankie couldn't believe she hadn't seen the signs earlier. She'd spent plenty of time over the last two weeks discreetly studying Evan from afar. Anytime she'd walked into the kitchen and they were busy at the dish pit, or when they'd arrive hours early for their shift and sit in the back of the pub with a sketchbook in their hands. That first week, Evan had come in on their birthday and never once spoken about how they'd planned to celebrate with friends, even though Sloane had asked. Last week for Christmas, Frankie had considered asking Evan what their plans were—not that she did much herself—but Evan never came in. She'd just figured they'd had somewhere to go after all.

Frankie swallowed, watching as Evan's eyes welled up with tears. How long had there been bags under that resplendent blue and brown gaze?

"No." Frankie widened her stance, folded her arms across her chest, and said in as even a tone as possible, "So that I could have offered you my spare bedroom."

Spare bedroom? Since when does the playroom classify as spare? Spare, equating vacant and ready for use?

"*What?*" Evan's mouth fell open.

"I have the space, and I won't have one of my staff sleeping on the street."

Fuck. Frankie would have her day cut out for her, moving things around. It's not as if she could leave her A-frame or freestanding St. Andrew's Cross in that room and toss a sheet over them.

"It's not up to you. Maybe I wanna live on the street. Maybe I like it."

Frankie would have laughed at how stubborn Evan was if the urge to bend them over her knee wasn't forefront in her mind. Taking a deep breath, she unfolded her arms and leaned closer to Evan. The height difference was significant, as Evan was even shorter than McCoy's five-foot-four, but she bent so that her face was inches from Evan's. Their hot breath fanned her cheeks, but she didn't back away. "You don't. You hate it and are often scared to fall asleep. Jesus, Evan, what do you take me for? A little thing like you would get eaten alive out on the streets."

"I can take care of myself." Evan moved to go around Frankie, but she caught their arm, holding them in place.

"I'm sure you can, but I want to help," she insisted, yet she was as confused as Evan at her decision. She'd never gone out of her way to help her staff before. What made Evan different? "Starting tonight, after your shift, you'll come home with me. Don't bother arguing. If you want to work for me, I suggest you take the offer."

Evan's jaw tightened, and Frankie couldn't help but follow the movement. They were angry with her, and truly, the knowledge shouldn't have excited her the way it did.

"Sloane said you were bossy."

"Sloane?" Frankie echoed, an unwarranted pang of jealousy hitting her square in the chest. She bared her teeth, something between a grimace and a smile that stared back at her from the mirror behind Evan. "You two talk about me often?"

Frankie hadn't been the only one to notice Evan. Sloane was revoltingly obvious when she had her sights set on someone. The worst part was how Evan had noticed her as well. Where they were wary around Frankie, with Sloane, they looked lighter and seemed to genuinely want to be around her.

Her question roused a chuckle from Evan. "Uh, no. Not really."

"Oh. Well, good then." Frankie released Evan's arm and stepped back. She straightened her shoulders, the tightness in her chest only increasing the further apart she got from Evan. Something about them in particular activated her need to protect, but judging by the way Evan quickly dismissed her question, the feeling was completely one-sided.

I'm being ridiculous.

Perhaps taking Kelsey up on her offer of Katie wouldn't be a bad thing after all. At the very least, Frankie would have the opportunity to spoil and play with a sub again, which would take her mind off the current butch lesbians in her life.

"This is stupid," Evan grumbled as they led the way out of the washroom. They stopped to stare at her, adding, "You don't know me, Frankie. I could be dangerous."

Frankie bit back a smile, Evan's defiance surprisingly endearing. "Believe me, honey, there isn't anything currently in my life scarier than me."

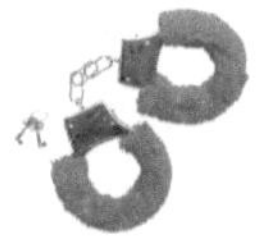

CHAPTER 10

Evan

"One batch ruined, okay. Manageable. But three? What the fuck, boss?"

Evan hovered on the stairwell leading to Frankie's second-floor apartment, scrolling through their phone so that it wasn't obvious to Frankie or Sloane they were listening in. Inside, they were gloating. Dumping mill dust into the fermentation tanks had worked! Frankie's sloppy workers would need to clean the mill station better next time. And the fact Evan was able to break into the basement, avoid the cameras, and do it mostly in the dark? *Fucking epic. Surely cranky Cecil would even approve.*

"That's what I'm saying. It's almost like they've been tampered with, but I didn't catch anything on the security feeds."

Even from across the room, agitation rolled off Frankie in waves. She'd been out most of the day, only making a lengthy appearance when the technician came to repair the walk-in cooler. Word around the pub was that Frankie had been miffed at how the fan motors had been unplugged from *inside* the evaporator electrical cabinet. It was too bad Evan had been on their break and missed how their hard work had paid off.

Unfortunately, now that Evan would be staying with Frankie, any further retaliation would only get trickier to execute. Ugh. Any time they pictured what the next several days would look like under the same roof as Frankie, it brought on some serious nausea.

"Ready to go up?"

Evan whipped their head up to find Frankie with her handbag slung over one shoulder. Tension lines marred her otherwise immaculate forehead, adding creases around her eyes, but she gave Evan a tight smile.

"Mm-hmm." Evan nodded, slipping off the stairs to let Frankie up first. They turned to say goodbye to Sloane, and a sigh escaped when she was nowhere to be found. Evan must have been too in their thoughts if they'd missed the part where Sloane left for the night. "Let's get this over with," they muttered, trailing behind Frankie to the second floor. The first half of the stairwell was only dimly lit, but it was bright enough that Evan still had a front-row seat to the distracting way Frankie's baby blue suit pants hugged her backside, so much that Evan could see the outline of the underwear she wore.

They dropped their gaze, ashamed of how hot their cheeks flushed. Hell, why couldn't Frankie be butt-ugly and wear baggy, less flattering clothes?

"I cleared out the spare bedroom as well as I could today," Frankie said as she unlocked her apartment door. At some point, she had tied her curly hair up in a loose bun, and when she turned to Evan, it bobbed with the movement. The messy do did absolutely nothing to make her less attractive. If anything, having her hair away from her face only added an unnecessary emphasis on her cheekbones and the small, almost indiscernible mole on her neck.

And fuck me for noticing.

Frankie pushed the door open, gesturing with one hand for Evan to go inside first. Evan tensed for about five seconds before the fatigue of the day and their sore feet had them gingerly stepping over the threshold. The apartment had an open-concept brick design with a small but functional kitchen. A cute built-in dining booth separated the kitchen and living room.

"Make yourself at home," Frankie said from behind Evan. They swallowed when they heard the deadbolt turn over, locking them inside the apartment with Frankie.

Maybe this wasn't a good idea. Not a good idea at all. They'd be alone with the same person who had killed Caleb. With just one small knife and no plan. Their stomach lurched. *Does she know who I am?*

"Is there a lock on the door of the bedroom you're putting me in?" Evan blurted, their pulse kicking up several notches.

Frankie was bent over, unstrapping her high heels, and she didn't reply until her bare feet were touching the entrance mat. She came a little closer, slanting her head in curiosity at Evan's question. "There could be, if you wanted one. Why?" she asked jokingly. "Are you worried I'll sneak in? Seduce you, maybe?"

Slowly, Evan shook their head. Having Frankie so close left them dazed, and it took a second of confusion before they fumbled out, "N-no. Of course not. You used to be a cop. You wouldn't do that."

"You're right, I won't. We barely know each other. Having said that, if there ever comes a time when you're interested, you'll be coming to me, sweet boi. Not the other way around." Frankie's grin was slow, confident, and full of promise, and the unfamiliar low swoop in Evan's belly had them horrified. They weren't immune to

Frankie's charm. How was that even possible, after literally *everything* they knew about her?

"You're delusional," Evan managed to get out before pushing around her to the door again. Their hands trembled slightly, and there was a tightness to their skin that hadn't been there a few minutes ago, but they held their ground and stared up at Frankie. "If fucking you is the payment for my safety, I'll see my way out."

Been there, done that. And Evan refused to have a repeat, regardless of whether it meant they were huddled in a street alley until the job was finished. After all, there was more than one kind of prison in life.

"Wait, that's not what I meant." Frankie's hand landed on their arm, holding them in place. Regret burned in her brown eyes. "I'm sorry, I guess I'm worse at flirting than I thought. I just meant that ... I'm attracted to you, Evan. But I promise nothing will happen that you don't consent to."

Evan held her gaze for an uncomfortably long minute before offering a slight nod. "Apology accepted. And ... thanks for putting me up."

"Of course." Frankie's smile was back.

Evan slipped off their boots and followed Frankie down the hall to where the bedrooms and bath were. "The bathroom isn't very big, but the tub does come with jets," Frankie said, pushing the door open so that Evan could peek their head in. Frankie moved on to the next room, watching Evan intently. "This is my room. It also doesn't have a lock, as I've never needed one. I'm giving you the benefit of the doubt here, Evan, to be better than you were in the past. Unless you're visiting my bed, don't ever step foot in here. Understood?"

"Got it." Evan's eyes narrowed. They tried not to take Frankie's comment personally, but how else *could* they take it? Frankie had very bluntly called them out on their criminal background.

"Great. Now, I'll show you your bedroom." Frankie bowed her head, another smile tugging at her lips, as if the insult she'd inadvertently dished out had been humorous.

"This is actually the largest of the two rooms, so you'll have plenty of space to settle in," Frankie explained, opening the door and walking in. There was a queen-sized, handmade canopy bed in the center of the room, a bench with leather upholstery at the foot of the bed, and a tallboy dresser in the corner. Besides the two large paintings of nude women Frankie had hanging on the walls, the rest of the room was bare.

"That's the walk-in closet, but again, it's off limits. Sorry." Frankie shot Evan an apologetic smile. "That door *is* locked, and although I'm sure you can pick it, don't. You may not like what you find behind that door."

"Cryptic," Evan said, dropping their backpack onto the leather bench. They glanced around the room again before turning back to Frankie. "Is that all?"

Frankie nodded. "That's all for now. Oh, wait, I'll grab you towels. Be right back."

Evan watched her go, then slumped down on the mattress. Being in a room that belonged to the enemy was a strange feeling. They kept waiting for the ball to drop, for the plot twist in Frankie's fucked up narrative. From the way she handled her problems, it was shocking to see any other side of her. It'd have made more sense to Evan that Frankie had discovered their identity, and taking them in was her roundabout way of kidnapping. Keeping the enemy closer and all that.

Frankie appeared in the open doorway, her suit jacket discarded now and the cuffs on her white dress shirt open and rolled up. Thin gold bracelets dangled from her wrists as she entered the room to place a set of towels on the dresser. "This should get you started. I've also set out a new toothbrush for you in the bathroom. You'll have to use the soap I have if you're lacking, but I can pick up your preferred brand on the next shopping trip."

Evan remained silent, and when she glanced at them for acknowledgement, they gritted their teeth and bowed their head slightly. "Thanks. I'm sure it's fine." They could live with whatever super feminine scent Frankie used if it meant they wouldn't need to ask her for anything else.

"Okay. I'll leave you to it and just let me know if I missed something." Frankie looked almost kind as she peered down at Evan. The red and blonde highlights in her hair shone under the scrutiny of the bedroom light. Her entire aura seemed different inside the apartment. Softer, more at ease.

Vulnerable.

A light went off in Evan's brain at the realization, and laughter bubbled out past their lips before they could stop it.

"Ah ... everything okay?" Frankie tilted her head in confusion. "Are you the type to randomly laugh when you're nervous?"

"No, sorry." Evan clamped their lips shut, trying desperately to smother their grin. Frankie wasn't aware of it yet, but tonight, she'd made a fatal mistake. She'd welcomed a lion to sleep inside her wolf den.

And the end was closer than she realized.

CHAPTER 11

Frankie

It was too quiet in her apartment. Too still. She'd have thought inviting someone into her home would disrupt her usual tranquil atmosphere, but Evan barely made a sound. Frankie slipped out of bed and yawned. The night had been rough. For as many horrors as she'd been through over the years, actual nightmares rarely plagued her. She'd been lucky that way, faring better than Emily ever had with hers. She often had night terrors, but at least she couldn't remember them upon waking. Except last night, Frankie had dreamt of Emily. It wasn't a nightmare exactly, but when Frankie had woken calling out her name, she was too shaken to fall back to sleep.

"What did it *mean*?" she whispered, rubbing her hand over her face. She shook her arms loose, waking them up, and then stretched the kinks out of her neck. Reaching for a hair tie on her nightstand, she fastened the unruly locks into a messy ponytail and immediately dropped down into a pushup. Frankie preferred to get her workout over with as soon as she woke up in the morning, unless of course, other, more horizontal, methods of self-care took precedence.

Emily's youthful, freckled face and the dream she'd had came to mind as she counted out her pushups. It was so odd that Frankie had woken in a sweat. She remembered the elation she'd felt, followed by confusion, when Emily cupped her face and whispered, *"Be careful. They aren't what they seem."* And then she kissed Frankie and disappeared. That's what woke Frankie. Even now, she wasn't sure what she was more shaken up about—the warning or the fact that Emily had kissed her. When she was alive, Emily only ever hinted there was something between them once. Even then, she'd been quick to shove the idea away as quickly as it surfaced. Perhaps it was because they'd been such close friends, or that Emily was her foster sister, but back then a kiss would have been just more wishful thinking in Frankie's juvenile mind.

Unrequited love was often like that.

Frankie's pulse thrummed in her throat as she moved into her morning bicycles. She liked to do thirty or forty of each exercise. It helped keep her fit for her classes and did wonders waking her up. By the time she was done, her muscles burned, and she'd begun to sweat.

After a quick shower, Frankie pulled on a pair of slacks and a camisole and made her bed before heading into the kitchen. It was still early, earlier than she usually woke, but she wanted to cook something for Evan to have when they woke up. The reason behind it nagged at her. Why did it matter that she cooked? In all the time she'd known McCoy, she'd made breakfast maybe a handful of times, and it was well after they began sleeping together. She hadn't even kissed Evan yet, and she was doting on them.

Frankie's lips twitched. She imagined how small they must look sleeping under the covers on her queen mattress, unaware that there were wrist and ankle restraints tucked into the bed rails. The thought made her chuckle.

Opening her fridge, Frankie went over the options before pulling out the heavy cream, butter, and eggs. She set about making her favorite gluten-free, low-carb almond flour pancakes. As they were cooking, she sliced fresh strawberries and bananas and then made coffee. Frankie was setting the table when the sound of the bathroom fan came on down the hall. The door clicked shut, and Frankie's belly fluttered. She couldn't put her finger on the why or how, but there was something special about Evan. It didn't matter that they'd done time, or that they had a chip on their shoulder and liked to avoid eye contact. She wanted to be around them, but she wasn't the only one.

Sloane's going to be a problem.

"Hey, what's all this?"

Frankie glanced up from where she was placing cutlery on the table of the breakfast booth. Evan was dressed in the same jeans as yesterday, but instead of the leather jacket they always wore, a black hoodie hung well past their waist. Their hands were clasped loosely together, but Frankie assumed it was an act since Evan was using the fingers of one hand to pick at the other. They were nervous, but at least they didn't have their shoes and jacket on yet.

"I made us breakfast," Frankie said, her gaze roaming over Evan a second time. Wariness was evident in the way they scanned the table first, followed by the kitchen where Frankie had yet to pull the pancakes from the stovetop, and then back to her. "How did you sleep?"

Evan chewed their lip, seemingly at war with themself. "It was fine," they replied after a moment. A sigh left them, and Frankie's lips quirked up when they finally took a seat on one side of the booth.

"Great." Heading back to the kitchen, she returned with the pancakes, placing the plate on the trivet already on the table. "I usually eat low carb when I can help it, so I hope you don't mind trying pancakes made with almond flour."

"Erm ... sure. I'm not allergic as far as I know." Evan frowned at their empty plate.

"What's wrong?" Using her fork, Frankie dropped three pancakes onto Evan's plate. Next, she slid the butter and syrup closer before peering at her houseguest again.

"You're acting ... not how I expected."

"And how's that?" Frankie dished up a serving for herself, but kept half her attention on Evan. "Go ahead, eat. Do you drink coffee or tea?"

"Ah ... no, I don't. Never liked the stuff," Evan admitted, pushing up their glasses. As they spread butter over the pancakes, they continued, "You just seem ... I dunno, nice, I guess."

That made Frankie laugh. "Who is going around saying I'm a bitch? Sloane, right?"

Evan shrugged, neither agreeing nor disagreeing. They piled fruit on the pancakes with syrup. Frankie did the same but patiently waited for Evan to dig in first. She hadn't been this captivated by anyone since McCoy had first come into her life. It was such a strange, all-consuming feeling, and it wasn't as if Evan and McCoy were even remotely similar. Evan frowned as much as McCoy grinned, and it was clear to Frankie how different their childhoods must have been. Evan had grown up hard, that much was clear in the way they moved and interacted with her staff, not to mention the little she knew about their time in prison.

"How is it?" Frankie watched intently as Evan chewed. They ate almost … politely, if that was the right word, cutting their pancake into squares and placing one at a time on their fork. A drop of syrup escaped down their chin. Frankie gripped her utensils tighter so she didn't do something too impulsive, like reach over and wipe the sticky sweetness off with her thumb.

They aren't into you yet. Evan is not your sub so cool your jets.

It was incredibly difficult since every instinct Frankie had screamed at her to go full-on possessive mode with Evan.

"It's good. You not eating?" Evan shot her a look rife with suspicion, then dropped their gaze to the pancakes again. "What'd you do to them?"

Frankie bit back a smile. "Nothing. I was waiting for you to start." *I like watching you eat the food I cooked for you*, she almost added, but it was too soon for all that. She didn't want to scare them away. For the first time in a long time, there was a lightness in Frankie's chest, a buzzing in each of her nerve endings as her brain flooded with possibilities for the future. Why go looking for a sub when there was one right in front of her?

All Frankie had to do was make Evan crave her too.

Frankie was rushing through traffic that evening on the way to her class when a phone call came through on her Bluetooth. Her cousin's name was on the display, and for a moment, she debated answering it. Besides the wonderful, albeit awkward breakfast that morning with Evan, the day had been one pile of shit after another. The last thing she needed was more from her family.

Reaching forward to hit the decline button on the dashboard, she hesitated. It'd been weeks since she'd touched base with Danny. That was a long time for someone she considered like a brother. Frankie heaved a sigh, answering just before the call went to voicemail.

"Hey, Danny. Everything okay?"

"I could ask you the same thing, little cuz. I was beginning to think it'd take an SOS to reach you."

Danny's deep voice boomed through the car's speakers, which was awkward as hell now that she was stuck at a red light. She glanced around her and turned the volume down. "Now that you have, what's up? I can't talk for long. I'm on my way to a meeting."

"You never do, but I won't keep you. Just wondering about the radio silence lately. You leave me on read more times than dudes who ghost their girl do. What's it take to get some attention?"

Frankie shook her head and chuckled at her cousin's dry humor. "One, that was a bit sexist, and two, what are you, twelve? You know how busy owning a business can be."

Blaming her avoidance issue on work was a pathetic excuse, but thankfully Danny didn't call her on it. Instead, his voice grew so soft that Frankie had to adjust the volume again. "Mom missed you over Christmas, Frankie. Two years in a row now. Quit pushing her away."

Frankie clenched her teeth and glared at the dash display, wishing Danny could see how far past the line he'd crossed. "Now she's getting you to speak for her? Auntie B pushed *me* away first, Danny."

Danny's long, drawn-out sigh had Frankie gripping the steering wheel harder. "You know she didn't mean what she said. It was just

...” He trailed off, sighed again, then added quietly, “So complicated, Frankie. She didn't understand.”

“Bullshit.” Frankie's chest tightened, and the argument she'd had with Auntie B two Christmases ago flooded her memories. Emotion swelled in her throat, and she forced out, “What's so complicated about loving someone?”

“It's *who* you loved, Frankie. The who is what made it complicated. Em was—”

“Not blood related, so Auntie B's full of crap.” The light turned green, and Frankie pushed the Audi forward once more. She swallowed, ignoring the burn in her sinuses as tears threatened. “It doesn't matter anymore, does it? I've gotta go now, Danny. Talk soon, okay?”

She ended the call with a jab of her thumb, hating how quickly her family could sour her mood. Was it so awful that she'd wanted to reminisce about Evan a little longer? They'd been in her apartment showering when she'd left.

“Fucking Danny,” she said, snatching her water bottle from the cup holder. Out of all the things her aunt could be a judgmental ass over, it had to be *that* fact. And then to have Danny ring her up only to jump to his mother's defense yet again ... Hell, it was no wonder Frankie had avoided them all as much as possible.

She was ten minutes late by the time she reached the fitness center. She grabbed her duffel bag from the passenger seat and climbed from the Audi, locking the door on the way into the building.

CHAPTER 12

Evan

"Bullshit. What's so complicated about loving someone?"

Evan held their breath, straining their ears to hear Frankie's voice from the front seat. Despite the late December chill, it was hot and stuffy where they hid. Learning the location of wherever Frankie slipped off to twice a week had become an obsession for Evan over the last couple of weeks, ever since Sloane had dropped the hint in conversation. How could she have worked for Frankie for years and never bothered to ask or dig up the information on her own?

It was suspicious as hell that Frankie didn't tell anyone, and something someone who was into illegal things would do. Evan was determined to find out, if for nothing else than the peace of mind of knowing that Frankie was exactly the kind of person their stepfather had described. That she was exactly like them, and the only thing that had kept her out of prison was the badge she'd worn at the time.

Even if she made you breakfast.

"It's *who* you loved, Frankie. The who is what makes it complicated. Em was—"

Evan's eyes narrowed as they heard the deep baritone of Frankie's cousin. They'd uncovered Danny's name while digging for information on O'Rourke's Pub weeks ago. Evan hadn't found much, just that he now lived in B.C.'s wine country with a wife and kids. Kids Frankie apparently wasn't attached to.

"Not blood related, so Auntie B's full of crap. It doesn't matter anymore, does it?"

The tightness in Frankie's voice had Evan holding their breath for more. That was genuine, unmasked hurt, and it filled Evan with questions. Who had Frankie loved that was so wrong in her aunt's eyes? Another cousin? No, she only had Danny, and besides, the O'Rourkes were blood relatives of Frankie's.

Why was Evan getting so caught up in this? *Who cares who she loved? I loved Caleb, and she took him away.*

"I've gotta go now, Danny. Talk soon, okay?"

The call disconnected, and the car filled with silence once more. Somehow, it made the darkness inside the trunk ten degrees more stifling, and let's face it, it was a damn good thing Evan wasn't claustrophobic.

"Fucking Danny," they heard Frankie mutter, and if Evan wasn't mistaken, there was a hint of tears with that statement. Rather than it being a welcome sound, Evan scrunched up their nose. Was mentioning an old relationship all it took for someone as evil as Frankie O'Rourke to cry?

That didn't fit her personality at all.

The moment the car came to a stop, Frankie got out, slamming the door behind her. Evan popped open the interior latch to the trunk but held on to the strap so that the lid didn't blow open. They waited a full minute before inching the lid open bit by bit, making sure no one was near the car to see them.

Shit! Panic stole Evan's breath as they spotted a woman getting out of her car beside Frankie's. They inched the trunk lid down silently, listening intently for the sound of the woman's footsteps on the asphalt. It took another minute or so before it came, and yet another for Evan to calm their racing heart enough to try again. A slick, clammy sweat had formed on their forehead and neck, but it was hard to know if it was from the stuffiness in the trunk or the fact they were under duress.

Hey, at least you can tell the old man you made the switch into illegal territory again, Evan thought with an eye roll. They took another deep breath and inched the trunk lid up once more, relief flooding them when they saw the coast was clear. Quietly, they opened it far enough to climb out onto the cold, slushy pavement, clicking it shut a final time. The car was parked in a backstreet, alleyway entrance of some kind of strip mall. Evan spotted a set of apartment complexes looming far above them on the opposite side of a divider fence and gulped. They were still far too out in the open. Who knew who might have seen them?

Quickly getting to their feet lest anyone spot them lurking near Frankie's car, Evan very casually made their way to the end of the alley, then further to the street corner. The neighborhood was one they hadn't seen before, but with a little effort, Evan made out the street sign. Fishing out their phone, they pulled up the map app and said into the microphone, "Brunswick and Broadway, Vancouver to Davie."

"That checks out," Evan said when the nine-minute route popped up on their screen. It'd been about twelve, but Frankie had hit several red lights on the way. *What's she doing here?* It was time to find out. Evan pocketed their phone again and adjusted their beanie so that it covered their ears. Unfortunately, they lacked body heat on the warmest of days, so they all but froze in the winter.

They continued to the Broadway entrances of the strip mall, noting the various businesses as they passed. A sushi restaurant, an acupuncture clinic, Pilates ... unless there was a back-room poker game in one of the businesses, it didn't make sense for Frankie to be there. Not to mention, they were all closed except for the restaurants.

"Not all," Evan corrected themself as they stopped in front of a martial arts academy. There was no open sign lit up, but the lights were on and noise coming from within. Evan tilted their head in consideration. Frankie was an ex-cop. It made sense she'd know how to take care of herself. Evan recalled how confident she'd looked the first night they'd officially met. She'd snatched the glass from that guy without a second thought, kicking him out as if she could take him down if necessary. So unless she'd parked in a random alley and hoofed it elsewhere, chances were, the academy was Frankie's great big secret.

But why?

Knowing the risk, Evan said the hell with it. Impulsively jumping into the back seat of Frankie's late model Audi and crawling through to the trunk had gotten them this far. It was too late to turn back now. They took another deep breath and pulled open the door.

Hours later, tucked snugly under the heavy duvet in Frankie's guest bedroom, Evan stared at the ceiling, unable to fall asleep. They were tired enough, but every time they closed their eyes, images of Frankie in loose joggers and a ribbed tank top tortured them senseless. Her big secret wasn't nefarious at all. It was good, *too* good for a person as supposedly evil as she was. Frankie dedicated her time to vulnerable people, abused women and the like, and taught them how to protect themselves in a fight. And she was *incredible*, deadly even, at least in the takedown moves she'd shown as an example with her sparring partner.

What level of fucked up was Evan to find that attractive?

It wasn't as if Frankie couldn't still be a horrible human yet put on a charade where she helped people. Many powerful people did that, looked good in public and were the worst of the worst in private.

Still, why hadn't Evan known about this beforehand? They needed to backtrack, go over the information Cecil had given them. It included a printout copy of the police report he'd paid some clerk off for, as well as anything and everything about the femme's personal life—as Frankie, but also when she'd gone by Katheryn. Maybe rereading the report of Caleb's murder would help ground them again.

Knowing they wouldn't be falling asleep anytime soon, Evan flicked on the lamp and got out of bed. They'd arrived by cab long before Frankie returned, yet had done nothing productive in the free time they'd had in the apartment. Breaking into Frankie's personal space had been the first thing to come to mind when Evan moved in the night before, but besides helping themself to a beer earlier, they'd been huddled inside the bedroom. The things Evan had learned about Frankie that evening didn't sit well with them.

When they opened the bedroom door, Evan almost tripped over the shopping bags blocking the entrance into the hall. "What ..." Frowning, Evan crouched to peer inside the closest bag. A brand-new faded pair of denims caught their eye. In addition, there were two crew neck T-shirts, one black and one white, and a pullover hoodie, all with the tags on them. Surprise filled Evan, and they quickly glanced inside the two other bags. One held a set of pajamas, new boxers and socks, and the other toiletries. Suspiciously, the exact same brand Evan had been running out of in their toiletry bag. All they'd bought for the trip were travel size bottles of shampoo and body wash. Frankie must have spotted them sitting on the counter in the pub washroom the day before.

Dumbfounded, Evan picked up the gift bags and carried them to the leather bench in front of their bed. They glanced down at the clothes they'd put back on after their shower, the same clothes they'd worn for the better part of two weeks. They had alternated between a few extra pairs of underwear, but only had room in their backpack for another T-shirt and their hoodie when it got too hot indoors. As for their duffel bag, it'd been stolen the second night on the streets.

"I wasn't sure about your size." Frankie's low voice rang out from the open doorway.

Evan turned to see her watching them, still in her usual pub attire. It was as if she hadn't taken a break from work earlier and gone to get all sweaty. She looked very well put together, albeit tired perhaps. Her long hair was down, and once again, her jacket was off. Evan zeroed in on the several open buttons on her blouse, giving them an ample view of her cleavage.

"I can exchange them if they don't fit, but I think I matched your style correctly." Frankie leaned her head against the doorframe, soaking Evan up with a tired smile.

"I ..." Evan trailed off, swallowing past the growing lump in their throat. Their gaze dropped back to the bags, where one hand was subconsciously tracing the fabric of the pajama pants. They couldn't remember the last time they'd worn new threads, let alone been given anything by anyone. Had it really been the wallet Caleb gave them? But that was … seven years ago. So much had happened during that time. Most of it had been spent locked up, and inside the prison walls, the only "gift" Evan had been grateful for was the choice of trading sex for protection. Some of the inmates never got that option. *Some fucking gift that was.*

But what would it say about them if they accepted Frankie's generosity? Evan's cheeks and throat flushed hot, and they reached up to rub the back of their neck. They didn't look at Frankie as they mumbled, "Thank you."

I'll throw them away when this is over. It's just part of the act, they thought as they lifted the pajamas out of the bag. But they knew they wouldn't, and it wasn't.

"Try them on for me."

Frankie's demand was laced in silk and drenched with innuendo, and Evan's body instinctively responded to the gentle direction. Breathing became a challenge, and a sort of yearning clawed at them from the inside. Their gaze met Frankie's almost helplessly, watching her eyes darken as if she'd read the room and knew exactly what was happening.

"Try them on, Evan. Show me what a great job I did choosing your clothes." Frankie's tongue darted out to lick her lips, and then she turned around so that her back faced Evan. "Go ahead, honey. I promise not to peek."

"Okay," Evan heard themself murmur, and it was like they were having an out-of-body experience. There was no other reason for it, because if they were in their right mind, stripping in front of Frankie wouldn't have crossed it. Even so, Evan found themself removing their sweater and binder too, so that they could rip off the tags and feel the new clothes against their skin. Emotion clogged their throat at Frankie's kindness. By the time they were fully dressed in the long-sleeved thermal top and flannel pajama bottoms, their eyes were misting with tears. "You can turn around."

Frankie did, at once picking up on Evan's mood. Her arrogant once-over did a one-eighty, her face pinching in concern. She crossed the room in three long strides, her hand reaching for Evan's. The shock of her touch on Evan's skin was nothing like they'd have expected. In fact, on the plane ride to Vancouver, Evan had day-dreamed of the many violent things they vowed to do if Frankie ever touched them. They weren't expecting a temporary loss of their independence and function of their limbs. God help them, but they *melted* into her touch.

"What's wrong?" Frankie's lips were parted as she stared down at them. Her thumb caressed Evan's skin. "Were you not okay with ..." She paused, imploring gaze fixed on Evan's. She swallowed as if she'd just considered something she wasn't okay with. "If you weren't okay with me—"

"No one's given me gifts like this before. That's all," Evan admitted, their stomach bottoming out at the honesty. What possessed them to speak their mind in front of Frankie? She was the *enemy*.

"Well, no one has appreciated one of my gifts as much as you, so thank you." One sculpted eyebrow raised, and a teasing grin appeared on Frankie's face. "At least, not one of my G-rated gifts."

"You're pathetic. A child."

Frankie didn't need to say it; Evan could read in between the lines. It was humiliating how in their feelings they got over something so simple. Especially considering who it was from.

"That outfit looks wonderful on you," Frankie whispered, pulling Evan from their misery. They swallowed, blushing under

Frankie's slow exploration of their body. Her eyes met Evan's, lips curling in a flirtatious smile. "I didn't think anyone could make a set of pajamas look so good."

Whelp, there went their cheeks again, flooding with intense heat at Frankie's rapt attention. They averted their gaze to the hands still joined, considering pulling away.

"Have a good sleep, Evan," Frankie said, and before Evan could respond, Frankie's lips were grazing their cheek with a light kiss. She straightened, her smile widening at what Evan was sure was their gaping mouth and silently left the room.

Oh my god.

Evan flopped backwards onto the mattress, covering their face with an arm and groaning.

What have I done?

Chapter 13

Frankie

One night in mid-January, the pub's annual holiday staff party was well underway. It was one of the few times throughout the year that Frankie closed to the public, and the only time when she allowed her staff to drink for free. This year her generosity came at a price.

"I'd cap everyone at two freebies, boss, or at least limit the evening to drinking only what we have in surplus. Some of our domestic beers haven't been selling well, and the same goes for some of our cooler flavors." Sloane tapped the laptop screen, showing January's estimated income in comparison to the inventory. "Since you lost three batches of microbrew, we've already got a deficit in your supply. We'll already have to stretch what's made, and order in a larger quantity from Barry's Brewery in case we run out."

Frankie's lips thinned at the news. She'd known the spoiled batches would have put a damper on the following month—all they ran was a microbrewery, after all—but she hadn't foreseen it possibly affecting tonight's party.

"I don't know what happened." Frankie shook her head. "I can't cap the drinks. I haven't done that since I took over from Danny."

"Hey, as much as we all love the free booze, we aren't gonna fault you for it." Sloane pushed out of the office chair and shrugged. "The customers come first, or else we won't have a job to go to."

"I *know*, Sloane. Quit being cheeky." Frankie eyed Sloane's outfit for the night. The moment the pub had closed at four, she'd swapped her black-on-black uniform for a leather skirt and a gothic style mesh skull crop top with individual, matching slip-on mesh sleeves. She was in what she liked to call her "emo era." Since they'd met, Sloane had shown many other eras of fashion to go along with her eccentric personality. Frankie pointed to the vintage leather heeled Dr. Martens on her feet and tsked. "And hey, don't get so trashed tonight you break an ankle in those."

"Ugh, you're such a mom right now." Sloane rolled her eyes and started for the door, laughing over her shoulder. "And besides, 'trashed' with what high income? I'm a broke bitch, boss."

"Such a brat," Frankie huffed, watching as Sloane shut the door behind her on the way out. Frankie groaned, turning her attention back to the numbers on the screen. Her microbrew flavors were her best sellers, hands down. She didn't want to think about how it might impact her business if any further batches were compromised. A professional had been by to service the tanks, but they had found no issues. It had been Jon that suggested the ruined batches tasted like dust from the mill table. Somehow it must have gotten into brew tanks.

Unfortunately, Sloane was right. Tonight would be the first party since opening the microbrewery that Frankie wouldn't have the means to give her staff free rein over her commercial selection. She sighed, closing the laptop and heading out of the office as well.

There was something not many knew about Frankie. Something she'd struggled with since she was a little girl, a reluctant personality trait she'd fought tooth and nail to conceal since she'd allowed Emily to talk her into going to that damn party as teenagers. In a lot of ways, she was a people pleaser, to the point where her fear of disappointing those she cared for had gotten someone she loved killed.

I'd just be offering up my less popular inventory, not ending the world.

When she reached the front of the pub, Frankie spotted Evan almost immediately. They were dressed in the black shirt and blue denims she'd purchased for them, wearing a black beanie over their buzzed blonde hair, and looking so cute that it took a moment to realize Evan wasn't alone. The twins stood holding pool sticks on either side of Evan, and the trio were in deep conversation. Andy sat with his hip perched on the opposite end of the pool table, chatting with Dakota. Frankie's other staff and their guests for the night were scattered around the rest of the pub. Some had pushed the tables back in one section and made a makeshift dance floor, and others were drinking in the booths and playing cards. Balloons and party banners were strung up on as much surface as Sloane and Lian had managed earlier that day, completely covering the typical Irish pub theme in places.

And sitting alone in a booth adjacent to the pool table was Sawyer. McCoy's girlfriend was well dressed in a cardigan and navy-blue denims, with her thick black hair cascading just past her shoulders. From what Frankie had seen so far, Sawyer seemed like the no-nonsense type. A complete opposite of McCoy, and yet, exactly her type.

"Not enjoying the party?" Frankie asked, sliding into the booth across from Sawyer.

"Frankie, hi." Sawyer paused the glass of water that was on the way to her mouth, slowly setting it back down on the table before scrutinizing Frankie. "No, it's lovely. You've given me some ideas for staff parties at Desmarais."

"Great." Frankie smiled, recalling how McCoy had told her Sawyer was the owner of the French fusion restaurant on Vancouver's west side. Her ex-lover certainly had a type. "However, I don't deserve any of the credit. It's Sloane who's been organizing the staff parties for years."

"Really," Sawyer deadpanned. She pointed past the booth to where Sloane was trying to climb on top of the pool table while McCoy held her back. "*That* Sloane?"

Frankie chuckled, watching the twins a moment longer, especially the way McCoy remained gentle even while lifting her sister over her shoulder. "You'd be surprised. She's also my bar manager and handles all the bookkeeping. When I hired her, I swore her business management certificate wouldn't go to waste."

"I'm sorry, but I think we know two different Sloanes." Sawyer leveled Frankie with a hard stare. "That girl did her best to break McCoy and me up."

Oh, Frankie was aware of what Sloane was capable of. McCoy herself had told her all about the first date sabotage, but Frankie also knew what it was like to feel deserted. It made the best people do ridiculous things they weren't necessarily proud of.

"Tried and failed, remember." Frankie tilted her head in the twins' direction. Her gaze softened slightly when she saw McCoy standing by herself, watching her and Sawyer, but her heart didn't race like it did with Evan. Frankie swallowed, turning back to Sawyer to say, "Think of it like this. You won over the best person imaginable, and now, your prize is putting up with her family."

"I suppose so." Sawyer's lips twitched, and she finally took a drink of her water. "McCoy's been ... not like herself since Christmas. I think the tension between her and Sloane gets stressful at times."

Frankie's stomach tensed, and she inhaled sharply. It had been a constant struggle to detach herself from McCoy since they'd parted ways. Cutting ties with a sub was every bit as torturous as Natasha had warned so long ago. Even now, while Frankie spent much of her free time fantasizing about Evan, with just one mention of McCoy not doing well, the urge to go full Domme was a powerful thing.

"What do you mean 'not like herself'?"

"I think a part of her misses a part of you." Sawyer's response was crisp and to the point, but the feigned confidence was no match for the sudden tic in her clenched jaw.

"It's not necessarily *me* she misses, Sawyer." Frankie took another deep breath, letting her eyes close for a second before refocusing on the older woman. "More than likely, McCoy misses what I represent. Is there a part of her feeling guilty over the issues with Sloane? She might be feeling adrift because a part of her longs to be punished."

"Punished?"

Slowly, Frankie nodded. She glanced at the bar, wishing she'd poured herself a beer before coming over. She sat up straighter, wringing her hands together on the tabletop as she eyed Sawyer. "Yes. BDSM is more than restraints and blindfolds, more than anything else the average light kinkster enjoys. It delves into the mind, far beyond what some can imagine. And every sub is different. Over the years, I learned what McCoy responds to the most. What scenes she likes or how they vary depending on her mood. Have you spanked her yet? Used a flogger?"

"No, not yet. It was mentioned in the beginning…" Sawyer trailed off, her storm grey eyes clouding over. "What if… I can't be what she needs?"

The tightness in Frankie's chest dispersed a little bit with those words. Sawyer's dedication to understanding McCoy and her obvious love for the much younger woman was everything McCoy deserved.

Frankie gave her a wan smile, reaching across the table for Sawyer's hand. She gave it a gentle squeeze. "So long as you're open to learning, I can teach you the basics."

The look of disbelief on Sawyer's face was comical. "*You* will teach me?"

Frankie shrugged before sliding out of the booth. She brushed off her suit. "McCoy means the world to me, so yes. Let's keep in touch, but for now," Frankie leaned down to whisper into Sawyer's ear, "I suggest you learn how to use a strap-on. That's simple enough." Pausing, she smirked. "McCoy likes her wrists and ankles to be restrained while it happens."

Chapter 14

Evan

"Are you much of a reader? It's been mostly eBooks or audio for me these days, but I love print, too."

Evan blinked at Coy's question, baffled by the enthusiasm surrounding her latest random conversation opener. She seemed to have an insatiable zest for life, which only burned brighter whenever she glanced at her girlfriend.

It was a toss-up for Evan whether to instantly like Coy or to allow their own insecurities and baggage to fester inside the possible new friend bubble. It was hard not to feel jealous of the joyous, carefree attitude.

"I'm not. To be honest, I ..." *That's funny. When have you ever been honest? All you do is lie.* Evan cleared their throat, shaking off the less-than-helpful silent commentary. "I'm dyslexic, so reading's always been a struggle for me. Kind of lost interest in the idea over the years, but I'll borrow an audiobook from the library if need be."

"You're dyslexic?" Coy and Sloane, who stood on the opposite side of Evan, echoed in unison.

"So that explains why you got so flustered reading the menu that day," Sloane added, and winked. She took a drink of her vodka cooler, adding, "I assumed it was because you were nervous around me."

The tips of Evan's ears grew hot, and they grinned sheepishly. "I mean, you're not wrong. I was."

"Still are, from what I can tell," Coy teased, reaching around to poke Sloane. "I dunno why. Unless she's being a bitch for absolutely no reason, Sloane's the nicest person around."

"Fuck off, Coy," Sloane shot back, shoving at Coy, but the mechanic barely moved. "Just because you're clueless doesn't mean my reasons aren't any less valid."

Evan squeezed out from between them in case fists started flying. They didn't get far before a hand was snaking through theirs, tugging them to a halt. Evan turned around again and over Sloane's shoulder, spotted Frankie carrying in a platter of appetizers from the kitchen. Behind her, Rain followed with another platter, and they set both out on the waiting tables. Then they were gone again, without Frankie looking Evan's way once. Evan gnawed on the inside of their cheek and wondered at the strange sting they felt beneath their chest. Frankie always looked at them, regardless of whether Evan wanted her to or not.

They sipped the ale being offered complimentary to the staff that night. Evan had heard through the grapevine that it wasn't the selection Frankie usually offered, and that it was the basic, run-of-the-mill brew that anyone could make, but Evan was digging it. They had also heard gossip floating around about how Frankie was running on short supply of her best-selling microbrew.

Evan tried hard not to feel guilty.

If Cecil knew how heavy-chested they were, or how their gut had churned with the news, he'd have certainly given Evan something else to whine about. Frankie deserved much more than she'd received so far as payback. Evan should be elated if her business went under, so that she could learn what it felt like to lose everything. There was nothing like watching someone else's world crumble around them, especially when they learned how avoidable it could have all been.

Or so Cecil says.

"You should hang out with us some night when the rest of the Fab Five are around," Coy said, holding her mug of beer out. "To new friends."

"Yes, to new friends!" Sloane agreed, clinking Coy's mug before Evan's. Her smile was wide and infectious, her green eyes glistening under the dimly lit pub lights.

"To new friends," Evan said, toasting them both before taking another drink. The ache in their chest grew larger, and they weren't at all surprised when the bridge of their nose started to burn, the threat of tears stinging their eyes. Did their friendship count if it'd begun under false pretenses?

Andy and his girlfriend sidled up beside them. "Hey, how 'bout another game? Then it'll be the best out of three."

"You sure you want that? Best out of three takes a bet," Sloane drawled, holding her drink out with her index finger pointing toward Andy. "And you know I rarely lose, my sweet, handsome Newfie friend."

"Are ye drunk already, b'y?"

"Sloane, c'mon. We can shoot a game without needing to bet on it," Coy told her sister, annoyance crossing her features.

"Ugh, you're no fun anymore," Sloane pouted, before tossing her drink back and finishing it in three long swigs. She handed the empty over to Coy, who shot her another peeved look, and tugged on Evan's hand. "When I'm finished giving Evan a proper tour, I plan to wipe the floor with you guys."

"But I already got the—"

"C'mon. It'll be fun." Sloane winked at them, something she did at an alarming rate once a few drinks were in her, and led the way through the pub.

Evan allowed it, assuming they were headed for the washroom. They'd been dying to relieve their bladder for the last thirty minutes or longer and practically whimpered when Sloane pulled out a set of keys in front of Frankie's office. She waggled her eyebrows suggestively. "Finally, I'll be able to get you to myself."

"Um, yeah." Evan's smile was unsure, because the idea of them *together* was the ideal scenario to be unsure about. Sloane was everything they should want, but ...

Evan glanced around them, waiting for Frankie to pop out of her hiding place and demand to know why Sloane was helping herself to her office.

"Benefits of being the manager." Sloane's hand was on the doorknob. She cast Evan a heated look and turned the handle with another wink. The unconscious movement might have worked on others, but for Evan, it was distracting.

"Whoa!" they exclaimed as Sloane yanked them inside Frankie's office. She quickly pressed Evan against the closed door, cupped their cheeks in her palms, and kissed them.

The first sensation to hit Evan was the sickeningly sweet odor of vodka as Sloane breathed into their mouth. The next was the extreme lack of sexual tension between them, but perhaps it was because Sloane had caught Evan off guard.

"C'mon. Have you been in here before?" Sloane asked, draping her arm around Evan's waist on the way to Frankie's large, rectangular desk. Her lips found Evan's again, kissing them longer this time. Evan returned the kiss because, why not? They couldn't—and wouldn't—entertain how magical it'd felt the other night when Frankie's lips had grazed their cheek.

Evan's ass pressed into something solid, and then Sloane whispered, "Get on the desk, Evan."

They felt a bit dazed looking back at her but did as she requested. Sloane shot Evan a devilish look, her fingers landing on the seam of fabric leading into her cleavage. "Close your eyes."

Evan laughed in disbelief but did as Sloane asked. "We're gonna get in trouble."

"No way. And don't peek."

"I'm not." Evan couldn't help but smile at Sloane's silliness. The whole thing was ridiculous, but it was turning into one helluva night.

They heard Sloane moving around, and then the distinct beep of numbers being punched into a keypad. Realization hit Evan like a tidal wave. They cracked one eye open, just enough that Sloane wouldn't notice, and sure enough, their new friend was drunkenly attempting to disarm the safe's code. A sly grin crept over Evan's face as they watched Sloane get it right finally. Breaking into Frankie's safe later would be too easy. Sloane opened the door and started pulling bills out of Frankie's safe and stuffing them into her boot. As she was closing the door, Evan caught the gleam of a silver handgun.

Holy shit!

Evan squeezed their eyes shut again, old images of Caleb's coroner report flooding their memories. Seeing him on a slab, cold as ice. The ME had stitched up his wounds, but nothing about the sharp entry and exit points of the bullet could have stopped Evan's imagination of what happened that night.

"Have you ever broken in anywhere just to hook up with someone?" Sloane's voice was close now, so close, her hot breath tickling Evan's ear seconds before her lips did.

"You're a bad influence." Evan clenched their hands to their sides, struggling with the urge to shove her off. When their eyes opened, Sloane was stripped of her shirt, and her bra-clad breasts were doing their best to caress Evan's chin.

The office door opened, and Evan and Sloane jumped when it crashed against the wall. Evan swiveled around from their place on top of Frankie's desk, almost knocking their forehead into Sloane's, and stared, mouth agape, at the stormy look in Frankie's eyes.

"Get the fuck out of my office. Sloane, you should know better." Frankie marched toward them, her glare bouncing between Sloane's half-naked state to, well, whatever current hellish state Evan was in. She grabbed Sloane's arm, pulling her away from Evan, and didn't stop until she'd pushed Sloane out into the hallway. "This is *my* office. You work for me. Don't fucking forget it."

"Jesus, Frankie, we were just having fun." Sloane's whine died off when her discarded shirt struck her in the face, compliments of Frankie.

Evan slid off the desk on wobbly legs. They hadn't drunk too many beers, perhaps three, but damn did it feel like they were leaving the office intoxicated. Evan was almost to the door when Frankie caught their arm, turned them around, and pulled them closer. Unhelpfully, Evan's breath hitched with a dramatic flare, as if they were a couple intakes away from an orgasm. The reaction caused Frankie's entire demeanor to drip with a kind of hate-fuck possessiveness Evan had never seen before.

Then Frankie let go of Evan and turned away. "Leave," she growled, "before I do something I regret."

The next morning, Evan stared at the locked closet door, just as they had for the last ten minutes after their shower. If their focus was enough to melt the door or see through it, both would have happened already. Evan was curious by nature, and hearing that something was off limits just made them want it more. And if someone like Frankie kept a closet locked when her own bedroom didn't even have one, that could only mean one thing.

Secrets lay beyond that door. Fuel for Evan's vendetta, something they could use to con Frankie, or tangible proof they could expose, stating what a horrible human she was. Something Evan could later reason with as to why they'd done what they'd done to her.

Isn't Caleb's death reason enough, you fucking coward?

Evan ground down on their molars. Their hands clenched the bed sheets, and with a deep breath, they pried them open and got to their feet. More evidence was necessary for their peace of mind. Obsessively hanging on to an old news clipping of Frankie in uniform—during a time when she went by Officer Katheryn O'Rourke—and reading a printout of the police report, all seemed so different now that they'd gotten to know Frankie. If Evan didn't know better, they'd question if Frankie was the one who'd shot

Caleb. What if the police report Cecil had received was wrong? Yes, Frankie had confirmed she'd once been a cop. And she had a gun in her safe—but those things alone didn't tell much.

"Just do it already." Evan sighed heavily, checked that the bedroom door was shut, and retrieved their lock pick from inside the dresser.

It was stupid that hesitation was now a factor. It was as if a part of Evan didn't *want* to displease Frankie, but that made zero sense. They were a thief. Breaking into places and stealing was what they'd always done, and who the hell cared what offense they did toward the enemy anyway?

"Fuck. How you gonna kill her, hmm?" The endgame seemed further away each day, especially after the humiliating way Evan had reacted in Frankie's office. Instead of feeling threatened and defensive, they'd gotten more turned on than ever before.

Evan got to work using the lockpick. The closet door was child's play, really, and within seconds, they were granted access to the mystery that lay beyond. Their eyes widened.

"Holy shit."

CHAPTER 15

Frankie

"I should fire you."

The blatant threat didn't seem to ruffle Sloane's feathers one bit. She gathered up another stack of dirty dishes from the deserted pub table and tossed an irritating smirk Frankie's way. "But you won't, and besides, quit pretending you're not more upset over me kissing Evan than you are about me helping myself to your office. I know you like them."

Frankie's gaze narrowed to slits. The tightness in her chest crept up her throat, strangling her. Watching Sloane's eye roll and assessing glance made her want to throttle the younger woman. "If you know," she growled, then clamped her mouth shut. Taking a deep breath, she tried again. "Don't fuck with me, Sloane. I saw more of your skin last night than I ever wished to. Not to mention, I still sign your paychecks."

"Relax. I didn't mean it the way you took it." Sloane shook her head and headed for the kitchen. Frankie followed. She'd left the apartment earlier today, knowing there would be plenty of cleanup to help with before the pub opened. When they arrived in the kitchen, Donnie and Dakota were busy with prep. Sloane stacked the dirty dishes onto the rack and pushed them through the dishwasher before turning to Frankie, resignation clear in her green gaze. "I've got the worst luck. I swear, every time I like someone, someone else beats me to them. Coy snatched up Ash before I could work my magic, and—"

"Don't remind me." Frankie scowled. She would always regret agreeing to an open relationship with McCoy. Since Frankie couldn't ever be a switch, and McCoy had no interest in being a full-time sub, she hadn't known how else to keep her. Still, watching McCoy play the field right in front of her had been a slow torture, one Frankie vowed never to repeat.

"My point is," Sloane continued, louder this time. "Now it's you, with Evan, who I happen to really like, by the way. So when will it be my turn?"

"You barely know them."

"Same goes for you, boss, and yet, it doesn't stop you from marking your territory." Sloane rolled her eyes, but it did nothing to disguise the hurt. She grabbed the empty tray and started back out to the dining room.

A mental image of her pissing all over Evan popped into Frankie's head, and she wrinkled her nose. *I don't mark my territory.* She followed Sloane, almost crashing into her when Sloane suddenly swiveled around.

"And what *was* that last night, anyway? Evan left the office after me, looking all hot and bothered. Can you sniff out a sub, or was it coincidental?"

Frankie arched a brow. "First off, your two assumptions aren't necessarily related, and second, show some respect when you're referring to Evan. And third, I'm not having this conversation with you, Sloane."

"Fine."

A barely discernible sigh of relief left Frankie. She relaxed her shoulders. "Good. Now let's get to work. There's a lot to be done before opening."

Needing distance between them, Frankie decided to restock the bar rather than wait for Sloane or Andy to do it. It gave her time to reflect not only on their earlier conversation, but also on what she was doing with Evan. Just because their body responded to Frankie didn't mean they were on board mentally. Hell, at times Evan looked like they hated Frankie. What was up with that? *It's probably a defense mechanism, but still.* It would be wrong to take advantage of their chemistry if Evan wasn't completely into it.

As Frankie rotated and filled the beer fridge, thoughts of the soft butch teased her relentlessly. It'd been, well, years since she'd taken so quickly to someone. Something about Evan screamed out to her. It went deeper than their looks or the harsh chip on their shoulder. Behind their enigmatic, bi-colored eyes, Evan was calculating, hard-working, intelligent, and—

Mine.

"Fuck, Sloane's right." Frankie shoved the possessive notion away. Going full alpha on someone who shot figurative daggers at her half the time would *not* be a good look for her *or* the business.

"I'm headed upstairs for a bit. Text if you need me before one," Frankie said later as she finished wiping down the counters. Everything was restocked and sanitized, ready for another shift. She'd checked on the brewery as soon as she'd come down that morning, and everything looked as it should. After screwing up the last batch, she'd been paying close attention to it.

"Will do, but we should be good. Lian's on her way in, and Andy's on call," Sloane reminded her, not stopping to look at Frankie as she mopped. Frankie had a lot of complicated feelings toward Sloane, mostly tied in with McCoy, but one thing was certain: the woman wasn't afraid to work. "Have fun with Evan."

"Evan?" Frankie echoed. "I don't even know if they're up there. Quit making something out of nothing, Sloane. It's beneath you." With that, she marched to the back stairwell to the private entrance of her apartment. She'd told Sloane the truth; she *didn't* know Evan's whereabouts, but that didn't mean she wasn't hoping they were inside the apartment. She'd barely seen them since the party the night before, and honestly, Evan hadn't exactly been speaking to her after she caught them with Sloane in her office. Evan, who had sat on her desk and been an equal participant in Sloane's kiss. Frankie rolled her lips inward. She was far too jealous to be with someone who wasn't totally committed to her. So why was she so fixated on Evan when Evan was paying a little too much attention to Sloane?

The apartment was quiet when she let herself inside, and her gaze immediately dropped to the boot rack to see the footwear Evan always wore. A smile tugged at Frankie, and she slipped out of her wedge heels and placed them beside Evan's boots. It was a different feeling, sharing her space with someone else after all these years. Especially with someone like Evan, whom she had fantasies about that no typical roommate should.

"I reek of stale beer and fries," she grumbled, entering her bedroom long enough to grab her robe off the hook behind the door. She needed a shower, pronto. Evan's door was closed as she passed on the way to the bathroom, but there was a lingering scent of Evan's woodsy soap when she closed the door behind her. "Maybe not asleep after all." Frankie inhaled, humming with pleasure as she stripped out of her clothes. She hurried with her shower, successfully getting her hair out of the way and half her body washed before the loofah snagged on one of her nipple piercings.

"Oh my sweet fuck!" Frankie sucked in a sharp breath, her fingers tightening around the loofah to hold it in place. Shit, that stung! It had only happened twice since getting her nipples done, but twice was plenty. Unexpectedly yanking on her piercing was significantly different from purposefully attaching a chain to the nipple hoops and letting it dangle all day. "Not that you let anyone see it. Or anything else." She carefully detached the loofah from her piercing before finishing her shower.

Her hair was still damp as she donned her teal silk robe and made her way out of the bathroom. She didn't get far as the sound of Evan grunting and swearing beyond their bedroom door made Frankie pause. She gave a soft knock. "Everything okay?"

Silence, then Evan said in a voice so low Frankie had to strain to hear, "I'm stuck."

"Stuck?" How could they be stuck? There wasn't anything in the guest bed ... oh. Annoyance rippled through Frankie. "Are you in the closet?"

Evan sighed. "You might as well come in."

"I seem to recall telling you not to go inside there. Not to mention, it was locked," Frankie bit out, turning the doorknob and pushing the bedroom door open. "Your issue with authority is ..." Her voice died off as she got a good look at the situation before her. Evan had not only broken into the closet, but they'd torn it apart by the look of things. Frankie's toys were spread out over the made-up bed, her St. Andrew's Cross leaning up against the long wall, and in the dead center of the chaos was Evan. Wearing just a binder and a pair of boxers, one of the handcuffs from Frankie's now set up bondage frame was securing Evan in place.

A laugh bubbled up inside Frankie, but she smothered it by clearing her throat. "Do you play, Evan? You should have waited for me."

"Do I ... No. I saw it and was just ..." Evan's voice trailed off. They wouldn't meet her gaze, and that wouldn't do.

Frankie closed the space between them with three long strides, reached a tentative hand out to cup the crook of Evan's jaw, and tilted their face up. "Look at me. There's no need to feel embarrassed. This is a safe, non-judgmental space, Evan. Want me to uncuff you?"

Evan's eyelashes fluttered as they finally looked up. Their gaze widened slightly when they noticed her piercings beneath the bathrobe's thin material, and by the time their eyes finally met, Evan's cheeks were tinged pink.

"What do you think of them?" Frankie husked, and together they watched as her nipples tightened further under the attention.

"They're sexy," Evan admitted, blushing even more now. They glanced around the room at the toys spread throughout. "Are you, like, into crazy sex parties or something? Why have you got all these ..."

"Sex toys?" Frankie finished for them. When they gave a helpless nod, Frankie ducked her head, grazing her lips across Evan's ear as she purred, "I'm a Dominant, but I have a feeling you already know what that means. Don't you, Evan?" She pulled back, caressing Evan's free arm, dancing her fingers along the skin. "Otherwise, why would you willingly handcuff yourself to my bondage frame?"

Evan licked their lips. When Frankie stepped away, they tried to follow, only for the handcuff with their wrist still attached to jangle against the steel frame. They didn't ask to be set free, and she was enjoying this too much to rush. "Who do you dominate?"

Frankie sashayed over to the bed for a closer inspection of her toys. Evan had organized each one meticulously. She chose one of her favorite beginner crops and picked it up. "Any submissive that I connect with. It could be you, if you're willing. Tell me what you were thinking when you broke into the closet and discovered my toys. What crossed your mind when you realized what the bondage frame was for?"

Frankie turned back in time to see Evan close their eyes. An unmistakable hitch of breath left their lips, and they swallowed hard. "I wanted to know what it felt like to be trapped under your spell. I-I could see you torturing so—"

"Not torture," Frankie interrupted, closing the space between them again. Their eyes met once more, and Frankie teased the crop up Evan's bare legs. Satisfaction grew when she felt their body shudder. She set the crop back on the mattress and continued. "Pleasure. And punishment, but only with consent."

"C-consent?"

"Yes, consent is key. Consent and safety, or all this"—she gestured around the room at her various toys and equipment—"wouldn't be possible." Evan squirmed under the heat of Frankie's gaze. Her words were having the desired effect on her little thief. *Good.* But today would be an introduction, no more. Evan needed time to reflect, to decide if going further with Frankie was something they wanted.

Frankie reached up and flipped open the handcuff's quick-release lever, freeing Evan. They stumbled forward into her arms before regaining their footing. Still, they didn't move away from Frankie's close proximity. A delicious sensation raced through her as her piercings scraped across Evan's exposed clavicle. Frankie reached out, tilting Evan's face to hers.

"Frankie." Evan's chest rose and fell heavily now, their blue and brown eyes darkened with lust.

"May I kiss you, Evan?"

Evan's fingers closed around hers. Uncertainty mounted in their expression for an agonizing moment, but they nodded, licking their lips again. Frankie didn't wait for them to change their mind. Her mouth was on theirs in seconds, a firm kiss cementing whatever new connection they'd found together.

CHAPTER 16

Evan

EVAN COULDN'T THINK. MINDLESS, boneless in the arms of the enemy. Frankie's lips were possibly the softest in existence. Velvet soft, which was a stark contrast to the hard edges Evan knew she was capable of. Plans to escape Frankie's mind games had evaporated the moment they'd opened the closet. There, Evan's repressed desires came to light in the darkened walk-in space. They'd had fantasies of being held down during sex ever since they'd watched the stash of old porn Caleb had kept under his bed. Discovering Frankie was a Domme ...

So much about her now made more sense.

"I want you to be mine. No one else's," Frankie murmured against Evan's mouth before capturing their bottom lip between her teeth. She gave it a gentle tug, and a cross between pain and pleasure raced up Evan's spine. "If you were my sub, we could play for real. Just imagine what it would feel like to be fully cuffed and at my mercy, little thief."

Evan's lips parted, and they were certain something sensible would eventually come forth, a polite decline of the offer perhaps, but Frankie took the pause as an invitation to devour them once more. Evan's eyes fluttered closed again, and they stifled a groan as Frankie's tongue expertly fucked their mouth. Arousal shot straight to Evan's core, but it didn't stop there. The delicious sensation of Frankie's silken tongue owning their mouth set fireworks off inside them. Their legs buckled, but before Evan could fall, Frankie scooped them up in her arms without ever breaking the kiss.

The fuck is happening right now? was all Evan could manage as Frankie carried them to the bed. They weren't just an observer, however. Evan's arms somehow found their way around Frankie's neck, and they were pulling her closer, gasping for breath when Frankie broke their kiss long enough to shove her toys aside to make room for them.

"If you were my sub, I'd spend hours testing out each one of these on you. Filling you up, fucking you with them while you are tied and begging me to let you come."

"Oh shit," Evan moaned, and images of Frankie doing just that flashed across their mind as Frankie kissed them again. So hot, she was so fucking hot that Evan gleefully welcomed the fantasy of being bound and pounded into oblivion. An orgasm from Frankie would be wild.

Frankie nibbled on Evan's bottom lip again, before placing wet kisses along their jaw. "Can I touch you, Evan?"

Evan blinked through the sensual fog of their arousal, Frankie's question reaching them slowly. She was on top of them, the part in her silk bathrobe far enough open now that Evan caught the flash of areola with each movement. Wait, was that the edge of one of her piercings? Evan's mouth watered, completely preoccupied as they watched the robe slip open and close.

"You can look, but no touching," Frankie said between kisses. Arousal flushed her cheeks as well, but it wasn't until Evan stared up at the smoldering intensity of her brown eyes that the spell broke.

"N-no, get off me!" Evan drew their leg up sharply and knocked their knee as hard as they could into Frankie's backside.

Frankie fell forward, but just as she would have landed heavily on top of Evan, Evan rolled away. "The fuck, little thief, stop." Frankie grabbed them up in her arms easily, holding them in place. "Calm down."

"Let me go!" Hot, panicked tears sprung forth, and Evan thrashed against Frankie, successfully catching an elbow to her face before she released them again. *Holy fuck, I just made out with Caleb's killer.* Evan fell off the bed, taking a handful of sex toys with them. A dildo landed on their face. They were going to be sick all over the floor if they didn't hustle ass.

"Evan, talk to me." The concern in Frankie's voice was just another lie. Evan stood and stumbled out of the room to the bathroom. They slammed the door and locked it before collapsing in front of the toilet.

What have I done? Nausea thundered through them, making their mouth water, but the only thing that left them was more tears. *You're pathetic and weak.* Cecil wasn't there to remind them, but they knew. It was no wonder Cecil had favored Caleb. Evan's brother wouldn't have botched an assignment and developed an attraction to the target.

"Stupid, stupid," Evan spat, banging their fist against their forehead. They weren't just stupid, they were *sick* to find Frankie alluring. The same woman who had taken Caleb from this world and gotten away with it.

A soft knock sounded on the bathroom door. "Evan? Please talk to me. I'm sorry if I overstepped. I got carried away."

Evan covered their mouth, smothering a sob. They squeezed their eyes shut, desperate to block out the bullshit worry in Frankie's muffled voice. Tension radiated through them, coiling their muscles until they sat rigid on the floor. They would not utter a sound. Frankie didn't deserve an ounce of explanation from them.

"I'm so sorry, honey. I-I'll give you space."

Frankie's retreating footsteps weren't enough to release the grip around Evan's chest, but at least they could go back to sobbing openly.

"Hell, no." They were *not* going to do that. Crying was for pussies. That's what Cecil had always told Evan and Caleb growing up. Channel the unnecessary feelings into something useful. Like revenge. Take back the control. *Just take Frankie out of the picture and move on. Fuck trying to bring down her business.* After they were done with Frankie, she'd be too dead to care about her business anyway.

Evan forced their body to uncoil enough to stand. They flicked up the lever on the sink tap and stared themself down in the mirror as they splashed cold water on their flaming cheeks. Their eyelids were puffy and red, not at all indifferent like the vigilante they'd set out to be weeks ago. It made no difference. Evan shut the tap off and patted their cheeks and hands dry. Their stomach still rolled slightly, like a washing machine at the beginning of its cycle, but they took a deep breath and squared their shoulders anyway.

There was no sign of Frankie as Evan crept through the silent apartment. Both bedrooms sat with the doors ajar, so chances were she was beyond one of them. Likely hers, unless she was sitting in wait for Evan to return so they could have a friendly chat. Evan inwardly scoffed as they padded silently into the entranceway. They wouldn't risk trying to get to the backpack in their room in case Frankie was waiting, but luckily, all they needed was tucked away in their leather jacket. Usually strapped to the inside of their boot, Evan retrieved the small hunting knife from the jacket's breast pocket and carefully unsheathed it. The hand with the knife trembled slightly as they hid it behind them on the way to the bedrooms. Their mouth had gone dry, but thankfully, so had the tedious tears. They could do this. They could avenge Caleb and go home. Cecil would be so proud that Evan would finally get to see their mother again.

Seven years later, did she still blame Evan, too?

They inched Frankie's bedroom door open first, wide enough to peek inside. Her bed was made, and a yoga mat rested unrolled by the bay windows looking out onto Davie St, but she wasn't there. Evan crept back out, swallowed the massive lump lodged in their throat, and continued to the guest bedroom. The largest, nicest room out of the two, and now Evan knew it was because it wasn't a guest room at all. It was Frankie's kink room.

Fuck off, Evan reprimanded their traitorous body as tingles of awareness flared low in their belly. Taking a deep breath, they nudged the door open with one foot. If they could catch Frankie unaware, they'd sneak up—

Evan stilled as Frankie came into view. She was cleaning off the bed and putting her many toys in the large leather bag they'd come out of, and she was crying. Nothing loud and messy, but enough that she had to pause every few seconds to wipe the tears away. Evan's chest clenched at the sight, and they gnawed on the fleshy part of their cheek until blood oozed over their tongue. *What does she have to cry over? She didn't almost fuck a killer.* It was then that Evan noticed Frankie was speaking to someone.

"They looked at me terrified, Danny. L-like I was about to … *assault them.*" Frankie choked out the last two words. Evan caught the Bluetooth earpiece as she turned to sit on the bed. She was so distracted that she hadn't yet seen Evan watching from the doorway. "A-after what I went through, I would *never.*"

What she went through? Evan narrowed their eyes. An uneasy feeling niggled at them as they backed out of the room. Something about this didn't feel right. A cold killer wouldn't break down because she thought she'd harmed Evan. Frankie was supposed to act nonchalant, making Evan's decision undisputable. This new information was unplanned. Evan couldn't lash out now no matter how in their feelings they were. Despite their upbringing, Evan liked to think they were still a decent person. No, they wouldn't kill Frankie.

Not until she'd shown all her cards.

CHAPTER 17

Frankie

"How can one small human do this?" Frankie grumbled into the bathroom mirror as she applied concealer over the bruise under her eye. Evan stood just over five feet tall, was very lean, and probably weighed no more than a hundred and ten pounds soaking wet, yet not only had they successfully knocked Frankie over, they'd hit her hard enough to cause swelling and a bruise.

I deserved it.

Frankie pinched her lips together, taking a deep breath in and out through her nose. She should never have grabbed Evan after they'd knocked her off the first time. She wanted to call it instinctual, but honestly, she wasn't sure what had happened. At first, she mistook Evan's aggression as an attack, but after, Frankie had freaked out a little, worried she'd somehow hurt them. In response, Evan had done what any cornered animal would do—attack.

"Let me go!"

Goosebumps broke out over Frankie's arms whenever she recalled those words. Evan had screamed them in such a way that it could only mean one thing. Something Frankie had said or done had triggered them.

"Who hurt you?" Frankie whispered, reaching for her lipstick. She hadn't seen Evan since the "incident," as she was calling it, but could guess they weren't anywhere in the building. If they didn't show up for their shift, Frankie would deal with it. Regardless of the fact that a huge part of her wanted to find Evan and hold on to them for dear life, the last thing she should do was chase them down when things were so volatile between them.

Frankie finished getting ready and had just enough time to make a protein shake before heading out the door. She locked up and headed downstairs, checking her purse to make sure she'd packed her cell. It was surprisingly therapeutic to speak to Danny earlier. Frankie may have called in a panic, but they chatted for quite a while after. Only he and Auntie B knew everything about Frankie's past, and her inability to open that ominous door was why she continued to fail with relationships.

A better Domme would have read the room and not pushed for more than a kiss, Frankie thought bitterly on the way to her office. It's why McCoy had left her. She'd said it wasn't, but what else could Frankie think? She'd only had two other subs before McCoy, and neither one had wanted Frankie as their Domme for long.

A knock landed on her open door. "Hey, boss, any idea where Evan is?"

Frankie set her purse and protein shake on her desk, taking a moment to gather herself before turning. Rain looked at her expectantly. "Evan wasn't feeling well. I doubt they'll be in, so I'll need to do some rearranging in the kitchen."

"Want me at the dish pit?"

Frankie tapped her chin and slowly shook her head. "No, I think we can all help with the dishes in between other tasks for now. Spread the word for me?" Rain nodded, taking off again. Frankie sank into her office chair, eyeing up the shake for lunch instead of the salad she'd gone upstairs for in the first place. She sighed, picking it up and taking a sip. Somehow, she needed to push thoughts of Evan and her own insecurities aside for, oh ... about twelve hours.

Good fucking luck with that.

Evan was situated at the dining booth when Frankie got home that night, sitting lengthwise on the bench with their back against the wall, boots barely reaching the edge. Two empty bottles of Frankie's homemade brew sat on the table next to them.

Frankie's throat worked overtime as she swallowed. It'd been awful not knowing where Evan had disappeared to. "You're here."

Evan glanced up from where they were working in their sketchbook, an unreadable look on their face. Their gaze landed on the floor past Frankie, and she turned to see Evan's backpack. "I left, then remembered I was homeless before this, so ..." Evan shrugged one shoulder and briefly met Frankie's gaze. "I bought new doorknobs for the bedrooms. You need a better toolkit, by the way."

"Doorknobs?"

"Yes." Irritation crossed Evan, but as swift as it'd come, it was gone again. "Ones with a lock. As your tenant, I have the right to feel safe in my personal space. Don't I?"

"Of course. Of course you do, Evan. I never intended ... Earlier when we ..." Frankie couldn't get the words out. She cleared her throat. "At what point did you no longer consent? I should have explained safe words, and then you could have said something. I would have stopped, Evan, I-I, I didn't mean to ... I would have stopped. Did something happen to you? Before, in the past?"

"Who's Emily?"

The abrupt change in topic threw Frankie off guard, but then, she had a feeling Evan had done it on purpose. Her shoulders sagged, and she slumped into the dining booth across from Evan. "Emily? How do you know that name?"

"I heard you on the phone this morning. Was she a girlfriend?"

Frankie frowned. "You eavesdropped on my private conversation? You had no right."

"You were in my bedroom, cleaning up."

Unease settled over Frankie as she recalled her conversation with Danny. The past had been brought up throughout the call, and with it, the topic of Emily. There hadn't been a phone call where Emily wasn't discussed. Even gone, she played a pivotal role in Frankie's relationships.

"Did she give consent in the beginning too?"

"Stop talking about her," Frankie snapped. She shoved herself out of the booth and glared down at Evan. "Next time, knock instead of skulking around." She had to get out of the room before she did something she regretted, like break down in front of Evan. Frankie fled to her bedroom, noticed that the handle on the door was indeed swapped for one with a lock, and shut it firmly behind her. Exhaustion from the day weighed down on her as she stripped her clothes off and crawled into bed. Tears burned her eyes, and she wiped them away angrily.

"Fuck you, Evan," she said in a choked whisper. Fuck them for making her worry, for causing her heart to bleed tonight when all she'd wanted was an honest conversation. And fuck them for amplifying the self-doubt she already had as a Domme.

Brushing more tears away, Frankie leaned over and pulled open the drawer of her bedside table. She rummaged around for the picture of Emily she always kept there, frowning when she came back empty-handed. Sitting up now in the bed, she sniffled and reached for the drawer again, this time pulling it out completely. She turned the contents over on her bed, sifting through the small pile. A pair of suede wrist cuffs, vibrator, lozenges, phone charger, e-reader, but the picture wasn't there.

"Shit."

Had it fallen out in her mad search for her charger the other night?

Frankie didn't throw the drawer, even though she wanted to. She placed everything calmly back inside and returned it to the bedside table. She was too mentally and emotionally depleted to get down and look for the picture tonight. Tomorrow she would, and perhaps then she and Evan could have a proper conversation. She'd finally met someone she felt she truly connected with, yet at every turn, Evan seemed to take a step forward with her only to take two giant leaps back. What if Frankie was wrong? What if Evan wasn't submissive enough?

What if Frankie were no longer dominant enough?

CHAPTER 18

Evan

"Why isn't it done by now?"

Evan pulled the phone away, wincing at the voice barking in their ear. Cecil was loud enough on a good day, let alone when he was angry.

"I'm still fucking with her business." *And looking for clues about Frankie's character.* Evan started to move again when the walk sign lit up and had to sidestep a woman pushing a baby stroller.

"Yeah, well, my contact says the pub still stands. So I suggest you quit screwin' around and get it done, Evan."

"Sir, I don't think ... How sure are you that Frankie is the one who—"

"Are you doubting my history with that bitch? Or Jerry, who stood just feet away from her two months ago?"

Evan swallowed. "No, of course not. It's just—"

"That bitch cop killed Caleb. Get the job done, Evan, or so fucking help me I'll come out there and kick your ass before offing her myself," Cecil yelled, and before Evan could get another word in, the call was dropped.

Evan pocketed the phone. "Shit." Apprehension clawed at their insides. Cecil showing up was the last thing they wanted. What was Evan going to do? Nothing about Frankie was how Cecil had described her. *Cold-blooded, unpunished dirty cop.* Frankie seemed good. Mischievous at times, maybe, but she was caring and protective. And she was very into Evan. But what else could Frankie show them to confirm how wrong Cecil was? Because he had to be wrong. Perhaps he'd been holding onto the wrong police report all these years.

Why not just ask Frankie over breakfast one morning? Oh yeaaah. They could already imagine how *that* conversation would go.

"So ... did you by chance fall into a fit of rage and shoot my brother seven years ago?"

"What? No, of course not, honey. Now, would you care for more toast?"

Evan smirked. They rounded the corner of Davie St., immediately spotting the European bakery and coffee shop Sloane had mentioned in their text thread earlier that morning. Stepping inside the building, Evan relaxed a fraction as the gentle warmth and delicious smells enveloped them. They peeled off their fingerless gloves, glancing around the café for any sign of Sloane and Andy. Since the staff party the week prior, the three of them had become friends to some degree. Andy was friendly and charismatic, and honestly, too damn good a person to be hanging with the likes of Evan. But whatev. It wasn't as if any of Evan's new friends were aware of all the shit they got up to when no one was looking.

Once they'd ordered a hot chocolate with whipped cream, Evan found an empty table near the back and took a seat. From other interactions with Sloane, they knew there was a high chance that she'd be late. Work seemed to be the only place she *wasn't* late. Andy seemed like the punctual type, but Evan wouldn't hold their breath. People in general were usually unreliable.

Evan took a careful sip of the hot chocolate, toying with their wallet resting on the table. They flipped it open to see the picture they'd stolen from Frankie's bedroom. A pretty, teenage girl with auburn hair and freckles stared back at Evan. The portrait was several years old, with some wear and tear on the edges and a crease down the middle. Evan had recognized the name Frankie had written on the back the moment they'd spotted it. After returning to the apartment with the new door handles to install, there hadn't seemed like a more perfect time to snoop inside Frankie's personal space. Evan even wore gloves for the occasion—latex ones they'd taken from the pub kitchen. And they had been careful, not leaving an inch of Frankie's bedroom unchecked or after, making sure everything was put back in the right place. Becoming a con artist like Cecil might have been out of the question, but no one could fault Evan's attention to detail when they were motivated.

So, who was Emily? That was what Evan wanted to find out. They wouldn't stop until they'd discovered everything there was to Frankie, if for nothing else than to have a proper case when it came time to be judge and jury. When they'd arrived in Vancouver, nothing had seemed more important than killing Frankie and going home. As awful as Evan's life had sometimes been before they'd wound up in prison, it was still home. A place they could lie their head or spend time with their mom when she got out of the psych ward.

Since getting to know Frankie and wanting her in ways they shouldn't, Evan wasn't so sure they'd been tasked with the right job. Maybe they weren't the revenge type. Caleb had always said that Evan thought too much, felt too much. Maybe he'd been right.

"If you frown and think any harder, smoke's gonna come outta yer ears, b'y." Evan blinked, Andy's face coming into focus as he pulled up a chair. He shrugged out of his insulated parka and nodded to Evan's exposed wallet. "Who's that?"

"No one," Evan hurried to say, swiping up the wallet and tucking it into the back pocket of their jeans. One of the new pairs Frankie had purchased. Evan had paired them with one of the long-sleeved shirts under their leather jacket. Frankie noticed that morning as she passed by to the bathroom. Her eyes had lingered a few seconds longer than was polite, but Evan had warmed to her gaze.

Lust was a confusing emotion. Since they'd shoved Frankie off and ran out of the room, Frankie had been a lot more subdued in her attraction. In fact, besides the two times she had tried to sit and talk things over with Evan—which were equally annoying and repentant—they had mostly tiptoed around each other.

"Where's Sloane?"

"Up front, ordering." Andy pulled off his winter beanie and ruffled the curly mop that was his hair, then shot Evan a smirk. "Occasionally, the cheap ass gets generous with her money and offers to buy. I think she's getting you a muffin or something too."

"She's cheap because she doesn't pay for your food?" Surely, Evan didn't hear that right. Their eyes narrowed at their new friend, but Andy only laughed.

"No, she's cheap cuz she usually bums money off me and says she doesn't have enough. It's whatev though, honest. I love that girl, no matter how many lattes she owes me."

Evan thought back to the night of the staff party, the image of Sloane taking money from Frankie's safe as clear as day in their mind. There was a lot about her that didn't add up in Evan's eyes. They turned toward the front counter, spotting Sloane in the lineup right away. Her hair was thrown up into a high ponytail with its pink tips acting as a personal marker. She had her head down in her phone and purse slung over one shoulder, and not one ounce of sexual or romantic feelings stirred in Evan. *We're better off as friends anyway.*

Late that evening, Evan wiped the sweat off their forehead with the back of their hand, secured the dishwasher hose, and said loud enough to get Rain and Dakota's attention, "Hey, gotta piss. I'll be right back."

They were in the middle of a rush, and as Evan had anticipated, Rain waved them off and kept cooking. Evan hurried from the kitchen to the hallway, making the short trip to the restrooms. Chatter and music from karaoke night were in full swing, which meant the front of house staff would all be too busy to worry about Evan's whereabouts for ten minutes. Evan knew well enough by now that Frankie never left the bar when it was busy, which was perfect for what they had in mind.

After quickly using the washroom, Evan crossed the few steps to Frankie's office. They removed a lock pick from their jeans, checking once more that the hallway was empty, and got to work on the office door. There was just one deadbolt on top of the lock on the door handle. "She needs better security," Evan muttered after granting access almost immediately. The door opened with a soft *click*, and Evan slipped easily inside and closed it over again.

Breaking into the office had been their plan all along, but since getting a peek inside the safe the night of the party, they hadn't been able to stop thinking about it. What other secrets lie inside that steel box? What about her laptop, or the filing cabinet? Surely there was evidence somewhere of her past as a cop. She seemed the type to carry around a file of someone she'd killed. *If she did kill Caleb.*

Without turning on the light, Evan swapped the lock pick for the small flashlight in their jacket. Judging by the time illuminating from the desk clock, five minutes had already passed since they'd left the kitchen. Evan took a deep breath, expelling it slowly. *Let's do this.*

Breaking into the safe would have been significantly trickier than the average door Evan had picked lately, especially considering this safe came with a keypad as well as a keyhole. It would involve a coat hanger and more time than Evan could spare. Thanks to Sloane and her sloppy "cover your eyes" scheme, Evan knew the code.

Click! Evan grinned devilishly at the sound. Finally, they'd see what Frankie deemed important enough to be locked away. They cracked the safe door open slowly, half convinced an alarm would still go off. Frankie's 9mm was the first to come into view, and just like the last time, the sight stole Evan's breath momentarily. It wasn't hard to picture the determined, capable woman gripping the gleaming gun in her strong hands; it wasn't far-fetched to imagine Frankie using it either. What *was* hard to swallow for Evan was the fact that the woman they were very likely at least halfway obsessed with had not only pointed a gun at Caleb but had opened fire on him. Why? Why him, why then? Caleb wouldn't even have been in the alleyway if it hadn't been for Evan.

"Why'd you come anyway? Dad's gonna skin you alive when he finds out." Caleb shoved Evan, annoyance evident in the way his dark eyebrows comically slashed together. His mouth sat in a tight grimace. For being only twenty-three, Evan's big brother looked like the weight of the world was on his shoulders, and they told him that.

"You'd look old and stressed out too if you had a kid tailing you to every party you tried to go to."

"Well, I hate being left home with him! Lately, all I've gotta do is walk in the kitchen and it sets him off."

Caleb's face softened. "He doesn't understand you, Ev."

"Yeah, well, he doesn't need to understand me to show a little re-spect." Emotion swelled in Evan's throat. They grabbed the beer out of Caleb's hand and took a long swig. Some of the liquid dribbled down their bruised chin, and they swiped it away with a shaky hand. "It sucks being cooped up in the bedroom all the time, especially since you get to strut around like a fuckin' golden boy."

The distinctive tap of stilettos coming down the hallway broke Evan out of their silent reprieve. "Shit, shit." Evan's heart thudded frantically as they scraped their lock kit from the floor and stuffed it back into their jeans. They hadn't even gone through the entire safe, too checked out in the past to focus properly. Had they locked the door? How much time did they have? Evan pulled out their phone and quickly snapped a picture of the inside of the safe before closing and locking it. Evan gave a terse glance around with the flashlight, making sure everything was in order. If they survived this, then breaking into Frankie's filing cabinet would have to wait for another day.

Flicking off the flashlight and jamming it into their jeans again, Evan scrambled to the front of the desk just as the door to Frankie's office opened. Their heart was in their throat as they came face to face with the woman they were supposed to hate more than anything else in the world.

"Jesus!" Frankie's hand flew to her chest in alarm, and she hit the light on with the other. Evan caught the flash of fear in her eyes, and then it was gone, replaced with the kind of hardness Evan had suspected to see. "What the hell, Evan? You're supposed to be at the dish pit."

Panic chilled Evan's insides. Frankie showing up this soon hadn't been in their plan. She never left the bar during a rush. *Stupid, stupid! I can't go back to prison.* Evan took a deep, steadying breath, and shot Frankie a shaky smile. "I-I knew you'd come looking for me."

"Come again?" Frankie shut the door and folded her arms across her ample chest. An indiscernible glint shadowed her brown eyes as she walked toward them. "Did you break into my office?"

Evan swallowed and forced themselves to relax enough to lean against Frankie's desk. "Maybe, but only so I could surprise you. It's been hard trying to get you alone today."

"So you ... what? Thought it'd be appropriate to help yourself to my office during one of our busiest times?" The confusion on Frankie's face was paramount. "I don't believe you. You have me to yourself morning and night, and it's been a week since you spoke a full sentence to me, Evan. Do you realize that?"

Evan thought for certain Frankie would take the bait. She was always so eager to flirt and touch and tease them. Hell, a part of them was disappointed that she wasn't falling over their feet yet. The other, more rational part of them was glad they might escape the mess they'd found themself in without taking off their clothes.

"What's really going on? And don't lie."

"It's true," Evan insisted, forcing themself to keep eye contact. If they looked away, Frankie would know it was a lie. Evan relaxed their breathing, going so far as to grin a little. "Listen, I'm not great at discussing my feelings, Frankie. I figured ... what better way was there than for you to find me in your office again? Wasn't there some kind of sexual punishment promised?"

Frankie's jaw sagged, and for an uncomfortable stretch of time, she stared at Evan. "You clearly don't understand as much as I'd hoped about Domme/sub dynamics. I'm not built that way, Evan. I can't just forget how terrified I made you feel that morning. As a Domme, hearing you scream for me to let you go ..." Frankie trailed off, visibly upset now. She turned toward the door. "I'm not sure what to think about this situation but know this: if you seriously want to get involved with me, we will sit down and discuss matters like adults."

Like adults. Humph. Evan tried not to let the comment sting. It was a well-deserved dig, they'd give her that. After all, Frankie wasn't the one breaking into someone's office and lying in wait. Evan cleared their throat. "Okay."

Frankie opened the office door before looking at them again. "And Evan?"

Fuck, the broken shards in her voice were enough to choke Evan up. Something was seriously wrong, and they'd hazard a guess that it went well beyond Evan rejecting her in the bedroom. "Frankie?"

"If you ever break into my office again, I'll have you arrested."

CHAPTER 19

Frankie

EVAN WAS LYING. FRANKIE wasn't sure how she knew, but she did. There was no way they'd broken into her office in hopes she'd walk in. In fact, she'd be willing to bet they had broken in on the assumption that she *wouldn't*. That everyone working would be too busy to notice.

"What were you doing in my office, little thief?" Frankie wondered, pocketing her keys as she got out of her Audi and headed into the gym. She had combed her office after Evan had left, yet found nothing unusual. Knowing what she did about them, Frankie wouldn't be surprised if Evan had broken into her filing cabinet or desk. But what were they looking for? If Frankie had any sense whatsoever, she'd have fired Evan on the spot. They had a snooping problem that needed to be kicked to the curb, and fast. It would be a lot easier if Frankie weren't so damn captivated by the little shit.

"Hey, Frankie," Courtney greeted as Frankie set her bag on the bench in the changing room. The younger woman's skin was flushed and sweaty, evidence of how hard she'd worked during her kickboxing class. "How's business?"

Frankie hesitated. How *was* her business? In the last two months, the pub hadn't yet recovered from the ruined batches of microbrew, the walk-in cooler had broken down twice, she'd been slapped with a health and safety citation and shut down for a day, and— "Good, same as always. How about you?" The lie came easily. Frankie wasn't one to talk shop with acquaintances, especially not to the COO of Cairn's Corp, an internationally leading investment and acquisitions company.

"Good, same as always." Courtney pushed an auburn curl off her cheek and smirked. "So, question for you. Ever heard of a stunning woman named Kelsey? She's a Domme in the community."

"I have. She and her sub are lovely. Why do you ask?" Frankie checked her watch. Her class should start piling into the change rooms any minute.

"Aren't they? I had the pleasure of meeting them both the other day." Courtney shouldered her bag, glanced around the space, and lowered her voice. "Kelsey invited Lex and me to a kink party she's putting on this weekend. Have you ever been?"

"I haven't, but I've been to some others in the past. Was Kris not invited too? I've been away from the scene for a while, but as I recall, the parties are inclusive to everyone in the kink community." Frankie knew a little of Courtney's partners, though she'd only met Lexi once when they'd come into the pub.

A breathy laugh escaped Courtney, and she shook her head. Behind her, Rachel and Patricia entered the room. They were chatting with one another, so only Frankie heard Courtney's reply. "Crowds and a bunch of dominants in one space would *not* be good for him, trust me. Considering his shitty past, I count myself lucky that he lets *me* dominate him sometimes."

Unbeknownst to her, the constant guarded look in Evan's eyes came to mind. From what little Courtney had told her about her boyfriend, Kris had the same jaded personality as Evan. *My little thief.* Warmth blossomed in her chest. "Be patient. Who knows? Maybe he'll come around."

"Mm-hmm, maybe." Courtney nodded, a small grin appearing, as if she were contemplating it. "Anyway, take care and say hello to Coy for me." Frankie opened her mouth to correct the assumption that McCoy was still with her, but Courtney was already rushing out.

A few others trickled into the room, and once Frankie changed into her tank and sweats and headed out to the dojo, she noticed a handful of other familiar faces waiting. "Evening, everyone," she greeted warmly. Her gaze landed on a lone figure standing a few feet away. "Toni, three classes in a row. That's a record. Great job."

Ninety minutes later, Frankie was driving back to work with Evan situated deeply in her thoughts. Beyond the flurry of new feelings that came with a crush, there was an underlying worry that lingered like a bad cold. Who was Evan *really*, and why had they come to Vancouver to get a job at the pub of all places? What did they truly want from Frankie? The chemistry was there, but something about Frankie scared them.

It was time to give her old partner on the force a call. Hopefully, Sean could uncover some answers.

The following morning in her office, Frankie stared in shock at the pictures Sean had sent over. A much younger Evan stared back at her, their chin-length blonde hair unruly. Mismatched eyes, same stubborn set in their chin, but who they stood next to was the real kicker.

Caleb fucking Deroche. The man she'd had nightmares about for at least the first week after the incident. Side by side, Frankie could only vaguely make out the similarities between siblings. Evan had the same hook to their nose, but perhaps it only meant that Caleb had also broken his nose a time or two. But then there was the familiar way they postured and walked. Caleb had been a good seven years older than Evan, and, judging by the public records Sean had accessed for Frankie, they'd had different fathers. *That at least could explain why I never put two and two together after I saw Evan's license.* Caleb Deroche ... and Evan *Landry.*

"Fuck my life." Frankie reached up to pinch the bridge of her nose. Her stomach rolled incessantly, a side effect of the predicament she now faced. *And poor Evan.* Had they always known she was responsible? How long had they planned to continue the cloak-and-dagger stuff before acting on the real reason they'd come to Vancouver? Frankie would be naïve if she believed for one second Evan showed up with plans to "talk things out". No, that wasn't her little thief at all. Evan lashed out, using unconventional means of revenge, and did a shit poor job of it.

Frankie's eyes widened. It was like a bulb had come on, shedding light on questions that had dumbfounded her for two months. The ruined batches, the walk-in breaking ... all of it. "It was them all along. Fucking with my business." But *why*? Why not just kill her and get it over with? As soon as the thought was out, Frankie already knew. For the same reason she couldn't think of anyone else since Evan had introduced themself over a glass of her whiskey. The attraction and emotional chemistry Frankie felt, Evan felt it too.

Knock, knock.

Frankie's gaze flew to her office door, as she half expected it to be open and for Evan to have heard the whole thing, but no. It was exactly as she'd left it. She heaved a sigh. "Yes?"

The door opened wide enough for Evan's handsome face to appear. "Everyone's heading out for the night. Can I do anything else for you?"

Talk about a loaded question. Frankie studied what she could see of Evan, her stomach dipping low like it often did when she was around them. Sean might have successfully uncovered their true identity, yet Evan was still someone Frankie was dying to know in a profound way. And not just sexually as her sub, but emotionally, intellectually. She wanted ... no, *needed* to know just how far Evan would take things. Were they caught in the middle like she was? For the right price, could they give up their revenge?

"Help me lock up, then we can go home together."

"Home," Evan slowly echoed like they were trying the word out for the first time. Their face grew tense, making Evan look much older than their twenty-four years. Frankie dropped her gaze and cleared her throat, ignoring the pang of guilt trying desperately to resurface. *What's done is done.* Now that she knew who Evan was, it didn't change the past. Wishing she hadn't needed to pull the trigger wouldn't bring Caleb back.

But did it have to be me in that alley?

"So, I've noticed you and Sloane are less touchy-feely since the staff party," Frankie said as they walked to the front entrance. Sure enough, as they reached the bar, only Sloane remained. She was pulling on her jacket, her headphones covering her ears, which coincidentally was the perfect cover to Frankie's question.

"There goes that incredible skill of deduction again." Evan shot Frankie a wry look, teasing, by the slight smirk they held.

Frankie took a deep breath, her nostrils flaring as she caught Evan's scent underneath the kitchen odors still clinging to them. The soft, woodsy odor somehow made both her heart and pussy flutter.

"We'll need to discuss that sharp tongue of yours, and how it fits into this relationship." Frankie sent Evan her best pointed look, a grin threatening to break forth when Evan's cheeks flushed.

"Oh, hey, you're still here." Sloane pulled her headphones off and smiled in Evan's direction, completely disregarding that Frankie was present as well. The urge to grip Evan's hand and shield them from Sloane's clutches was intense, so much that her fingers tingled even as her body subconsciously moved closer to Evan.

"Evan was waiting for me to finish up," Frankie interjected before Evan could. She pulled the door open. "Have a good night, Sloane. Thanks for the hard work this shift."

"*Every* shift," Sloane drawled, glancing between her and Evan before rolling her eyes. "Remember what I said about marking your territory? Prime example, Mommy Frankie. I told you I'd back off. No need to go around pissing."

"Actually, she prefers 'Daddy'." Evan was teasing, but Frankie couldn't deny the heady rush she felt at the witty declaration. The swift spark of desire made her stomach tighten and heat flood her pussy.

Well fuck, new kink anyone?

Fingers closed around hers, and when she turned, the barest hint of a smile tugged at Evan's mouth as they looked up at her.

"Ohmigod, that's TMI, people." Sloane shuddered, shouldered her bag, and gave them a little wave. "Night, you kinky shits."

Frankie locked the door and closed the blinds before reluctantly letting go of Evan's hand. "You stood up for me." Amazement colored her words. Why would Evan do that? Was putting on an act for Sloane another piece of their long-term game? Just how far would they take it? Frankie's stomach dropped a little. She turned away to check that the windows were still locked, a sizable lump in her throat that hadn't been there a moment ago. She saw Evan in the window's reflection, checking they were locked as well. There was finally an ease between them, as if they now shared an inside joke Sloane and everyone else wasn't privy to. Evan hadn't gone past first base with her, let alone learned which respective terms she preferred.

Is their plan to make me crave their body, their mind, or their heart before they attempt to kill me?

"I was hoping to have that talk tonight, if it's not too late," Evan said, tugging on the final window to make sure it was secure. Their build might have been small, but Evan packed a lot of lean muscle in their torso and arms. Frankie loved watching them at work throughout the day, lifting the trays of dishes, or when they helped carry cases of drinks to the bar.

"Frankie?"

She met Evan's watchful gaze. "It is late, but if it's important to you that we do it now, you've got my undivided attention, little thief."

"Why do you call me that, 'little thief'?" Evan swallowed, their resplendent gaze with those gorgeous long eyelashes lowering to Frankie's mouth. "You used to be a cop. You should hate that about me."

"If we're to play that game, then you should also hate that I used to be a cop." Frankie stepped closer, reaching for Evan almost helplessly. She brushed her fingertips lightly along their exquisite jawline. Standing so close, sharing one breath, it was unfathomable that Evan was out to hurt her. They appeared so soft, submissive in the way they responded to her. "Once a pig, always a pig, correct?"

Evan's eyes fluttered closed from the touch, their breath growing ragged. "But I don't hate you."

"No." *But you want to, desperately.* Frankie could see it plain as day now—the constant push and pull of desire versus expectation. "My little thief, I don't hate you either." Their mouths were a hairbreadth away from touching when Frankie got hold of herself. She blinked, and then sighed, stepping away. For a second, she'd forgotten her own decree. No kissing Evan until they'd set some ground rules.

A gust of air left Evan, and they raked their nails through the fine hair on their scalp. Evan's cheeks were rosy, and their blue and brown eyes glittered with the promise of that would-be kiss. Their pouty lips looked so tempting Frankie almost went back on her word. Almost.

"Let's go upstairs. I'll put on tea, and we'll chat," she forced out, not waiting for Evan to follow. Frankie shut the lights out in the dining area, then headed for the back staircase. Evan's soft footsteps followed, and neither one spoke until they were locked inside the apartment.

"I don't like tea."

Frankie held in her smile, unstrapping her pumps before walking barefoot into her kitchen. "I remember you telling me that. What would you like instead? I could warm you up some milk."

Frankie caught the flash of teeth Evan bared her way as she filled the kettle. "Maybe you are a Mommy Domme."

"I was being serious." Laughing, Frankie shrugged out of her blazer jacket, heading into her bedroom to drape it over her chaise chair. She left the door open, raising her voice as she unbuttoned her blouse and tore off her bra. The moment the cool air reached her bare skin, she moaned in contentment. Ahhh. Much better. "I don't like alcohol getting in the way of deep topics."

"Well, I never had warmed up milk. Sounds disgusting," Evan replied from the doorway. The typical sarcastic edge to their voice had shifted into something soft and husky. Frankie turned fully to face them, fought the urge to grab her blouse again to cover herself, and allowed Evan to see her body. No one had seen her half naked in a *very* long time. There was never a good reason for it, at least no excuse she assumed others might have. But being naked usually led to touching, and Frankie hadn't dared go down that road. She didn't consider herself a service top for nothing.

"Fair play, I suppose. I've seen most of your body," Frankie acknowledged, and the blatant desire that shone in Evan's eyes made her breasts feel heavier and the nerves under her skin ripple in excitement. It made her want to pull Evan to her and have them feast on her nipples, regardless that having them so close would no doubt bring up questions about the scar on her chest she wasn't ready to answer. If Evan saw it, Frankie couldn't lie. Withholding information was significantly easier to live with than an outright lie.

"You're fucking gorgeous."

"Thank you, Evan. So are you." Frankie ignored her body's demand for Evan's lingering gaze and went to her closet in search of a hoodie.

"I'm serious. You could be a model. I'd love to draw you sometime."

Frankie smiled softly, pulling the material over her head. She worked hard for her body, trained it in and out of the gym, and loved how it was both curvy and strong. She gave up years ago trying to shape her body the way other, thinner girls were and embraced what she had to work with.

"Maybe one day I'll let you. For tonight, though, I believe a conversation is overdue, don't you agree?" Frankie held her hand out to Evan and wanted to laugh at their crestfallen expression. The idea of drawing her must have been right up there with how she'd wanted them to pleasure her breasts. And that was an odd desire for her. She'd never let anyone near her breasts except for the few minutes it took for the body piercer to accessorize her nipples. And Naz swore never to mention it to her friend McCoy.

Frankie led the way back into the kitchen area, directing Evan to the diner booth. "Have a seat, honey. Let me get my tea, and we can chat."

Chapter 20

Evan

"So, do you not ever have normal relationships? Like, without all the BDSM role play stuff?"

It felt like a fair question to ask, but regret burrowed a pathway to Evan's chest nonetheless. What was defined as normal these days anyway? They had long since concluded that they hadn't had a "normal" childhood growing up. But Frankie didn't look at all offended by the question. In fact, she reached across the table and patted Evan's hand.

"It's okay. There are no wrong questions here. And no, I don't. Not for ... perhaps ever." A faint smile touched Frankie's lips, but Evan couldn't decipher its cause.

"Why not?"

Frankie shrugged. "Many reasons. I prefer to remain in control in the bedroom. I love giving to my partner, and having a sub allows me to take things deeper. I get off on their pleasure. It entices me to see bruises on their skin after a scene that I put there. I love knowing I control their pain or pleasure, but also that they've put their trust in me enough to give me permission to do so. I love rules, pet names, and safe words."

"And restraints."

Evan thought of the restraint-based adult-sized toys hidden away in the guest room closet. Not allowing subs the freedom of movement seemed to be a kink of Frankie's too. It should sicken Evan, but instead, their traitorous body responded wholeheartedly to the idea of them being the one restrained.

"Being restrained turns you on." Frankie's soft gaze was knowing, and the glaring fact she was the enemy blurred even more. She didn't seem like a killer. The index finger tracing soothing circles across Evan's hand certainly didn't feel like it once pulled a trigger to kill Caleb. She was just ... Frankie. A fierce personality bursting with passion and sensuality and an ample figure Evan craved like there was no tomorrow. They didn't have a lot of experience giving, as they somehow attracted dominant lovers, and had never truly cared one way or another. But Frankie made them want to fall to their knees and spread her thighs open.

Cool it. She literally just said she didn't like that.

"Maybe." Evan licked their lips, looking away. For a moment, they studied the minimalist furnishings around Frankie's apartment, their gaze finally landing on the four-by-six picture of Frankie and McCoy together. A bitter taste filled their tongue. "What would we be to each other if we did this?"

"Well, speaking in a broad sense, there are plenty of Dominants and submissives who navigate open relationships, or never label themselves as anything more outside the bedroom." A sigh left Frankie, and when Evan turned back, she was also looking at the picture of her and McCoy. "I tried that, and it didn't work well for me, Evan. Letting someone in is hard for me, and I don't think casual suits my life anymore."

"You mean being exclusive?" Their eyes met, and Frankie watched them so long that Evan began to squirm. They pulled their hand away and pushed their glasses up on their nose.

"Yes, but more than that. If you're truly interested in what I have to offer, and I think you are, I suggest we start on a trial basis. Get to know each other better outside of the bedroom first."

"So, no sex?" Evan's shoulders slumped. How could they navigate a relationship with Frankie when their life was nothing but a web of lies and deceit? On the other hand, it would enable Evan to get closer to Frankie and uncover all her secrets.

"I don't want just sex anymore, little thief. I want to be more than a body to someone." Frankie swallowed, her gaze dropping to where her hand still rested on the table. She pulled it away, tucking it with the other one on her lap. "I want a partner that's just mine. I'm tired of sharing and then losing them. If practicing kink and getting off is all you want, then I'm the wrong person."

"What, no, I ..." Evan hesitated, allowing Frankie's words to sink in. Hadn't sex been the only thing on their mind when it came to the two of them together? Entertaining anything longer in Evan's predicament was not only foolish but unrealistic. If they failed, Cecil would just take Frankie out himself, and Evan had a feeling their stepfather wasn't exactly the merciful type. No, dying would be the least of Frankie's worries if Cecil got his hands on her.

Still, the idea of having nothing with Frankie made Evan's stomach tighten. The past week had been gruesome without their normal banter. Even when Evan was trying to keep distance between them, Frankie's attentiveness and ready smile had worked miracles in softening them. How could they give that up?

"I wanna get to know you, too." The words spilled breathlessly from Evan's lips, as both terror and elation filled them at speaking the truth.

"You do?" A tentative smile appeared. "You genuinely want to know me?"

"Of course, why do you think I can't seem to—" Evan broke off, realizing they were about to say, *"Can't seem to get the job done and go home."* Their lips clamped shut. Heat rose up Evan's neck to their cheeks as they stared mindlessly at Frankie for an agonizing moment.

"Why you can't seem to stop thinking about me?" Frankie guessed, and there was nothing tentative about her smile now. It was wide and as gorgeous as she was. Evan's breath caught as Frankie leaned across the table, her lips grazing Evan's cheek, and then their ear as she whispered, "The feeling is entirely mutual."

Evan breathed in the lingering scent of Frankie's perfume that still clung to her. A strong desire to bury their nose in the collar of her hoodie filled them, and before Evan realized, they were nuzzling the small gap of exposed skin on her throat.

"You're like a drug. Bad for me, but I think I might die if I don't get it." Evan pulled back in search of Frankie's mouth. They reached up with the intention of cupping Frankie's cheeks, but she grabbed hold of their wrists, securing them to the table.

"Dying is the last thing I'll let you do." She met Evan's kiss halfway, and the moment their lips touched, Evan swore they died and went to heaven. The stars aligned just for them, and every doubt Evan had of the two of them fled like a runaway bride. Frankie kissed in the same fashion she did everything else. Full of restrained passion and power, with deep, erotic hints of all the pleasures to come. Evan opened their mouth and groaned at the silken feel of Frankie's tongue pushing inside, invading them, owning their mind and body.

Evan's nub throbbed and pulsed as they envisioned Frankie one day licking and sucking them senseless.

Unfortunately, Frankie pulled back shortly after, her movements slow and reluctant. She pecked wet kisses along Evan's mouth and jaw, those gorgeous brown eyes greeting theirs. "Not rushing will be a challenge, but it'll give us time to figure out if we're compatible in other ways. You'll have more time to get to know me and understand what I will and won't tolerate when it comes to intimacy. Like putting your hands on me without permission."

"That's why you have restraint frames." Evan's eyes widened, understanding dawning on them. "You don't like to be touched."

Frankie's jaw tensed. She looked away. "That wasn't the point I was getting at. Everyone needs boundaries, especially while we're in the stages of getting to know one another. Just like I won't assume you want me to touch you."

"Will you ever let me touch you?"

Frankie hesitated, pulling away from Evan to sit once more in the breakfast booth. Regret burned in her gaze. "Not in the way you're asking. If I'm expecting it, like in a hug or if we're making out, for instance, then your arms around me are fine. But as I said earlier, I'm a service top, Evan. It's the only way I know how to be. It's the only thing I want. So you would have to be okay with being a submissive bottom."

Fuck, what happened to you? Evan bit back the question. It was neither appropriate nor compassionate, and despite Evan's sole reason for coming to Vancouver, they cared about both of those things. Evan didn't want to hurt Frankie, not like that. *Besides, getting topped by her all the time sounds hot as hell.*

"It's late, honey." Frankie got to her feet, holding out a hand for Evan to take. "Let's get some sleep, and I'll make you breakfast in the morning."

"Sure, thanks." Evan had to actively tone down their grin at the thought of Frankie cooking for them or doing anything that involved taking care of them. She did it so effortlessly that Evan had come to look forward to being pampered now and again. Frankie pulled Evan to their feet, and their lips met briefly once more.

"Which would you prefer, my almond pancakes or bacon, eggs, and toast? I picked up some of that sourdough bread you like."

"Either one sounds great. Thank you, Frankie, for real." Frankie's constant attentiveness had Evan choking up. They swallowed past the lump in their throat, unable to look at her. Humiliation lit their cheeks ablaze.

"I should be thanking you, little thief, for giving me a chance." Frankie's cool hand grazed Evan's hot cheek, and they shivered. "It means more than you'll probably ever realize."

"Damn, kid, you look like a fish out of water right now." Andy patted Evan on the back as he took a seat. He gestured around the Board Game Café that the group had invited Evan to. "Busy spot, b'y. I keep begging Frankie to head up a board game night but she won't have it. Says it'd be more trouble than it's worth."

"Yeah." Now *that* Evan believed. At least this place had its own library of board games. Where would they ever fit something like that in the pub? They wrapped their hands around their spiked hot chocolate, and the heat radiating from the mug took the chill out of Evan's fingertips, "Thanks for inviting me, hey."

"It was Sloane's idea, so I can't take all the credit." Andy grinned, jerking his thumb over his shoulder to add, "Not gonna lie, I think she likes you, Ev. Claire's been shipping you since the staff party."

"Oh, well." Evan squirmed in their seat, before busying themself by taking a drink of the hot chocolate. "Not to burst her bubble, but I'm sort of seeing someone."

"Already?" Andy laughed. "You just moved here, b'y. Who is it? Anyone I know?" He leaned closer, eyes widening and cheeks flushed from excitement and the warmth of the café. "Someone from O'Rourke's?"

"I'm not telling, so quit while you're ahead." Evan smirked but knew there was only a limited time before their new friends found out. Frankie must have been feeling a bit possessive to see Evan go out with Sloane so soon, so she hadn't held back in her office earlier that evening. If anyone had walked in, they would have witnessed Frankie's tongue halfway down Evan's throat.

"Okay, I won't pry. Good to see you're settling in." Andy raised his glass in Evan's direction. "To new friends and potential lovers."

Evan narrowed their gaze on the glass, then back at Andy, who chuckled. "C'mon, kid, don't make it awkward. Acknowledge the toast, or I can't drop my hand."

"You totally could. Talk about making shit awkward." Evan picked up their glass to toast Andy's.

Claire returned from the washroom a moment later without Sloane, and Evan glanced around the café in search of her. "Lose someone?"

"Sloane got a call and took off outside," Claire explained, but something like worry lines creased her forehead. She turned to the exit, before shifting in her seat and plastering a smile on. "What'd I miss?"

"Ev's seeing someone, but we can't know yet who," Andy summed up before Evan got the chance to speak.

"Yeahhhh, about that." Claire opened the next game on their list, another one Evan hadn't played before called Ticket to Ride. "Sloane was grumbling in the bathroom about how much you reek of Frankie's perfume. I didn't notice 'til she mentioned it but ..." She leaned in to take a big whiff of Evan's jacket and grinned. "Wow! Smells like Frankie crawled all up inside you."

Evan's cheeks burned, and they sputtered, "Well, I mean, I'm staying with her right now. It's a small apartment."

Sloane returned to their table flustered, out of breath and looking faintly red-rimmed around the eyes, as if she'd been crying while outside. Evan sat up straighter, tensing. "What's wrong?"

"Nothing. Fuck, you look so worried." Sloane ran her fingers through her long hair, a breathless laugh escaping, but the feigned nonchalance did nothing to diffuse Evan's curiosity. She'd been fine when she left the table. What had happened in those few minutes?

"I'd hoped you slowpokes would have set the game up already." Sloane pulled the board out and spread it open on the table.

"Nope, 'cause we were too busy razzing Evan about Frankie, which I had no clue about." Andy shot Sloane an accusing look. "How am I a bartender yet the last one anyone spills the tea to?"

"It's new, and kind of still on the down-low," Evan said, then winced as they thought of the gossip mill reaching Frankie.

"All you needed was to activate your eyes and nose, friend. The boss isn't exactly discreet with her affections." Sloane glanced around the noisy café and sighed. "It's weird being here without Coy."

"You could've invited her," Andy reminded her.

"Nah, she wouldn't have come." Sloane snatched her drink from the table, taking a long drink before she shrugged. "It's, whatever."

"You didn't invite her because you knew she'd wanna bring her girlfriend." Claire rolled her eyes so hard for a second it looked as if they'd get stuck.

"Not true. At all." Sloane sniffed as she handed out bags of game pieces to everyone. "Help set up. Have you ever played this one, Evan?"

Evan shook their head and gave Sloane a hopeful smile. "Explain it to me?"

"Yeah, sure."

Listening to instructions had always been much easier for Evan than reading them. It, of course, didn't hurt that Sloane was an excellent teacher, and after five minutes, it felt like Evan got the gist of how to play the game. As Andy and Sloane gossiped about the bar, Evan began organizing their trains in rows on the table in front of them and studying the destination cards.

"You're kind of quiet. How'd you become friends with these two? They never shut up," Claire asked from beside Evan.

"Hey now." Andy waggled his eyebrows at his girlfriend. "Sometimes I do. During sexy times, for instance."

Claire laughed. "Not even then, babe. Your chatter just turns to moans and cries of ecstasy."

Evan met Sloane's gaze for a second before they both cracked up. Andy just shrugged. "What can I say? You got mad skills, b'y."

"Ohmigod, the Newfie slang is top-notch," Sloane guffawed, her hand holding her stomach as she laughed.

Evan couldn't stop the big grin even if they wanted to. Being around Andy, Sloane, and now Claire, it was simple to forget about

Cecil and the responsibilities Evan was currently doing a poor job of handling. Their friendship was light and easy, a breath of fresh air, and as Evan watched the tightness disappear from Sloane's shoulders, they thought that perhaps she felt it too. Coy might have been elsewhere, but there was still something of a familial bond forming between the four of them.

Chapter 21

Frankie

FRANKIE PULLED A BEER and paused, staring across the bar at her good friend and ex-lover. "I didn't think you'd come."

Confusion creased McCoy's forehead momentarily before she broke into a grin as Frankie placed a beer in front of her. "Thanks, Frankie. And why would you think that? Can I not be here without Sloane acting as a sarcastic buffer?"

"Of course you can, pet." The nickname carelessly slipped from Frankie's lips, making them both wince. "Sorry, old habit. What I meant to say was, I didn't think you'd come without Sawyer."

"Oh, well." McCoy took a long drink before lifting one wide shoulder in a shrug. "She trusts me, and we aren't tied at the hip. The messages you sent implied there was room for only one audience, so here I am."

"Jesus, you're starting to sound like her." But the knowledge only made Frankie smile. It meant Sawyer was having an impact on McCoy. It meant that McCoy found someone to stick around long enough to rub off on her. She picked up her own beer and signaled to Lian. "You're on your own for a bit, but I won't be far."

Lian saluted, and Frankie motioned McCoy toward an empty booth in a secluded area off to the side of the bar.

"Where's Sloane? I never heard from her today," McCoy said.

Frankie slid into the booth across from McCoy. It'd been a slower night for the pub, so it wasn't overly loud as they sat across from one another.

"I think they all went to the board game place. Sloane, Andy, Evan, and Claire." Frankie crossed her legs, studying her old lover. "Let me guess. She didn't invite you."

Hurt flashed in McCoy's meadow green gaze, and she shook her head. Her teeth were clenched. "Apparently not. I don't get it. Why does she hate Sawyer so much?"

"I think Sloane feels she has to compete for your attention now that Sawyer's in the picture. Self-sabotage at its finest. She's distancing herself from you before you can." *It's what I'd do too,* Frankie almost said, but reined her words in at the last minute. Pushing people away was something Frankie had a lot of experience with.

"Yeah. Sawyer mentioned something similar. She did a lot of that when we were getting to know each other. It hurts." McCoy looked troubled. "So, how have you been? I'm sorry I don't drop in as much. You're usually gone when I come to help out."

"I know, and I'm grateful you haven't quit." Frankie reached for McCoy's hand resting casually on the booth table and was caught off guard at how different in size and feel it was compared to Evan's. How hadn't she noticed before now? McCoy's hands were thicker, stronger from her days spent as a mechanic. The skin was calloused as well, with traces of engine oil embedded under some of her blunt fingernails. Evan had what Frankie could only refer to as artist's hands. They were smaller, like the rest of Evan, and thin, with too-short fingernails from years of biting them.

Why was she even comparing the two? It was silly; McCoy and Evan's similarities stopped at their preference for femmes. Frankie pulled away quickly, clearing her throat.

"The topic you'd wanted to discuss," McCoy began with a faint smile. "It doesn't have anything to do with Evan, does it?"

Frankie tried to keep her face impassive, but she was surprised. McCoy was as astute as ever. She was about to ask how McCoy knew when Rain approached their table with the large serving of nachos Frankie had ordered.

McCoy whistled, beaming up at Rain as the cook placed small dishes of sour cream and salsa on the table as well. "My favorite! Damn, you sure know how to treat a girl."

Rain jerked her thumb Frankie's way and laughed. "I just cooked it, bro. This deliciousness is all Frankie's doing. Later."

"It's nothing. I just know you think better on a full belly," Frankie explained, waving away McCoy's gratitude, but her cheeks felt warmer. That annoyed her. Surely, she was too old to get embarrassed over such a simple thing. "How long have you known about Evan?"

The hand holding the small nacho pile stopped inches from McCoy's mouth, and Frankie caught the mischievous wink thrown her way. "Oh, since probably the staff party. I doubt anyone else noticed, but you looked hella jealous when Sloane pulled Evan away to go make out. We were lovers long enough that I've got that look ingrained in my head."

"Not that you bothered to heed the warning," Frankie said, her tone dry as flaking paint.

"Evan's young. I hope you know what you're doing."

Frankie bared her teeth, fixing a scowl on the mug of warming beer. She gripped it in her hands but didn't take a drink. "You're young too," she reminded McCoy.

"Not *that* young, and I don't just mean in age. Evan seems less mature, but I guess I don't know them all that well," McCoy reasoned, biting into the nachos.

Frankie's throat thickened, at a loss for words. For a moment, she had the strongest desire to snap at McCoy. "You're right. You don't know them. Evan is significantly more mature than you were at twenty-four, and you and I worked for almost six years before you left me for someone else."

"Whoa, take it easy. I'm sorry, I shouldn't have said that." McCoy licked salsa off her fingers, then wiped them off on the napkin before reaching for Frankie. Her strong hand landed gently on Frankie's forearm. Regret shone bright in her eyes. "I just don't want you to get hurt, Frankie. I love you, okay? Maybe not in the way you expected, but you're important to me."

Emotion swelled in Frankie's chest and throat. She reached out to palm McCoy's cheek, swallowing thickly. "I love you, too. For a long time, I thought if only I could ... change, then maybe you would have too. But then you met Sawyer. I'm happy for you, truly."

McCoy shook her head, smiling sadly. "I'm needy and a slut when it comes to physical touch, Frankie. We weren't compatible. You deserve someone who breaks down your barriers without you even realizing they're coming down, or at least unable to stop them from falling. You've known me for a long time, and yet they still shield you from me. I know nothing of your past except that you were a cop, and you visit Emily's grave every year on her birthday. I don't even know who she was to you."

Frankie opened her mouth to reply, but no words came out. Her hand fell away from McCoy's cheek. McCoy pointed a finger at her before digging into her meal once more. "That's exactly what I'm talking about," she said between bites. "You don't trust anyone."

"I can't," Frankie ground out, her heart racing now. She took a long drink of her beer, unable to look at McCoy.

"You're scared, and I understand." McCoy cleaned her fingers off again before lifting Frankie's hand to her mouth, pressing a gentle kiss against the knuckles. Their eyes met. "But one day, you're gonna meet someone who makes you want to. You deserve someone special enough to hold all your secrets and who loves you even more after learning each and every one of them."

Evan's face flashed behind Frankie's eyes, the way they looked at her that morning over breakfast. Was it all an act? Evan already suspected Frankie was to blame for what happened to Caleb. If what McCoy said was true, then Evan could never be that person for Frankie. Who could blame them? The moment the truth was out, it'd be all over for Frankie.

"Which brings me to my earlier point," McCoy said, unaware of Frankie's inner turmoil. "Something about Evan doesn't feel right. My gaydar is off the charts around them, sure, but sometimes, when they look at you, the hair on my neck stands up. Just like that one time I was up in my nana's attic and the old dresser moved by itself. Spooky as fuck, I'm telling you."

"You're being ridiculous. So far, you're the only one who doesn't like Evan." The reply came quickly, but deep in Frankie's gut, McCoy's concern expanded like a tumor growth. Her stomach churned. Why couldn't Evan be anyone other than Caleb's sibling? Why couldn't she have been the arresting officer in Evan's case, rather than the unpunished cop who'd taken their brother away?

Bullshit. You've been punished, just not in the eyes of the media. Her name might not have been published in the paper, but she'd been beating herself up for years over that night.

"Maybe I am, but watch yourself anyway." McCoy scooped up another mouthful, and Frankie raised a brow as McCoy's eyes shut in what could only be described as blissful contentment. She patted her stomach. "You not having any? I swear I'll eat the whole thing."

Frankie tried for a smile, but if McCoy's squint was any indication, she'd failed miserably. Knowing what she knew of them, was she just setting herself up with Evan? She was no saint and would make an appallingly terrible therapist if that was what Evan needed. So what made Frankie think she could take Evan on in the first place?

Sloane, Andy, and Claire returned to the pub close to midnight, heading straight for the bar counter with Evan trailing sluggishly behind. Their cheeks had a rosy tinge to them, and as the group got closer, the unmistakable scent of marijuana saturated Frankie's nostrils.

"Not a chance." Frankie shook her head, blocking Sloane from trying to come behind the bar. "You're off-duty and intoxicated."

"Hardly, boss, but fiiine, I was just trying to help you out." Sloane huffed, skulking her way to an unoccupied stool beside Andy, who was mid kiss with Claire.

Frankie ignored both the kiss and Sloane, instead zeroing in on her favorite butch. The pulse under her jaw thrummed with excitement as she studied Evan's outfit. They were wearing a new-to-them black and blue plaid button-up shirt under the open leather jacket. A joint was tucked haphazardly under their beanie, resting directly over the sword tattoo near their ear. Frankie's throat went dry at the sight. "Hey, how did the evening go?"

"Alright, but I'm not sure board games are for me." A wan smile appeared, and Evan shrugged out of the jacket before taking a seat.

"I didn't know you smoked."

"That's my bad, Frankie." Andy glanced at her guiltily. "I rolled two in the bathroom but passing around the one was enough. Ev was kind enough to hold on to the second for me."

"It wasn't my first time, Frankie. I used to smoke a lot before I was locked …" Their mouth clamped shut, and Frankie could only assume it was because Evan hadn't told anyone else of their incarceration.

Lian returned from taking an order, slipping easily behind Frankie. The moment Sloane spotted her petite frame pulling beers from the fridge, she rapped her ringed knuckles on the countertop and drawled out, "Lian! Hand me one of those, will you? The service here is shit."

Lian looked at Sloane's pleading expression before lifting her gaze to catch Frankie's eye roll. She shook her head. "Finish your order, Lian. I've got these guys."

"Okay." Lian shrugged, which caused the beers on her serving tray to rattle. She gave Sloane an apologetic smile for her efforts. "Some of your friends were here earlier. The engaged ones, and then I saw the tall, super tattooed one. She was asking about you."

"Naz." Sloane wrinkled her nose. "I'd rather break my arm again than go down that slippery slope."

"So what would everyone like?" Frankie asked once Lian disappeared again. After their drinks were made, she propped her hand on her hip, looking at Evan expectantly. "Can you follow me for a minute? There's something I need to go over with you in my office. Time sensitive, so I'd rather not wait until tomorrow."

Andy choked on his beer, and Claire giggled. Sloane let out a long whistle. "Wow. Now I know why you used to get me to deliver notes to Coy when she was here. You suck at this."

"I dunno what you're talking about."

"They know, Frankie. About us." Evan hung their head, as if waiting for Frankie to reprimand them. Which was ridiculous. How could she ever fault Evan for something she should have been more careful about?

"Oh, well in that case," Frankie took Evan's beer bottle and set it aside, then reached across the bar counter to fist Evan's shirt collar. She pulled them in, her lips a hairbreadth away from theirs. "Is this okay?"

"Yes, Daddy." Evan's teasing murmur only made what they were about to do that much hotter for Frankie, and as her mouth claimed theirs in a hungry kiss, she ensured she gave everything she had to it. If Evan was going to gossip to their friends, nothing short of a ten out of ten, boxer melting, orgasmic kiss would suffice.

Besides, there was something heady about having an audience.

"You taste like cannabis and Skittles," she murmured, licking Evan's swollen lips and ignoring the cheering around them. She nipped their chin.

"Cannabis," Evan chuckled. "So clinical, but I guess that's what I get kissing an ex—"

"Shh." Frankie placed a finger over Evan's lips. She tilted her head slightly to indicate the three spectators eagerly soaking up their interaction. "They don't know about that."

"Really?" Evan's eyes widened momentarily before a humbled expression fell over them. They nodded. "Well, thank you for telling me."

"Likewise." Frankie smiled, going in for another kiss. She'd almost succeeded too, but then Sloane did the same rap-rapping of her rings on the countertop.

"Not that we're not collectively enjoying the view, because we are, and by 'we' I mean my kitty and me, but you've got a couple of bashful customers waiting, boss."

Andy and Claire broke into laughter, but Sloane managed to snap the spell. Frankie let go of Evan and straightened, clearing her throat and shooting daggers at the three smirking faces staring up at her. Her gaze shifted to the couple a few feet away. Plastering on a smile, Frankie once again propped her hand on her hip. "What can I get you?"

CHAPTER 22

Evan

"Opening up isn't easy for either of us, is it, little thief?" Frankie rested the washed plate in the dish rack, viewing Evan expectantly.

"I guess not." Evan's cheeks flushed, still finding it difficult to believe just how attentive Frankie was. When they were together, no matter what they were doing, she gave Evan her undivided attention. Her cell phone was usually in her bedroom or her purse in the hallway, so that her focus never wandered. If someone needed her downstairs, they knew to ring the landline.

"How about we play a game, one that will help me get to know you, and you, me?" Frankie's hand, still damp and warm from the dishwater, settled on Evan's bare arm, making the skin prickle with goosebumps. Their eyes met. "Because I want nothing more than to get to know all of you."

Evan's mouth went dry. "O-okay. What kind of game?"

"How about we start with ... two truths and a lie? It'll give me a glimpse of your creativity at the same time."

Evan's mouth went dry. They weren't ready for this. At all. Evan had been lying for what seemed like forever some days, about small, unimportant things, and big, heavy, character-shaping things, but this game Frankie wanted to play felt like a landmine. One wrong step and it could be all over for Evan.

"You look pensive. What else is hidden behind those intriguing eyes I adore so much?" Frankie's fingers grazed Evan's cheek, reining their thoughts back in, and they blinked up at Frankie.

"I'm not."

"Here, I'll go first. Try to pinpoint the lie." Frankie smiled, turning back to the waiting dishes in the sudsy water. Her hands sank past the bubbles, and she washed their supper glasses before speaking again. "I love to hike, I'm adopted, and I hold a black belt in Krav Maga."

An unexpected pang of guilt hit Evan in the chest. It didn't seem fair now that they knew more than they should have about Frankie. They'd have to lie just to seem less suspicious. "I'll say the black belt is a lie. You practically live at the pub."

"And you would be wrong, honey." Frankie grinned, leaning into Evan so that her lips brushed theirs in a soft kiss. "I hold a black belt in Krav Maga and a brown in Muay Thai. The lie is my love of hiking. Nothing sounds worse than huffing and puffing in buggy woods or up a mountain."

"Wow, that sounds ... That's impressive. And hot. Also, you're adopted?" Evan feigned surprise. "Since you were born?"

"Now, we wouldn't want you to discover everything about me all at once, would we?" Frankie kissed Evan again, murmuring, "Your turn, little thief."

Fear skittered up Evan's spine, and for an agonizingly long moment, their brain drew a blank. What parts of them did they want Frankie to discover? Most of their life brought shame to the table, no matter how it was sugar-coated. Good deeds were few and far between, and honestly, hobbies were the same. Nothing had been the same for Evan after prison. They'd been out long enough to realize all their previous friends had moved on or disappeared. And while on the inside, the only passion had been for drawing, unless they counted their penchant for pickpocketing the occasional inmate or prison guard.

"Don't overthink it," Frankie said softly. "This should be fun. I want to get to know you, but only as far as you're willing to let me in."

Evan nodded, their thoughts drifting to Cecil. He *had* to be wrong about Frankie. The woman didn't have an evil bone in her body. After living with her for over a month, Evan should know that better than anyone else.

"Use your words, Evan. A nod doesn't go far with me, I'm afraid. I want verbal consent, 'yes' and 'no' and 'I understand'."

"I understand." Evan licked their lips, daring to look at Frankie. Her stunning brown eyes were full of warmth and desire. For Evan. "I...um, used to play hockey, my favorite color is green, and I never went down on a girl before."

One of Frankie's brows shot up, and she stared at Evan, no doubt trying to figure out if that was their lie or not. Her lips twitched. "I had a feeling you'd be good at this. But I'll have to call it. Surely, the third is the lie."

A blush warmed Evan's cheeks, and they broke Frankie's intense eye contact. "Actually, my favorite colors are black and blue." What possessed them to divulge such an intimate, honest fact? What happened to making something up on the fly to keep the game going long enough so that Frankie spilled something useful? Frankie commanded Evan in a way no one had before.

"You've never ...?" Frankie trailed off. Shaking her head in wonder, she dried her hands off and headed into the living room. Evan followed, a strange kind of apprehension sinking low in their belly as they sat on the sectional beside Frankie. Had Evan's fact been too honest too soon? Fuck, was Frankie now having second thoughts about them together?

But why would it matter when she doesn't like—

"Why haven't you?"

Evan gave her a small smile. "Now who's prying?"

Frankie's eyes widened, and she bit her lip. "You're right, I'm sorry. I just ... I want to make sure you'll be satisfied with me, if giving wasn't an option. Confiding in me makes it sound as if giving to your partner has been on your mind often."

"No, it's not that. Not really." Evan glanced away, embarrassed at how much they'd let slip. Why was it that their brain got all scrambled around Frankie? Was it because she was a Domme? "I-I just have a type, I guess. No one's ever let me ... do that. I dunno why. Maybe I don't look like I'd be good at it."

"I doubt it's that, little thief." Frankie's strong fingers gripped Evan's jaw, and she turned their face toward hers. Her sympathy was etched plain as day onto her face. "Offering yourself fully is a terribly vulnerable thing for some. I would never demand someone to go out of their comfort zone if they weren't ready. And I would never push back against a hard limit. Respect in the bedroom must go both ways."

"I understand, Daddy."

Frankie's nostrils flared, and her voice dropped several octaves, her husky reply floating over Evan in a gentle caress. "Three times you've called me that."

"Do you want me to stop?" Evan swallowed, their eyes trained on Frankie's full lips. As if their wishful thinking had willed it, Frankie's tongue darted out to lovingly trace the bottom one.

"No, I find I rather enjoy hearing you call me Daddy. It makes me want to do ... certain things to you."

Evan licked their lips. "Y-yeah?"

"Mm-hmm." Frankie smirked, relaxing further into the sofa. "I believe it's my turn, two truths and a lie."

"Huh?" It took a minute to remember the game, and Evan's shoulders slumped. They could think of at least five other things they'd rather be doing with Frankie that evening. "Yeah, I guess."

"Very good. Now let's see." Frankie tapped her finger on her chin, and the longer she took, the more serious her expression got. That vulnerability she spoke about flickered in her eyes but was gone so fast Evan wondered if they'd imagined it. "I've never been bowling, I don't have any tattoos, and ... I-I took a life in the line of duty."

Evan reeled back, slack-jawed at Frankie's confession. Their pulse began to race, and it felt as if their heart had lodged itself inside Evan's throat. Their voice cracked. "What?"

"Two truths and a lie, little thief. I used to be a cop, so which one is the lie?"

Evan could barely hear Frankie over the buzzing in their ears. They clamped their hands over them to muffle the sound and flinched away from Frankie when her hand landed on their thigh.

"That bitch cop killed Caleb. Get rid of her, or I will."

Cecil's cruel voice penetrated Evan's chaotic whirlwind thoughts, the threat to Frankie's life causing their stomach to lurch.

It's true. It's really fucking true.

With as much force as they could muster, Evan schooled their features in front of Frankie. Later, when they were alone, they could fall apart. They ignored the concern shadowing Frankie's gaze and choked out a laugh. "Offing somebody, obvs. Gotta admit, it's a solid way of filtering out your possible submissives."

Frankie studied Evan for what seemed like forever, an unreadable look in her eyes. Finally, she bowed her head slightly before getting to her feet. "That's right, but hey, I just remembered there's something I need to finish up in the office. I won't be too long."

"Okay."

Evan watched her go, their hand sliding over the still rapid beating of their heart. Evan's stomach churned violently, and they feared the delicious tacos Frankie had made would soon come back up.

She cooked you food, touched you, with the same hands that killed your brother.

Forbidden tears stung Evan's eyes at the reminder. They hated it when Cecil was right. They hated it even more that Frankie was the one who had to die.

Why couldn't Frankie have been anyone other than Officer Katheryn O'Rourke?

It was so quiet in the apartment that Evan could just make out the constant ticking of the grandfather clock outside the guest bedroom. It'd been late when Frankie returned to the apartment, so late that she didn't knock on Evan's closed door as she passed to the bathroom. With the lights off, Frankie probably assumed that Evan was fast asleep.

Not fucking likely.

They gripped the handle of their hunting knife tighter, the serrated blade gleaming under the streetlamp. Evan's bags were once again packed, but this time they were resting on the bench in front of the bed. Dressed all in black, Evan had lain in wait for hours, first listening for the telltale signs of Frankie readying herself for bed, and then for any sign of activity in her bedroom.

Tonight, Evan was going to do what they'd sworn to their old man. They'd make Cecil proud, avenge Caleb's death, and leave their new friends behind. It was the right thing to do. It was the only outcome for Evan, and they'd been fucking foolish to think otherwise.

I wish I wasn't gonna miss them.

Evan swiped the sweat off their forehead with the hand not gripping the knife. Every single time they thought of sinking the blade through Frankie's soft, silken flesh, their body cramped up. Evan's heart and mind warred with one another, tearing them to shreds in the silence. The darkness grew suffocating, and Evan deserted the bed on weighted, trembling legs. Bile burned the back of Evan's throat, and as they padded barefoot to the closed door, light-headedness made their vision spotty.

"Fuck," Evan whispered, leaning against the wall to gather their bearings. They fumbled with the lock on the door, wincing at the loud *click* of its release, and crept out. When they reached Frankie's bedroom, the door was ajar slightly, which was nothing new. She always left the door partially open, almost as if she hoped Evan would join her. They would join her tonight, just not in the way she'd been expecting.

Evan's gut twisted even tighter, like an ulcer ready to burst, and they gagged on the acid forming in their throat. *Don't you dare get sick before this is done!*

Evan shut their eyes briefly, drawing slow breaths in and out, trying desperately to calm down. Frankie, no, *Katheryn,* was only getting what she deserved. If it wasn't Evan, it would be Cecil taking her life. Evan was doing her a favor.

They pushed the door inward, an inch at a time, and immediately took in Frankie's still form under the covers of her queen bed. She looked dead asleep, and Evan hoped to all hell she remained that way. The last thing they needed was an angry black belt fighting for her life.

By the time they reached Frankie, Evan's whole body shook. Dread consumed them, but they'd gone too far to quit now. She slept soundly on her back, completely unaware. Evan peeled back her covers carefully, just far enough to gain a clear opening of her throat. Or should they stab her in the heart, like the bullet that had pierced Caleb's? A sob wracked Evan's shoulders, but before they could chicken out, they raised the knife high in the air and brought it down with all their might.

Chapter 23

Frankie

Frankie had finally dozed off when instinct kicked in, and she lurched out of reach seconds before the blade made contact. Evan squealed in surprise, but she didn't wait for them to regain the upper hand. She swung her foot out and around, hitting Evan in the back with her heel. The move had them toppling onto her, so she grabbed hold of their wrists.

"Evan, stop!"

"You killed my brother!" Evan growled, struggling to pull out of Frankie's iron grip.

"It's ... more complicated than that!" Frankie was still on the bed, Evan thrashing above her with mad intent. Sweat poured from their face like they'd visited a sauna before delivering their attack. They looked enraged, fearful, and ... and *heartbroken*.

I caused this, Frankie realized. No matter which way she looked at it, she'd played a part in who Evan had become in the last seven years.

"So that makes it okay?" Evan screamed so close to Frankie's face that spit and tears sprayed her just above the eye. They stilled their arms, chest heaving as they glared down at her.

Finally, they were getting somewhere. Now that the tug of war had stopped, perhaps Evan would listen to—

"Ugh!" Frankie groaned as Evan's knee came in sharply against her ribs. And then their whole body was over hers, pressing down on her, nowhere near as heavy as the last person who'd tried, but that didn't matter. Panic filled Frankie, and before she could stop, she was throwing Evan onto the floor and straddling them.

For several long heartbeats, they stared each other down in the semi-darkness. Blood trickled from a cut on Evan's lip, and their cheeks were so flushed that their glasses had fogged slightly.

"Murderer," Evan spat out, blood and spit oozing down their chin.

"*Survivor.*"

"Caleb was killed during an arrest. You shot him at point-blank range."

Evan's knife came up swinging toward her face, but before she could duck out of the way, the blade's tip sliced into her cheek. Frankie hissed, the fresh wound stinging, but she didn't retaliate. Hurting Evan further was the last thing she wanted. As she restrained Evan's wrists in her hands once more, a thought occurred to her.

I have to let go.

Let go of Evan's wrists, let go of her solid stance straddling their thighs, let go of her power and her pride. She owed Evan that much and more. Evan was a *good* person. She had to believe that.

Taking a deep, trembling breath, Frankie loosened her grip. The second Evan realized her apparent slip-up, they grabbed her arms instead and shoved her backwards. Frankie fought the urge to shield herself and disarm Evan, crashing back-first onto her hardwood floor. Evan was on her in an instant, their compact body grappling hers in a surprisingly firm hold.

Frankie's breath caught in her throat, and she had to rein in her panic. Once again, someone was on top of her with a weapon inches from her throat. Tears sprang forth, and Frankie blinked, letting them fall. The warm fluid trickled down her cheeks, stinging her wound further as the salt mixed with her blood.

"Your brother had me on my back just like this." Frankie panted, losing herself in Evan's feral eyes.

"You're lying. Just like every other pig out there." Tears wet Evan's cheeks as well, slipping off their chin to splash in Frankie's hair.

"I'm not. I would never lie to my little thief." Frankie gasped as the tip of the blade pressed into her throat.

"There was no arrest, okay? I lied in my statement. Caleb caught me by surprise. There was a-a struggle. He stabbed me with a blade just like yours, Evan. I couldn't see anything but him, and then he had his hand over my mouth and nose, I—" Frankie quaked, unable to stop the sob that escaped.

"Why are you *lying*?" Evan screamed.

"I would never lie to you. I respect you too much. I love you too much to lie." The words flew past her lips, but she'd be damned if she went back on them now. Because it was the *truth*. Despite the short time they'd known each other, Frankie had been steadily falling in love with Evan, a surefire feeling that hadn't diminished once she'd learned the truth about them.

"I clawed at the pavement, blindly searching for my firearm. If … if I hadn't found it in time and pulled that trigger, I wouldn't be here with you, baby."

"Caleb would never have attacked you unprovoked. He was good. He protected me from Cecil!" Evan shook their head wildly, and with each jerk, the blade's flat side slid against Frankie's throat.

"Examine the scar for yourself, see that I'm speaking the truth. It's on my chest, a quarter of an inch from my heart."

"Don't fucking move," Evan warned between sobs of their own. The knife shook in their hand as they trailed it down Frankie's throat to the buttons on her pajama top. With each slice through the buttons, shadows danced around the edges of Frankie's eyes. Her vision dimmed.

"I need you to get off me now," she growled. Her fingers ached to grab Evan, to disarm Evan, to flip Evan around and put them in a sleeper hold. Violence and desperation clawed at her until she was groaning, but for Evan, she held still.

"Caleb ... stabbed you." Evan's wet lashes fluttered as their tortured gaze met hers. The knife clattered noisily to the floor, each bang sounding like percussion cymbals in the still room. Evan's shaking hand flew to their mouth, and when they spoke, grief and disbelief strangled their words. "It was self-defense. Why? Why would he do that? Try t-to kill you? Why, Frankie? Why?"

Frankie's panic subsided, and she reached a tentative hand toward Evan. Before she'd made contact, Evan collapsed into her embrace, their chest heaving as broken sobs erupted from their small frame. "I'm sorry, baby. You have no idea how sorry I am," Frankie whispered, both arms wrapping Evan in a secure, comforting hold. She cradled Evan's head to her chest, still lying under them on the floor. For once, she let her old insecurities wash away. For now, she was right where she needed to be, acting as both a pillow and a shield for her little thief.

"Will you tell me more? I-I need to understand."

Frankie paused mid stroke down Evan's back. She let her fingers trace their shoulder blade, closing the gap to place a sweet kiss on Evan's forehead. While she didn't want to cause Evan further pain, she understood the desire for closure. Years ago, long before Caleb, long before becoming a police officer, Frankie had been a heartbroken teenager grappling with her own loss. She'd learned the hard way that some things couldn't achieve closure. Still, if it meant that Evan could see her as more than a villain, she would be happy to share the story. She resumed the light caress along Evan's back, speaking softly.

"It was a Friday, one stifling hot summer night. My partner and I were driving around in the patrol car, cooling down with the AC after chasing some thug through the park. I'd had bad sushi or something that day, and the effects were starting to kick in, making me sick. When we got a call from dispatch around midnight about a possible domestic dispute in the area, Sean had to rescue me from a washroom in a nearby 7-11. When ... when we went to check out the call, the front door was broken open and the couple inside were dead. We swept the house, me on the first floor and Sean on the second. I was in the bathroom when I got sick again, only to find a small figure jumping out the window. I hollered at Sean but didn't wait, instead chasing the suspect on foot. I"—Frankie closed her eyes, images of that night returning—"should have waited for Sean, but wasn't thinking clearly. The suspect had just turned a corner when someone body checked me from behind, about two blocks away from the house. I-I was so focused on the suspect, and depleted from being sick, that the idea of anyone else being in the house hadn't occurred to me."

"It was me." Evan glanced at her with a pair of seemingly haunted eyes, their throat bobbing up and down as words came with great difficulty.

"What do you mean, baby? You didn't knock me to the ground and stab me."

"No. It was me you were chasing." Fresh tears fell past Evan's long lashes.

Frankie's eyes widened, digesting Evan's confession. A small figure escaping through the window, dressed all in black and disguised beneath a hoodie. Reaching up slowly, Frankie used the pads of her thumbs to wipe away Evan's tears. "Caleb was protecting you."

Evan nodded, their eyes drifting closed from the contact. "He was always protecting me. And I was always getting into trouble. That night was my fault, everything. I shouldn't have gone in there, shouldn't have left the party, I … When I saw those people, I-I froze. I couldn't just … *leave* them there, a-all alone."

"So you called it in and waited for us. But why lie and say it was a domestic dispute?"

"I didn't want any evidence that I broke in."

Frankie was confused. "But the door *was* broken, which was a clear indication of possible foul play."

Evan shrugged, sniffling. "I didn't know about that. I came in through an open window."

"Oh, Evan." Frankie tightened her hold, brushing her lips on their soft skin once more. Emotion choked her, and as she pecked gentle kisses, she fought back her own tears. Even then, when they were just a teenager, Evan was a good person. They'd stayed behind at the risk of getting caught themself. "I'm sorry this happened. I wish I could change the past, believe me."

"Me too."

Silence fell over Frankie's bedroom, and Evan remained in her arms on the floor for a long time after the final word was spoken. Frankie wasn't sure how much time passed, only how often Evan dozed in and out of sleep on top of her. The frame of their glasses pressed into her chest, and muffled, nasally breaths came and went through their swollen, cut lips. They both could use some ice, as the slice on her cheek from Evan's knife still stung. Ice and disinfectant, not necessarily in that order.

The hardwood floor dug into her already stiffening back, and martial artist or not, Frankie anticipated a day of hobbling around if she didn't soon get up. Evan stirred as she slowly pulled them both into a sitting position, rubbing their puffy eyes under the wireless glasses.

"I'm sorry, I was trying to move you to the bed," Frankie said gently, watching as Evan's gaze flitted around the room before settling on her. Exhaustion and wariness made their movements sluggish as they climbed off her.

"I fell asleep."

"Yes."

"On you. But you don't like to be touched." Evan stood up, still glancing around.

"It's fine, Evan. If I didn't want you to be on me, I wouldn't have allowed it." After Frankie's initial panic had subsided, holding Evan close to her body had felt unusually wonderful. In the past, she'd gotten fairly close to McCoy during aftercare, but she'd never allowed her old sub to lie directly on her. In fact, no one else had since …

Nope. Nu-uh. Fuck off with that.

Frankie swallowed, her gaze landing on the deserted knife at the same time Evan's seemed to. For a tense moment, neither one moved, and then slowly, Frankie forced her legs to. She left the knife where it lay, instead walking out of her bedroom to the kitchen. She didn't see the point in confiscating Evan's weapon, not when they could try to kill her with something else in her apartment if they were hell-bent on doing so. At least now she wouldn't worry about one of her kitchen knives going missing.

"What happens now?"

Evan's small voice splintered Frankie's weathered heart, and she slowly retrieved an ice pack from the freezer. Therein lay a throbbing, deep-seated ache in her chest for what she'd done seven years ago and again last night. Why had she confessed to killing Caleb through a game of all things, instead of sitting Evan down and explaining things clearly?

She closed the freezer and grabbed a towel, clearing her throat as she headed back to where Evan was slumped on the sofa. Sitting down beside them, she held the ice to Evan's lip. "Nothing, if you don't want it to. But I meant what I said." Frankie met Evan's eyes, her free hand reaching up to cup their bruised cheek. "I love you and want you with me."

"I tried t-to … just like he did." Fresh tears glistened just beyond Evan's eyelashes, begging for release. Their jaw twitched and clenched beneath Frankie's fingertips, and she knew they were trying hard not to cry.

"I suspected you would, little thief, but even after I stopped defending myself, I'm still here. You might hate me for what I've done, but you also care for me too."

"Where do we go from here?" The column of Evan's throat bobbed up and down as they swallowed, those stubborn tears falling at last. The ache in Frankie's chest grew, guilt and heartache alike festering like a disease inside her. Was it wrong of her to ask Evan to stay? But she was selfish and lonely, and if Evan could get past what she'd done, then surely the two of them could surpass any relationship hurdles.

"You learn to trust me. Trust that I would never willingly hurt you emotionally. Trust that I still crave for your submission, for your body and heart to be mine, and mine alone. In turn, I will trust that you won't try to kill me again."

"You still want me after what I did?" Evan's lip trembled, and when Frankie traced the temptation with her thumb, their lips parted.

"Yes, always. I want to care for you, Evan, to nurture your emotional needs. And then, when you're ready, I also want to restrain you to your bed and fuck you with my strap-on."

The faintest squeak left Evan upon hearing that. She watched with satisfaction as their cheeks pinkened. "I need to ... Can I think it through? About you, a-and everything else?"

"Of course. Take all the time you need." Frankie gave them a small smile, getting to her feet.

"Where are you going?" Evan asked as she headed to the bathroom.

Frankie slowed, looking over her shoulder at them. Evan looked so small, hunched down on her large sectional. She wished a thousand times over that they'd never been put in a position to avenge Caleb.

Evan was built for playful mischief and creating masterful illustrations with gifted hands, not professional subterfuge and murder.

"I'm going to clean up, and then after, I'll make some tea." She was almost to the door of the bathroom when she heard Evan mutter.

"Still don't like tea."

CHAPTER 24

Evan

CECIL: WHAT DO YA mean you're not doing it? Quit fucking with me and get the job done.

The voice of Evan's stepfather boomed into their earphones as they departed the transit bus in Richmond. Listening to the message a third time did nothing to dampen Evan's terror or the unmistakable threat in Cecil's tone. Kill Frankie or suffer the consequences. While Evan wasn't positive about what those would entail, they knew there was no real love lost between them. Getting rid of Evan for good wouldn't keep Cecil up at night. Not like Caleb's death had.

Evan pressed the voice-to-text button, lips parting to reply, but no words came. How could they explain the nuances in Frankie's character that would make Cecil just a little empathetic? Yes, she had done it, she'd killed Caleb, but she wasn't evil. *You don't, you lie,* Evan realized. Cecil would never accept the truth.

Evan: She didn't do it. You got the wrong person.

"What a shit-show," they said, flicking over to the map app with directions to Sloane's apartment. As Evan neared the end of the block, they squinted at the street sign and glanced at the map once more. They took a left just as their phone buzzed twice. When they paused to look at it, someone slammed into them from behind, and the phone flew out of Evan's hands.

They swiveled around to glare up at the clumsy fool, who happened to have his own phone in his hands. "Watch it!"

The teenager rolled his eyes before side-stepping Evan and continuing down the street. "Whatever."

"Ass," Evan grumbled, scanning the ground and dodging two other people until they spotted the discarded cell in a pile of snowy slush a few feet away. Snatching it up, they continued to grumble under their breath, using the tail end of their hoodie to wipe off the phone. *Just fucking great.* Evan grimaced at the water inside the charging port. They shook the device, watching as a dribble of liquid escaped. Evan's throat burned as anger flared hot inside them. They scrambled to unlock their phone, getting as far as their SMS inbox where a new message from Frankie waited, but when Evan clicked on the thread, the phone wigged out.

"Fucking asshole," Evan spat, referring to the idiot who walked into them. They jabbed the cell into their bag before taking off again. It was a guessing game to Sloane's apartment now. All Evan remembered from her description was that she lived a few blocks away from the Miller Mechanic and Restoration shop, and the civic address. No problem, they had time. It wasn't as if Evan was actively avoiding going home to Frankie's apartment. They definitely *were not* doing that.

They'd slipped out the moment Frankie had gone for a shower early that morning, too much of a coward to face off with her again. The memory of falling asleep curled into Frankie on her sectional still made Evan's cheeks warm and their gut tighten. They'd woken filled with shame and desire for Frankie, utterly confused at how the two emotions could go hand in hand. They needed Frankie like they needed air, and yet, they hated her, too. They *needed* to hate her, even if they couldn't kill her for what she'd done. The problem was that it had felt wondrous in Frankie's embrace. Equal amounts strong and feminine, she'd held Evan against her body as if they were something precious, something she feared would crumble or disappear. Her affection scared the shit out of Evan. It was so wrong on so many levels, yet Evan couldn't shake the warmth blossoming in their chest hours later.

The heart was full of nonsense emotions and contradictions.

Falling for Frankie would bring nothing but agony to them both. And that's why Evan left that morning. To rebuild their collapsed boundaries. To make a stand, one Frankie understood and respected.

Once Evan caved and asked for directions, it took no time at all to locate Sloane's apartment in a clean, middle-class neighborhood. Evan approached the building's entrance, debating their plan now. It was barely eight in the morning. They knew Sloane worked the evening shift, and although she'd left Evan an open invitation to visit, she wasn't expecting them *now*. They stood just inside the main door, eyeing Sloane's apartment number on the intercom, indecision warring when an older gentleman pushed open the security door and left the building without a glance at Evan.

Evan moved quickly, shoving their foot between the door and the threshold before it could click shut again. Surely a gentle knock to Sloane's door would be less abrasive than using the buzzer. Evan knew they'd prefer to be woken up by someone's gentle knock than the alternative. It took a few minutes, but eventually they heard movement within Sloane's apartment. Then deadbolts were unlocked, and before Evan was ready, Sloane swung the door inward. Surprise, followed by a flicker of concern, crossed her face. She reached for Evan's arm, dragging them inside with her.

"Fuckin' hell, what happened to you?"

Evan froze, letting Sloane's words sink in. They swore under their breath. How could they have forgotten the attack on Frankie the night before? She wasn't the only one sporting nicks and bruises that morning. An uneasy laugh left Evan, and they busied themself with taking off their boots.

"You should see the other guy."

"You were jumped? By who? What'd he look like?" An edge of fear coated Sloane's usually smooth voice, and something about it made Evan look up. She was gripping the handle on the door she'd just shut and relocked, her lips slashed in a tight line. Sleep clung to her features from being jostled awake but Evan realized the big bags under her eyes shed light on a different story. Something was going on with Sloane.

"It was a joke. Me and Frankie, we …" Evan removed their last boot, trailing off. There was no way they could tell Sloane what really happened. Besides the fact that it sounded crazy, Evan was certain Frankie had kept that part of her life hidden. "She's been teaching me some self-defense moves."

"Oh. Okay, wow." Sloane scrubbed a hand over her face. Evan followed her into the kitchen, watching as she finger-combed her long hair and got stuck at the pink tips. She yanked them free, muttering about needing a trim. "Bit early for an impromptu visit, Ev."

"I know, sorry."

"You're lucky I was up for a pee, or I wouldn't have heard you. You could have sent a text," Sloane said, setting about making coffee. She wore a black tank top and navy-blue space pajama pants, looking a helluva lot less edgy than Evan would have guessed. When she bent to retrieve milk from inside the fridge, Evan spotted the butterfly tattoo on her lower back. It was one they had seen before at the pub, as Sloane often wore tops that rode up.

"I know, I just ... I needed to get away for a bit."

"From Frankie, huh? Sounds about right. She is allll-consuming." Sloane met Evan's gaze with a snicker, gesturing to her empty coffee mug waiting by the percolator. "You want one?"

Evan shook their head. "Nah, but I'll take a hot cocoa if you've got any of that."

"Sure."

Once they were sitting on Sloane's sofa with drinks, Evan relaxed, taking in the living room. It looked very much lived in, but tidy, with a flat-screen TV and two bikes secured to the wall. Evan turned to see Sloane watching them. "Does your sister still live here?"

Rolling her eyes, Sloane lifted a mug of coffee to her lips. She took a sip before saying, "Not really. She spends most nights at Sawyer's. Why? You need a new roommate?"

"Yes" was on the tip of Evan's tongue, but nothing came out when they opened their mouth. It made sense to move out of Frankie's place. Now that the ruse was up, nothing was stopping them. Nothing but the paradox of emotions Evan experienced whenever Frankie walked into the apartment at the end of the night. It had become a home for Evan these last couple of months. Frankie had become a home.

"What's going on with you?" Evan said instead, scanning Sloane's face for answers. "You looked like you'd piss yourself when you saw me."

Sloane shook her head, but her free hand trembled slightly as it pushed hair away from her eyes. "Just haven't been sleeping well lately. It's weird living here by myself, you understand. It's been Coy and me for years."

"Yeah, that must suck." Evan wasn't sure that was the whole truth, but they chose to let it drop. Sloane looked the type to clam up if she felt pressured at all, and besides, whatever was going on wasn't Evan's business.

They made small talk until their drinks were finished. Sloane announced it was time to shower, so Evan occupied themself while she was in the bathroom. They tried their phone again, and when it still flickered to the home screen each time, Evan went on a hunt for rice. When it was safely in a bag and covered, Evan browsed the apartment. They headed toward where Sloane had disappeared, stopping to take in the row of pictures in the hallway on both walls. Friends and family of the twins, Evan's eyes widened as they came across one with them in it. It was a group shot taken during the staff party, just two weeks before, and Sloane's arm was draped across Evan's shoulders. The memory of Sloane's drunken, winking come-ons made them smile.

Evan was curious by nature, so when they noticed one of the two bedrooms was open, they couldn't help but peer inside. By the thong and push-up bra strewn on the messy floor, they could only assume it was Sloane's room. Coy didn't strike them as a wearer of thongs. *It could be Sawyer's.* They stepped into the room, a bereft feeling crossing them as they scanned the well-used space. Even as a child, Evan had never *lived* lived in their bedroom. They'd never owned enough personal things to clutter a room. Cecil had made sure of that, as he'd break whatever was in his path on the way to whoop Evan.

"What's this?" Evan spotted an open notebook on the bedside table. Sloane didn't seem like a journal keeper, but that didn't stop Evan from swiping it up to inspect. What they discovered was shocking.

Instead of letters they would need to read repeatedly to understand, the notebook was some kind of ledger. Columns drawn on each page, with numbers under at least three categories. Evan didn't pretend to know everything, but Cecil was involved in enough shady shit for them to recognize a wager logbook when they saw one.

"Fuck, Sloane."

What had once started as small, harmless bets against Coy had somehow exploded into a different matter entirely. Sloane was gambling heavily by the looks of things, and Evan had a feeling they were the only one that knew.

Sloane drove like she was the star in a high-speed chase with ten cop cars on her ass and laughed crazily when Evan gripped their seatbelt tighter. Strapped across their chest, it was the only thing in Sloane's Trans Am to utilize as a lifeline.

"How haven't you got yourself arrested or killed yet?" they shouted over the blaring rock music. Evan's stomach rolled as Sloane swerved to miss a pothole, coming way too close to an oncoming car in the opposite lane.

Sloane's eyes were as feral as the grin she shot Evan, and she lowered her face to kiss the steering wheel before hollering back, "Sara hasn't let me down yet. She's my good luck charm."

Evan's brows shot up, unsure if Sloane's affections for her car were endearing or concerning. They didn't have much time to think about it when she stopped abruptly for a red light. Evan slammed into the seatbelt's restraint, gagging hard as the toast Sloane gave them earlier threatened to come back up.

"You're fucking crazy."

"No way. Going fast is one of life's greatest rushes, Ev. Right up there with—"

"Gambling?" Evan deadpanned without any thought.

Sloane whipped her head in Evan's direction. "Come again?"

Evan blanked, pulling back slightly from their friend's accusatory glare. They gestured to the stereo. "It's hard to hear you."

Sloane didn't move to turn the music down, just gave Evan an odd look before turning back to the road. A small sigh left them, relief making it possible to relax more in the seat. Sloane didn't speak to Evan again as they drove toward Vancouver's downtown. She just chugged her energy drink, bobbed her head to the music, and checked her phone half a dozen times. Reckless, that's what Sloane was.

How am I just noticing?

"Dude, you need to lighten up," Sloane said once she had parked and they were walking the two blocks to work. She laughed again, giving Evan a light thump on the shoulder. "You look like I just pushed you out of a fucking airplane. I wasn't even going that fast."

Seriously, she was going to resort to gaslighting now? Evan scoffed, not bothering to mention how she'd looked while driving. Like she'd done a line of coke in the bathroom before they'd left.

As Evan entered O'Rourke's, it felt like entire days had passed, not hours, and the deep sigh of relief that escaped was the perfect de-stressor after their precarious drive. Sloane disappeared toward the washrooms, and Evan took a moment to let their eyes adjust to the surroundings. It was mid-afternoon, so it was no surprise that several of the booths were occupied. The flat screens above the bar and in the corner of the pub had an MMA match on mute, while a much more relaxing genre of music played through the speakers.

Evan's pulse tripped as their gaze fell to Frankie, who was just coming from the direction of her office. Even from across the pub, Evan noticed the dark circles under her eyes and faint slouch in her shoulders. Well, that, and the small bandage covering part of her cheek where Evan had cut her the night before.

Guilt hit them with such force that they swayed on their feet before latching onto the nearest chair for balance. Grainy images of last night trickled through Evan's mind. The unabating need to avenge Caleb had completely taken over. In a broken fit of rage, they'd attacked the very woman they'd spent weeks falling for.

That wasn't Evan.

No matter how hardened Cecil tried to make them throughout the years, they were no murderer. Not when the victim was Frankie, the same woman who made Evan's toes curl with just a kiss. She was the woman who looked at Evan like *that*, exactly as she was doing now, with her entire resting bitch face softening. Subdued joy sparkled in her brown gaze as she watched Evan cross the room to her.

"You came back."

Evan gave her a slight nod, taking the stool next to her at the bar. Andy was busy making drinks, and Lian and another server walked past them a time or two, but Evan only noticed Frankie. Their shoulders were touching, Frankie's presence beside them comforting in a way they never understood before.

"I'm sorry, Frankie."

Frankie shifted on the stool so that her knees brushed against Evan's thighs. She reached for them tentatively, her palm heading for their cheek, but just before she would have touched them, she changed course and pulled them into a tight hug.

Frankie buried her face in Evan's neck, uttering, "And I'm sorry, baby. More than you'll ever know."

Her arms felt like safety nets wrapped around Evan, and they sank into the sensation, inhaling the floral scent of her shampoo.

"How are you?" she asked after several moments. Pulling back slightly, Frankie's gaze softened even more as she took Evan in. Her fingertips skimmed Evan's hairline just under the neckline of their hoodie. "Did you manage to get any sleep last night?"

She didn't kiss Evan, which Evan was grateful for. They couldn't guarantee their reaction in front of any onlookers and didn't want to hurt Frankie by pulling away. It was difficult to put into words how Evan felt, knowing what they did and feeling what they felt for Frankie. Her involvement had always been a glaring possibility, but Evan had never considered what would happen if they tried for a relationship after all the dirty laundry had been aired. How could Frankie ever trust them after what they'd done? Moreover, could there ever come a time when they didn't look at Frankie's hands and envision Caleb's blood coating them?

"Some," Evan quietly replied. The deep-seated ache in their hollow chest lifted a little at Frankie's small smile.

"Mm-hmm, good. Wouldn't want you getting hurt on the job because you're sleepy." Frankie tilted her head, her fingers still tracing Evan's skin. She looked deeply reflective, as if she was trying to figure out how best to voice her question. It was unlike her to be unsure about anything. She was Frankie O'Rourke. Fierce and proud in nature. Evan melted a little at the awkward display.

"Frankie?"

"What happens now, little thief? What do you want from me?"

"Holy shit, did Evan do that?"

Sloane's overzealous voice snapped Frankie and Evan out of their private bubble. When they looked up, she was hovering across the bar counter, shock and awe on her face as she gawked at Frankie. "Self-defense class, right? Ev said you were teaching them, but damn, they got you good, boss."

"Self-defense?" Frankie slowly echoed, glancing from Evan to Sloane and then back to Evan. They tensed under her touch, and just as Evan was certain their earlier cover-up would be blown, realization dawned in Frankie's expressive eyes. She switched her attention to Sloane once more, a smooth reply slipping off her tongue. "You're welcome to come to the next class if you've warmed up to the idea."

Evan couldn't hide their surprise, and they turned to Sloane as well. "You said you didn't know where she disappeared to twice a week."

"I think the better question is, when did you learn where I disappear twice a week?"

Evan realized their slip as Frankie's eyebrow shot up, her pretty face inquisitive. Yup, so Evan would need to explain that story later. Maybe. They weren't sure they were ready for everything they'd done to be revealed.

Rather than respond to Evan, a whoosh of air left Sloane, unknowingly saving Evan from an awkward explanation. She nodded to Frankie. "You know what? That might not be a bad idea."

"Great, I'm sure we can rearrange the bar schedule a bit. Now, both of you, time for work."

It wasn't until Evan was pulling on their apron in the kitchen that they realized Frankie's question had gone unanswered. What *did* Evan want from her now that revenge was out? Could they try for a genuine relationship?

The desire to submit to Frankie was still there, despite everything that had happened in the last twenty-four hours.

And the desire to run away and never look back was there, too. Evan knew, without a fraction of a doubt, that if they stayed, it would only be a matter of time before Frankie claimed their entire body and soul.

But what about Cecil? No matter what they decided, at the very least, Evan owed Frankie a warning.

Chapter 25

Frankie

Frankie pulled a stack of twenties from her safe and carefully counted them out onto her desk. She set them up in groups of five before unlocking her desk and fishing out the petty cash. There she traded the twenties for hundred-dollar bills, put the petty cash back, and secured the safe.

The chore numbed her thoughts of Evan, which was precisely what she hoped it would do. Three days had passed since they'd snuck out of her apartment while she was in the shower. She was trying so hard to be patient, waiting for Evan to seek her out rather than Frankie going into full possessive mode. After everything that had transpired between them, being tactful was key.

And Evan wasn't the only one struggling. Frankie wasn't sleeping, and when she finally caught a few winks, the nightmares weren't too far off. Ones of Caleb, and Emily. There had even been a nightmare where she'd defended herself against Evan's attack and killed them.

Frankie was exhausted. And *lonely*.

Having Evan so close, yet being unable to touch them, was torture in and of itself. She'd expected to feel fury over Evan's attack, betrayed even. How could she ever trust them not to try again down the road? But she didn't.

In fact, since she'd first learned of their connection to Caleb, a quiet acceptance had overtaken Frankie. She had never been the type to leave things in the hands of fate, but with Evan, the words "It will be what it will be" had become an everyday mantra. For someone who had spent most of their life remaining in control, that was a tricky phrase to abide by.

She slipped the money into a black sleeve before tucking it into a manila envelope. Next, she added the printout of Auntie B's address to the front of the envelope, making sure not to include a return address. The last thing Frankie wanted was a discussion about the funds she budgeted and mailed out each month. It was best for everyone if her aunt received the envelope anonymously. That way, no concern was had, old wounds remained suppressed, and no feelings got hurt. No matter how much she wished it were possible, Frankie couldn't change the past. But she could send money to help where needed.

"It's the least I can do for you." *For you and for her.*

Frankie thought of the boy she'd seen in so many of Auntie B's pictures over the years. Well, at twenty-one, she supposed Maddox was now a man. Frankie couldn't begin to understand the responsibility of raising a child into adulthood, but she imagined that at his age, there must have been something he required. Perhaps her aunt was putting the money into a college fund. She wouldn't know.

Because you lost those rights a long time ago.

"Oh, fuck off," Frankie chastised, jerking the adhesive off the lip of the envelope and securing it. She spent the next few hours poring over the finance reports and scheduling. Evan's half-assed devotion to sabotaging her business had unfortunately created a dent in the pub's overall balance. A budget for miscellaneous expenses was a necessity, but Evan managed to screw Frankie over so much that Sloane had had to dip into other accounts just to keep the pub afloat. After two months, Frankie expected things to start looking up again, but the longer she studied the numbers, the less they made sense.

"This is why Sloane's in charge of all this." Frankie pushed her chair away from her desk. She let her eyes close and reached up to massage her temples. Something in the books wasn't adding up, but she was too exhausted to figure it out. Sloane had been working the bar a lot lately. Maybe Frankie needed to pull some of her hours there, so she'd have more to dedicate to the bookkeeping part of her job.

A tentative knock pulled Frankie from her thoughts. "Come in," she said and winced at how rough around the edges she sounded. She stood up just as the door opened, and her eyes widened fractionally at the sight of Sawyer hovering over the threshold. Frankie waved her in and headed to the water cooler in the corner of her office. Filling two glasses, she offered one to Sawyer before nestling into her leather chair once more.

"Thank you. And hello," Sawyer greeted, her tone and mannerisms stiff yet as polite as always.

Frankie took a long drink of her water before setting it on the coaster on her desk. She quirked an eyebrow. "Do you ever smile?"

"Coming here to ask my girlfriend's ex for help doesn't exactly justify a smile, wouldn't you agree?"

Frankie stared at Sawyer's pensive expression, her mind drawing a blank for a good five seconds before the reason for the visit hit her. "We had an appointment."

"Yes."

"I completely forgot, I'm sorry." Frankie leaned closer, resting her elbows on the table. A smug smile threatened to take over, but she smothered it. She wasn't a monster. It wouldn't serve anyone well if she made Sawyer more uncomfortable than she was already. Still, she couldn't help the words that came out. "You want to learn how to fuck McCoy with a strap."

A kaleidoscope of emotions crossed Sawyer's face, from surprise to embarrassment and finally to annoyance. "Per your suggestion, yes," she responded through clenched, almost perfect white teeth. One day, when and if they ever crossed into proper friend territory, Frankie would have to ask Sawyer what her dental regimen was like.

Frankie opened her hands, palms up, in the most non-threatening posture possible. "Hey, there's no shame in that. McCoy deserves everything you can offer, and soon, strapping up will be one of those. How's she doing since we last spoke?"

"She told me of your meeting a few weeks ago. How you told her you loved her."

"Okay." Frowning, Frankie stood again, heading to her filing cabinet this time. McCoy blurting out private conversations between them irked her, but what did she expect? McCoy was as loyal as they came, and these days, her loyalty was to Sawyer. "Then I can only guess that she told you the entire conversation, not just the part where it looks as if I'm attempting to steal her back. Because I'm not, in case you're interested."

"I ... do know that. I suppose I just needed to hear you say it," Sawyer finally conceded. Frankie heard her clasp her hands together. "So, what do you have in mind?"

Right to business. My kind of woman. Frankie smiled, retrieved a bag from the bottom of the filing cabinet, and brought it back to her desk. "I went shopping after our last talk. Excuse me if it was a bit presumptuous on my part, but I couldn't picture you browsing this kind of store."

"What— Oh." Sawyer's brows shot up as Frankie emptied the contents of the bag across her messy desk. An adorable blush darkened her tanned complexion as she eyed the selection of dildos and strap accessories Frankie had purchased.

"I know McCoy has some already," Frankie began, biting back a laugh when Sawyer's gaze darted around before finally settling on her lap. "But it would be good for you to find something you can get personally comfortable with. The more your confidence builds, the better the outcome will be."

A noncommittal grunt left Sawyer, and when she didn't look at the toys again, a small sigh left Frankie. She rounded her desk to where Sawyer sat rigid in her seat. Frankie leaned against her desk and folded her arms across her chest. She kept her voice soft as she asked, "What about this scares you the most?"

"It doesn't scare me," Sawyer refuted, her gaze lifting to Frankie's now. She scowled, but the deepening blush on her cheeks was hard for Frankie to ignore.

"Mm-hmm, I think it does. A little bit. So why not tell me?"

Sawyer clamped her mouth shut, refusing to speak. She looked away. Frankie sighed again, pushing herself off the desk. The hour hand on the wall clock loomed overhead as she made her way back to her seat, and she silently cursed. It was well past noon. She should have checked with her staff by now.

"I-I'm afraid of failing. At this."

The vulnerability in Sawyer's voice had Frankie's tense shoulders relaxing slightly. She eyed the clock again. She could spare a few more minutes. If not for Sawyer's benefit, then for McCoy's.

"You don't need to make decisions today." Frankie studied Sawyer's features, silently appreciating all her natural beauty and imperfections. It was a shame she didn't smile more. Frankie trailed a hand over the selection of toys. "All you have to do is choose a couple you think you might like. You can take them home and first get comfortable with how they feel, how they look on you in the mirror. And you can ask McCoy her opinion if you're worried at all."

"No." Sawyer shook her head, and Frankie's hand fell away. Sawyer cleared her throat, repeating, "No. I need to go into this like a Domme."

Frankie hesitated. "Okay, but part of being a Domme is discovering what your sub likes. McCoy understands—"

"I know," Sawyer cut in. She blew out a breath. "I mean that I want to act confident when I do this. Otherwise, McCoy will unknowingly switch things around, and I'll be the one on my back. And that won't help her when she's feeling ..."

"Submissive?" Frankie finished for her. Sawyer nodded. "Okay, well, let's go over it then. And no shying away this time. You're a fucking gorgeous femme and the only one in the city who's been able to steal McCoy's heart. That alone should have your head up high, honey."

To Frankie's shock, Sawyer smirked. "You're right."

As Frankie explained what each of the toys and accessories were for, McCoy's preferences somehow got into their conversation. And then, the general topic of McCoy stole the conversation. The longer they spoke, the softer Sawyer became, although Frankie was willing to bet the older woman would never have admitted it. But damn, as she watched Sawyer's eyes sparkle as Frankie told stories of her old lover, a tight knot grew and festered inside Frankie's chest, strangling the space where her heart should be. Not because of leftover feelings for McCoy, but for the little shit likely still sulking up in her apartment. Evan had wormed their way into her heart all while trying to stab her in it. How was that even possible? The chemistry between them was magnetic, their passion like a burning inferno.

But what if it burned too hot, too bright? What if neither of them could trust the other long enough to tame those flames?

"McCoy told me about Evan, too," Sawyer said as Frankie walked her to the door. She fought the urge to check the clock again. If her staff needed her, they would have phoned.

"Did she now?" Frankie assumed as much, but didn't say.

"Don't forget what I said when I came here looking for McCoy all those months ago." Sawyer glanced back at Frankie, clutching her bag of goodies in front of her. Her eyes softened with such sympathy, Frankie had to look away. "When the time came, I chose her over my insecurities. Do you know yet what you're willing to give up, if Evan's the one?"

By the time Frankie was climbing the stairs to her apartment hours later, it was close to midnight. After four nights with hardly any sleep, she was dead on her feet. Her lower back and calves ached from standing for the last several hours, and all she wanted to do was strip and stretch out on her sectional with a drink in hand. A homemade lager or a few fingers' worth of bourbon, she wasn't sure just yet.

A yawn slipped out as she fumbled with her keys, and she dropped them twice before she found the right one and let herself in. The lemony scent of disinfectant, combined with the baked apple candle burning on the ledge near the entryway, lifted Frankie's spirits somewhat.

"You've been busy. The place smells great, Evan," Frankie said, setting her keys and purse down. She bent to unfasten her pumps, grimacing at how her back protested with the movement. A heating pad might do her well, too.

Evan appeared from the kitchen, quickly noticing her struggle. They dropped to their knees in front of Frankie, one hand reaching out to touch her foot. "Can I?"

"Mm-hmm." Frankie watched them with hooded eyes as they carefully unstrapped her pumps and freed her of the footwear. The softness of Evan's featherlight touch on her skin made her chest constrict, and it took every ounce of willpower she possessed to keep her hands to herself. It was all she could do to not caress the fine hairs on Evan's scalp for a job well done. "Thank you," she husked, satisfaction blooming when Evan's cheeks pinkened.

"Yeah, of course. Can you ... Are you too tired to talk?"

"No." She was, but she would take a win with Evan when she could get one. "Just let me change and I'm all yours."

Once Frankie was dressed in a loose pair of joggers and T-shirt, she met Evan in the kitchen just as the kettle on the stove began to whistle. Her lips curled up at the two mugs waiting on the counter, and she met Evan's expectant gaze.

"You're being very considerate tonight, little thief."

"Deep conversations require tea." When Frankie continued to stare at them, Evan added a bit sheepishly, "You said that before."

With the desire to kick back and relax—with alcohol—silently taunting her, Frankie forced herself to cross the kitchen to where the mugs sat. She lifted the steaming kettle off the burner. "Is that what this is tonight? A deep conversation?"

"Yes. No. I mean, maybe?" Evan heaved a sigh, appearing beside her. Frankie poured the hot water into the mugs, noting the hot chocolate mix in Evan's. She added a drop of milk from the carton in the fridge, and for a comforting moment, the only sound in the room was the slight *clang* of their spoons against the ceramic as they stirred their beverages.

"I've tried to give you space the last few days," Frankie said at last. She studied Evan across from her in the breakfast booth, from their mostly bare, untatted arms in a crew neck tank top, to the lone chain around a slender neck, to the recently buzzed blonde hair. When they blushed and dropped their gaze to their hot chocolate, Frankie caught the sword tattoo just below the arm of their eyeglasses. Her stomach did a low, delicious swoop at the sight. "I've tried and, while difficult, I think I succeeded. Don't you?"

Evan nodded in agreement, still not looking at her fully. "It gave me a lot of time to think. I realized that ... you know tons about me, Frankie. Deep, personal things and shit I'm not proud of. But I don't know you, not really. You said you didn't wanna be just a body to someone into kink, and I don't think I want that either. So I figure ..." Evan trailed off, took a long sip of their hot chocolate, and lifted their face to Frankie's at last. Nerves made them restless in the booth, and a rosy flush appeared on their throat, but determination shone in their eyes.

"What do you figure, honey?" Frankie asked when Evan's pause stretched out.

A gust of air left them. "I know that what happened with Caleb must've fucked you up a little bit, but only 'cause I figured it out. I want ... I need something else. How else am I supposed to learn to trust you?"

An obnoxiously loud strum of her pulse started in Frankie's ears, the kind she got when her body began to panic. She reached for her neck, kneading her fingers into the overwrought ball of tension there. "You know I'm adopted."

"I knew that before I even met you."

Evan's confession came as a surprise, but then, why would it? They had managed to find her even after she'd legally dropped her first name, Katheryn. She swallowed. "And do you know why?"

Evan nodded once, a flash of sympathy showing. "Your parents were killed in a car accident when you were four. Your aunt and uncle raised you. In this apartment, actually." They glanced around the home Frankie had spent so much of her childhood in. "That's all. You guys moved, but I don't know where."

Frankie leveled Evan with a long look, trying to keep her voice steady. "Honey, you already know more than most. What else could you possibly need at this stage in our relationship?"

"This." Evan reached for their wallet tucked off to the side of the table. Flipping it open, they took out a picture and set it in front of Frankie.

Emily's face stared back at her past the photograph's frayed edges. Frankie's breath hitched in her throat, and her gaze collided with Evan's. Her voice was steely as she gritted out, "Why did you steal this? You had no right! Investigating me is one thing, but Emily is—"

"Of course I stole it. You were my *enemy*, Frankie." Evan held their hands up like they were calling a truce, a pleading expression on their face. "Please, just listen, okay? You know about Caleb. He was one of the most important people to me, and you *fucking shot him*. The *least* you could do is tell me who this girl was to you."

"No." Frankie wagged her head back and forth, her movements jerky as she shoved out of the booth and pointed a shaking finger at Evan. "I shot him because *I had to*. Because if I didn't, he would have *killed* me, Evan. Don't fucking dare try to manipulate the narrative. Emily is off limits."

"You clearly cared for her if it tears you up just saying her name. I'm not trying to manipulate you, but how can you love me if you can't even trust me?"

Fuck the tea with conversation. Frankie retrieved the bottle of whiskey kept in the cupboard above the sink, followed by a tumbler, and almost dropped the glass as she poured out a few fingers' worth. She tossed it back in one gulp, enjoying the burn on the way down. Her hands were a lot steadier as she refilled the glass before setting the bottle on the counter.

Evan didn't know what they were asking. Excluding her family, no one currently in her life knew about Emily. The past hurt too damn much to dredge up. The mandatory therapy Frankie had endured while on the force had helped her move on from that god awful night, but that didn't mean her ghosts weren't still lurking in the dark, waiting for a chance to resurface. Over the years, she'd thwarted every single one of McCoy's attempts to find out. Surely she could bury this one with Evan easily enough.

Slowly, Frankie turned and leaned against the counter, finding Evan's shifty gaze across the room.

"I-I can't."

"Do you know yet what you're willing to give up, if Evan's the one?"

Sawyer's question from hours earlier popped intrusively into Frankie's thoughts. She hesitated, her glass halfway to her lips. Evan slipped out of the booth, their posture slouched in defeat. They turned to leave the kitchen, and Frankie knew she might never have another chance. She might wake up tomorrow and find Evan gone. For good this time.

She opened her mouth, her voice cracking as she said, "Emily was my foster sister."

Evan stilled as if waiting for Frankie to continue. So she took a big swig of her drink and said something she'd only ever admitted twice before.

"I was also in love with her."

CHAPTER 26

Frankie

"SHE'D BEEN LIVING WITH us for a couple of years before any romantic feelings came to light. She was ... my best friend. Even though I was a year older, we did everything together. It was hard at first to distinguish between normal friend affections and ... something more. But then her changing around me became a whole other thing." Frankie could still remember the first time she'd noticed Emily in a sexual way. *Damn bikinis.*

"She didn't want me, not like that." Shaking her head, tears blurred Frankie's image of Evan before her. She let them fall down her cheeks, hot and full of old pain. A droplet landed on the picture in her hand, and she used her thumb to wipe it clear of Emily's hair. Her chest ached, all the lingering emotions from years past causing a steady, dull void in a piece of her heart. "I loved her, but she didn't ... not like that. Like how I wanted." Emily had tried, for a time. After that damn party, after the attack ...

"What happened to her?" Evan reached across the breakfast table to grasp her hand in theirs. They had managed to sit down again after Frankie's initial outburst. She was calmer now, no doubt from the whiskey she'd drunk. She was nursing her third glass, swishing the liquid around gently as she thought of how best to answer Evan. It was hard to deliver the "how" of Emily's death without explaining the "why".

"She died." Frankie swallowed, the lump in her throat as raw as her heart was right then. She tugged her bottom lip between her teeth, unsure how much of her past she should share. Or if she could at all. Her chest squeezed as the night of the party came back to her.

It had been the beginning of the end for her and Emily.

"It was my fault. I knew we shouldn't, but ..." Frankie shook her head, lifting the tumbler to her lips again. The whiskey no longer burned going down. "Emily wanted to go to a party in the neighborhood. A guy she liked from school was going. You know, typical jock douchebag who didn't deserve a girl like Emily. Auntie B had already said no, which I was secretly grateful for, but Em was so crushed. She wanted to sneak out to the party anyway and begged me to go with her. I never could say no to her, and honestly, would have done anything for the smile she gave me when I finally caved."

Emily had been so excited to see Brett, and regardless that it killed Frankie at the time, seeing how happy she was had been everything. *Stupid teenage love.*

Voice cracking, Frankie continued, not daring to look at Evan as she did so. "We were ... drugged and ... and raped at that party."

Evan cursed, and as much as her brain screamed at her to stop, Frankie took another drink and pushed through. *Liquid courage.* "Years and many therapy sessions later, and I still can't stand the smell of a certain brand of body spray. Funny, isn't it?"

She didn't give Evan the explicit details, like how long it'd taken her to mistakenly accept a drink from a stranger near the beer keg. She'd been so proud of herself for sourcing beers for her and

Emily without needing the help of Brett and his loser friends. And watching as Emily chugged it back like it was her tenth party instead of her first. God, Frankie had been so in love with her. And then after—she'd never been able to pinpoint how long after—hearing Emily's sobs stop and feeling the crushing weight on top of Frankie.

No, she didn't tell Evan how the rumble of excitement let her know others were in the room, watching, waiting for their turn. That the sound of their jeers still sometimes echoed in the recesses of her mind on days she felt low. She didn't describe the relief she'd felt when the weight on her lifted, only for fresh panic to set in as rough hands grabbed her wrists and someone else took their place. Over and over before she'd finally lost consciousness again.

She didn't tell Evan how pathetically grateful she'd been to have woken the following morning in an unfamiliar backyard, *three* blocks from where the party had been. Because Emily had been there beside her, bruised and bloody as well, but *alive*. She didn't explain just how long it'd taken her and Emily to figure out that it was their word against the boys. They'd been left with zero evidence of the attack. Frankie had spent years digging for answers around that night, trying to find proof that Brett had been involved since the attackers had worn masks. The grainy images haunting her hadn't been substantial enough for a case. Evan didn't need to know about any of that.

It wasn't until therapy that she chose to let it all go. The attack had stolen too much of her life already. What better "fuck you" could she give than to dedicate her career to helping stop future rapists? After the incident with Caleb, Frankie had decided helping women in a different way would be less self-sacrificing.

"Fuck, Frankie. I'm so sorry." Evan's eyes were leaking tears as well, yet another reason Frankie knew their feelings for her were genuine. It wasn't an act; Evan truly cared for her.

She squeezed their hand, knowing that if she didn't finish the story, she'd never bring it up again. It was the biggest scar on her heart, bigger still than what killing Caleb had cost her. "Emily was five months along before any of us realized she was pregnant. She'd sat me down in our bedroom one day, hoping that if she told me, I'd figure out a way to break the news to Auntie B. Since she was fifteen and a foster kid, we had no idea what would happen to her or the baby when her social worker found out."

Frankie swallowed hard, faint images of Emily's thigh touching hers all those years ago. What an exhilarating feeling it had been back then, just to have her close enough to touch. "I comforted her, we cried for what happened to us, I wiped her tears away, and then she kissed me. For the first time ever, she'd acknowledged that there could be anything more between us. It'd been ... everything I could ever hope for. We kissed for hours, long into the night. She fell asleep in my arms.

"I-I promised I'd take care of her and the baby. When she woke up, though, she wanted to forget what happened. So I said okay. Her happiness was all that mattered to me and, well, neither of us was the same after the attack. Emily's moods had been up and down for a long time, but a part of me clung to the hope that she'd change her mind down the road."

"No more," Evan said when she reached for the bottle of whiskey again. They passed her a glass of water instead. Frankie scowled, but took it from them anyway, downing half the contents.

"And so I sat Emily down with Auntie B and explained what she couldn't. I told Auntie B everything—about the party, the drugs, and t-the ..." Frankie's voice caught on the last word. Her throat bobbed up and down as she swallowed past the raw memories. Her eyes drifted closed as more tears fell. They had suffered in silence until that night. It wasn't until Auntie B learned of the attack that the police were notified. By then, it'd been too late.

Evan's hand slipped into hers. "This is hurting you. That wasn't my intention."

"No, it's okay. More than anyone else, you deserve to know me, little thief." Frankie blew out a breath, squeezing Evan's hand again before releasing it. To get through the next part, she'd need all the strength she could get, and touching Evan made her feel anything but strong. "Fast forward several months. Auntie B had it worked out that Emily and the baby stayed with us, and she fostered him too. They talked about Emily giving him up for adoption, but she didn't want that. If it had been me ... but not Emily. In her eyes, she was trying to right a wrong."

Frankie lifted the bottle of whiskey, brushing Evan's hand away when they tried to stop her. Her hand shook as she poured a couple of fingers into the empty tumbler. She picked the glass up, downing the amber liquid in one big gulp before setting it back down with a hard thud. Her hazy eyes met the blatant concern in Evan's, and before Frankie could chicken out, she spoke the words she'd never told anyone.

"Emily hung herself a month later."

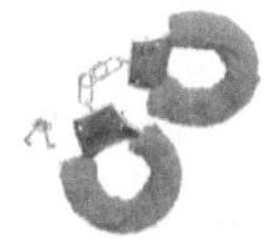

CHAPTER 27

Evan

CECIL: YOU'RE A FUCKING disappointment. If only you got killed instead of your brother then I KNOW business would be taken care of.

Evan read the message again. After the fourth time, they'd pieced together enough to confirm that not only was Cecil a complete asshole, but he was also an idiot. There was no way Caleb would have been sent to take out Frankie had Evan been the one killed. Not unless Caleb acted alone. No one except him had ever cared enough about Evan.

Not true. Mom cared, once upon a time ago.

That wasn't fair. Leah had struggled silently for a long time after Caleb died. Evan going to prison must have been her breaking point.

Evan locked the phone and set it down on the bar counter, scrubbing a hand over their face. It had been a blessing and a curse when the device had started working again after its slushy plunge. Since then, Cecil's threats were a daily occurrence, so much that Evan wasn't sure what his plan of action truly was.

"The boss is taking her time today," Sloane remarked from behind the bar. She'd come in earlier than usual to put in the alcohol order and was now restocking the beer fridge.

"Yeah, we, uh, had a late night."

After a few attempts, Evan had successfully gotten the bottle of whiskey away from Frankie, but by then, she'd been good and drunk. They'd helped her to bed, tucking her in and making sure to leave a bowl close by and the bottle of Gatorade they'd found in the fridge. Then Evan had sat with Frankie for the better part of the night, watching her sleep as they rehashed the night's confessions. They didn't know it was possible to regret a conversation as much as they did. Prying into Frankie's life before she was ready was bullheaded and uncalled for. But fuck, Evan had expected her to say Emily was an old girlfriend or something, not all of ... *that*.

Poor Frankie. And poor *Emily.* The world was a cruel place, Evan knew that intimately. It pushed and pushed until you either collapsed from the weight or learned how to push back and never stop.

"You're fucking now, I take it?" Sloane ripped open the next case of beer, seemingly agitated. "Well, she better treat you right. You and Coy both act like nothing bothers you, but I know better. You're just gooey marshmallow on the inside, mistakenly assuming the dominant femme you fall for won't tear your heart out and stomp on it."

"Jesus, Sloane, not this before I've had my coffee." Frankie's tired voice sounded behind Evan. They turned to say hello, words dying on their lips at the sight of her. All they could do was stare.

"Jesus yourself," Sloane said, her jaw dropping open. Then she snorted a laugh. "You look like shit rolled up and baked, with more shit poured over top. The flu finally get you?"

Sloane could use some tact, but Evan had to admit she wasn't too far off in the description. Frankie's hair was combed, sort of, haphazardly tied in a low ponytail. And if that wasn't enough to raise a flag or two, then the smudged makeup still on her face from last night, and the dark, almost sick-looking circles under tormented brown eyes would. Hangovers did not suit Frankie.

"Shut up. She looks great," Evan lied, but no way would they sit there and listen to Sloane insult Frankie after the night she'd had. On second thought, they *never* wanted to hear Sloane's verbal vomit when it came to Frankie.

Sliding off the barstool, Evan offered Frankie their kindest smile to date. "It probably doesn't feel like it, but good morning."

Frankie's exhausted smile shifted into a wince as she peered down at Evan. She took their hand in hers, giving it a light squeeze. "Any morning you're here is a good one."

Warmth spread across Evan's chest with her gravelly murmur. It was a miracle she still felt that way after all that had happened. Not only had Evan got a job at the pub to purposely sabotage her business, but they'd tried to take her out assassin-style. And then, the night before, Evan had pushed Frankie so far that she'd become a drinking, sobbing mess.

Yeah. It was a *real* good morning alright.

"Sit down, let me grab you some coffee," Evan said, guiding Frankie to the stool they'd just vacated. They ignored Sloane's eye roll on the way to the coffee station, pulled a mug off the shelf, and filled it about an inch from the top. Next, they located the mint non-dairy creamer Frankie used whenever she forwent her usual Irish coffees, giving it a good stir before setting the drink in front of her.

Frankie smiled again, clearly pleased and not caring that they had an audience as she drew Evan closer. "Thank you, baby. You're very sweet."

"You're welcome," Evan quietly replied, but the number of butterflies that erupted low in their belly at Frankie's latest term of endearment made their cheeks burn.

"You two are nauseatingly sweet," Sloane grumped, brushing past Evan.

"How are you?" Frankie asked the moment Sloane disappeared into the kitchen. She took a drink of her coffee, her gaze never wavering from Evan. Her fingertips brushed the back of Evan's hand before catching the cuff of the hoodie sleeve. "I'm sorry about last night. I wasn't very good company, was I?"

Frankie drunkenly weeping until she passed out in the bed sparked in Evan's memory, but they shrugged, admitting in a teasing voice, "I always love your company. It's been a curse since we met, you being my enemy and all."

"That must have been so hard for you, little thief."

"You're still at it, and now, with the nicknames," Sloane huffed, walking past them to the dining room. Chairs clanged as she pulled them noisily off the table to the floor. "At least it's not 'pet', 'cause that would be a major ick after Coy, know what I'm saying?"

Frankie's eyes narrowed, and when it looked as if she would snap a response, her lips clamped shut. She turned on her stool to face Sloane, eyes squinting. "You'd do well to re-engage your filter, honey. I'm working with a hangover from hell, and almost exclusively in the 'fuck around and find out' mood today."

"I don't think she can help it," Evan said, covering Frankie's hand that still held lightly to their sleeve. They used their thumb to stroke her soft skin, which brought Frankie's focus back to them.

"Well, she needs to learn. She can't keep bringing McCoy's name into the conversation." Frankie looked adorably perturbed, and Evan couldn't help but reach up and kiss the side of her mouth. Their nose pressed into her skin, and even smelling faintly like whiskey, she was delectable.

"It's okay, Daddy."

The title had Frankie instantly brightening, and with slow but steady fingers, she grasped Evan's chin. "Are you sure?"

"Yes."

Truthfully, Evan wasn't, but the desire for Frankie to be their Domme was stronger than ever. She was protective, caring, and perhaps if Evan was secured in her whims, they could take some of the burden from one another. Evan understood now exactly why Frankie restrained her partners. It was a chance to reclaim her control. A chance to indulge in sex in the safest way she knew how. Now, more than anything, Evan wanted the freedom Frankie had teased about for months. What with everything with Caleb and Cecil, it was too much. It felt like they were stuffed inside a too-small suit, and each time they tried to stand tall or take a step, the fabric tore at the seams. It was suffocating and confined them just as the bars in prison had. Frankie could help them, and in return, Evan could help her.

"Fuck, not now," Evan said hours later, spying the rack full of half-washed glasses. It was the second time they'd gone through the cycle. Taking a deep breath, they pushed it back into the dishwasher, noticing the lukewarm temperature inside. It was usually much hotter.

"Hey, Nathan, it's still booming out there. Frankie wants you to run through inventory, and let her know," Andy called from the doorway, turning to give Evan a playful salute before disappearing again. Evan didn't have time to warn him about the possible shit-show brewing, and sure enough, when the dish cycle ran its course, the glasses still came out streaked and smudged in fingerprints. Evan checked around them, half-heartedly hoping someone else in the kitchen was available to lend a hand, but Nathan was racing around, and Rain was belting orders to Dakota from the hot line.

Maybe I can fix it myself. How hard could it be? After all, Evan had managed to break the walk-in cooler on purpose. Surely, they could problem-solve a simple industrial dishwasher. Swiping perspiration off their forehead, Evan shut the machine off first and checked it over. Maybe a reset would help with the temperature issue. Next, they braced one hand on the frame for support and reached inside the dishwasher, tugging on the bottom spray arm. They knew the food could sometimes get clogged and—

"What are you doing?"

Evan jumped at the sound of Frankie's throaty demand, their head smacking into the sliding door of the dishwasher. Evan grimaced, rubbing the fresh sore. "Trying to fix this. It's not washing properly."

"Really." Frankie shot them a weighted glance before assessing the issue herself. "Move aside, let me turn it on."

"It was just on," Evan protested, but did as they were told. Folding their arms, Evan almost rolled their eyes as Frankie followed the exact steps they had. She turned the dishwasher on and then off before closely inspecting the interior.

"Looks okay. Let's try a load to see," Frankie instructed, moving out of the way and gesturing for Evan to take over. Their femme was a lot better put together now than that morning, but apparently, still moody as fuck.

"I tried like three times, but okay." Evan stepped forward, sliding the rack of dishes into the chamber once more. The intensity of Frankie's gaze set Evan aflame as they pulled the door closed. There was a charge in the air between them as they waited for the cycle to finish, and Evan had never been more aware of someone else in their bubble. Restless energy emanated from Frankie, as if she was doing all she could to keep still, but inside she was dying to either fight or fuck someone.

And then the dishwasher died mid-cycle.

"What? No, no. Fuck." Evan jammed their thumb into the power button once, twice, three times. Nothing happened, so they grabbed the handle on the door to open it, but the locking mechanism was still in place.

"We don't have time for this, little thief. Just reverse whatever you did in the first place," Frankie said from behind Evan, her body pressing closer to theirs.

Evan's pulse picked up when Frankie's hands fell to their hips, and they turned in her arms, their gaze darting behind Frankie to the rest of the kitchen staff. Thankfully everyone was too busy to pay attention to them. Evan gulped at the look in Frankie's eyes, quickly averting their gaze. "I-I didn't do anything to it. I swear."

"Really?" Frankie purred, her hands tightening a fraction on Evan's hips. She yanked them closer so that Evan's nose grazed her collarbone through her blazer. "Because I can think of a few things I'd rather you be doing late tonight than washing all these by hand."

"By ... hand?"

"Yes. How else do you expect this pile to disappear?" Frankie's hands moved from Evan's hips to their wrists, locking them in place between them. When she brushed her lips over Evan's earlobe, a groan almost escaped. "You'd better get started."

"But ... Yes, Daddy." Evan's shoulders slumped. There was no point arguing. Evan was too tired, and after what the two of them had been through the last couple of nights, Evan just wanted to do *something* to please Frankie.

"That's it, be a good boi for me." Evan sucked in a breath at the new endearment. There was a spark in Frankie's eyes as she released Evan, and judging by the deep rise and falls of her chest, Evan wasn't the only one affected.

"Dude, the boss has got a chokehold on you," Rain crowed from nearby the fryer the moment Frankie disappeared.

"Haha." Evan rolled their eyes, but at the way their pulse pounded in their throat, Rain's assumption might not have been too far off.

CHAPTER 28

Frankie

I'M GOING TO TIE them to my desk for that stunt, Frankie thought, baring her teeth in a smile as she took another order. It had taken great effort on her part not to get angry with Evan. For all she knew, the dishwasher breaking was something they had planned weeks ago, long before Evan began responding to Frankie's dominant side. But the idea sounded ludicrous even to her. Was pre-scheduling an appliance breaking something that could be done?

"Who knew we could get slammed on a Thursday?" Andy said, halting in his tracks seconds before they would have collided. He maneuvered his tray of drinks easily away from Frankie's shoulder.

"I bet it's because of the new rom-com being filmed. Half the supporting cast are gay as fuck, or at least that's what's going around most of my feeds. Hey, what can I get you?" Sloane asked the next patron.

Frankie surveyed her pub with fresh eyes. There were dozens of new faces milling about, either watching the hockey match on the big flat screen or hovering around pool tables. A few people had even taken to the small, unoccupied floor space, creating a makeshift dance floor. She didn't recognize anyone famous, but Frankie wasn't one to keep up with the news and didn't watch many movies. Whatever was the cause of the unusual influx of patrons, it was a bad night for the dishwasher to break—accidentally or otherwise.

They ran out of plates first, and the only reason Frankie could come up with was that Evan must have been making sure the customers didn't run out of glasses for all the alcohol they were consuming. Ensuring her front house staff were alright, Frankie announced she was going to check in with the kitchen, aware she'd need to save Evan. She hadn't even pushed the swing door to enter when she heard the shouting match.

"Why would you wait till we're fucking out before saying anything? We could've helped wash!"

"If you were focused on anything besides Rain's tits, you would've seen for yourself!"

Evan's cheeks were flushed with anger and, Frankie assumed, the rising warmth of the small kitchen. She watched the stare down between her little thief and Dakota for perhaps ten seconds before she clapped her hands.

"Dakota, get out there and bus the tables."

Dakota swung his gaze to Frankie standing in the doorway, his mouth clamping shut the moment he spotted her. Then he grabbed the clean apron hanging on the back wall and stormed past her in silence.

"You've got yourself knee deep in dishes, I see." Frankie looked Evan over as she unbuttoned her blazer and hung it on a hook. Even hungover with her bed still calling to her, Frankie had made herself shower and dress to impress for her shift. She was of the assumption that the better she looked on the outside, the better she'd feel on the inside. Today it only seemed to have about a 50 percent success rate.

"I thought I had to do them myself."

"As much as I'd like that, my business comes first. You dry, I'll wash," she instructed, putting on an apron and pulling a hair tie from her pocket. She clasped the flowing curls in a loose ponytail in the back.

"Okay. Umm, thanks." Evan grabbed a clean, dry cloth while Frankie got to work, dipping her hands into the already sudsy hot water.

It was a good thing she had plenty of fond memories of doing exactly this when she was younger. Helping with the dishes, cleaning tables, or lounging in the office with her cousin while her uncle worked the pub. Although she'd never pictured herself following in his footsteps. That had been her cousin's dream, not hers.

"This is just like at home. Er ... upstairs, I mean."

Frankie glanced Evan's way, really looking at them since she suspected they'd broken something of hers again. None of the earlier frustration simmered to the surface like she expected. Instead, a tingly kind of warmth spread over her chest at the hopeful look in Evan's eyes. They were impossible to stay angry at.

"It's kind of like a date, right? Although if you wanted a date with me, you didn't need to go through such extreme measures," Frankie reasoned, easing another plate into the rinse water.

"Date?" Evan stared at her blankly for a second, and then, much to Frankie's delight, turned red and stammered out, "I didn't break the washer on purpose. Why would you think that?"

"Oh, I dunno," Frankie drawled. "Maybe because you've been sabotaging the pub since you arrived? The walk-in, the beer tanks? And, well, I saw you break into my office. All part of a grand scheme of revenge, I'm guessing."

Evan's enigmatic gaze flashed in defiance, and just when Frankie was certain they'd lash out at her, Evan bowed their head like a punished child. "Yeah, well, I didn't break this on purpose. Why would I make more work for myself?"

"To disrupt my business, to be petty." Frankie reached for Evan, wrapping her hand around the base of their neck and pulling them closer. "To get my attention. Which you have, my little thief."

"Mm-hmm, well, I actually didn't. Fucking thing broke all on its own. And your attention should wait while we're at work, Frankie."

At work. Right. Sighing, Frankie released Evan, even if what she wanted was to bend them over and kiss them senseless before dragging them up to her apartment. Their apartment, for the two of them. Hadn't Evan just called it home? *I love the sound of that.*

"Then after, when we're home, I'll show you exactly what my attention looks like," Frankie promised, not missing the faint squeak that left Evan.

"We haven't gone over safe words yet. Are you aware of the color system? Or the traffic light system, as some call it," Frankie asked back in the apartment late that night. She stripped off her blazer, tossing it on the chaise in the living room, before turning back to Evan. She reached to undo the first several buttons on her blouse, raising her eyebrow when Evan just stared at her newly exposed skin, slack-jawed. "Eyes up, little thief."

Evan blinked as if in a daze, slowly lifting their gaze away from Frankie's cleavage. "Umm, color system?"

"Yes. Unless you already have a safe word in mind, the color system can be great for communication during a scene. You'd tell me if you're feeling green, yellow, or red when I ask, or at any time you feel uncomfortable or unsure about something. Green means you like what we're doing and to continue, yellow is for me to slow down, and red is to stop everything immediately." Frankie leaned against the back of the chaise, making sure not to sit on her blazer. She reached for her hair clip, letting her long curls tumble out past her shoulders. Evan watched her intently, not missing a thing. The battle between apprehension and lust in their eyes was one Frankie wanted to put to rest, once and for all. "Whatever we do, it's because you've told me you're comfortable enough to try it, but that's not to say you won't change your mind midway through a scene. If that happens, red brings everything to a halt."

"Okay. I ..." Evan's gaze roamed slowly over Frankie, from the tips of her now bare toes to her legs still in dress pants, and back to her eyes. They licked their lips, one of several nervous habits that Frankie had picked up on. "I want this. I wanna try. I have this need ... There's a part of me I don't understand fully."

"And I can help with that, little thief. Take your boots off and come to me." Frankie watched as Evan bent to untie their footwear, waited until they were pulling them off before adding, "Don't forget to place them on the rack."

Evan's movements slowed for a millisecond before they dutifully did as requested. Frankie's mouth curled up in a smile. Evan approached her with uncertain steps, taking her hand when Frankie held it out for them. "That's good, you've made me very pleased."

Evan blushed, but there was a light in their eyes now. "Thank you," they mumbled.

"Thank you, what?" Frankie angled her head, studying the glaze of confusion in Evan's eyes, smirking when they figured out just what she was waiting for. The flush on their cheeks deepened.

"Thank you, Daddy."

"Mm-hmm, I do love it when you call me that." Frankie had loved it when McCoy would call her Mistress; in fact, she was the one who insisted on it in the beginning. Being called Daddy hit her in an entirely different way. It made her feel hyper sexy and naughtier than she'd ever been before. She liked that.

Frankie stood and led Evan to the bedrooms, pausing between her room and theirs. "Do I have your permission to use your space for play tonight? Or would you be more comfortable in my room for the first time?"

"Maybe just yours tonight?"

Frankie nodded, understanding the need for space and privacy all too well. Now more than anything, she wished she owned a house that came with multiple bedrooms as well as a playroom. Then Evan could retreat to their bedroom when they wanted alone time. In all the BDSM romances she'd skimmed of McCoy's, the Dommes always seemed exceptionally wealthy. In reality, most were just regular people like her. "Very well, little thief. Come."

Once in Frankie's room, she drew Evan to her so their back pressed against her chest. Nuzzling their ear with her nose, she inhaled the woodsy scent of their body wash. "Is there anything you're uncomfortable with when it comes to sex and your body, Evan? I want to make sure no lines are crossed."

"I don't mind my chest or nipples being touched accidentally, but I don't like them being played with. It makes me ... It weirds me the fuck out." Evan's voice was pensive, and when they tilted their face up to look at her, Frankie saw a plea for understanding. "I'm not ...

I'm not often comfortable in this body, so you know, I-I like the idea of getting out of my head with you."

"Okay, that's not a problem. Anything else?" Frankie had suspected something like that, but discussing matters first was crucial in this type of dynamic. She slid her hands up and down Evan's arms in a soothing gesture.

Evan shook their head, a small sigh escaping as she caressed their shoulders. "I'm okay with everything else, except maybe ..."

"What?"

Evan peered up at Frankie, though how they could see her with those long lashes almost covering their eyes, Frankie didn't know. "I sometimes don't like calling my ... down there ... by the clinical names. It can affect my headspace. So just ... front hole, back hole, sexy bits, downstairs, bud, nub. Occasionally clit is okay, but I haven't settled on a certain term yet."

Frankie nodded, considering this new information. She would do anything to make things easier for her sub. She wanted them to feel as comfortable as possible around her. "What about while referring to my body?"

"I'm okay with it." Evan's eyelashes fluttered, a relatively shy smile appearing. "I like it, Daddy. You have a gorgeous body and great tits."

"I do not call them tits, and neither will you." Frankie huffed a laugh, giving Evan a light pinch on their hip where their hoodie had ridden up. "Call them breasts and nipples, clit and pussy, all of which you will not see tonight."

Frankie smirked when Evan let out an audible groan. They were rather cute when they were sulky. "Take your clothes off, as many as you're comfortable with. Tonight, I'll go easy on you. We'll practice restraint play, and perhaps, if you're a good boi, I'll even let you come before we've finished. Do you have any hard limits I need to know of tonight? Are you against me using a beginner flogger on you?"

"No, I don't think so. Just what I already said." Evan shook their head, and Frankie watched intently as they unfastened the belt on their jeans before pushing the denim off their narrow hips. Frankie ran her tongue over her bottom lip, her pulse picking up at the view. Next went Evan's hoodie, then their socks, until they were stripped down to just their boxers and tank top. They weren't wearing a binder tonight, or a bra, and Frankie was instantly grateful she hadn't pressured Evan into removing their top.

"You're being such a good little sub for me, aren't you?" Frankie reined in her urge to touch them. She turned to her closet to give them privacy if they chose to remove anything else and called over her shoulder, "When you're ready, climb on the bed and lie face down for me with your arms out in front of you."

"Yes, Daddy."

Evan's eager reply made Frankie smile. She could hear them doing as asked, and she took her time locating one of the few toys she kept in her closet. The mahogany flogger was well used and dependable, with its strips of leather worn around the edges. It would do nicely for Evan's first time. Next, she retrieved her blindfold and finally, a small, recently purchased dildo. She hadn't had a chance to try it out and was looking forward to Evan possibly being the first to experience it.

"There is so much I can do to you without you needing to face me," Frankie explained, keeping her voice low and purposely seductive. It was a tactic she'd learned years ago, as one of only a handful of female officers in her department. It helped to contain the misogyny on the force. Her male counterparts hated her less when they spent too much time dreaming of the day they'd fuck her. If only she'd been as insightful when she was sixteen. It might have helped her and Emily.

Stop. Don't you fucking ruin this for me. Frankie gave herself a hard mental shake. Losing focus during a time like this wasn't a price she was willing to pay. She took a deep breath, turning to see that Evan had pulled the covers all the way back on her bed and climbed in, exactly as instructed. Pleasure skittered down her spine as she took in Evan's bare ass. They'd also rolled up their tank top so that it sat midway on their back. All that soft skin was exposed to Frankie's view, looking as tempting as ever. She could already envision just how flushed and pretty her marks on their skin would be.

"My, my, aren't you a good boi, all splayed out like the feast you are and waiting for your Domme? If there is one thing you'll learn from playtime with me, little thief, it's that good subs get rewarded."

A breathy noise left Evan as Frankie approached the head of the bed. Their fingers had the faintest tremble to them, which Frankie instantly zeroed in on. A smug smile appeared as she reached for Evan's left wrist, at the same time reaching under her mattress for the restraint strap she had secured there. She met Evan's eyes behind their slightly fogged-up lenses. They were hot already, and the two of them had barely started. Hell, Frankie hadn't scratched the surface on things she wanted to do to Evan before the night's end. She fit the cuff carefully around her sub's wrist. "Tell me what color you are right now."

"Green, Daddy."

"Excellent." Frankie finished with the clasp before tugging on the restraint. Another airy breath escaped Evan, their gaze steadfast on Frankie. Frankie reached out and very gently traced her fingers along the sharp angle of Evan's jawline. "I've wanted you at my mercy for so long. From the moment I laid eyes on you, I just knew I had to have you."

"I-I'm yours." Evan's eyes fluttered closed, and they leaned into her touch.

"Yes, I do believe you are." Frankie didn't waste time securing Evan's other wrist. As she moved to the foot of the bed and reached for their ankles, she asked what color they were.

"Still very green, Daddy."

"Mm-hmm, good. I plan to bind you fully to my bed and then, I'll tease and torment your body until you're a sopping mess for me. What do you say to that? You can end it all right now, just say the word."

Evan gave a vehement shake of their head, craning behind them to see Frankie. "I say ... thank you, Daddy. Y-your pleasure is my pleasure."

"Mmm, I had a feeling you'd be a natural at this. And you're absolutely right. Turning your tantalizing ass and thighs into a ripe, plump, tomato red would bring me immense pleasure."

Frankie reached under the mattress again, pulling out the two ankle restraints before carefully securing them on Evan. Desire flared hot in her belly as she examined her handiwork. She trailed the flogger lightly up and down Evan's legs, relishing the breathy shudder to leave them. "Remember," she said, and quickly flicked her wrist. The flogger's thin strips brandished into a fan shape before making contact with Evan's lean thighs. Evan hissed, tensing momentarily. "Yellow tells me you want me to slow down or pause. If you say red, I'll stop what I'm doing immediately. What color are you now?"

"Still green, Daddy."

"Good, because I've been dying to give you a good flogging. One where your pain becomes pleasure and you think of nothing else but how generous your Domme is, and how thankful you are." She snapped the flogger again, her pussy clenching at the crack as it made contact with Evan's flesh again, and once more they flinched, sucking in a breath. Frankie's breasts were heavy inside the fabric of her blouse, her stiffening nipples jutting the piercings against her bra. It had been so long since she'd derived pleasure from teasing a submissive, and Evan was so much more than that. Frankie brought the flogger down across Evan's ass cheek, not too hard, just with enough force to make Evan's skin sting. An audible groan left them, and the blossoming red on their skin was immediate.

"You're doing so well. Seeing you tied up like this is turning me on. What do you think, six, seven more? Can you handle that?"

Evan's breath hitched, their ass muscles flexing, and hell, it was hot. Frankie wanted to dip low and run her tongue over Evan's hot flesh, over every inch the flogger had touched. But she didn't want to stop there. She couldn't wait to make her way further, sinking her tongue deep into Evan's sex from behind, and then, sinking the dildo in as well.

"I'm wet for you, Daddy."

"Mm-hmm, and that makes me so pleased." Frankie snapped the flogger twice in rapid succession over Evan's thighs and ass, her pussy pulsing with each point of contact. Damn, this was going to be a good night. By the time the flogger made contact for the last time, Evan's hisses and groans of pain had transformed. Frankie sank her teeth into her bottom lip, eyes flashing with excitement as she watched Evan writhe and moan in erotic pleasure. Or as well as they could while bound to her bed.

"How are we?"

"So good." Evan's soft voice cracked a little, and they looked up at Frankie with aroused, out-of-focus eyes.

"You look exquisite spread out for me," Frankie said and set the flogger down on her nightstand. Evan kept their eyes trained on her as Frankie removed her jacket, hanging it up behind the door. Then she slipped out of her socks and pulled her blouse loose from where it tucked into her dress pants. She made her way back to the bed, crouching low to face her sub. "Can I touch you, Evan?"

"You can always touch me, Daddy."

Behind their glasses, Evan's gaze darkened. It couldn't have been comfortable to wear them in that position, so the first thing Frankie did was reach up and remove them. She set the glasses beside the discarded flogger with her attention still on Evan. Without them, Frankie could make out every detailed emotion her sub tried so hard to conceal from her. "No more hiding, little thief. During playtime at least, I want to see all of you."

CHAPTER 29

Evan

EVAN WAS DYING TO swallow the growing lump ascending in their throat, but they nodded in understanding. Hiding had been a coping mechanism for as long as they could—they gasped when Frankie kissed them, eyes drifting closed at the contact. Her scent clouded their senses, set the blood running through their veins ablaze. Evan returned the kiss with abandon, and when they attempted to wrap their arms around Frankie's shoulders, they were quickly reminded of their shackled limbs.

"Patience," Frankie cooed, circling Evan's throat with one hand. She grazed Evan's jaw with her teeth, her hand squeezing lightly. Evan's breathing grew labored as their Domme locked eyes with them. "Tell me again who you belong to."

Fuck. Evan shuddered as another bout of arousal thrummed through their pleasure points. Frankie's husky voice, her body so close to theirs, was the only thing they could focus on. Evan's skin where Frankie had struck them was hot, but they found they wanted more, *needed* everything their Domme would offer.

"You. I belong to you, Daddy."

"Mm-hmm, that's right. And do you know what I do with good bois who belong to me?"

"W-what?"

Frankie stood, and Evan had to crane their head up to see what she would do next. They didn't need to wait long. Frankie climbed onto the bed with Evan, the feeling of her slacks rough over Evan's already sensitized skin. An involuntary yelp left Evan when Frankie's soft hands landed on their back. Seconds later her lips were warm and moist against Evan's ear, the feel of her breath causing Evan's toes to curl. "I make them beg. I own your orgasm, little thief, and only when I'm good and ready will you come for me. Understood?"

Evan couldn't stop the whimper that came out, though hell if they knew if it was out of complaint or excitement. A scorching ball of heat dipped low in their stomach when Frankie suddenly spanked their ass cheek. "Answer the question, little thief."

"Un-understood, but ..." Evan inhaled sharply, and ground their pelvis harder into the mattress. There was a tremble in their voice as they continued, "What if I accidentally come?"

A low, yet compelling chuckle filled the room. Frankie's fingernails scored Evan's legs before slipping between them. Evan sucked in a sharp breath as Frankie's skillful fingers slid along their slit, teasing the growing wetness. Her thumb found Evan's tightly coiled bud, and when she gave it a gentle rub, pleasure zapped through their body like an electrical current. "Fuck."

"And to think, we've only just gotten started."

"Daddy, I don't think ... it's possible I won't be able to—oh, fuuuck." Evan's eyes rolled back when Frankie sank a finger deep inside.

"You were saying?" There was a sly smirk in Frankie's voice. She pressed Evan's ass down with one hand, and with the other, she began slowly pumping her finger in and out of Evan's heat. "Goddamn, you feel amazing. So wet for me, aren't you, little thief?"

Evan buried their face in the mattress and forced their body to relax. Even from behind, Frankie knew just where to angle her fingers and thumb to hit every erogenous zone. It wasn't long before she added a second finger, and then a third, thrusting painfully slowly inside Evan. A long moan escaped Evan, and their pulse sped up, the muscles in their bound arms and legs constricting and releasing as they got closer to a climax.

And then Frankie retracted her fingers, retreating from Evan's body altogether. A whine left them at the loss of contact. They'd been so close!

"That's my orgasm you're building, remember?" Frankie's lips caressed Evan's ear, her hot breath against their skin exciting them even more. Her hands clasped Evan's still caught in the restraints. "And I'm not ready for you to come just yet."

"I'm sorry, Daddy." The sting of Frankie's words caused Evan's cheeks to flush. But Frankie's lips and tongue didn't let up, sucking their earlobe into her mouth before trailing teasing kisses down their neck and across their exposed shoulders.

"You're forgiven. After all, you're still learning precisely what pleases me." Frankie's hands tightened on Evan's right before she bit down gently on Evan's shoulder. Evan's breath caught, another groan forming in their throat when Frankie straddled their thighs. She still wore her pants, absolutely nothing had changed, but when she began pumping her pelvis into Evan's ass and exposed sex, she might as well have been fucking them with a strap. That same slow, all-consuming fire began to spread through Evan once more, curling their toes and tightening low in their belly. Their sex fluttered.

Once again, the moment Evan was sure they'd come apart, Frankie brandished the flogger.

"What color are you, little thief?"

Evan's arms broke out in goosebumps as the leather tips of the flogger danced along their skin. They squeezed their eyes shut, a faint tremor washing over them. "Green."

"Yeah? You don't need me to slow down or anything?"

Evan let out a huff at the humor in Frankie's voice. Through clenched teeth, they managed, "I need more, *please*, Daddy. I need you."

"I know you do, and you're being so patient waiting for me. But I'm not finished with you yet."

"Frankie." A sob caught in Evan's throat when Frankie's weight lifted off them a third time. Fucking hell, what would it take to get an orgasm tonight?

"Shh, baby, you're doing so well for your first time. I'll make this worth your while, I promise." Frankie trailed the flogger along Evan's spine, passing over their ass to the meaty part of their slender legs. Evan knew at once more pain would ensue, but as the flogger came down on their feverish skin, a surprised cry of pleasure escaped instead. Arousal coated the sheets underneath them.

"Fuck, c-can I please come?"

"While I'm loving your manners, not just yet." Frankie chuckled, and another sob left Evan when the flogger came down on their thigh once more.

Deep breaths, deep breaths.

But Frankie was everywhere, touching, whipping, kissing, and licking. Evan sucked in another breath when her teeth nipped the flesh on the inner part of their thigh before sinking her fingers into their sex, only to pull out again. Evan whimpered. "Fuck, you're drenched for me, little thief. All this, mine."

Evan's head turned just as Frankie was sucking their arousal off her fingers. She looked beautifully wild, leaning back on her haunches, the crotch of her dress pants damp and full of Evan's scent. Her blouse was agape enough that Evan could make out the scar on her chest, but it didn't turn them off or snap them back to reality. In fact, Evan couldn't remember wanting anyone more than they did Frankie.

"Taste yourself on me," she told Evan, grabbing their cheek in one hand. Then her lips were on Evan's, her tongue in their mouth, and they could indeed taste their arousal in their kiss. Evan's sex throbbed, begging for the release they knew Frankie could give them. And then they felt the hard tip of something pressing against their entrance. Evan broke the kiss and pulled away from Frankie with a sharp inhale.

"What color are you, my gorgeous boi?" Frankie asked, leaning into Evan for another deep kiss. While their mouths were occupied, Evan felt Frankie trail the dildo through their wetness, but not inside.

They tensed for a heartbeat. Evan wanted the release they knew Frankie could provide, but there was one thing they'd forgotten to mention. "Green, Daddy, but I-I've never actually used one before. A-a dildo. Or any toy."

"Thank you for telling me. I'll take it slow, then." Frankie bit down on Evan's shoulder at the same time she inched the dildo inside. Soft moans left them both. Evan clamped down on the toy, their choppy breaths sounding loud in the bedroom. The dildo was tight and a bit painful, but each of Frankie's slow thrusts was oh-so-fucking delicious. A hot flush broke out on Evan's chest and on their throat where Frankie's fingers still rested. Perspiration dampened their forehead. The swollen bud Frankie had been relentlessly teasing spasmed as she passed her thumb over it once more. Secured to the restraints, Evan's legs began to shake.

"Goddamn, I think you might be my new favorite addiction."

"Please," Evan begged, so overstimulated now they were beyond full sentences.

"Come for me, then. Come apart all over my hand as I fuck you."

Evan did *not* need to be told twice. As soon as the dildo hit a certain pleasure spot at the exact moment Frankie pinched their bud, a cry erupted from Evan, and their entire body went rigid as waves and waves of pleasure washed over them.

"Fuck, you look so good coming for me." Frankie's low voice sounded somewhere close by. Evan couldn't gather enough energy to lift their head. They felt Frankie carefully slip the toy out, and then she was climbing from the bed. Exhaustion settled over Evan to the point where they dozed off for a minute. They were only vaguely coherent when Frankie removed the restraints around their wrists and ankles. Then she was smoothing her hand down Evan's back, tugging their tank top down so that it wasn't revealing. "I'm going to rub a little ointment over the tender areas, okay?"

Groggily, Evan licked their lips. "'Kay."

Frankie disappeared, and Evan dozed off again. They startled awake a while later when a cool balm touched their hot skin. "Shh, it's just me, baby," Frankie said softly. Evan relaxed into the touch, appreciating how diligent and caring their Domme was. A lazy smile formed. They had a Domme. Who would have thought a few months ago that being someone's submissive was something they'd one day yearn for? The gentle massage stopped, and a sweet kiss landed in Evan's hair. "I'm so proud of you, little thief. And beyond grateful. Thank you for trusting me with your body."

Evan turned over, grimacing at how sore their freshly flogged skin was. Frankie sat beside them, staring down at Evan with a soft smile. She'd removed her pants and changed into a loose-fitting T-shirt, looking so casual and homey that emotion clogged in Evan's throat. "You're welcome."

Frankie reached for Evan, the back of her finger stroking their cheek almost lovingly. "How are you feeling? Can I get you anything?" Even as she asked, Frankie was lifting a glass of water off the nightstand for Evan to take. "Drink."

Evan did, gulping down half the glass before handing it back. They wiped their mouth with the back of a hand and swallowed, peering up at Frankie shyly. "Don't suppose you have another one of those shirts I can put on?"

Frankie's smile widened, and she nodded, hopping off the bed in search of one. Evan watched her rummage around in her dresser before pulling out another long, baggy T-shirt. "This will be perfect," she commented, returning to Evan's side on the mattress.

"What do we do now?" Evan asked, dutifully lifting their arms as Frankie slid the shirt over their head. It smelled like her, which was way more comforting than Evan would have thought. Burrowing their face into the sleeve, Evan took an unabashed whiff, batting their eyelashes over their arm at Frankie.

"Whatever you want, so long as it's relaxing and brings you comfort." Frankie tugged her bottom lip between her teeth as she watched Evan, as if she was trying not to bring attention to the fact that they were totally scenting her. She placed a hand on Evan's thigh. "We can cuddle or watch a movie and cuddle. I could run you a bath."

Evan shook their head. "I can't imagine getting out of bed right now. I'm ... I feel exhausted." A barely-awake idea formed, but Evan blushed at the thought. There was no way Frankie would—

"Tell me what you need. Aftercare is important after a scene, as important as the scene itself."

"Will you read to me?" Evan grimaced. Their brain wasn't braining at the moment, but it was something their mom used to do when they were little. Reading had always been a barrier for Evan, a skill they lacked, and because of that, had never taken joy in. But listening to Frankie's sensual voice as she snuggled and read to them? Evan could think of nothing better.

Frankie gave Evan another one of her full-on open smiles that made her brown eyes sparkle with warmth and affection. Evan wasn't certain, but they had a feeling she didn't smile like that for just anyone.

"I would be honored to do that for you. What kind of genre are you into?"

"Will you choose?" It didn't matter so long as Evan didn't need to return to their bedroom right away. They liked it here, sharing precious space with Frankie.

As Frankie left in search of a book, Evan sank back into the mattress and let out a contented sigh. They were tired, but happy, and also something else they refused to name. All they knew was that Frankie was no longer the enemy. No, now the only one Evan feared was their father. Cecil would come, of that Evan was sure.

I need to protect Frankie.

But how?

CHAPTER 30

Frankie

NEVER IN FRANKIE'S LIFE had watching a lover sleep been so appealing. But looking at Evan, her sleeping, peaceful sub with their typical scowl gone and face serene, Frankie found herself riveted to where she sat on the mattress. No one had ever transfixed her quite like Evan had in just a few months. The night before teased at the recesses of Frankie's memory. Her mouth curled up at the corners. Evan had been very good indeed. The way their body responded to each one of Frankie's whims was exquisite to watch unfold.

Frankie reached out to trail her finger lightly over Evan's eyebrow, whispering, "I promise to never take you for granted."

It's what she'd done with first Emily, and then McCoy, assuming they'd always be there. She'd vowed to protect and love them both, and in the end, Emily was lost to her, and McCoy left Frankie for someone else.

How will loving Evan be any different? You always get left behind.

"Fuck off, brain. Not helping." Frankie reluctantly stood up. She left Evan asleep in her bed, slipping on her bathrobe before quietly pulling her bedroom door closed. She took care of business in the bathroom before making her way into the kitchen, wrinkling her nose at the time on her wall clock. Considering she and Evan had been playing well into the night, 8:23 a.m. was too early to be up. It was good she hadn't woken Evan. They'd need all the sleep they could get for their afternoon/evening shift at the pub. *Not to mention they're grumpy when tired,* Frankie thought, smirking through a yawn as she turned on the kettle. It was the perfect morning to make coffee in her French press.

Her future, and Evan's place in it, filled her with new doubt as she nestled into her breakfast booth with the French press, empty mug, and non-dairy creamer. Last night, they said they'd stay, but that was during sub drop. In the light of day with a clear head, Evan could have an entirely different answer. No matter how real things felt between them, it would be foolish of Frankie to bank her life on such a juvenile faith. She'd been burned multiple times before, and trusting the wrong people was what took Emily from her all those years ago.

"Don't ruin this for me, okay?" Frankie said to the empty room, speaking to Emily as if she were there and alive. Frankie wasn't one to believe in ghosts, but now and again, it sure as hell felt like Emily dropped in from time to time to warn her about things. Like that nightmare Frankie had the night Evan moved in, and now, with doubt plaguing her chest, threatening to smother out the warmth and love bursting forth for Evan.

"Talking to yourself?"

Frankie started, her head snapping up mid-pour to see a sleepy Evan a few feet away. "I ... Good morning. How are you feeling?" Frankie managed not to overfill her mug and set the French press down on the table. Evan's presence had her sliding out of the booth to greet them properly, and she closed the small space between them to drop a kiss on their cheek.

"I'm ... okay. A little sore, but manageable." A shy smile tugged at Evan's sensual mouth, and tired eyes lifted to meet hers.

Frankie smiled. "That's understandable. I imagine your ass will be tender for a few days, especially if you're not used to it." She took Evan's hand in hers and gave it a light squeeze. "How are you feeling about everything we did?"

The question was direct and ill-timed, but Frankie was never one to beat around the bush. Especially when it involved her sub. It was important that they were on the same page and communicating freely. And with Evan, Frankie had to account for a number of things in their growing relationship. As much as she wished it were so, she could never forget the reasons Evan landed on her doorstep to begin with. Or that they might never fully trust or forgive her.

"I am ... I dunno, Frankie. I just woke up." Evan lowered their gaze, staring down at their entangled hands a moment before pulling out of Frankie's grasp. Their movements were stiff as they headed for the fridge.

Frankie fought for composure, fought the urge to grab Evan up in her arms and kiss them senseless. Surely once she'd reclaimed their lips with hers, they'd remember that she wasn't the enemy. But driving her will home wasn't the way to Evan's heart, even Frankie knew that. She needed patience and sympathy. There was a long road ahead of them before Evan could think about committing to her.

"Right. Well. I hadn't had a chance to cook breakfast. Are you in the mood to go out at all? We could grab something at the diner up the street."

Evan put the cap back on the orange juice and returned it to the fridge. "Not really. I could just have cereal, if that's okay with you?"

"Of course." Frankie bit her tongue as disappointment washed over her. She left Evan in the kitchen and instead headed to the bathroom to start the shower. Unfortunately, standing under the hot spray didn't silence her internal monologue or need to snatch back the control she seemed to have given to Evan. It shouldn't bother Frankie that Evan was acting standoffish. They could still have been experiencing a bit of sub drop from last night's scene, but even if that wasn't the case, how they were feeling was normal under the circumstances. Not only had Evan slept with their brother's killer, but they'd allowed her to restrain them to her bed and take a flogger to their flesh.

And then I read to them. The memory of Evan curled in her arms made Frankie smile. Caring for her sub had always been one of her favorite parts of the whole experience. Not in a maternal way; no, more that for a period of time, someone trusted her enough to be innately vulnerable. They relied on her for protection.

After her shower, Frankie toweled off, spending extra time on her hair. She brushed it out and then flipped it upside down to add curl serum to the damp strands. Next she did her makeup. By the sound of dishes clanging, Evan was still busy in the kitchen, so Frankie quietly crossed the hall to her bedroom and closed her door. No matter how difficult it was, she planned to give them whatever space they needed that morning. She took her time getting dressed, choosing her azure-blue blazer and slacks rather than the burgundy solely because they reminded her of Evan's right eye. Once she donned her jewelry, she stood in front of the freestanding mirror to study herself.

"Not bad at all." Some people thought Frankie was insane for dressing so formally when she owned a pub, but that was only because they didn't understand. She'd spent years giving away her power while on the police force, and before that, her power had been stolen in a brutal assault. Frankie would never forget the first day she'd worn a suit to work, rather than a dress or any other typical gender-conforming clothing society expected. It'd been the grand reopening of the pub after she'd taken it over from Danny. Frankie bought a suit specifically for that night, hoping the outfit would act like a shield and give her the confidence she lacked. And it worked. She'd worn a shield for years as a cop, but donning a suit was the figurative armor she hadn't realized she'd needed until that night. It became a coping mechanism, another way to leave her old life behind.

A knock sounded, breaking Frankie out of her thoughts. "Come in," she called, turning away from the mirror just as the door opened.

"I'm sorry for ..." Evan's eyes widened slightly as they took in her outfit, bottom lip disappearing between their teeth. "That's one of my favorite outfits on you."

"Why, because it's the same color you see in the mirror every day?" Frankie held her hand out, waiting for Evan to take it before she tugged them against her. She dipped her face close, her lips grazing their ear. "I love it for the same reason."

Evan hadn't changed out of the oversized t-shirt Frankie had lent them the night before, and when she breathed them in, the skin along their neck still bore remnants of Frankie's lipstick and floral perfume. "You smell like mine, little thief," she uttered against their ear.

A full-body tremble erupted in Evan at the declaration. "I am yours. Sorry for being weird earlier. I-I feel uber emotional for some reason. Like, all over the place kind of."

Frankie pressed a kiss to Evan's forehead, then another on their cheek, her eyes fluttering closed at the contact. "I suspect you might still be in sub drop. What do you need from me? Space, cuddles, sex?"

"Not space. I know that much." Evan's grip on her hand tightened. "I don't understand, but I felt like I was gonna cry when I woke up without you. And that isn't me, like at all. I'm not the clingy, co-dependent kind, I promise you."

"Can I kiss you? Like, really kiss you?"

"I might cry … or die if you don't, so fucking please just—"

Frankie's lips silenced Evan's ramble, her mouth parting in time to whatever else they were about to say. She felt the gush of air between her teeth as Evan gasped, and then they were returning the kiss with fervor. Frankie cupped Evan's cheeks, holding them in place and teasing their mouth with her tongue. The sweet aftertaste of the cereal they'd eaten for breakfast clung to Evan's lips and tongue, and Frankie moaned softly at how delicious and eager they were for her.

"I can't get enough of you." She licked Evan's lips before placing wet kisses along their jaw and throat. Evan's head lolled to the side, granting her better access, but it wasn't enough. She needed her mouth where her fingers and dildo had been the night before. "Do you want this?"

"Yes," Evan breathed, accepting another deep kiss from Frankie. Their hands came up to rest on her arms. "But not like last night, if that's okay."

They didn't want another scene so soon. Frankie assumed that would be the case since their emotions were running high, but still she hesitated. She couldn't remember the last time she'd fucked someone without flogging and tying them up in some fashion. *But this is Evan.* They watched her, waiting, Frankie's suit reflecting in their captivating blue eye. Vulnerability shone clearer in their brown one, almost luminescent under the bedroom light.

"Okay," she said at last, kissing Evan once more. Moving her hands slowly down their arms, and then further, to where the hem of their long T-shirt rested against their lean thighs, Frankie pushed the material up until she was gripping Evan's ass. Without breaking their kiss, Frankie lifted them off the floor, silently directing their legs around her waist. She didn't let go as she walked to her bed, relishing Evan's soft groan as she nipped their kiss-swollen lip.

"I won't take my clothes off." It was important Evan knew that. That they were aware of her boundaries, even in moments like this. Being naked with someone, fully exposed emotionally and physically, wasn't something Frankie did. Ever. She wasn't about to start now.

"What are you willing to give up, if Evan's the one?"

Frankie almost growled at the irritating voice that popped in her head. Sawyer could fuck off and stay in her own damn lane.

Evan's awkward chuckle switched to a sigh when Frankie lowered them to the mattress and began kissing them once more. "I'll never see your ... piercings again at this rate," they said between kisses.

"One day, little thief, but this morning is all about you." She slipped her hands between their bodies, her lips and tongue teasing Evan as her fingers grasped the hem of the T-shirt again. The material slid up an inch at a time, and Frankie moaned her appreciation over Evan's bare thighs and ass. They felt exquisite underneath her.

"Don't ... please don't take it all the way off."

Frankie paused, her attention flickering to the apprehension in Evan's gaze. One hand let go of the shirt to palm their cheek. "I would never. I want you as comfortable as possible. Now ..." She flashed a grin, climbing off Evan and lowering herself to her knees on the floor.

Evan pushed themself up on their elbows. "What are you—oh!"

Frankie hauled them to the edge of her bed so their legs dangled over the side, and the dark thatch of blonde hair covering their sex was within kissing distance. *Perfect.* "Still okay?"

Nodding, a rosy tinge blossomed on Evan's cheeks. They parted their legs slightly. "Please, I need you."

"I know, baby." Frankie didn't want to tease this time around. Evan needed the comfort of an orgasm and the closeness she offered. The teasing could wait for another day.

Frankie held Evan's gaze, spreading their legs further apart. Flashing a salacious grin, she dipped her head and went in for that kiss she craved.

CHAPTER 31

Evan

THEY DIDN'T KNOW WHICH was hotter: the fact they were watching intently as their Domme ate them out, or how much of a boss Frankie looked in her suit while doing it. She was beautiful. No, scratch that. *Frankie O'Rourke was sexy.* And by the way the femme held Evan's trembling thighs still while giving long, slow strokes of her tongue along their sensitive flesh, they suspected she was well aware of the effect she had on people.

"Fuck, Daddy, you're so fucking good."

Evan's legs burned from being held so far apart, and they could feel the heat rising under the shirt they wore. But a little discomfort was worth it to have Frankie devour them. Her slender fingers pumped in and out of Evan while she masterfully worked her lips and tongue over their hot, swollen sex. Their breath hitched in their throat when Frankie curled her fingers just right, hitting their g-spot at the same moment she closed her teeth over Evan's throbbing nub. A long moan escaped.

"Oh god."

Frankie chuckled, and the breathy vibration had Evan mewling.

"Careful," came the huskiest voice Evan had ever heard leave Frankie. The sound wrapped around them, trickling down their skin like the warmest honey.

It was unfortunate she was too far away for Evan to touch. Her long, multi-colored curls were loose and all gathered over one shoulder. Evan had the strongest urge to sink their hands through the thick locks. Frankie grasped their swollen nub between her lips this time, giving it a gentle suck at first, and then harder, increasing the pressure until Evan released another ragged moan. Their elbows shook from supporting their weight, slipping down further on the sheets, so Evan repositioned. Frankie's head was closer now, and they couldn't resist reaching for her hair. Their body was so taut, desperate, and so close to the edge, and Evan could think of nothing better than touching Frankie while they came.

Their approaching orgasm halted just before its glorious crescendo, however, because the moment contact was made, Frankie wrenched away. Her chest rose and fell with unsteady breaths, and her mouth, slick with Evan's arousal, curled into a snarl. "No. Hands on the bed, or I tie you up."

A flash of hurt stabbed Evan at the words said so callously. Frankie's dislike for touch flickered in and out of their lustful haze, like a lightbulb shorting out. It was something she'd stated more than once since they'd met, so the information wasn't new. How did the importance of *not* touching slip Evan's mind?

Tears sprang forth, and the abrupt change from butterflies to the sinking anchor in the pit of their stomach did a bang-up job of chasing away any chance of an orgasm.

"Fuck, baby, I'm sorry." The mattress dipped, and then Frankie was tugging Evan's hands away from their tear-soaked eyes. "Evan, please."

"I-I forgot."

"It's not your fault. We weren't doing a scene. I always do a scene. Always remove temptation. That way, I don't get hurt. I-I don't like my hair pulled. I don't ..." She was muttering to herself more than Evan, staring vacantly at their hands tangled together. Her tortured expression was enough to quiet Evan's sobs. They pulled up into a sitting position on the bed.

"Frankie?"

It was a long time before Frankie lifted her face to theirs. Tears shone in her eyes, but she stubbornly clung to them.

"Will you let me hold you?"

"Will you ..." Frankie trailed off. She cleared her throat, scrubbed a hand over her face, and glanced around her bedroom like she was seeing it for the first time. "No. I'm fine. I'm sorry, but I just remembered the repairman is coming this morning."

Evan stared in confusion. "Repairman?"

Frankie practically jumped off the bed, answering Evan while she smoothed down the rumples in her suit. "Yes, for the dishwasher. Sorry again. Do some self-care this morning, okay? I need to..." She didn't finish her sentence, just bolted from the bedroom.

The fuck?

Heaving a long, frustrated sigh, Evan fell backward onto the soft sheets.

Hours later and no one had seen Frankie. According to Andy, after spilling coffee on her paperwork that morning, she'd locked up her office and rushed out of the pub. He'd also said in all the years he'd worked there he'd never seen her so rattled.

It's my fault.

Why couldn't Evan have kept their damn hands to themself? This was precisely why Frankie couldn't have a vanilla relationship. To be fair, who would want one? Not Evan, to be sure, not after discovering they had a submission kink, or how freeing it felt to be restrained and used by Frankie. But Frankie had explained her aversion to touch. Perhaps not in so many words, but after learning about Emily and what happened to her and Frankie, Evan had *understood*. Of course touch during sex could be triggering. So why hadn't Frankie insisted on restraining them?

Where are you?

And Sloane was an hour late to her shift. She had at least texted Andy with a heads up, but punctuality was surprisingly something Sloane rarely had an issue with. Despite her restless—often chaotic—nature, it seemed as if Sloane took great pride in her job.

"Closing can't come soon enough," Rain grumbled on the way back to the hot line. Evan knew the day was doomed if it started drizzling on Rain's cheery parade. And here they'd thought nothing short of a terminal diagnosis could ever dampen her mood.

"Boss's phone goes right to voicemail," Dakota said while throwing together a club sandwich. He shot Evan a look rife with suspicion. "You live in her back pocket. Care to share why we're down two people during one of our busiest nights?"

Evan opened their mouth, about to lie and tell him Frankie had forgotten her cell phone on her nightstand, but decided it wasn't their place to do even that. Besides, as the boss, Frankie didn't owe anyone an explanation. Also, Dakota could go fuck a duck for all Evan cared.

"No response? What a surprise."

"Actually, I was gonna tell you to go fuck yourself, but figured it wasn't 'workplace' appropriate."

"Picking a fight will only drag out the shift longer. I'm in charge of the kitchen when Frankie's not here, so buckle up and shut up. Both of you," Rain said, once again surprising the shit out of Evan. Their respect for her only grew.

They kept their head down, focusing on the steady flow of dirty dishes Jessie brought in from the eating area. Besides the noise the pub carried into the kitchen, and hollering orders back and forth, Evan worked in silence for the next half hour. When they were finally able to grab a quick break, they let Rain know and headed out to the bar for a soda refill. Evan didn't enjoy being out front when it was so busy but worry for Frankie and Sloane made them a little more than curious.

Lian was filling up a tray with drinks, so Evan stood off to the side and waited for her to finish. They scanned the occupied tables for any sign of Frankie or, Evan cringed to think, Cecil. They had fully intended to warn Frankie about him that morning, but their emotions had already been all over the place. And then the whole hair-touching thing happened and ruined everything.

What if…

No, Cecil wasn't so bold as to show up without some preparation beforehand. He was probably still home, brewing up a dramatic concoction. Even when Caleb and Evan were kids, Cecil loved to add flair to whatever revenge scheme he planned out. A teacher dished out detention for Caleb? Cecil left dead mice in the man's car for seven days—the length of Caleb's detention—before Cecil took a bat to both kneecaps in the staff parking lot on the eighth day. That was just one story of many. For as long as Evan could remember,

Cecil had brought nothing but chaos to their life. It made them wonder why they'd wasted so much damn time trying to gain his love and respect over the years.

A quick squeeze to their arm pulled Evan back to the present, and thoughts of Cecil and their screwed-up childhood drifted away. They caught the departing figure as they passed on the way to the restroom, her familiar pink-tipped hair swaying across her back as she walked. And she wasn't by herself.

"Sloane?" Evan's eyes narrowed on the man gripping Sloane's forearm. It wasn't a light touch either. It looked like he was dragging Sloane down the hallway.

Evan took off after them, their gut clenching with aggravated anticipation. Calling for backup would have been a good idea, but fuck they seemed to be fresh out of those, because before they knew it, they were shoving open the door to the larger restroom on nothing but false bravado.

"Hey!" Evan said, just as the man pulled his fist back to strike Sloane again. She was between the hand dryer and the second stall, her body turned in toward the wall. One hand clutched the hand dryer for support, causing it to continually run.

Evan bent over, quickly yanking out the small knife they kept sheathed inside their boot. It wasn't the same one they'd attacked Frankie with, but it was sure as hell better than nothing. Coming up on the man's left side, Evan shoulder-checked him as hard as they could. "Get away from her!"

Unfortunately, Evan's lightweight ass only proved to piss him off more. The man struck Sloane first and then rounded on Evan. "Goddamn, you look just like the losers I used to stuff into the school lockers back in the day. Fucking bring it, shorty."

Evan was fast and quickly dodged his first swing. *Shit, those fists look like sledgehammers!*

"You were supposed to get Frankie, you idiot."

That came from Sloane, sounding awfully fiery for someone Evan was about to get an ass whooping for.

"Not here," Evan grunted, feinting right before slashing their knife out toward the man's left side. It barely grazed his jacket before Evan got hit with that sledgehammer of a fist. The air seized in their lungs as they dropped hard, toppling over the garbage can on the way down.

"Evan!"

"Fuckin' hell," they wheezed, their mouth watering as the burger they'd eaten earlier threatened to make an appearance.

The knife was pried from their hand, and then a voice growled, "Stay down."

Evan's vision spotted. Their face hurt like a motherfucker, and there was a good chance their head was leaking. So when the restroom door opened and the comforting, familiar scent of Frankie wafted under Evan's nose, they chalked it up to a hallucination. And wow, it was a good one.

"Daddy?"

She still wore her azure-blue suit, but her hair had been tied back at some point. She spared Evan a quick, reassuring glance before turning her focus on the man. They squared off in the center of the restroom, Sloane on one side and Evan struggling to sit up on the other. They watched as the man wielded the knife, *their* knife, and circled Frankie.

"Come get it, bitch." He lunged at Frankie, aiming straight for her chest. Evan's heart stuttered, the memory of Frankie's scar flashing before their eyes.

"Look out!"

But Frankie laughed, dodging the knife easily. She danced around the man while wearing heels and a wolfish grin, looking every bit like she'd prayed all day for this exact outcome.

"You hurt what's mine. That was a mistake."

Mmm 'kay, but why is that so hot?

It had been years since anyone went to bat for them, let alone a fierce, dominant femme with a killer aesthetic appeal. Not that the last part mattered so much, but hot *damn,* Frankie was wearing the shit out of that suit. *And kicking ass doing it.*

Evan watched the fight with rapt attention, half listening to Sloane cheer on Frankie like she was a die-hard fan at an MMA match. When the knife came at her again, Frankie knocked the man's arm to the side. He then swiped up and around, coming at Frankie in a different direction, but she thwarted his attempts again, grabbed his wrist, and quickly disarmed him. The knife clattered to the floor, and Frankie kicked it away. The man punched her in the gut, but unlike Evan, she barely moved. Instead, Frankie returned a few punches of her own before her opponent somehow put her in a chokehold from behind.

"Fuck, Frank—"

Frankie rammed the man into the closed stall and kicked him hard in the shin. The second he loosened his grip a fraction, Frankie flipped him over her shoulder and slammed him onto the floor.

"Evan, hand me your apron," she instructed, only marginally out of breath.

"Ugh ..." Evan scrambled to remove it while Frankie forcefully turned the man onto his stomach and shoved a knee into his back. When he fought her to get up, she knocked him unconscious with a quick jab to the face.

"Sloane, call the police."

"Already did, boss," Sloane squeaked.

"You know him?" Frankie asked before accepting the apron from Evan. Her eyes softened. "Thanks, baby."

"Never saw him in my life," Sloane answered. "He grabbed me just outside the pub."

"That fight, what you did, was …" Crazy? Impressive? Scary? "Attractive," Evan finished lamely. They'd been in a few fights in prison, but never with such finesse. Mostly, it was Evan getting beaten up by bigger, tougher inmates.

One corner of Frankie's plump mouth quirked up. "Duly noted." She made quick work securing the man's wrists and ankles by using the apron strings. When she stood up, she glanced between Evan and Sloane. "Are you two okay?"

They both nodded, but Sloane added, "Just glad you came to the rescue."

"I did try," Evan grumbled.

Frankie stepped closer and reached for Evan slowly, giving them plenty of time to back away. But distancing themself was the last thing on their mind. Her hand grasped the back of Evan's neck, and she guided them into her warmth. "When I go to greet the police, I need you to disappear. Go back to work or something, but don't stay here. Can you do that for me? And hand me the sheath for your knife. I'll say it was mine."

Evan nodded mutely, kicked up their leg, and effortlessly removed the sheath from inside their boot before handing it over. In response, Frankie gave them the sweetest kiss. It was fleeting, airy almost in the way their lips pressed together, but it felt like their Domme was rewarding them for their obedience. And despite their new aches and pains from the fight, Evan's body tingled with the knowledge.

Frankie left, leaving them alone with the man once more. Something nagged at Evan about the whole thing. The attack seemed too random, especially when they considered how late Sloane was for her shift.

"What was that about?" Sloane grumbled, now examining herself in front of the mirror. She'd certainly have a shiner come morning, if not sooner. Her lip was split as well, but she still had that same attitude Evan was used to.

"I just got out of prison," they said without thinking, then wanted to kick themself. Not *just* but surely being involved in an altercation wouldn't look good for them.

Sure enough, Sloane's bruised eyes widened a fraction. "For what?"

"Stealing." Burglary, to be specific, but there was no need to hash out all the details.

"Well, fuck. You know, I didn't expect you to jump to my rescue."

Evan lifted one shoulder. "You're my friend." They reached up to feel the back of their head, finding moisture there they'd thought was blood earlier. They sniffed their damp fingers. Huh. It was sweet-smelling, like someone had dumped a take-out cup of soda into the garbage.

"You better go."

"Hey, are you sure this doesn't have something to do with your gambling?"

Sloane stilled. "Excuse me?"

Might as well go all in. Evan sighed, their hand on the door. "You gamble. A lot. And I bet Coy has no idea how bad shit is."

She glared at Evan in the mirror for several awkward seconds before snapping, "And *you* aren't gonna tell her. Stay in your lane,

Evan. If you're my friend, then be one and mind your fucking business."

CHAPTER 32

Frankie

SIX HOURS EARLIER …

I should go back. I need to go back.

But no matter how many times she willed herself to turn the car around, she wouldn't. *Couldn't.* It had been three hours or more since she'd run out of the pub, and she'd done everything she could think of *but* go back. She'd hit the bag at the gym for an hour, and when that hadn't helped, she drove to her favorite sex shop. Browsing the newest kink toys was nice, but it was perusing the gender affirming section that truly acted as a temporary distraction. All Frankie could think of was gifting Evan a new, top-of-the-line binder. She would have done it, too, had the sales associate not suggested Evan come and personally try them on.

It wasn't long after that Frankie stopped by the graveyard. Usually a visit with Emily would put things in perspective, but not today. Evan had barely touched her, and yet, the panic trying to claw its way out felt eerily familiar. She was hot, her skin felt tight and uncomfortable under her clothes, and the usual comfort and safety of being in her car had disappeared.

Center yourself. Breathe, goddammit.

Frankie pulled the car onto the shoulder of the road, put the gear in park, and ripped off her seatbelt. She was breathing hard, her throat swollen and raw against her blouse buttons. Why did she insist on wearing such confining clothes day in and day out?

Too hot, it's too hot.

Shifting back and forth in her seat, she shimmied the blazer off and tossed it onto the passenger side. Next came the buttons, and it wasn't until they were halfway undone and a chilled, rainy breeze was coming in through the open car window that Frankie felt like she could breathe again. Her eyes drifted closed. But, almost like clockwork, the pesky, meddling voice of Sawyer blared like a foghorn in Frankie's head.

"Do you know yet, what you're willing to give up if Evan's the one?"

Frankie cursed, her eyes flying back open. Slamming her hand down on the steering wheel, she glared out at the noon-hour traffic whizzing by on the highway. A minute passed, maybe more, and then Frankie reached for her phone. She pulled up Sawyer's text thread, still unnamed in her inbox, and connected the call to her car's Bluetooth. As it rang, she maneuvered the Audi back onto the road, not yet knowing where she was headed. She was a pub owner, for Christ's sake, she couldn't play hooky whenever she felt like it. There wasn't enough staff scheduled for stunts like that.

The call eventually went to voicemail, Sawyer's slightly accented voice coming in over the speaker as she apologized for missing whoever was on the other end. Frankie scoffed when she heard the beep. "You know what? I'm sorry you missed me too, because I wanted to say 'fuck you' directly. I don't know what kind of voodoo shit you planted in my head, but it needs to stop. Your voice plays like a broken cassette in an old car radio. Over and fucking over, Sawyer. Knowing what I'm ready to give up for Evan and succeeding in doing it are two very different things."

Disconnecting the call, she heaved a ragged sigh. That had been foolish. *No fear, not anymore. Don't let them see your pain.* That mantra was something she'd shared with Emily all those years ago in a steadfast hope they could take back some of their power.

Frankie turned onto her old street before she realized where her subconscious mind had taken her. North Burnaby, one of Vancouver's suburbs, looked the same as it had the last time she'd visited. The neighboring lawns were snow-free and soggy with rainwater, but the flowers had already started to grow, and soon the cherry blossoms lining the sidewalks would bloom. Once upon a time, she had loved living in such a close-knit community. After moving from above the pub, she and Danny had made friends with kids in the neighborhood. It was there Emily had come to live with them, and regardless that Frankie was adopted and Emily was fostered, it had felt like a true family for a long time.

Frankie slowed the Audi down to a snail's pace when she reached her old home, hesitating for a fraction of a moment before pulling the car into the driveway. She parked beside an older-style van, scrunching her nose up as she took in the dent on the passenger side door. When had they bought a van? And more to the point, *why?* She was out of the loop, sure, but as far as she knew, her aunt and uncle were done with fostering. Had been for a long time, too.

As she walked the short distance to the front door, she found herself wiping clammy palms against her dress slacks. It was a strange feeling, the nervous anticipation knotting her insides like a tangled ball of yarn. Perhaps it was the memories, the nostalgia she faced, that had kept her away far longer than family contact had.

Grasping the door handle, Frankie was about to open it when she stopped. Over two years had passed since she crossed this threshold. She had no rights to this house, not anymore. She took a deep breath, gushing out an exhale as she rang the doorbell.

And then she waited.

And waited some more.

About to ring the bell again, Frankie drew back in surprise when the door swung inward. Her heart squeezed as she took in the tall, six-two, maybe six-foot-four man in his early twenties. His reddish-brown hair, which leaned closer to a cinnamon shade, was cut a lot shorter than the last time Frankie had seen him.

Maddox tucked his cell phone away, deep blue eyes squinting like he wasn't sure she was really there. "Kitty Kat?"

The age-old nickname brought on the faintest tremble in Frankie's lower lip. She bit down to stop it, breathing in and out through her nose as they gawked at one another. God, he looked just like Emily, right down to the small, pert nose and carefully placed freckles scattering his cheeks. At twenty-one, Maddox had already surpassed his mother's age by five years.

Life is a fucking tragedy.

"How ..." Frankie cleared her throat and tried again. "How's my favorite nephew?"

Frankie's smile felt tentative, as if it was as unsure as she was of the situation. It seemed wrong to be someone's aunt, let alone Maddox's. Not only was she just generally not aunt material—Danny's kids could attest to that—but with Maddox, she'd been prepared to be a second mother to him.

And then you skipped out on him and everyone else. Class act, you are.

"If I were a favorite, I'm sure you'd see me more." Maddox held the door open for Frankie to enter, his tone as dry as peeling paint. He gestured to the boot rack, calling over his shoulder as he headed to the kitchen, "House rules haven't changed."

"Figured," Frankie murmured, bending to unstrap her high heels. Since the day Frankie had come to live with her aunt and uncle at four years old, Auntie B had been a stickler for placing their footwear on the boot rack. It was nice to know some things hadn't shifted in her life.

She followed Maddox, his words from before stinging a little. She'd never been a kid person. When she was thirteen, the only reason she'd taken a babysitting course was because Emily hadn't wanted to do it alone. She'd never had that nurturing side so many girls that age did, and had Emily not been pregnant, Frankie would have gone through life without a second thought. But Emily was, and Frankie had loved her, so it had made sense to Frankie that she would love Maddox too. That if Emily had deemed it so, she could have been a part of their lives in a truly meaningful way.

Auntie B adopting Maddox was the best outcome, Frankie knew that. She would have made a shit mother. And Maddox was right. He might not have said the words, but she was a terrible aunt, too. It's just ... how could she explain how it hurt just looking at him? He was a constant reminder of what she'd lost. Of what they'd both lost.

"I'm sorry," she began, knowing she should say *something*, "but you know, keeping in touch goes both ways." Fuck, no, that wasn't supposed to slip out. Yes, Maddox might have been fully grown now, but he wasn't always. Even before the tiff with Auntie B, Frankie had been the adult pushing everyone away. Hell, the moment a position had opened in the Toronto police department, Frankie had transferred just to get away from her family for a while.

Small puffs of air escaped her lungs as she tried to keep her control. "That didn't come out right. I meant to say ..."

Frankie's mouth clamped shut as she spotted the slouched figure in a wheelchair by the kitchen table. Her eyes widened, and she gasped out, "Uncle?"

"I was just getting him into his chair when you showed up," Maddox said, taking a seat beside their uncle. He waved her over before picking up a spoon filled with what appeared to be mashed-up food.

"What happened?" The question left her lips with a croak. Her throat ached from trying unsuccessfully to keep her emotions in check. Uncle Eamon barely registered her presence, just a grunt behind a well-kept mustache.

"He had a stroke a year and a half ago." Sympathy brimmed in Maddox's blue eyes as he watched their uncle struggle with his food. He used a cloth napkin to wipe the corners of the older man's mouth before meeting Frankie's blurry gaze. "Auntie B didn't think you were ready to know."

"Not ready?" Frankie choked out. She tore her eyes away, instead taking in the updated kitchen. Sliding doors to an outdoor patio had taken the place of the old hutch. In fact, nothing in the kitchen looked familiar. She was a stranger. She'd pushed them away for so long that they'd stopped trying to hold on.

Goddamn. Her life today was like a nonstop train ride to the land of shit. First with Evan, and now all of this. *Fuck's sake.*

"I-I shouldn't have come. I don't know why ..." Why she'd turned into this neighborhood of all places. Frankie scrubbed a hand over her face, a sob building in her chest as she backed away. "I'm sorry. Maddox, I am."

"Uh-huh."

Frankie fled the kitchen, not waiting to see if he'd say anything more. The first splash of tears on her cheeks came while she struggled to put her heels back on. When she opted to go barefoot, she swung open the door and almost tackled the woman on the other side.

"Frankie, you're not leaving already?" Auntie B exclaimed, gripping Frankie's arms to hold herself upright. Her weight was on the plumper side than years ago, and she looked slightly breathless as she took Frankie in. "I'd just run over to grab more potatoes from Dorothy across the street when I saw you pulling in through the window. She got to talking my ear off, like always. I was about to make a run for it, but then she made a mad dash for the bathroom, if you know what I mean."

"I can't ..." Frankie clenched her teeth so hard she worried they'd snapped when she heard a crack. "Why didn't you tell me? I deserved to know."

"Like how you told me you'd been stabbed?" Auntie B smiled sadly. "Oh, right, you told Danny not to tell us."

"I didn't want you to worry."

"And I didn't want you to worry about Eamon." She reached her hand up as if to cup Frankie's cheek, but let it fall away at the last second. "Dear, you've already sent too much money over the years for Maddox."

"I don't know what you're talking about." Frankie balked, turning away so the older woman couldn't see her wiping away more tears.

"You do, and we both know that if I'd told you, your need to protect would kick in and you'd have tried to set Eamon up with his own nurse. Even if doing so put you in a deficit."

She was right. Frankie would have done whatever she could to make things easier for them. Despite how dysfunctional it had always been, the O'Rourkes were her family. Through adoption, yes, but through blood as well. She owed her aunt and uncle the world. They'd taken her in and not looked back once.

"Don't leave, honey, *please*. It's been two years, and you're still punishing me. Can't we get past this?" Auntie B's hand was back on Frankie's arm, squeezing it gently through the thin jacket she wore.

"Get past it?" Frankie echoed and wrenched her arm free. Old pain and betrayal crept over her, filling her throat with despair as she croaked, "You called me sick for having feelings for Emily. For loving someone years ago who wasn't even related to me. She wasn't my real sister!"

"I was three sheets to the wind by the time that conversation started between you and Danny. I am *sorry*, okay?" Auntie B was crying as well now. Frankie watched her wring her hands together. "I loved Emily like a daughter. W-when I introduced her to people, I would leave the foster part out. Surely you remember that? When I looked at you two, I saw sisters. I look at you and Danny and see brother and sister, not cousins. You're my kid, Frankie. And so was Emily. Overhearing your conversation that night, it just set something off in me. I can't take it back. Believe me, I wish I could."

"I never saw her as my sister. It wasn't like that for me," Frankie bit out with a scowl. "If she hadn't died ..."

"You two possibly dating would have ruined her placement with us," Auntie B cut in, staring up at Frankie. "I know you weren't a social worker, but surely you can understand that? Would you have risked it knowing social services might have caught on and ripped Emily away from us?"

Well, fuck. Frankie had never looked at it from that angle before. Her shoulders slumped in defeat. "I guess we'll never know."

"I know *you*, Frankie. You'd have put her safety and well-being first."

A tear hit Frankie's cheek. She brushed it away, nodding a little. "Always."

"All these years. I still miss her."

"Yup." Frankie dragged out the word, emphasizing the "p" sound so it popped.

"Will you stay awhile? I miss you too, honey. Terribly. You can catch me up on your life and visit with the boys. Not that you ever need a reason to visit, but it feels like maybe you came here with one."

Frankie shook her head. "I can't go back in there. Not yet."

Auntie B nodded, a kind, understanding look crossing her face. She'd always been able to read Frankie better than anyone else. It's why it hurt so much when her feelings for Emily came to light. It'd sent a shockwave through Auntie B, and here Frankie had assumed she'd known already.

She didn't want to know. How does that saying go? Denial is a river in Egypt.

"How about we chat in your car, then?"

"I'm sorry for running out on you." Frankie pressed the gel ice pack gently against Evan's cheek, rubbing her other hand across their mostly bared back. Evan smelled clean and fresh from their shower, wearing just a binder across their chest and a pair of boxers. Frankie's fury at what happened in the pub's washroom had been set on a mid-range simmer most of the night. After the assailant was arrested and statements taken from Frankie and Sloane, they'd started their shift alongside Evan and the rest of her staff. Now, hours later, she was tending to Evan's swollen cheek in the privacy of her apartment. A dozen questions filled her regarding her lover's part in tonight's fight, but it was late. All she wanted to do now was offer reassurance and maybe, if she was lucky, reestablish her role as Evan's Domme. More than anything, she needed reassurance for herself.

"It's okay. I get it."

"It's not. I'm your Domme, little thief. You need to be able to rely on me." Frankie hung her head, admitting, "I went to see my aunt. We cleared the air about a lot of things. And ... and I told her about you."

Evan's back grew rigid at her words, and Frankie quickly amended, "Not about any of that. I would never. Your reason for coming here is between the two of us. But I told her what kind of person you were, and what you meant to me."

"Oh." Evan's face softened. "What'd she say?"

Thinking back on her conversation with Auntie B pulled a sad smile from Frankie. "She thinks I should start therapy again. To help get past my aversion to touch." Her aunt didn't believe they could last long term if mutual touch wasn't on the table, but Frankie kept that to herself.

"And what do you think?"

Frankie set the ice pack aside, slid her hand up Evan's back to their neck, and drew them in for a long kiss. "I think we could continue to do scenes and I'd be fine," she acknowledged, her lips resting against theirs. She peppered slow kisses along Evan's jaw, breathing them in.

"But I believe you require more than that sometimes. And as your Domme, as ... as the person who's fallen in love with you, I want to meet your needs."

"I wanna meet yours, too. I wanna be a good sub for you."

"Baby, you're already well on your way to achieving that."

Evan's cheeks grew warm under the gentle caress of Frankie's lips. She chuckled softly. "You are too cute."

"Can we play tonight?"

The soft question lit a fire inside Frankie and made her pussy clench, eager as hell at the prospect. But she hesitated, pulling back to catch the hopeful look on Evan's face. "It's been a long day. Are you not tired?"

A cheeky grin appeared. "Not in the way I'd like to be."

Frankie's lips twitched, and she had to hold her laughter in. God, she adored this little shit. She cleared her throat. "We need to discuss what happened this morning. While I know it was accidental, touching me without consent crossed a boundary I'd very clearly laid out in the beginning. If we're to go any further in our dynamic, then there needs to be a punishment for what happened."

"Punishment?" Evan's face fell, their previous joy deflating right before her.

Frankie quickly amended, "Consider it more like a funishment—a fun punishment. And of course, even those are done with your consent."

"Like flogging again? I liked that a lot."

This time Frankie did laugh, just a breathy chuckle past her lips. "Little thief, I wasn't punishing you last night. But I imagine you'll like this one just as much. So while I set up, you can head to the bathroom. Remove as many clothes as you're comfortable with and then put on the bathrobe hanging on the door. Meet me back here. Understood?"

"Yes, Daddy." Evan jumped off the bed, their swollen face and ice pack forgotten. They hooked her with a purely suggestive smile, like they were already dreaming up all the naughty ways their Domme would use them before the sun came up.

CHAPTER 33

Evan

FRANKIE WAS WAITING IN the armchair when Evan entered their bedroom ten minutes later, one long leg crossed over the other. She'd set up several toys on what appeared to be a protective cloth at the edge of Evan's bed. The restraint frame they'd accidentally cuffed themself to weeks ago sat off to the side, along with the St. Andrew's Cross.

"Stop." Frankie held her hand up. When Evan did, she continued, "Are you alright to continue using the traffic light system, or would a safe word work instead?"

Evan considered the question. "A safe word."

"We can do that. Do you have one in mind?"

"Mustard." Evan hated everything about the condiment, so it seemed the ideal word to halt a scene.

"Very well. So to be clear, you will obey, like a good boi, everything I do or say. Unless you use the safe word. Then everything stops at once. Agreed?"

"Yes." Frankie was in full Domme mode now, and Evan was *there* for it. Fucking hell, she was sexy. Frankie had the ability to turn them on like no one had before.

"Excellent. Now remove the bathrobe, get on your hands and knees, and crawl to me."

Evan's palms were sweaty as they hurriedly unfastened the robe ties. Their knees quaked as they pulled open the fabric, letting the robe slip off their shoulders. Standing mostly nude before Daddy Frankie, Evan was at once grateful they'd increased the temperature in the room earlier.

"So tempting." Frankie's brown gaze darkened, watching intently as Evan sank slowly to their knees. It was an odd experience for them, baring themself to a lover while crawling across the floor. But crawl they did, eyes trained on their femme in a decidedly non-demure way, but witnessing the outward pleasure on her face was worth the risk of being reprimanded later.

"You take orders so well," she crooned when Evan reached her side. There was a flogging whip in one hand, different from the one last night, and Evan held their breath as she trailed the thin, leather ribbons slowly up their torso. It tickled their bare skin, setting fire to the blood coursing beneath.

How am I so turned on already?

"Now to begin your funishment." Frankie leaned forward in the chair, dipped her head down so that her plump lips grazed Evan's ear, and whispered, "I want you on my cross, my good boi."

Evan's heart skipped a beat, and they leaned into her, trying to chase the contact, but she was already standing up and stepping aside. "Since you're already on your knees for me, I'd like you to crawl your way to the St. Andrew's Cross. And as you do, I'll warm up my whip on your delectable ass."

Evan's bravery wavered for a millisecond, and Frankie noticed. "Trouble? Just say the magic word if you don't want to continue."

"N-no, Daddy. Please, I want this." Hell, did they ever. Evan wanted to explore so much with Frankie, including any shared desires she'd lain awake at night thinking about when Evan wasn't warming her bed. More than anything, they wanted to chase the majestic cloud-like feeling that came over them the night before.

"Crawl then, little thief. Head down. Let me see what that ass can do."

Evan's face flushed, the intense awareness of being on display as they crawled had heat pooling low in their belly and between their thighs. Receiving their Domme's attention was powerful. And *arousing*.

"Very good," Frankie purred, and Evan gasped as the whip came down across their ass. *Oh, fuck.* Pain and pleasure rippled through them, and Evan had to stop in their tracks to squeeze their legs together. Frankie didn't wait for them to recover, and when the whip connected with their flesh again, something between a moan and a cry left their lips.

"Remember, you don't come until I say you do," Frankie said, voice so husky it sent shivers racing down Evan's spine. The leather ribbons of the whip brushed their cheek gently. "You can stand now."

Evan lifted their gaze to hers, waiting for her nod of confirmation before slowly rising. Their ass stung, and their knees burned a little from crawling on the wooden floor, but the discomfort fled the instant Frankie drew them into a hard kiss. Her tongue stroked the seam of Evan's lips, demanding entry. When they parted, she kissed Evan with abandon. By the way she fucked their mouth, there was no doubt in Evan's mind who was in charge. They were lightheaded when Frankie pulled away, her fingertips dancing along the column of their throat. Both were breathing hard.

"That was a reward for taking my directions so well," she murmured, her hooded gaze still focused on Evan's lips, like she wanted to claim them all over again.

Evan bowed their head slightly. "I'm grateful. Thank you, Daddy."

"But your funishment isn't over, yet." She clasped her fingers around Evan's wrists, their eyes locking as Frankie gently backed them up against the waiting St. Andrew's Cross. "Tell me your safe word."

"M-mustard."

Frankie's lips twitched. "Very good. Remember it if things become too much. I'll stop at once."

"I understand." Eager anticipation flitted through Evan as Frankie secured their wrists and ankles to the frame. Their heart was in their throat with her standing so close, her loose curls grazing Evan's bare collarbone as she checked the shackles. Then she was retreating, and the loss was enough to make Evan whimper. They expected her to whip them some more or spank them, but instead Frankie reached for the buttons on her blazer. Their gazes caught and held, and completely entranced, Evan watched their femme slowly undress. The blazer disappeared first, and then she unbuttoned her dress slacks and freed her blouse. Evan was certain she was done, and their eyes widened as Frankie began undoing the buttons on that as well. Inch by tantalizing inch, the swell of her full breasts came into view, cupped in a black lace bra. She stood close enough that Evan could see the outline of her nipple piercings. Their mouth watered for a taste.

"Fuck."

"You may watch, you may enjoy the view, but you won't touch, and you won't orgasm until I say so. Is that clear?"

Evan bobbed their head yes, but the only words to leave their mouth were a hushed, "Fuck me."

Frankie's blouse was off now, and they stared with rapt attention as she slid the slacks slowly off her curvy hips and down her long, lush thighs to pool around her bare feet. Then she did the same with her black thong, until the bra was the only thing remaining.

"Was that a 'yes, Daddy'?" she asked, sashaying her way over. Evan beheld her like they were taking in the sunrise for the first time; shocked that such beauty could exist, and humbled they were there to witness the moment.

"Yes, Daddy," Evan croaked out, their pulse kicking up when she stopped so close her bra tickled their cheek. She smirked, reaching behind to unfasten it. The bra fell away slowly, too slowly for Evan's liking. And then her bare breasts were so close Evan could stick their tongue out and taste them, twirl their tongue around the barbells through each nipple. Being in this proximity was a delicious torture, exciting and frustrating Evan at the same time. Another moan slipped out when Frankie's palm found the aching pleasure point between their legs, and it only increased as she dipped her fingers into their wetness.

Out of nowhere, the image of Frankie protecting them earlier popped into Evan's head, using those same exact fingers now stroking them to knock a man unconscious ...

Their breath quickened, muscles growing more rigid with each stroke. Evan's eyes fell to Frankie's breasts, to the little bounce they gave as she worked them into a frenzy.

"I-I-I'm ..."

"No, you're not," Frankie warned. Her fingers retreated at once, and Evan gasped as she smacked their inner thigh. "Who owns your orgasm, little thief?"

"Umm ..." Evan's eyelashes fluttered. "You do, Daddy."

"Mm-hmm, that's right." Frankie smirked. When she turned away, a petulant whine left Evan, or at least until they realized the rear view of her was almost as good as the front. Even without their glasses on, they could see how her luscious backside jiggled as she went over to Evan's bed. Her skin was so deliciously creamy, the muscles underneath flexing as she moved. There was a small tattoo on one hip that Evan hadn't seen before.

"What're you doing?"

"Teaching you a lesson on patience," Frankie purred, picking up a short chain from the selection spread out on Evan's bed. She turned their way, the scorching heat in her eyes shooting straight to Evan's core. *Fuck, what'll happen if I come too soon?*

"Sometimes, I like a little pain as well." Opening the clip on one end of the chain, she guided it carefully over one nipple before doing the same on the other breast. *Well, hell.* Instead of putting the nipple clamps on her sub like she'd probably done so many times in the past, Frankie put them on herself. *God, why is that so hot?*

Next, she picked up a wand-shaped vibrator and closed the distance between them in three long strides. "Look at you, at my mercy and cuffed to my cross like a good boi." A slight tremble began in Evan's legs, and they thrust their hips out as she neared.

"Please, Daddy." They didn't know if they were pleading for their femme to fuck them or herself. Either, both, the only thing that mattered was how insane with need Evan felt. They were about to come apart from the anticipation alone, fuck anything else.

"I love it when you beg," Frankie crooned, placing her hand on their bare chest above the binder. She pushed them back against the cross, holding them there—as if there was any chance they could escape. Then she raked her nails over Evan's skin, down the binder to their abdomen. When she reached the sopping heat, she smacked the sensitive flesh.

"Fuck," Evan hissed, pleasure and pain flooding their sex.

"So wet for me. So needy." The low buzz of the vibrator started in Frankie's other hand, and Evan, half out of it with desire, sobbed when she turned the toy onto herself.

Frankie moaned softly, her chestnut brown eyes almost black. Her bottom lip disappeared between her teeth. Evan rattled the chains attached to their wrist cuffs, wanting to cry from the injustice of it all. They wanted to bite and tease that plump lip, wanted the wand pressing against their swollen nub. They *craved* it, needed it like lungs needed air to breathe.

"I need you."

"Yeah? How bad, little thief?" One corner of Frankie's mouth curved up, and before Evan could answer, she removed the wand and placed it against their sex.

"Oh!" Evan cried, their pelvis bucking in shock. The wand's low pulse had even their toes curling. Heat and arousal spread through them like wildfire. Their breaths became ragged, and just when they were about to climax, Frankie pulled back the toy.

"Not yet," she said, her voice hoarse as well now. She spread her legs slightly, met Evan's feverish gaze, and turned the wand on herself again. The sound of the toy increased, like Frankie had dialed up the intensity. Arching her back, she thrust her pelvis toward Evan at the same time she tugged on the chain attached to the nipple clamps.

"Oh fuck, yes. So good." Frankie stepped closer, breathing heavily as well, and began stroking her body against Evan's. The nipple clamps tickled their oversensitive skin, but it was the wand's throbbing vibration sandwiched between them that pulled a long, guttural moan from Evan.

"I'm going to get myself off grinding against you while my tongue fucks yours. But you still can't come until I say so," Frankie said huskily, gaze roaming their face. "What do you say to that?"

Evan licked their lips, faintly aware of not only the response she expected, but one that they wanted to give. "I'm grateful, Daddy. Thank you."

"Mmm, very good." Her fingers slid to the back of Evan's head, her nails gently digging into their scalp as she pulled their face closer. When their mouths connected, Frankie's throaty moan damn near sent Evan over the edge. She held them still, kissing them exactly as she promised, angling their heads so that her lips could seduce theirs. It wasn't a gentle seduction either, not this time. Frankie's mouth was hot and hungry against theirs, her tongue slipping in to stroke Evan's as she ground her pelvis and the wand against them. Evan felt her body stiffen, and without breaking their kiss, Frankie's hand disappeared from their scalp. Seconds later, it was sliding between their torsos to quickly remove the nipple clamps. And then she was groaning into their kiss, massaging the wand faster over her clit as she rode out her orgasm.

"Such a good sub," Frankie gushed, her swollen lips trembling against Evan's.

"Y-you ..." Evan closed their eyes, fuzziness coming over them. They breathed deeply before trying again. "You're gorgeous like this. Thank you." The why wasn't clear to Evan, but it felt like Daddy had just given them the greatest gift. The answer was within reach, but Evan couldn't focus on anything other than the desperate ache between their legs. They were dripping with arousal. Their limbs shook with need and fatigue, muscles taut from clenching every time they neared an orgasm.

Frankie pressed a kiss to Evan's sweaty forehead. "You're welcome."

Another whine left Evan when Frankie pulled away, the wand disappearing as well. A sob broke free. "Come back, p-please."

"I could, but doesn't my good boi want their reward?" Frankie's soft laughter floated over to Evan from near the bed. They weren't sure since their eyes were still closed. It felt like just inhaling wrong could cause them to combust.

Evan flinched when Frankie's soft hands landed on their thighs. Their eyes shot open to find her down on her knees between the opening of the cross, her face a hair's breadth away from Evan's sex. She glanced up and smiled. "Come for me, baby."

The first climax came the instant Frankie's tongue touched Evan's unbearably engorged nub. Their head fell back as they screamed their release, waves and waves of ecstasy washing over them. They were still coming down off the first when Frankie pulled a second orgasm from them. She gripped Evan's ass in her hands, nails biting into skin, and used her tongue to stroke them like she was licking her favorite chocolate chunk ice cream. Deep licks where she flattened her tongue through the folds, and then occasionally a nip of her teeth against the still-swollen nub.

She stopped long enough to say, "Again."

Evan gasped, breath hitched halfway up their throat and stomach tightening. "I-I can't."

Frankie gave them a knowing look, three of her fingers sinking into them only for Evan to clench around them. She smirked, her hand beginning to thrust. Evan moaned at just how good she felt. "You can, little thief, and you will."

She was right, of course.

CHAPTER 34

Frankie

THERE WAS NOTHING LIKE forcing an orgasm from a sub. Or several. It was a close second to her absolute favorite during a scene—edging her sub until they were sobbing, they were so desperate to come.

And tonight, her little thief would accomplish both. She'd wound them up until they begged for release, and now, she'd get to witness them come apart over and over until they were a spent mess in her arms.

"You're doing so well," Frankie crooned, her thumb rubbing slow circles around Evan's bundle of nerves. She was on her feet again and pressed against them, her tongue tracing a lazy path over the rapid pulse along their throat. "But I think you can take another. What do you say?"

Evan gave her a jerky nod, their mismatched eyes dropping down to the toy nestled between them. "With that?"

"Yes." Frankie stroked the length of the dildo attached to her harness. It wasn't too long or too thick, so she had no worries about hurting Evan. "If you don't want it, all you have to do is use your safe word."

"W-will you feel it too?"

"Mm-hmm. I'll feel it enough."

"Good." A ghost of a smile appeared. Evan craned their face forward, pursing their lips.

Frankie kissed them, gently this time, continuing to massage their clit with her thumb. With her fingers, she teased their front hole, building their arousal still. Even after six orgasms, Evan was wet and needy for her. She broke the kiss slowly, lining the dildo up to Evan's entrance and carefully pushing inside.

Evan sucked in a breath. "Mmm, fuck."

"Yes." Groaning, Frankie pumped her hips, enjoying how the base of the toy knocked against her clit with each thrust. She gripped Evan's ass, fucking them slowly. It was such a turn on, watching the dildo slide almost all the way out of her little thief before she thrust it back in. Panting, she leaned forward and nipped Evan's shoulder. "Look, baby. Just look at how fucking good you take my cock."

"So good." Evan's head lolled to the side, exposing their neck. Frankie scratched the skin along their throat, relishing the flush in their cheeks.

"Like you were made for me."

"I-I love you," Evan rasped, biting their lip as another moan slipped out. Perspiration trickled down their hairline. By the glazed expression as they stared at her in wonder, Frankie guessed they were deep into subspace, blissed out beyond reason, and vulnerable.

"I love you too."

Fuck, she was going to come. Quickening her thrusts, her fingers found Evan's nub, working the pleasure point into a frenzy once more and panting out, "Come with me, baby. Now." When Evan climaxed, she quickly joined them, her pussy clenching as they rode the orgasm out together. Frankie's clit was still twitching when she reluctantly pulled out of Evan.

"That was amazing," Evan whispered, accepting her kiss. They were nearing the pass-out stage, and Frankie wanted them in bed when that happened.

Frankie cupped their cheek, whispering back, "It was. You were amazing. My perfect sub."

She got to work removing the harness and uncuffing Evan from the cross. For the first time ever, she wondered what it would be like to be with Evan without the need to restrain them. To have them touch her, to wring pleasure from her body the way she did them. To have them hold her afterwards, fall asleep in each other's arms.

Yeah, and suffer a panic attack or worse every time. Fuck off with that.

"Baby, I'm so proud of you. Thank you for trusting me," Frankie said, unhooking the last wrist cuff. Evan fell into her arms. She scooped them up easily and carried them to the bed, glad she'd thought to remove the protective cloth and unused toys earlier. Pressing a kiss to their lips, she slipped them under the covers. "Can I get you anything?" But Evan was sound asleep.

Frankie retrieved a wet washcloth and container of salve from the bathroom before heading back to Evan. She pulled the covers off again and gently used the cloth to freshen them up. Then she applied the salve over the marks she'd left on their backside and inner thigh. It had already started bruising in areas. Evan would no doubt be sore for a couple days, but the salve would be a significant help to the healing process.

When Frankie finished, she was about to climb in beside Evan when she froze, glancing down at herself. She muttered a curse.

Still naked. Frankie had *never* been naked after a scene before. She sighed. Well, at least she was alone to sit in her self-doubt. Evan didn't deserve anything less than the best from her and showing even a modicum of vulnerability when they were in subspace would just amp up all the emotions. Evan's earlier declaration of love came back to her, and she reached out to trace her finger along the sword tattoo next to their ear, smiling softly. There was a chance Evan had been too out of it to remember the confession when they woke, and that was okay.

Frankie, on the other hand? She would remember those three words forever.

Evan was still sleeping when Frankie left the apartment hours later. She'd considered waking them with her face buried between their thighs, but surprise morning sex without verbal consent beforehand wasn't something they'd talked about yet. And besides, a sub drop could last a day or two, which meant Evan's emotions might already be at an all-time high. *I'll make a point to check on them later.* Evan had the day off, the lucky duck. Unlike Frankie, who had more than her share of work waiting. Starting with getting the latest batches of brew going and ending with mounds of paperwork after closing.

Once she was in the basement, Frankie switched on the fluorescent lights and watched the brewery slowly come to life. As shadows lifted off the large steel tanks, a small smile appeared. Frankie didn't have many hobbies. Her self-defense classes stemmed out of necessity and responsibility. She couldn't draw like Evan and didn't enjoy the outdoors like Sloane and McCoy. But the process of making beer? Now that she could do. In fact, it was one of the few things that truly shut her brain off. No more flickering images of the past, or of worries she had at present. Just gentle repetition and the comforting smell of yeast and malted barley.

It was closing in on 9 a.m. when Ted and Jon clocked in. After a few minutes of catching up, Frankie turned the job over to them and headed upstairs to the pub. Donnie was already prepping food in the kitchen when she walked by, so she called out a greeting. It was then she remembered that the new hire was supposed to start today, and she sighed. Time would need to be set aside for that as well. Because she had *so* much of it to spare.

Sloane and McCoy were chatting at the bar when Frankie slid behind the counter to make a coffee. She whistled when she spotted Sloane's black eye. "Morning. Quite a shiner you've got. Didn't Lian offer to take your shift?"

"No offense to Lian, but there's a reason I don't let her bartend. I'm fine." Sloane scowled before disappearing into the stock room.

"Moody brat."

"'Fine' my ass."

Frankie and McCoy spoke at the same time, glanced at one another, and snorted. "Seriously, I tried to get her to stay home. I slept at the apartment last night just in case. Crazy what happened, right? I'm pissed I wasn't here last night."

"I know you are." If she knew anything about McCoy, it was how vigilant she was in caring for her sister. She had one of the biggest hearts around.

McCoy let out a little huff and closed her eyes briefly. When she reopened them, her meadow green gaze glistened. "Thank you, Frankie. I'm glad you were there."

"Of course." Frankie took in McCoy's work overalls and topknot hairstyle tied back with the sides freshly shaven. There had been a time when she'd run her fingers over McCoy's undercut and not think twice about it. She cleared her throat, picked up her mug of coffee, and took a sip before saying, "You're never around this early. It's good to see you."

"Right back at you, beautiful." McCoy was visibly upset, but she winked at Frankie. It was so like her to put on a facade at will. Still, Frankie never thought a day would come when McCoy would put one up around her. And then McCoy smiled, making both dimples pop. Frankie tensed, waiting for the low swoop of her tummy that always happened when those dimples came out, but it never did. Huh.

Thank you, Evan!

"She's here because she's overprotective and likes to annoy me," Sloane said with an eye roll, sidestepping Frankie as she carried a case of cider to the fridge.

"You did get attacked at random," Frankie pointed out, thinking back on the man later carried away in handcuffs. She'd never seen him before last night, and when asked by both her and the police, Sloane had sworn the same thing.

"And with your car stolen, you needed—"

"Wait, your car was stolen?" Frankie cut in, jaw dropping in disbelief. Why was she only just hearing this? "When? Did you tell that to the police?"

Sloane shot her twin a glare before sighing. "Not yet. I'd parked a few blocks over, and it was gone by the time I finished work."

"You need to inform the police. It could be related."

"I'm sure it's a coincidence."

"Still."

Sloane heaved another sigh. She finished loading up the cider and stood to face them. For the first time, Frankie noticed the strain in Sloane's posture and a hollowness in her cheeks that hadn't been there before. She softened toward the other woman, reaching out to place a comforting hand on Sloane's arm. "Please, look after yourself."

"I am. God, now I know why you two didn't work. You both like to smother people," Sloane snapped and stalked off to the storage room again.

"Why is she so fucking stubborn?" McCoy bit out.

"She's scared. Give her time." On the one hand, Frankie wished she couldn't relate to Sloane's fear. On the other hand, she wished she had magic words to soothe it all away. An assault changed a person, no matter the circumstance. It had taken her and Emily months before they'd confided in Auntie B.

Frankie's phone vibrated in her pants pocket. She pulled it out, an unabashed smile taking over as she saw a message waiting from Evan.

Evan: I'm just waking up. Wish you didn't have to work.
Evan: Thank you for last night.

"Wow, I didn't think your face could do that," McCoy mused, slipping off the barstool. She picked up her keys, twirling the carabiner around on her finger.

"Do what?" Frankie said distractedly. She quickly typed out a reply.

Frankie: I know, baby. How are you feeling? You can come keep me company if you're lonely.

"Look so happy. In love. Evan really does it for you, huh?"

"Yeah, they really do." Frankie bit her lip, trying to bring the smile and her happiness down a notch. By McCoy's ensuing snort, she hadn't succeeded.

"Do you let them touch you? I'm sorry, I'm out of line."

She was out of line, but that didn't mean Frankie wouldn't answer. McCoy had been hers for too long not to reply honestly. "No. I don't."

McCoy grimaced. "That's too—"

"But I want to." Frankie nodded sharply, like she was trying to convince herself of her words. Evan touching her was a complicated situation. She did and didn't want them touching her. She'd never believed she could love someone so intensely before, or that another person could complete her so perfectly. She wanted Evan to experience the same level of trust that they'd given her each time with their submission.

"You ... want to?"

"Yes. I'm taking the steps toward it happening."

"That's great, Frankie. Truly. Evan's lucky."

Frankie gave McCoy a small smile. "So is Sawyer."

"No way, I'm the lucky one. I swear, every day I'm learning something new about her. Last week she pulled out a str—" McCoy slapped a hand over her mouth and flushed a deep red.

Frankie arched an eyebrow, mischievously playing along. "You were saying?"

CHAPTER 35

Evan

"THIS IS LIT, RIGHT? Great gig and we get away from O'Rourke's for a change."

"Def, my dude."

Sloane clinked her drink against Andy's, and Evan nodded, adding, "Scoring a night off together never happens, so the gig came at a good time."

They were across town at a different pub, sharing nachos and sipping a draft ale from the pitcher Andy bought for the table. Claire and her band were the entertainment there tonight, so Andy had thrown them the idea of coming to support her. It wasn't the first time Evan had heard the band, as they sometimes played at O'Rourke's, but their friend was right. No matter how much Evan wished they could attach themself to Frankie at times, tonight's change of scenery *was* nice. Scooping up more nachos, they studied the chip, cheese, and salsa ratio before popping it in their mouth. Really, there was just one complaint about the evening.

"O'Rourke's serves mozza sticks." Seriously, what kitchen didn't serve mozza sticks? *Should be a crime.*

Andy and Sloane pulled their gaze from the band at the same time to look at Evan. Andy seemed humored, but Sloane rolled her eyes. In Evan's opinion, everything anyone did lately agitated Sloane to some degree. "I'd say it serves Frankie, too, but we all know who serves whom in your relationship."

"That's subjective, though, right?" Andy piped up with a grin. "I mean, Frankie's a pleasure Domme, so in a way she's serving you."

Evan chewed the inside of their mouth as they fought back a grin of their own. It sure as hell felt like their Daddy was serving them the other night.

"Ugh, forget I said anything," Sloane said, and with the noise in the pub, Evan had to strain to hear her. Their attention returned to the band just in time to see Claire belt out a solo on the bass guitar.

"She's good." *Surprisingly so*, Evan thought. "What's she do again?"

"I know, b'y. I keep telling her that." Andy laughed and reached for his beer mug once more. "She works as a medical transcriber."

"Seriously?" Sloane laughed too. "Well, she found a great way to unwind."

When the band took a break an hour later, Andy disappeared to see Claire, which then left Sloane to keep Evan company. Things had been awkward between them since the assault in the pub washroom. Sloane had her guard up more times than not around Evan now, as if she was worried Evan was going to offer some much-needed advice or drill her with more questions. She was feeling insecure, having a weak moment. Evan understood that better than most. They'd hit rock bottom before prison helped straighten them out. Maybe it was time Sloane knew that about them.

"I did five years in prison for breaking into a pharmacy."

Sloane stilled, her mug of lager halfway to her lips. One eyebrow shot up. "Fucking random, but okay. Run out of toilet paper, did you?"

"No. I was there for prescription meds." Evan heaved a sigh, wishing they had told Frankie this first. She'd never asked, and when their stint in prison had come up, she had seemed satisfied not to have the details. *Tonight. I'll tell her tonight.* "After my brother died, I just wanted to not feel the pain anymore, you know? So I had a friend hook me up with Oxy he stole off his dad."

"Well, shit. That's a lot to unpack."

"Yep. Things went downhill from there."

Sloane whistled, her eyes still wide. She waved her hand around them. "Not that I don't appreciate the heart-to-heart, but why tonight?"

Evan frowned. "Because you're acting weird with me now. I don't love it, not gonna lie. And now you know something about me. Something I'm not proud of. I had an addiction, and as much as I hate to admit it, prison helped me get clean."

"But you were charged for theft, not drug possession."

"Yeah, that's right. I used to steal a lot back then. Besides, I never had any pills on me when I was arrested."

"I see."

"Anyway, you might not think the gambling is a problem. I didn't think I had one either 'til I was running down a back alley with cops after me."

Sloane's mug of lager hit the table with a thud Evan heard even over the surrounding noise. Sliding out of the booth, she snatched her purse from the vacant seat and shot Evan a look filled with unrestrained fury. "I should've known you were on about this again.

Just fuck off about it, okay? You don't know what you're talking about, Evan. I can take care of myself."

Since running O'Rourke's took up most of Frankie's nights, Evan had grown accustomed to their couple activities happening during mornings she didn't go in early. The day before, she'd taken Evan to buy more clothes, including a new binder, which was a pleasant surprise. The one they usually wore was an older style and wasn't as secure as it once had been. In spite of the "dangerous lone wolf" reputation Frankie had somehow built for herself over the years, she was always so thoughtful and attentive toward Evan. Frankie was made to be in a relationship. To serve and be served, never mind the assumptions Sloane and Andy had spoken of Friday night. Yes, Evan was positive it made Frankie feel good to do things for them, in and out of the bedroom. But it was the same for Evan.

They adored being able to get Frankie comfortable after a long day on her feet. Whether that was to take off her footwear, make tea, or something more subtle, like direct a fan onto Frankie whenever she broke out in a full-body sweat in the middle of the night. Her night terrors weren't something they ever spoke of, but Evan was often a silent witness regardless. It wasn't a bunch of screaming and crying in her sleep either, like what some of Evan's cellmates would do. Frankie's night terrors were quiet, composed, and if it weren't for the body sweats or the occasional tear tracks down her cheek, Evan would be none the wiser. Hell, they'd lived under the same roof as Frankie since December and hadn't realized.

"Daydreaming while we're on a movie date. Tsk tsk."

Evan blinked, Frankie's teasing smile coming into focus. They glanced past her to the TV still playing the latest drama Frankie had picked out. She was convinced that if Evan watched enough Julia Roberts movies, they'd love her acting as much as she did.

"I'm sorry."

"Don't be. What's on your mind?" Frankie's arm tightened around Evan's shoulders. She pulled them closer so that their head rested just below her chin. Frankie pressed a light kiss to Evan's head, and their eyes drifted closed.

"Are you nervous about therapy tomorrow?"

Frankie's first appointment hadn't exactly been on their mind, but it was related. Evan just hoped that returning to therapy wouldn't worsen the night terrors. She had been through enough already.

"No. I doubt much will happen in the first session. More of a get-to-know-you thing. Why do you ask?" Frankie reached for the remote, paused the movie, and tilted Evan's chin up so that they could face her. Affection warmed her dark brown eyes into a golden hue. Evan had never looked at someone before and thought, *That person loves me. I know because I can see it clear as day.* While Caleb had loved Evan, his eyes had never given too much away. Frankie's eyes were like a window, with Evan peering into her very soul. It was breathtaking. And terrifying.

"I have something to tell you. You might be mad," they blurted.

"Alright," Frankie returned slowly. "Spill." Her nails scored the length of Evan's cheek and throat lightly as she spoke. Besides the muscle in her jaw twitching, there was nothing to indicate their words had upset her.

"I-I never thought I'd come to Vancouver and decide to stay. I was supposed to complete the ... job—"

"Kill me, you mean."

Evan balked at how direct she was. *Of course she knew.* They nodded, cutting their gaze to the TV once more. The frozen image of Julia stared back at them. "A contact of my ... *step*father's," they practically spat, "saw you walking one day. He told Cecil when he went back to Toronto. That's ... Cecil is my stepfather. Anyway, Jerry showed him your picture. He's been obsessed with you since Caleb."

"And he couldn't find me due to the name and address change."

"Right. And then suddenly he could. I was sent because ..." Evan paused again, licking their dry lips and not missing how Frankie's gaze dropped to their mouth. "Well, at the time, it felt like the only way to get back on his good side. I-I'd just got out of prison, and he said if I took care of you, I'd be able to see my mom again."

"Your mom? How does she factor into this? Where is she?"

Evan clasped their hands together, wringing them out like a washcloth. Frankie's palm landed on them in a comforting gesture. Rolling their lips inward, Evan whispered, "She's in a mental hospital. Completely lost it while I was put away. I-I didn't even know until I got out. She just ... stopped coming to visit. Cecil's somehow in charge of the visitor list and refuses to put me on it."

Frankie cupped their cheek, averting Evan's gaze to her once again. "First of all, I'm so sorry you've had to deal with this alone, little thief. Understand that you can tell me anything, okay? Anything at all, I can handle it. Even if it's in relation to someone plotting my demise. And second, the term 'mental hospital' is outdated and brash, so please don't refer to it as that. Saying that your mother is in a psychiatric hospital is much more politically correct, yes?"

Evan's cheeks flushed with embarrassment. They tried to pull away, but Frankie held them in place, waiting. It took them a moment to figure out what for. Clearing their throat, Evan mumbled, "Yes, Daddy."

"Good, now tell me, honey. Since you've failed this 'job,' as you call it, what happens next? Cecil comes to off me himself?"

Evan cringed at how point-blank and aloof she was, as if Cecil trying to kill her was the most ridiculous idea she'd heard all day. Slowly, they nodded. "But I don't know when. I tried to stop him. Fuck, I'm sorry, Frankie. I-I told him Jerry got the wrong woman, but he won't listen." *He never has before, so why start?*

"It's okay. It's not your fault." Frankie dipped her face toward Evan's, pressing the gentlest kiss to the edge of their mouth. She pulled back a teensy bit to whisper, "Is this okay?"

"You never have to ask to kiss me," they whispered back, accepting another peck on the opposite side of their mouth.

"I do, in case one day you don't want my kisses."

"That day will never happen." Evan would more than happily make out with Frankie for hours. She always smelled delicious and could tease them to the begging point. Even now, after such a deep topic, a breathy sigh escaped them as Frankie's lips pressed fully against theirs. "I don't want anything to happen to you."

"Baby, it's okay, really. I'm not worried. I'll inform the police in the morning and stay vigilant." Frankie's gaze roamed over their face, her fingers of one hand lovingly stroking up and down Evan's arm.

They didn't know how she was so calm. Maybe it was because she didn't know Cecil like they did. Evan knew exactly what Cecil was capable of, the lengths he would go to when he sought revenge.

"C'mere, closer to me," Frankie said, her voice soft. She patted right between her legs which were reclined on the chaise part of the sectional. "Right here."

"Okay."

Once Evan was sitting between her thighs, their back leaning against her voluptuous breasts, Frankie dropped a kiss against their earlobe. "Tell me about your sword tattoo. I've noticed it's the only ink you have."

"Not much to tell," Evan admitted, studying Frankie's pale thighs in the silk sleep shorts she wore. They were thick and strong-looking from hours of training, and Evan longed for the permission to touch, to run their hands up the length of all that soft skin. "It represents courage and protection. I got it right after I was released."

"And has it helped?"

Evan hummed a sigh of pleasure as Frankie skimmed her fingers along the tattoo and then further, along their jawline and down their throat.

They tilted their face up to look at her, smiling shyly. "Only since I met you. I never felt like I belonged anywhere before. I was always in the way growing up, and in prison, my cellmate offered protection in exchange for ..." Evan trailed off, a shameful blush heating their cheeks.

"For what?" Frankie's voice had grown tight.

Evan swallowed, dropped their gaze away from hers. "Sex. She was easily twice my size and terrifying. Said trading it was the nicer option. So I did. Besides a few fights—which she got revenge for me—I was safe for five years."

Silence permeated the living room for several seconds before Frankie growled out, "You were sexually assaulted."

"No, I agreed to the sex so nothing worse would happen." Which Evan's cellmate had threatened in that first week. Often.

"Little thief, coercion is a form of rape." Frankie's arms went around Evan, holding them close to her. When she spoke again, her voice had grown husky, like she was battling the urge to cry. "I'm so sorry that happened. I wish I could've been there to protect you."

Evan smirked at that, trying for a joke. "If things had gone differently, you would've already arrested me a couple years before. By the time I landed in the pen, you'd have forgotten all about me."

"I'd never forget you." Frankie kissed their temple before burying her face in their short hair. "Even if it wasn't romantic, I would have taken notice of you. Maybe I would have looked into your stepfather, got social services involved."

"No offense, but I much prefer how it turned out. I love being your submissive."

"Mmm, me too. I love you being mine."

Frankie kissed them again, and as her soft hands caressed Evan's bare thighs exactly as they'd longed to do for her, the memory of her own tattoo returned. Evan had only seen it for a blurry second without their glasses on, and they wondered if Frankie had any more.

"What's your ink of? The one on your hip."

Frankie's hands stilled. She cleared her throat. "The Fire Rose Unity tattoo. It symbolizes unity and strength for sexual assault survivors."

Evan placed their hands on Frankie's, squeezing them. "Thanks for telling me."

"Thank you for asking. I hadn't realized you'd seen it."

A light chuckle left Evan. They tilted their head back to look at Frankie. "Just barely without my glasses. Maybe one day you'll let me see it a little better?"

As Frankie smiled, the earlier tension in her eyes vanished. "Perhaps, if you're a good boi and come for me now, I'll show you when I dress for work. What do you say?"

Evan grinned, already loving the sound of that. "Yes, please, Daddy."

CHAPTER 36

Frankie

SOMETHING WASN'T RIGHT. FRANKIE had gone over that month's bookkeeping twice now, and the numbers just weren't adding up. She pushed back from her desk with a heavy sigh, reaching up to massage her temples. The wall clock read close to midnight, not exactly a good time to do math calculations, and besides, numbers weren't her strong suit on the best of days. She had planned to come in early that morning to do it, but was pleasantly distracted by her sub. As it turned out, if Evan sat on their hands while nestled between her thighs on the sectional, she could access them easily and they could behave by not touching her. It was a position Frankie wanted to repeat, as it was perfect for movie dates or any time she didn't want to restrain Evan properly. *Mm-hmm, I wonder if they'd like it if I wore a strap-on. A reverse cowgirl position could be hot.*

"Sloane should have gone over this by now," she rubbed her eyes and watched as the numbers on her laptop screen blurred before her. Frankie could have sworn Sloane *had* gone over it. As busy as her brain often was with her ADHD, she was never late with month-end responsibilities. Speaking of, it was time to mail out the envelope for Auntie B. Frankie smiled as she considered her aunt. Since their overdue chat the day Frankie had run out on Evan, a morning didn't go by that they weren't checking in with each other. It felt good to be back in the older woman's good graces. Although Maddox may not have needed the monthly stipend as much anymore, Frankie was certain Auntie B could use it for Eamon.

She pulled her phone out, shooting off a text to Sloane to come to the office before heading home. If it were just a dollar here and there, Frankie would chalk it up to her math skills, but it wasn't. The ledgers showed a discrepancy of over a thousand. And that was just the drink order! The miscellaneous expenses seemed inaccurate as well.

A knock on the door had Frankie pulling her gaze from the screen again. "Come in," she called, expecting to see Sloane's dark hair pop in with its dyed pink tips. She broke into a smile when she saw who was on the other side. "Evan. Finished already?"

"Yep, slow night. Everyone's taking off." Evan closed the office door.

"Sloane?"

"Left already. Andy's locking up for her tonight."

"Oh?" That was news to Frankie. They were supposed to run any shift changes by her beforehand. There had been ample opportunity when Frankie returned from her class. Her throat felt tight. She didn't like being the last to know things. "Lock the door."

"Hmm, 'kay, Daddy." Evan's knowing grin was anything but submissive. Salaciously hopeful, if Frankie had to describe it, and the knowledge lessened the worry in her chest. If her little thief wanted to play after hours in her office, who was she to deny them? Asserting her dominance might be the ideal way to take the edge off prior to tearing a strip off her bar manager. Before she forgot, she quickly texted Sloane again.

Frankie: I have something to go over in the morning so don't be late.

"You look good tonight, baby. Have I mentioned how appealing I find you in those jeans?"

"Not verbally, but you squeezed my ass walking by me in the kitchen earlier. Dakota saw."

Shit. Frankie had forgotten she'd done that. Impulsive move, something she'd harped on to McCoy about in the past. She'd have to be more careful. Dating her employee was already breaking so many rules.

"What did he say?"

"Nothing worth repeating, Daddy."

Frankie considered pressing the issue, but it was late and she didn't want to waste time she could spend pleasuring her sub.

"And before you ask, I liked it. A lot. I've been wet most of the day thinking about how your fingers felt inside me this morning."

"Fuck, really? I love knowing that. You didn't slip to the washroom and get yourself off?"

Evan shook their head. "No way."

Interesting. Frankie got to her feet. "And why is that?"

"I ... um, felt like I needed permission. You said before that you own my orgasms, so it seemed wrong."

Frankie laughed softly, coming around the desk to kiss Evan. "You are too precious, my good boi. What I meant was during a scene, I own your orgasms. Or if we're playing and orgasm withdrawal is the focus, then I may make you wait for days. It would be agreed upon beforehand, and then I'd spend that time teasing you and enjoying the fact that you can't come until I say so. But since we hadn't talked about it, you're free to fuck yourself when the need arises. On your break, of course, or at home. Not during a dinner rush or something."

Evan frowned slightly, and she kissed them again. Longer this time, teasing her tongue along the seam of their mouth. She sighed as they opened for her, and she wrapped her arms around their waist and kissed them deeply.

"What's wrong?" she asked after, a little breathlessly.

"I wanna make you happy. How would getting myself off achieve that?"

"The power I have over you," Frankie explained as she teased the button on Evan's jeans. "Knowing I'm the reason you had to steal away and fuck yourself, or knowing that you're soaked right now, achieves that. Trust me."

"I am soaked." Evan rocked their pelvis, causing the seam of their jeans to push against Frankie's hand. A small groan left them.

"I love knowing that. You've been so patient, waiting for Daddy to fill you up. Would you like that? I could fuck you right here, in my office. Against my desk with a strap-on." God, just mentioning it had Frankie turned on. The bag of toys left over from her meeting with Sawyer came to mind. She grinned coyly. Her baby knew just how to take her mind off the bullshit of running a business.

"Please, Daddy. I'd fucking love that."

"So polite, too," Frankie purred. She leaned against the desk and watched them for a moment. When Evan tried to subtly squeeze their legs together, no doubt to release some of the building pressure, she said, "Head over to my filing cabinet. You'll find a bag with a harness and two dildos. Choose one and bring them to me."

As Evan scurried across the small space to do as instructed, Frankie set her laptop out of the way. When they returned holding the larger dildo of the two, with its ribbed girth, Frankie hummed. "Good choice, little thief. I can already imagine how it'll feel to slide inside you."

"Thank you, Daddy." Her sub looked up at her with hopeful, mismatched eyes behind their slightly crooked glasses. It took everything in Frankie not to pull Evan against her and ravish their mouth some more. She took the toys and quickly attached the O-ring on the harness to the dildo before handing them back.

"I want you to put it on me. Remove my slacks but leave the heels and g-string. Can you do that?" Satisfaction curled low in her belly as Evan licked their lips and nodded. "Excellent. And you know I reward good bois."

Desire pooled between Frankie's thighs as she watched Evan reach for the belt buckle. There was a slight tremble to the fingers pulling the belt free, but she didn't comment on it. Evan's eagerness to please her was a powerful tool in their dynamic.

"I rather like you on your knees before me," Frankie husked as Evan carefully lowered the garment to the floor. Her fingers tensed against the desk at how close their face was to her underwear, but she took a deep, controlled breath.

I'm safe with Evan, just like they're safe with me.

"Look at me. Who do you belong to?"

Evan glanced up at her from the floor, their eyes softening. *They know*, she realized. Somehow, they knew what she needed and why. "I belong to you, Daddy. I'm yours to use however you wish."

"That's right," Frankie said, lifting her legs one at a time as Evan helped her into the harness. The urge to speed things along took over, and she bent to yank the material up over her thighs. "You did a great job, but now it's my turn." She planted a rough kiss on Evan before swapping their positions and pushing them face-first over her desk. Spanking their ass through their jeans, she said, "Safe word? Tell me it."

"Mustard," Evan groaned out.

"Good, remember to use it if you want to stop." The dildo wedged between them as Frankie reached around to unfasten Evan's jeans. She shoved them down their legs, gripped their hip with one hand, and used the other to line the dildo up to Evan's front hole. With one thrust, she pushed inside, groaning at how Evan's sex tightened around the toy. "Fuck, baby, you feel so good. So slick and needy for me."

"I've wanted you all day," Evan panted, their elbows acting as support as they rested on top of her desk.

"You were so thoughtful to wait for Daddy," Frankie said between thrusts. She spanked Evan's thigh, enjoying another sting to her palm. "I enjoy rewarding good behavior." Then Frankie skimmed her fingers under Evan's long sleeve, scoring her nails up and down their back with one hand, from their binder to their bare ass, as the other held Evan in place against the desk.

"Ugh … fuck. You know exactly where to …" Evan gasped out a shaky moan and pushed their ass up more.

Frankie quickened her thrusts, pushing in deeper, groaning her own pleasure as the base of the dildo hit against her clit. She moved her hand to Evan's front, slid it between their thighs, and used her thumb and forefinger to tease the swollen bud waiting desperately for her touch. "I want you to come for me when you're ready, little thief. No holding back tonight."

Evan's cries became more urgent with each of Frankie's thrusts. They were so close, and she wanted nothing more than to give them that release they'd craved all day. Evan had craved *her*. No one else in the city could give her little thief the attention and dominance that she could. Frankie pinched Evan's bud, then drew her hand back slightly and spanked it.

"Fuck!" they screamed, and seconds later Evan went rigid in her grasp. Their sex clamped down on the dildo, trapping Frankie inside even as their legs began to shake.

"That's it," Frankie crooned, massaging the twitching bud beneath her fingers, wringing every ounce of pleasure from them. "I love watching you make a mess all over my cock. And on my desk, too. So hot, little thief. You're such a good little sub for me."

"Thank you, Daddy. I try." Another mewl escaped Evan as Frankie slowly pulled out.

"I know you do, my good boi." She hastily removed the harness before pulling Evan into her embrace. She scattered kisses over their damp forehead and cheeks, stopping at their mouth to give them a long kiss. Their eyes met. "Let's go home, shall we?"

Evan glanced down at their state of undress. Their jeans were bundled at the ankles, and Frankie still only wore a pair of pink pumps. They looked back up at her with a sheepish grin, "Maybe get dressed first?"

"Have you thought at all about another job now that the ruse is up with working for me?" Frankie asked the following morning. She and Evan were lying on their sides in her bed and facing each other, Frankie's fingers loosely tangled with Evan's. Although they had slept soundly through the night, Frankie was surprised to see Evan awake at 7 a.m. with her. Like many mornings before, she'd woken with a nightshirt clinging to her back and damp bed sheets, her tenacious night terrors a supreme pain in her ass. Today the bed linens had been changed by the time she returned from her shower, with Evan propped up against the headboard, sketching in their notebook. They hadn't mentioned anything to her, for which Frankie was grateful. It was too embarrassing to talk about.

Evan squinted, their forehead creasing in thought. "Do I need to? I'm not qualified for much else anyway. A GED diploma can only take me so far."

Frankie considered that. "You're still young; you could go back to school. Night classes are available for upgrading, if it's something you wanted to do."

"Is me being a dishwasher not good enough? I like working for you."

"No, no, that's not what I'm saying at all," Frankie rushed to say. She closed the distance between them, kissing Evan softly. "I love that too, but just know it's not expected in order to be with me. I want you to do whatever it is you dream of. You're free now. Do you understand what I'm saying?"

Evan nodded slowly. "You don't want me to go back home."

"I don't. Go and do anything but that, please. Now that I'm aware of how dangerous your stepfather is."

"But my mom—"

"By the time I'm done taking Cecil down, you'll be able to visit her. I promise, little thief. You and your mom will be safe." It would take reaching out to a lot of her old contacts in Toronto, but she wouldn't stop until Cecil was behind bars. How could she and Evan ever fully heal from the past while Cecil still roamed the streets?

"I believe you," Evan whispered, raising their hand to tentatively cup her jaw. Frankie's bottom lip quivered as Evan's calloused thumb passed over it. "If there's ever a day when Cecil isn't breathing down my neck, I wanna get top surgery. It's not going back to school or finding a different job, but it is a dream. One I've had for a long time."

"I can see how you'd want that. And I think it's a beautiful dream. One I'd love to be a part of making reality," Frankie whispered back with a smile. Spying the alarm clock on her nightstand, she groaned. "Sloane'll be in soon. I need to get going. There's a problem with the books that I need her help with."

"Problem?"

Frankie nodded, giving Evan a final kiss before slipping from the bed and hurriedly dressing. "Yes. Some of the expenses aren't adding up. Money not accounted for. I'm hoping Sloane can figure it out. She's better with numbers."

"What does that mean, money not accounted for?" Evan asked, an odd look crossing their face. They fidgeted on the bed, breaking eye contact with her. A trickle of unease crept over Frankie.

"It means money could be missing, inventory miscounted, or my math is worse than I thought," Frankie replied, watching her lover carefully. Knots formed in her stomach as she saw Evan swallow.

"Oh. Well, I'm sure Sloane can help."

"Mm-hmm. Okay, I've gotta run. See you later, honey."

A dozen scenarios, each involving Evan, flashed through Frankie's mind as she left the apartment. Evan had broken into her office at least once, but she'd never noticed anything missing, or she would have reviewed the security footage. There was one stationed outside her office and another, less noticeable one inside. There was no reason to steal from her now, was there? *Unless Evan is still really trying to hurt me.* Perhaps not murder, but there was more than one way to exact revenge on someone. Taking down their business, blackmail …

Quit fucking spiraling. You know them. They'd never hurt you.

But hadn't they done exactly that? Was it not Evan who'd snuck into her bedroom in an attempt to stab her in the heart *just like their brother had done years before?*

Sloane was just arriving via the rear entrance of O'Rourke's by the time Frankie approached her office. "Good, you're here earlier than I expected."

"Good morning to you too," Sloane yawned out. She ran her fingers through noticeably tangled hair and glanced up at Frankie with a bloodshot gaze. "I was in the area. Crashed with a friend."

Frankie assessed her wrinkled outfit, her eyes narrowing as it dawned on her. "Showing up in the same clothes as yesterday? Tell Naz to keep a change in her closet if she's planning on taking you back to her place."

"I wasn't with Naz. I can't stand her." Sloane feigned a shudder, and Frankie rolled her eyes. She didn't bother to point out the obvious blush or that now, come to think of it, Sloane reeked of Naz's cologne. Today wasn't the day to unpack all that nonsense.

"Let's get this over with, brat," she grumbled as she unlocked her office. "I'm tired and need a coffee."

"Want me to grab your usual while you set up?"

Frankie slapped a hand over her chest in mock surprise. "Did you just offer to fetch coffee? Fuck me sideways, Sloane, don't shock me like that."

Sloane, who was already walking up the hallway to the bar, flipped Frankie the bird and called over her shoulder with a laugh, "With that attitude, don't expect a repeat. Asshole."

Frankie let out her own chuckle and stepped inside her office. Flicking the lights on, the first thing she came across was the discarded strap-on from last night. "Jesus," she muttered with another, giddier chuckle. As she rushed to tidy up, thoughts of Evan and the bookkeeping plagued her like a mysterious illness. They wouldn't, *couldn't* steal from her. Not anymore. It must have been her math skills or another completely acceptable reason for the discrepancies.

Sloane returned with her Irish coffee, and they got to work crunching numbers over Frankie's spreadsheets. An hour or more went by before Frankie noticed Sloane worrying her lip and muttering. She must have been at it for a while as the skin was bloody. "What do you see? And stop doing that. Jesus."

"I just ... I didn't think they'd be so bold."

Frankie frowned. *They who?* "Don't talk in circles, brat."

Sloane met Frankie's gaze, tears shimmering in her green eyes. "I-I saw Evan dip into the tip jar a few times, but never said anything. I was worried they were using again and didn't want them in trouble."

Wait, what? "Using?" There was no way. Frankie would have seen it in Evan's file. *Would you, though? You read that file for one reason only.*

Sloane swallowed hard. "They didn't tell you? Fuck, now I feel even worse."

"Tell me what?"

"The reason they were arrested for breaking and entering. Evan was addicted to pills. And last week, I noticed some of my Concerta missing from my purse."

What the fuck? Frankie schooled her features, but inside, she was a hot mess. Why hadn't she ever asked for details? *Because it wasn't related at the time, and I was short-staffed.* Okay, but why hadn't Evan bothered to tell her? She had told them all her deepest secrets.

It's what Evan had wanted, what Sawyer had sworn would bring Frankie a real relationship.

"Who else knows about this?"

One of Sloane's shoulders went up. She wiped a tear away, stammering, "J-just me, I think. I'm really sorry, boss. I know how much you care for them. And I don't know for sure it's them skimming, but … I mean, if they can steal tips and meds out of my purse, what else are they up to?"

"No," Frankie gritted out, smacking her hand down on the desk. Her throat was raw, aching with pent-up fury and disbelief. She would not cry in front of Sloane. She needed to talk to Evan and get to the bottom of this. "I don't believe it."

"I don't want to either. Evan's my friend. Why don't you check the cameras? Maybe you'll catch something."

"Go to work. Leave me be now. Please, Sloane."

"Sure, boss." Sloane's smile was faint and wobbly, and it only worked to upset Frankie more. She lifted her arm and silently pointed at the door.

Once she was alone, Frankie pulled up the feed for the cameras. A string of curse words left her as she realized the security footage was disconnected or broken. How long ago had that happened?

Have I just been walking around utterly blind and lovesick these last few months? How could she have let her guard down so much?

Her gaze landed on her safe tucked away behind her desk. The tightness in her stomach grew to a cantankerous melon. *No, no fucking way.* Heart racing, Frankie dropped to her knees and reached for the keypad with shaking fingers. It took three attempts before she got it open, and what she saw splintered her battle-worn heart.

Besides the petty cash needed for the pub registers, the money she'd saved for her family and her handgun were gone.

CHAPTER 37

Evan

SOMETHING WASN'T RIGHT. THERE was a shift in the air around them that made the hair on the back of their neck stand up. A sixth sense or whatever people called it, but Evan had relied on that feeling for as long as they could remember. They'd known Cecil was bad before they'd even met, before Evan's mom had gotten back together with him. To a three-year-old, Cecil had been massive in size and had an energy as dark as the boogeyman Caleb would often try to scare Evan with stories about. When they moved in with Cecil, Caleb was happy to spend more time with his dad. Not Evan. They'd been so convinced Cecil was the real-life boogeyman that they'd barely slept for that whole first week.

As the years went by, that initial fear lessened to some degree, but that sixth sense remained absolute. Evan had known something was wrong the night Caleb was killed. When he hadn't followed them, they'd circled the block before returning, only to find the street sectioned off with crime scene tape.

And tonight at O'Rourke's, that very same feeling weighed heavily on them. From where they sat in a window booth, Evan could see Sloane sneaking looks at them from the bar. They were worried about her, the gambling, had even considered telling Coy about it. But in Evan's experience, becoming a rat never got a person far. Being here, being with Frankie, was a chance to put their old life behind them.

But Frankie's off today, too. Looking through Evan instead of at them when they'd crossed paths earlier. A nervous, almost sick feeling had begun in the pit of their stomach. Something was definitely not right.

"Lian, is Frankie still around?" Evan asked as the server walked past.

Lian shook her head. "Sorry, Ev."

Evan pulled out their phone and frowned. Frankie hadn't texted either, which was unlike her. They chewed their fry absently, unsure if they should reach out. Maybe she was busy. She'd had a lot on her mind when she'd left the apartment that morning.

A gust of air blew through the door as more patrons stepped into O'Rourke's. Evan glanced toward the entrance, only to do a double-take. Their mouth fell open and seconds later, their cell phone clattered right into the mound of ketchup on their plate.

Cecil.

Cecil was there.

Cecil was inside the pub.

Evan ripped the sweater hood over their head so fast that their elbow knocked the glass of soda onto their plate as well. Fuck, fuckity-fuck fuck. Evan's whole body was shaking as they snatched the phone out of the soda and ketchup before scrambling for the napkin dispenser. They yanked several out, patting the phone dry as best as possible.

Had Cecil seen them? *Fuck, I need to warn Frankie.*

Another breeze entered the pub as more people came or went, but Evan didn't dare look. They focused on cleaning up the mess they'd made. Soda was everywhere, dripping onto the floor as well now. That's what they were doing when two sets of familiar, shiny black combat boots appeared at their table. And as Evan slowly, cautiously, looked up, all the oxygen in their body seemed to leave them   at once.

Two cops stood before them, hands perched close to their gun holsters. The shorter, heavyset one spoke first. "Evan Landry, you're under arrest for ..."

Blood rushed to Evan's ears, pounding so loudly the cop's voice faded away. Frankie and Sloane were standing in front of the bar, staring right at them. "No, this is a mistake. Frankie! Tell them, please."

"Do you understand your rights as they've been read to you?" the other cop asked.

Evan nodded mutely. They clenched and unclenched their jaw as they were handcuffed. They were led toward the exit, and closer to the two people who should have known them better than anyone. Frankie had a hard, blank expression on her face as she met Evan's gaze. Sloane was pale, staring wide-eyed at Evan like it was the first time she'd come across them.

"Frankie, *please*. I didn't do anything. Tell her, Sloane."

"I-I can't." Sloane shook her head, choking out, "There's evidence, Ev. I'm so sorry."

Evidence? *The fuck did she do?* Evan's wild gaze collided with the woman they'd called a friend for the last three months. Apparently, they didn't know her at all because the Sloane they'd grown to like wouldn't have gone to such lengths to screw them over.

"Frankie, I-I love you. I didn't do this, I swear. You know me."

"C'mon." Evan's arm was tugged harder as the cops pulled them further away from their Domme, their friend, their lover. *Why won't she fucking look at me?*

Glee lit up Cecil's otherwise dead blue eyes as Evan passed. *Shit, I forgot about him!* They tried to turn around again to warn Frankie, but the pub door was already closing in their face.

An all-consuming panic surged through Evan as they were loaded into the police cruiser. Sloane had just eliminated the only person who knew what Cecil looked like.

CHAPTER 38

Frankie

FRANKIE STOOD WATCHING THE door long after Evan was hauled away in handcuffs. At some point in the last eight hours, numbness had taken over her thoughts, her limbs. She'd been walking around in a fog since the second it became apparent what would need to be done. Who she'd have to turn her back on. Never in her life had she expected to watch someone she loved get arrested. And more than that, know she couldn't do a thing to help them.

It had to be done. Yes, but that doesn't mean it was easy.

"I can't believe Evan stole your gun and then stupidly left it in their locker," Sloane remarked, wiping the bar counter Frankie had been leaning against.

"I'll be in my office," Frankie said, fatigue creeping into her voice. Her body felt trapped in a lethargic state as she dragged herself down the hallway. It was like she was inside a dream and walking, but reaching nowhere. Exhaustion and dejection made it difficult to be coherent.

I miss Evan.

Only thirty minutes had passed, but that half hour felt like a goddamn lifetime. Had it been just that morning when they'd been snuggling in bed and speaking of the future? Or last night, when Evan had helped her into the harness and afterward, happily bent over her desk while she'd fucked them?

This betrayal ran deeper than Frankie thought possible. The way it stabbed at her heart pained her in a way she hadn't felt in a long time.

Fuck McCoy's philosophy about loving and trusting everyone. That soft butch was nothing but a sappy golden retriever. In reality, untethered trust was for fools. The moment you started letting your guard down, people took advantage. And instead of asking for help, they preferred to steal right out from under her.

You might not know it yet, you slippery fuck, but you're dead to me.

Frankie wasn't, and never would be, a doormat. She gave a person one chance, that was it. No games, not with her. She hadn't pulled herself from the depths of hell—*twice*—just to be toyed with by a brat with apparent addiction issues. Hell, that information had been hard to wrap her head around. Frankie wanted to say that, as a former officer, she should have caught the signs. But if she were honest, there was more than one reason she'd left the force and not returned. She'd discovered that although she had a natural protective trait, her Sherlock skills left a lot to be desired.

The hours crawled by at a snail's pace. Frankie watched as the second hand reached the minute mark too many times to count, but still, she remained in her office. She was hiding, that much was clear, but at least she was on the premises if any of her staff needed her. Anger and just plain hostility burned a warpath inside her, but she couldn't escape work and go to the gym. She wanted to. God, she wanted to. Her body craved the kind of ferocious release only pain could offer, and yet, she stayed put.

At one point Rain came to check on her, and then Andy a little later, both offering their condolences and disbelief. It was comforting to know she wasn't the only one who'd believed Evan's innocence.

Thinking about her little thief caused tears to sting her eyes and her throat to tighten uncomfortably. *Why? Why did this have to happen?*

It was late evening when doubt began to creep in. Frankie was back from a brief, albeit emotional, stint behind the bar. She sipped a glass of scotch at her desk as silent tears dampened her cheeks.

She didn't feel like much of a Domme now. In fact, she felt pretty shitty about herself. Had she done the right thing, allowing them to carry Evan away like that?

"Frankie, I-I love you. I didn't do this, I swear. You know me."

For hours, she'd replayed Evan's words. They'd sounded genuinely scared. Was it possible Frankie wasn't seeing the whole picture?

"Frankie, I-I love you ..."

"I love you too." Fuck, but she did. Even after everything that had happened, she still loved Evan. And witnessing their arrest hurt *her*.

There was a knock on the office door. Frankie halted her bleak scroll through her phone's gallery and looked up to see Sloane stepping inside.

"What is it?" Frankie asked, wiping her tears away and despising Sloane's sympathetic look. She pushed her glass of scotch to the side.

"Umm." Sloane chewed her lip, an annoying habit she'd started over the last little while. Her eyes were bloodshot, like she'd been crying as well.

"Spit it out or fuck off, Sloane. I'm not in the mood." The words caught in Frankie's throat. Her shoulders trembled, and for a moment she feared she'd start sobbing in front of the other woman.

"Andy's at cash. He ... um, took over my till," Sloane said, pacing back and forth in short bursts before Frankie's desk. She started pulling at strands of her hair but appeared unaware of the action.

Frankie scowled, feeling less empathetic than she likely would have in any other circumstance. But she'd lost all her patience and then some. "Sloane."

Sloane's gaze, wide and wild, flew to Frankie. She noticeably paled at whatever emotion Frankie wasn't able to conceal on her face. "I-I thought I could do it. I'm so stupid. So fucking stupid." Frankie watched as she yanked at more hair, successfully pulling out a few strands. Pink and chestnut floated to the office floor.

"Jesus, will you quit that? And do what?" Frankie shoved her chair back and rounded the desk just as Sloane was going for more hair. She snatched her arms just in time. Sloane's chapped lips parted, and the column of her throat bobbed up and down as she lifted tear-filled green eyes to Frankie.

"P-put the blame on someone else. God, it's tearing me up inside. I can't breathe. All day I just—"

"What. Are you. Talking about?"

"It was me," Sloane whispered, and Frankie got hit by the stale stench of weed and vodka on her breath.

"Have you been drinking?"

"Yes, but not nearly enough for this conversation." Sloane pulled out of Frankie's hold, headed right to her desk, and swiped up Frankie's scotch, tossing it back in one gulp. "I am not a good person."

"What are you doing?" Frankie's eyes narrowed on Sloane, watching as the younger woman brandished a pair of scissors from the desk drawer.

"I hurt people I care about, like all the time," Sloane continued and yanked at her hair again. Tears soaked her cheeks, her gaze red-rimmed and feral as she stared across the desk at Frankie. "I can't quit. Mostly I like it."

"What the— Stop!" Frankie shouted as Sloane began chopping away at her long hair.

"No!" More strands fell to the floor. "I-I hurt people and don't know why. Hurt them before they can hurt me."

Frankie inched forward, but Sloane stopped long enough to wave the scissors at her. A high-pitched, hysterical laugh left her. "Did you know I came in here to confess? I did it, boss. I stole from you. And it was so fucking easy. Shit, I'm doing it again. Hurting people."

Frankie scowled so hard it was a shame Sloane didn't spontaneously combust. She stalked toward her, grabbed hold of the wrist with the scissors, and growled, "Explain to me why. Or *how* you could set your friend up like that. God, you let me think the person I love was stealing from me, you fucking coward."

"I know." Uncontrollable sobs racked Sloane's shoulders. She tried to dislodge her arm from Frankie's grip but was too weak. "And I'm sorry but framing them was easy too. I needed the money, you see? I'm so over my head in gambling. Cleaned out all my savings I had from mine and Coy's YouTube channel, but it wasn't enough. It's never enough with them, you know? So I started taking bits at a time from you. You never even noticed. A-and then I bet Sara since I didn't have anything else. My car, I bet my car! I didn't want to, I love Sara. Coy rebuilt her from the ground up for me, and I lost her.

I lost her. I-I figured I could borrow more money from you to get it back. I'm so stupid."

"Yes, you are." Frankie rolled her eyes as Sloane's weeping got louder. She wrangled the scissors away, and when Sloane got into her bubble trying to get them back, Frankie put her hand in Sloane's face and shoved her away. "Enough."

"Give them back, I'm not finished."

"Yes, you are. For good. Do you understand me? You are done here." Frankie moved around Sloane, picked up her office phone, and punched in a few numbers.

"Who are you calling? Not Coy? Please, not Coy."

"I've said it before, but some days I can't believe you're Mc-Coy's identical twin. You're nothing like her. You should be ashamed of yourself," Frankie said. To the 911 dispatcher, she relayed the necessary information and hung up. To Sloane once more, she barked, "Sit your ass down and wait. I wish I still had a badge 'cause I'd already have you in handcuffs."

"You ... you were a cop?" Sloane did sit, but she was still trying to rip her hair out as she rocked herself back and forth. She reminded Frankie of a disoriented, untamed animal as she peered up at her with tears dripping from her long eyelashes. "And yet you love Evan? I know they went to prison. Evan told me themsel—"

"Fuck you, Sloane. You have no right." Frankie ripped open her desk drawers, searching for something, *anything* she could use to *shut Sloane up*. Spotting a roll of masking tape and an old suit tie of McCoy's, her hands shook as she pulled them out. *This'll have to do.* Because if she had to listen to Sloane speak one more time, she was going to haul off and smack the bitch.

"What are you doing?"

"What I should have done earlier." Frankie tore a wide piece of tape off and wasted no time slapping it over Sloane's mouth. When she reached up to remove it, Frankie quickly grabbed her wrists and tied her to the chair. Then she turned Sloane around so that she was facing the wall. "There. Much better."

Frankie's pulse was racing as she sat back down. She took in the chunks of hair scattered on the floor around her desk and exhaled loudly. *Fucking hell, what just happened?*

When Sloane was finally arrested and lugged out the front doors just like Evan had been, Frankie trudged back to her office and made another phone call. It connected after the second ring.

"Hey, Frankie, I was sorry to hear about Evan."

Frankie took a deep breath, letting it out slowly. And then she spoke. "Hello, McCoy."

By the time O'Rourke's was closed for the night and the staff had gone home, Frankie was dead on her feet. Too many whispers had circulated among her employees after Sloane's arrest, and she knew she'd need to arrange a staff meeting sooner rather than later to discuss matters. There was so much piling up on Frankie's to-do list for the next several weeks. She had to hire an accountant for one, to help her figure out exactly how much Sloane had stolen. Plus, she was out a bar manager, but maybe that was for the best. Perhaps it was a position only she could fill. After all, she would never steal from herself.

As Frankie climbed the stairs to her apartment, she wanted more than anything to take Evan in her arms and beg for forgiveness. She reached the top, yawning as she fumbled for her keys. She unlocked the deadbolts first, and then the doorknob, sliding the keys back into her purse before swinging the door inward.

The hallway light was on, beckoning her to step inside. A tired smile lit Frankie's face as she crossed the threshold, shutting and locking the door behind her. "You were right," she called out, bending to take off her wedge heels. A faint cigarette smell hit her, like Evan had gotten close to someone who smoked. Frankie wrinkled her nose, stripping off her blazer and tossing it on the bench in the hallway as she moved further into the apartment. "Baby? Sloane confessed, just like you suspected. She was a little unhinged at the end, though, I think—"

Frankie stopped dead in her tracks at the sight before her. Fear crippled her voice. There in the middle of her living room was Evan, gagged, unconscious, and restrained to the bondage A-frame she'd set up that morning. Their clothes were torn and bloody, with more blood splattered on the floor. "Oh my god!" She charged forward, completely forgetting the years of training telling her *not* to do that.

Frankie registered the third occupant, and the gun, seconds too late.

Bang!

Chapter 39

Evan

HOURS EARLIER ...

The door to the apartment swung open, its handle bouncing noisily off the stopper on the wall. Evan looked up from their bowl of cereal to see Frankie standing in the kitchen entrance, dark brown eyes thunderous. Apprehension filled Evan as she glowered at them. They froze, spoon overflowing with Cheerios halfway to their mouth.

"What's wrong?"

"Did you ... God, I can't believe I need to ask this." Frankie jabbed ringed fingers through her loose tendrils, and when some of the curls caught, she swore, yanking her hand free. She was breathing heavily, like climbing the stairs had taken all her energy and then some. Like she'd faced a steep mountain and not the one flight she was accustomed to.

Evan set the spoon down, slid out of the booth, and took a few steps to Frankie. "Ask anyway. I don't keep shit from you, not anymore."

"Have you been stealing from me? The books aren't adding up and—"

"No."

"But my safe is cleaned out. I—"

"No."

Frankie's eyes narrowed. "Sloane said she caught you stealing from the tip jar. And then her purse—"

"She's lying." *Un-fucking-believable.* Evan's stomach lurched at that news. Sloane had betrayed them, even after they'd kept her secret. "Whatever she told you, they're lies."

"So did you or did you not break into a pharmacy to steal drugs years ago?"

The question felt like a thousand tiny shards of glass piercing Evan's back at once. It stole the breath from them, bowled them over at the waist, and for a moment, Evan worried they'd be sick.

That bitch.

"Not all lies then, I'm guessing."

Oh, god. The hurt in Frankie's voice caused tears to prick Evan's eyes. They stared up at her, pleading for her to understand. "I was gonna tell you, e-eventually. But I swear I didn't steal from you. Ever, Frankie, not since Emily's picture and never before. Snooped and broke shit, yes. I've admitted to that."

Frankie studied them for an agonizingly long moment before her shoulders sagged with obvious relief. Her lower lip trembled. "I believe you," she choked out. Nodding, she pulled Evan into her arms and squeezed them hard. "I believe you."

"Fuck, thank you. Thank you," Evan said, their voice muffled from where their face was buried in the crease of Frankie's cleavage. Sobs racked their shoulders, gratitude for Frankie making it hard to get the right words out. *Thank you for believing me. Believing in me,* was what they'd longed to say. No one ever had before.

"But why would Sloane blame you? It doesn't make sense."

Evan grimaced, knowing it was high time for the real truth to come out. "Because Sloane wants to take the heat off herself." They first guided Frankie to the breakfast booth to sit down and then explained everything they knew about Sloane's gambling addiction. Frankie was shocked at first, and then furious with herself for not catching on before.

An hour later, they were snuggling on the sectional and re-hashing ways to trap Sloane. "I don't like this plan, little thief. Too many ways it could go wrong." Frankie held Evan tighter. "I want to protect you, and regardless that I still know a few guys here from the academy, it feels a lot like I'd be throwing you to the wolves."

"How else do you expect to flush her out? Sloane's guilty conscience will kick in, trust me. She doesn't know what she's doing right now." Sloane was grasping at straws, trying not to get caught. Lying and stealing to feed the beast; Evan knew all about that and how hectic it made your thought process.

"I just ... I still can't believe she'd do this. I trusted her, Evan. More than anyone else in a long time. God, I'm such a fool. I should've caught on."

"It's because you trusted her that you didn't." Evan shrugged, adding sadly, "Love makes us blind sometimes. I spent way too much time trying to win Cecil over, and that prick's not even my real father. He was just the only one I knew."

"You deserve a much better life than the one you've had. I hope I can begin to change things for you." Frankie leaned in to kiss Evan softly. They heard a sigh right before she rested her forehead against theirs. "I do wish that I hadn't found out from Sloane about your addiction. I want to know things as you're ready to tell them."

"I know. And I promise that one day, I'll go into detail about it all. But for now, we need to plan this fake arrest."

"It'll need to be convincing." Frankie's palm came up to caress Evan's cheek.

Evan kissed her, grinning against her lips. "So make it convincing, Daddy."

In the end, Frankie had made it a little too convincing. Seeing how she'd looked through Evan instead of at them hurt like a bitch. They'd expected her to act, put on a performance, with words and perhaps some hint dropping that all was well with them. In the end, Evan was taken away and too stunned to warn Frankie properly about Cecil.

"Let me out. I need to go back," Evan said, jiggling their arms, "And fuck, why are these still on?"

The taller of the two cops eyed Evan in the rearview. "Frankie asked us to circle the block first to make it look convincing."

"She also said not to put the cuffs on so tight," Evan muttered, noting that they were *not* circling the block. Unless that was code for taking a scenic route around the downtown area. They tried not to let their panic swell any more than it already was. Being back in cuffs in a cop car wasn't nearly as fun as being restrained by Daddy Frankie and getting spanked. *Yes! Think of literally anything else than what's probably gonna happen if you don't warn Frankie in time.*

"Frankie needs help. My—" Evan clamped their mouth shut right before accidentally dropping Cecil's name. Feeding info to the police was not a smart idea. There was no way they'd look into Cecil without also discovering how Evan happened to be in Vancouver. With all the illegal activity they'd gotten up to since arriving in the city, there was a high chance of getting arrested right along with the old man.

But saving Frankie would make anything else worth it. Evan rolled their eyes. *Fucking sap, where do you come up with this shit?*

"Okay, kid, time to get out."

The patrol car pulled into a grocery store parking lot, and the shorter man who'd read Evan their rights stepped out. Evan's door was opened, and then they were being helped out of the backseat and uncuffed. Just as promised. Breathing a sigh of relief, Evan acknowledged the service with a thank you.

"You're welcome. Tell Frankie not to be a stranger," he said with an easy smile.

"I will."

Once the patrol car had driven away, Evan glanced around at the unfamiliar surroundings and groaned. What part of town had those two goons dropped them in?

Forty long minutes had passed by the time Evan made it back to O'Rourke's. They'd cursed for a good ten of those minutes for not having their wallet in order to flag down a cab. Talk about an oversight on their part. Now they crept around to the back of the pub like some spy, careful not to let anyone they might know see them. Prolonging the ruse as long as possible was the only way Evan's plan would work. So, for however long it took for Sloane to get in her feelings and pull out the morsel of humanity still left inside her, Evan would be waiting in the apartment.

It bothered them that they were essentially setting Sloane up like she'd done to them, but it couldn't be helped. What Sloane had done was infinitely worse. Hell, if Frankie hadn't been the type of person she was and asked Evan point-blank if they'd done the shit Sloane accused them of, then Evan really would be sitting behind bars. But she'd believed them, especially when Evan had reluctantly opened up about what they knew of Sloane. It felt really, *really* good to have Frankie's trust despite, well, all of Evan's past attempts at trying to sabotage her business.

Evan eyed the fire escape in the rear of Frankie's building warily, took a deep breath, and jumped onto the ladder. *Shit, don't fall. That's all I need.* Heights and Evan did not mix. It didn't help that the fire escape was made for someone much taller. And after going down it months ago to sneak into the trunk of Frankie's car, Evan still had intimate knowledge of just how "slippery when wet" the ladder could be. Trust that if there had been time to come up with a greater plan, it would have been taken.

The weather had worked in their favor, keeping the steel frame as slick-free as possible, so Evan had no issue ascending the rungs to the small landing above. When they reached the living room window, Evan checked their surroundings once more before placing their palms against the glass and sliding it open. They grinned, supremely glad they'd hashed the details out earlier. "Easy fucking peasy," they said, carefully climbing through the window one leg at a time. They landed on Frankie's soft decorative rug, turning around again to relock the window.

Something hard hit them from behind, slamming Evan's small frame into the window. Their forehead shattered the glass, and Evan's vision dimmed.

Then everything went black.

"Who the fuck doesn't own a dining room chair?" Evan heard as they slowly came to. They were being dragged across the floor by the scruff of the neck, and didn't need to see the intruder's face to know it was Cecil. Evan groaned, the familiar metallic taste of blood reaching them as they licked their lips. It was leaking from somewhere, but Evan wasn't sure where yet. Their nose, maybe, or their head. Every inch of them hurt in varying degrees.

"Lemme go," Evan slurred, weakly batting Cecil away. Cecil grabbed their arm and gave it a sharp twist. A bone snapped, and Evan cried out in sheer agony.

"I should've known I couldn't count on a piece of shit like you," Cecil grunted, hoisting Evan's limp body up off the ground. Dizziness and pain washed over Evan, and when they blinked away the spots in their vision, blood trickled into their left eye.

"Frankie ..." Evan moaned out, vaguely aware she would be due back soon. Fuck, there was no way to warn her ...

"Don't worry, that bitch is gonna get the surprise of a lifetime," Cecil thundered into Evan's ear. One at a time, he grabbed Evan's arms and shackled them to the bondage frame. When the injured one was raised above their head, their stomach clenching was the only warning Evan got before they threw up.

"Disgusting," Cecil spat, and drove his fist into Evan's gut. As they gasped for air and fought the urge to puke again, remnants of the past crept over Evan's semi-conscious mind. Striking Evan had always been one of Cecil's favorite pastimes while Evan was growing up.

"And fucking my son's killer? How very predictable of you, you disloyal fucking inbreed."

Strained laughter slipped out past Evan's bloodied lips, Cecil's ugly mug finally coming into view. "Have you ... looked in the mirror? Caleb took after Mom, thank fuck."

Another hard punch to the stomach. Evan's mouth watered as they gagged, and this time, they couldn't stop their body's natural urge.

"You make me sick," Cecil sneered as Evan's vomit landed close to his boots. "I dunno how you escaped the cops, but this works. I'll take care of you and that kinky bitch."

"She's gonna ... kick your ass," Evan said, grinning through pain and nausea.

"Oh, I'm looking forward to it," Cecil said, and pulled a folding knife from his back pocket. Flicking it open, a cruel smile crossed his face as he met Evan's eyes. Then he launched forward, stabbing the blade into Evan's side. They screamed as more white-hot pain sliced through their flesh. The living room tilted sideways once more, and as Evan lost consciousness, they heard Cecil's voice.

"It's about time she fought a real man again."

CHAPTER 40

Frankie

THE BULLET WHIZZED PAST Frankie, almost clipping her ear, and landed in the brick behind her. She dove for cover, not waiting for a second attempt. "Cecil, I'm guessing?" she called out, her pulse thumping loudly in her head as she crawled into the kitchen. The faint, pain-filled moan from Evan made Frankie's heart sore. "Baby, I'm here! Hold on for me, okay?"

Another shot rang out, the acrid odor of gunpowder trickling over her senses like a memory she'd forgotten. She both loved and loathed the pungent scent. "'Baby'," Cecil sneered. Another shot was fired, this one shattering the vase in the entryway. "You two disgust me."

Like you're one to talk, asshole.

"What's with your family striking first and asking questions later?" Frankie panted, reaching up and blindly searching her counter for a knife. She had a gun, but it was locked away in a safe in her bedroom.

"No questions. I just want you dead." Cecil sounded too close for comfort, and he had Frankie cornered. "Don't bother looking for a weapon, either. I threw 'em out before you got here." He laughed, a cringe-worthy, boisterous sound that raised Frankie's hackles.

Celebrating before the win. Pathetic.

"F-Frankie …" Evan moaned again. Fear had overtaken them, Frankie could hear it in their voice. And yet she couldn't get to them. *I have to end this.*

Frankie took a trembling breath, her knees quaking as she got to her feet, hands in the air. "And here I thought you'd want to play with me a bit first," she boasted, silently praying Cecil took the bait. "Evan talked you up, about how you like a little torture now and then. Surely you won't just shoot and be done?"

"Stay right there or I'll put a bullet in that pretty face," Cecil warned, his wide frame stiffening as Frankie came into view. Her eyes flared a fraction as she faced him head-on. Cecil was a *big* man. Not in a "so wide that he couldn't fit through the window he'd no doubt crawled through" way, but in a "several inches taller than she was with a build like Dwayne Johnson" way. *Fuck him, I've fought bigger.*

Cecil waved the gun in her direction. "Get into the bedroom. I saw handcuffs on the bed."

Frankie's breath caught but she did as he instructed. At least in there, they'd be safely away from Evan. "Not on the bed. Attached to the bed," she managed to say, and half a dozen ways she could subdue him while restrained on her back began to form. If she could get her legs wrapped around his—

"Get a move on," Cecil snapped, shoving Frankie. He was a lot closer than she'd anticipated. It was humorous how often a criminal with a gun assumed they had the upper hand.

Frankie spun around and disarmed him before he'd registered what happened. "No, I don't think so. How about you get on the bed? I'll cuff you and then call the police. I'm on a roll today, what's one more?"

Cecil's smile was full and missing a couple of teeth. He reached up and slowly removed a pack of cigarettes from his jacket. He lit one, taking a long drag. "Not gonna happen, ya dumb bitch. Not 'til I get a reason for what you did."

Frankie scowled, and then, in what felt like one of those slow-motion scenes in the movies, she watched in horror as Cecil flicked the lit cigarette onto the bed. The sheets began smoking immediately, and the distraction cost her. Cecil tackled her to the floor, and Frankie winced as a fist got her hard in the ribs. The gun slipped out of her grasp, skittering across the floor as she and Cecil traded punches.

Cecil got his hands around her throat and was laughing again. "You're gonna die tonight, copper. And my wife's traitor of a kid along with you, if my dagger hasn't done the job yet."

Frankie's heart stuttered. Evan had been stabbed? Her mind flashed back to the blood she'd seen. Fear slipped into her veins, but instead of letting it control her, Frankie focused on the rage burning a small inferno inside her. She grabbed hold of Cecil's face with her fingernails and jabbed her thumbs into his eyes as hard as she could. It worked to slacken his grip on her throat, and Frankie wrapped her legs around his waist in a grappling move, locking him in place. She tried flipping them over, but his arms still had too much range and ended back at her throat again. He was choking her, and as she stared up into a pair of feral eyes, she saw the gleam of flame illuminating in them.

My bed.

Her bed was on fire!

"Ack ..." Frankie struggled to breathe. She batted at his arms weakly. Her strength was waning, and her vision became spottier with each gasp and gurgle. The fire's heat felt closer than before as Frankie started to lose consciousness, and all she could think of was Evan. *Please, let them get away ...*

Bang!

A loud gunshot pierced the air. Frankie blinked back to awareness, gasping still. She wheezed, sucking in greedy gulps of air as the grip around her throat vanished. For an incoherent moment, she thought Cecil had shot her, but then he fell on top of her.

"F-Frankie." Her blurry gaze flew to where Evan stood a few feet away, their gun hand noticeably shaking. Their other arm dangled limply by their side. "Is he dead?"

Pushing down her own discomfort and pain, Frankie jumped into action, shoving Cecil off her even as flames licked up and down her bed, getting closer to the floor. She checked his pulse, croaking out, "Not yet." Grabbing Cecil by his jacket collar, Frankie felt half out of it as she pulled him from the room and yanked the door closed. Then she reached for Evan, pressing a gentle kiss on their busted lips. "Watch him, okay?"

She left them in the hallway to grab the fire extinguisher from the stairwell, trusting that Evan could handle it if Cecil woke up.

"I called 911," they said as Frankie ran back into the apartment. Tears and smoke burned her eyes and throat, but she gave Evan a grateful nod.

"Good work, baby. Now stay back."

As she entered her burning bedroom, Frankie hoped it wasn't too late to salvage most of it.

"Are you sure you're alright?" she whispered hours later. Cecil had been taken away long ago, statements were given, and then Frankie and Evan went to the hospital to have their injuries looked at. It was now nearing noon, and they were both exhausted and sore, Evan more so. Frankie had helped them in the shower and tucked them into their bed. Her room was temporarily off-limits as it aired out from the fire.

Frankie got upset every time she looked at Evan's wounds, angry that she hadn't been there to protect them in the first place, and devastated that they'd been almost killed by a man who should have been a father to Evan. Now, her little thief sported a broken arm and stitches on their forehead and side. The dagger had entered muscle and tissue and missed anything vital, thankfully. Still ... "The doctor said your concussion requires lots of rest and to keep that cast in a sling."

"I am, and I will." Evan was pale, though, and their jaw was clenched. They were clearly in pain, and the permitted aceta-minophen was doing little to help. It was driving Frankie insane that she couldn't make it better.

"I can't believe you shot him." She gathered Evan's hand in hers. It hurt like a bitch to talk, but she didn't care. Frankie would take the heavy bruising and sore throat and neck any day if it meant Evan was still there with her. She brought their hand to her lips for a soft kiss. "You protected me. I didn't think I could love you anymore, and yet ..."

"I told you I loved you," Evan said, as if that explained everything.

Frankie huffed a tired laugh, climbing into bed beside them. Her throat still ached from the fight and the smoke inhalation, but she and Evan were safe. Despite the bedroom renovation that would now need to happen, her pub and apartment were still intact.

Snuggling into them, she rested her head on Evan's chest and draped her arm across their stomach. Tilting her face toward Evan's, Frankie kissed them gently. "I love you too, my good boi. And I'm glad you're safe." The way Evan had earlier described their escape from the bondage frame had been almost comical. It was good that the self-release latch had come in handy.

"Ditto." Evan's newly-taped glasses slipped down on their nose as they yawned. They'd been broken at some point during the struggle with Cecil.

"Go to sleep now. I'll be here when you wake up."

"Mm-hmm."

Frankie watched as Evan drifted off, but didn't move from her position. It felt wondrous being so close, a small act she feared she wouldn't get again when she'd come across Evan strapped to the A-frame and bloody. So much had gone wrong in the last twenty-four hours that for just a moment, she wanted to breathe Evan in and thank her lucky stars nothing worse had happened.

The chime of her doorbell pulled Frankie from her thoughts. She groaned, not wanting to leave Evan's comforting warmth just yet.

"Maybe they'll leave if I ignore it." She traced her index finger along Evan's collarbone. The pub wasn't opening until five today, so Frankie wasn't sure who could be gracing her with their presence. She would have preferred to close completely today, but she had staff to pay regardless. Might as well make a little income to help with that.

The doorbell rang again.

"Why can't we be left alone?" Frankie grumbled, slipping reluctantly out of Evan's bed. The breeze from the open windows made her shiver, so she ducked into her ruined bedroom for a hoodie. She threw it on, walking to the door, and grimacing at the stench of smoke lingering on the material. The whole bedroom stank of charred satin and memory foam. Thankfully, it hadn't travelled to the rest of the apartment.

She squinted through the peephole in her door and sighed at the two figures in the stairwell. Unlocking the deadbolts, Frankie squared her haggard shoulders and pulled open the door. "I'm not really fit for company."

"Hello to you, too," McCoy said, her eyes widening comically at the state Frankie was in, but she didn't look so good herself. She was dressed in sweats and a wrinkled jacket, sporting deep bags under her eyes and an unruly, loose topknot hairstyle.

Sawyer, who was much more put together, placed a hand on her girlfriend's shoulder when she attempted to waltz inside the apartment. She met Frankie's tired gaze. "Are you and Evan okay? We came as soon as we heard."

"How..." Frankie shook her head. It didn't matter how they'd heard. It was just so good that they'd cared enough to show up. She swallowed, stepping into the stairwell with them and closing the door behind her. "Let's talk downstairs. Evan just fell asleep."

"I don't think I've ever seen you dressed so casually. I like it," McCoy commented as they descended the stairs. Frankie moved a little slower, still stiff from her run-in with Cecil.

Sawyer tsked. "Darling, you're lucky I find your constant flirting endearing."

"I wasn't—" McCoy started as Frankie punched in the keypad to get into the pub from her stairwell. From her periphery, she saw one of Sawyer's black eyebrows arch up, and a sheepish chuckle left McCoy. "I possibly was flirting, but unaware."

"Mm-hmm, better."

"I can't even find the energy to add my two cents," Frankie said, gesturing to the empty barstools. "Have a seat. Coffee?"

"Please," Sawyer and McCoy replied in unison. As Frankie set out to make coffee, they filled her in on Sloane.

"We decided not to post her bail, at least not yet. She could use a few days to de-stress in there," Sawyer said. Her facial expression told Frankie she'd be fine if Sloane was put away for a while.

"I don't know how it happened. She looks like she completely lost it, Frankie." Worry coated McCoy's exclamation, perking Frankie out of her daze. Memories of the night before returned. It felt like a lifetime ago.

"She did. I was there." Setting three mugs on the counter, Frankie carried the coffee pot over and filled each one, gently admitting, "It wasn't great to witness, but it doesn't excuse what she did. Sloane fucked me over. For months, by the sound of it, possibly years. I have no idea how much, nothing major until recently. Still, she needs to pay for what she's done."

Sawyer pulled a notebook from her purse and set it down in front of Frankie. "We found this in her bedroom. It looks like a ledger."

Frankie nodded. "Evan told me about it. Sloane kept track of all her bets."

"That's not all." McCoy flipped through the book until she'd almost reached the end, scanning the pages before offering it up for Frankie to see. "Looks like she kept track of everything she took as well."

The amount was less than Frankie feared, but still she scoffed. "More than she could ever pay back."

"Perhaps, but," Sawyer tossed a quick glance at her lover and then looked back at Frankie, blowing out a deep breath, "I'm willing to cover a portion of it. To help make amends, but also to tide you over until the insurance is sorted out. We both know that could take months."

The offer was too generous, something Frankie was certain McCoy had pleaded with Sawyer about. Instead of answering Sawyer right away, she addressed the younger woman. "You know you can't sweep in and make everything right for your sister, don't you? Even if I could excuse the financial loss, she crossed so many lines, McCoy. She framed her own friend and lied time and time again. I could never trust her again."

"She needs help, not to go to prison," McCoy argued. "Therapy, meetings to help with gambling, *something*."

Therapy. Shit. With all the excitement, Frankie had forgotten all about her appointment the day before. *Fucking Sloane.*

"Look, I am tired beyond reason. Excuse the fuck out of me for not caring about Sloane at the moment, but I can't do all of this right now. I just want to soak in a hot bubble bath and order takeout in my freezing cold apartment with its broken window and equally broken boifriend."

"Your window's broken? Why didn't you say? I can try to fix it for you." McCoy started to move, but Frankie held her hand up.

"I know you need to feel purposeful, but you're not listening. Maybe Sawyer can explain it better right now." Frankie shut the coffee pot off and headed toward the stairs without a backward glance. "Make sure to lock up when you're done."

As she was entering the stairwell, she heard McCoy say, "Sweetheart, what'd I do?"

CHAPTER 41

Evan

MOM: I'M DOING BETTER Ev. Thanks for asking. I miss you.

Evan: I miss you too. I want to try to plan a visit. Maybe I can take the bus there.

Evan set their phone on the table and smiled at the thought. It would be so good to see their mother. Now that Cecil wasn't in the way of the visitation, perhaps she'd get better and eventually come home. But what home? Toronto, with no one who cared enough to locate her? Or would a move closer to Evan be in the books?

"Talk about getting ahead of yourself." They picked their plate up one-handed to take to the sink. Still, the excitement over the possibility had been floating around since Cecil was arrested three weeks ago. They could be a family again. A *real* family. On top of the wonderful family Evan had found right there at O'Rourke's.

Their cell phone chirped on the kitchen booth table, indicating a new notification awaited. Evan took a moment first to fill the dishwasher with the supper dishes, knowing Frankie didn't like them sitting for too long in the sink. Thinking of their lover pulled a wider smile from Evan. Living with the femme, being loved and desired by her, was more than Evan could have imagined for their life. It had been a rocky three weeks for them both, from overcoming Sloane's betrayal as well as their injuries. Evan had been the one slowly bleeding out, but it was Frankie who suffered the longest. Cecil choking her had inadvertently dredged up a lot of buried memories, ones Frankie hadn't been ready to face. And while Evan's cast had offered immediate protection for their broken arm, it would take much longer for therapy to do the same for Frankie.

But she's tough. More than anyone realizes.

Evan's phone went off again. Making their way back to the kitchen booth, they unlocked their cell to see who had texted. Two sat unread, one from Evan's mother and one from Andy.

Mom: Can your girlfriend drive you? I'd love to meet her.

Andy: Claire wants to have you and Frankie over for dinner some night. If the boss can hire enough replacements LOL.

"Ugh, ain't that the truth?" The resumes were coming in, but Frankie was having a slight issue with trusting anyone enough to get past the hiring stage. She'd already had new surveillance put in, an updated safe for her office, and a quality lock set installed on her office door. Evan didn't have the heart to tell her they could pick that one too. Let naivete take her over, at least for another week. Perhaps Evan would shop around for a keypad entry and surprise Frankie one day.

Another notification popped up as Evan was trying to listen to the previous one.

Andy: P.S. I know I shouldn't, but I miss Sloane. In case I never said, I'm sorry she hurt you, bro.

Evan's jaw tightened. Sloane had been a shelved topic with Frankie, but maybe it was time to change that. The truth was, Andy wasn't alone in that feeling. As much as Sloane had wronged both

Evan and Frankie, Evan missed her too. It didn't have to make sense for it to be sincere.

Choosing to reply to their mom's message first, Evan went into the thread and hit the audio record button. "She runs a pub and is busy most of the time. But I'll ask." Leah Landry had been so cut off from life while Cecil had been taking control that she had no idea who Frankie truly was. Evan had zero plans to tell her, either. They might have been able to overcome her history with Caleb, but Evan didn't expect their mom to as well.

They decided not to reply to Andy just yet. The laundry still needed to be folded and the bathroom cleaned and doing it all with one working arm was a pain enough not to get distracted by text messages. For the first time ever, Evan had been invited out by Coy and the other friends who made up the Fab Five. They had no plans to replace Sloane in her circle, as they were certain Coy and the others didn't either, but the olive branch was a nice touch. In a twisted way, Sloane had brought them closer together. Everyone was worried about her, but that was muddled into other, more complicated feelings. A little hate, maybe, a lot of confusion, and hurt. Sloane not trusting Evan enough to ask for help was a plausible excuse. After all, they hadn't known one another for that long. But Sloane hadn't asked anyone for help. People she'd known and loved for years had been left entirely in the dark. Some, like Coy, weren't digesting that too well.

Evan met the Fab Five in the pub an hour later. Taunya let out an appreciative whistle as they approached their usual corner booth. "I'm loving the new glasses." The rest at the table nodded in agreement, offering praise and generally being a notch too enthusiastic to be considered "normal". The scene was a bit tense for Evan, but them hanging out together without Sloane was uncharted territory. It was natural to be nervous, right?

"Got you a beer," Coy said, sliding a mug across the table to Evan. The corner of her mouth tilted up. "Frankie said it's your favorite."

Evan bowed their head. "Appreciate it. How's things?"

"It's weird seeing you two face to face, being friendly." Abi glanced between them, her glacier blue eyes bright and full of mischief. "I don't know why, but I keep expecting, like, a pissing contest or something."

"Kind of like how it was with the barber, you mean?" Coy quipped back, laughing when Abi threw a fry her way. She turned to Evan. "Tess, Abs' girlfriend—"

"Fiancée—"

"*Fiancée*," Coy corrected, catching another french fry sailing across the table at her. She popped it in her mouth, chewing as she continued, "was too shy and uber jealous of my confidence around the ladies, if you know what I mean. Abi's my best friend, I was trying to support her—"

"Trying to get in her pants, you mean," Krystal, the fourth friend in Sloane's Fab Five circle, piped up. She was often less talkative, but by the looks of things, what little she did say packed a punch.

Evan joined in the laughter, loving how they were all able to tease each other yet still hold a massive amount of respect. As they sipped their beer, Abi and Coy took turns replaying the wedding party events from a year and a half before. And after, the conversation shifted to exactly what went on in Frankie's apartment to result in Evan being in a sling. They'd decided right then and there that they didn't want to be Frankie's age and not have anyone besides her know the truth. And so Evan shared what they could about that night, saying their abusive father had come for them. Which was the truth. Cecil had planned to kill Evan along with Frankie. But the rest of it? Evan didn't think anyone, save them and Frankie, needed to know. Speaking of …

Evan caught sight of the gorgeous woman working behind the bar; long, flowing brown curls with red and blonde highlights and dressed in the same white striped suit she'd worn the first evening they'd met. Although they couldn't see because the counter was in the way, Evan knew a pair of black, open-toed heels occupied her feet with blood red nail polish on her toes that they'd watched her put on that morning. Inappropriate footwear, but Evan had learned long ago that Frankie O'Rourke did as she pleased and got what she wanted. According to her, the moment she'd laid eyes on Evan, she'd wanted them. It was only a matter of time before she'd turned that desire into reality. And now?

Their gazes locked onto one another from across the dimly lit pub. A slow smile started on Frankie's beautiful face. She crooked her finger in Evan's direction, beckoning them over.

Evan couldn't help but smile back. Daddy Frankie wanted them. Who were they to deny their femme anything? "Excuse me," they told Coy and the others. "I'll be right back."

"Grab us another round while you're up!" Coy called after Evan. They answered with a thumbs up, knowing they would, because why not? That's what friends did. They took turns buying rounds and sharing stories.

I have friends, real friends. I've got a girlfriend who would die to protect me. Family. It's all Evan had ever truly wanted.

They took the only available stool at the bar, and it wasn't long before the bartender approached.

"Hey, are you waiting for a table, or is here fine?"

Evan looked up at her, surprised. And then laughed, catching on. "Here's good," they replied, thinking of their conversation months ago. "Can I get a whiskey? Straight and on the rocks."

"Depends," Frankie teased with a wag of her eyebrows. She placed one hand on her hip as if she were sizing them up. "You have ID?"

"For real?" Evan's mouth fell open. Damn, when their Daddy played, she didn't mess around. With an exaggerated sigh, Evan reached into their back pocket to retrieve their wallet. "I'm twenty-four next week," they said, assuming Frankie expected them to still reenact that first night.

"Anyone who looks under thirty, I'm afraid. Thanks." Frankie accepted the Toronto driver's license, which reminded Evan they needed to change the address. She examined the card before handing it back to them. Now both hands were on her hips.

Shit.

"It says your birthday has already passed and needs renewal. It's illegal to use an expired ID, you know."

Evan smirked. It was becoming increasingly harder to keep a straight face.

"Is that so? What are you, a cop?"

Frankie leaned over the counter, not seeming to care about getting her white suit dirty with spilled alcohol and stopped inches from Evan's face.

"No," she said, grinning widely now. Fuck, Evan loved her. They loved everything about her. "But I do own a few sets of handcuffs. If you want, we could play cops and robbers for a night. What do you say, my good boi?"

Epilogue

Frankie

Tonight was the night. It had to be. Too much time had passed in their relationship for Frankie not to take the leap.

"Diane thinks you're ready, so just go slow," she muttered, checking herself out in the mirror. Even with the low hum of her bathroom fan, Frankie could hear the muted conversation in the living room between Evan and their mother, Leah Landry. In the past ten months, she'd gotten comfortable enough with the older woman that leaving her and Evan alone to chat didn't make her feel like a bad hostess. Leah was a wonderfully eccentric woman whom Frankie adored, but besides their mutual love of Evan, they had little in common. Frankie found her attention with the older Landry waning at the best of times, but tonight especially.

She pulled the drawer open on the vanity, retrieving her rouge lipstick. She puckered her lips, reapplying the makeup as she held a steady gaze with her reflection. Evan might not know it yet, but once they got Leah out the door for the night, Frankie planned to take the terrifying next step in their relationship. For the second time that she could remember, she'd have sex without a whip or restraint in sight. If Evan would have her, then Frankie wanted to know what it felt like to be touched, to have pleasure pulled from every longing facet of her body by her love's careful ministrations.

And she would not panic. Surely, enough time and therapy sessions had passed for that not to be an issue. *Diane thinks I'm ready, and so do I.* Frankie took a deep breath, returned her lipstick to its drawer, and left the bathroom.

"That one took me ten hours to complete. I already sold several prints of it, but so far no one's grabbed up the original. It's worth too much to just give away, you know?" Evan was telling Leah as Frankie entered the decorated living room. They were lounging on the sectional, Leah on one end, with the large coffee table sitting between them. Evan was proudly showing off one of their favorite illustrations to date, of a woman wearing an open blouse, lacey lingerie beneath, bent over and straddling a lover. The model's breasts—*Frankie's* breasts—were practically falling out of the snug bra. In the last ten months, she'd found pieces of herself used as the inspiration for Evan's art on several occasions. Her hands, strong and calloused as they sometimes were, or her lips made to appear full and sensuous, her thighs or the curve of her ass, both naked and clothed, depending on the illustration. Frankie didn't mind. It was rather flattering, and if she was honest, she'd rather it be her intimate features on display as opposed to Evan bringing random women home to model for them. Just the thought raised her hackles.

She only hoped Leah had enough sense not to comment if she recognized the woman Evan was so proudly showing off. Nestling in beside Evan on the sofa, Frankie didn't miss their look of surprise as she slid an arm around their shoulders. She couldn't blame them. It wasn't too often that she got affectionate in front of Leah. It might be ridiculous, but if Leah was ever made aware, there would be a laundry list of things she'd no doubt despise Frankie for. If she could help it, overt displays of PDA with Leah's only living child wouldn't be one of them.

"It's a gorgeous piece, honey. They all are." Leah smiled, picking up another of Evan's illustrations. This one was drawn at the park during the fall. It was done in black ink, but the falling leaves and the person wearing a jacket as they walked their dog painted the scenery where color hadn't. "I think you've really blossomed as an artist, even just in the few months since I last saw you."

"Thanks, Mom. I started practicing with calligraphy brush ink, and it's like a whole other level." Frankie didn't need to see Evan's face to know they were blushing. They still had a long way to go when it came to their artistic confidence, but Leah was right. Evan had come a long way skill-wise from the sketches they'd been making when she first met her little thief. Frankie didn't cut into the conversation with her input, but Evan knew how she felt. By now she must have been their biggest fan. Their apartment was proof of that fact, as a good portion of the walls held at least one of Evan's art pieces.

She squeezed their shoulder in silent support, glancing around at the many Christmas decorations Leah had helped them with two days before. Frankie couldn't remember the last time she'd felt remotely festive; three Christmases ago, maybe, before her big fight with Auntie B. This holiday season was light-years away from the last in everything that mattered to Frankie. She was closer to her family than ever; she was sharing her home with the love of her life, a submissive she'd only dared to dream of before, and Leah was once again in Evan's life. They were free of Cecil's poison.

"Well, I better get going," Leah mentioned a while later, before helping herself to yet another of the cookies Sawyer had gifted them with. She moaned her appreciation, bits of crumb slipping down her sweater as she got to her feet. "The Holiday is showing at nine, and I don't want to miss it. Right in the comfort of my hotel room."

Frankie suppressed a smile as Leah bent down for another cookie. Sawyer and her daughter, Bree, were excellent bakers, she'd give them that. "Would you like to take the rest back with you?" she asked, standing as well. Evan was close on her heels.

"Oh no, I couldn't. Well, maybe I'll take one." The small woman swiped up another two, jerkily shoving them into a napkin before they disappeared into her purse. In the months since she'd known her, it was rare for Frankie to find Leah not munching on something. Evan sent her an apologetic look, but she patted their hand in reassurance. Leah's eccentricity didn't bother her one bit. If anything, she considered it endearing. She was glad Leah was doing well again. Visiting her in the hospital, in a whole other province, had been hard on Evan. Especially at first when they'd had to explain their broken arm.

"Thanks for helping with the shopping today. Merry Christmas, Mom," Evan said when they were at the door. They wrapped Leah up in a hug, kissing her cheek. "See you tomorrow."

"Are you sure I can't drive you? Or I can call an Uber," Frankie offered, although she'd much prefer the second option. If it took much longer to get Evan alone, she feared she'd chicken out of the whole thing.

"I'll be fine, honey." Leah opened her arms to Frankie, pulling her into a gentle embrace. Her hugs weren't warm and safe like Auntie B's, but considering they were closer in age than she knew Leah preferred, it was a welcoming peace offering Frankie had come to expect. When Leah released her, she brandished a knife from her purse with a smirk. "It's only a few blocks, and I've got this. Us Landry/Deroche bunch are tough cookies, right, baby?" She directed the question to Evan, reaching out to gently pat their cheek with the tips of her fingers.

And then she was disappearing over the apartment's threshold and down the stairs, leaving Frankie and Evan to stare mutely after her. Finally, Frankie closed the door and relocked it, huffing a soft laugh as she glanced at Evan. Her heart did the usual skip, dance, and melt it usually did whenever she saw them, but she didn't let it control her. She probably would never be a hyper-romantic woman who gushed over their lover all the time, but Evan knew exactly how she felt.

"Your mother is quite something, little thief." It was hard to believe she'd spent a year in a psych ward, though Frankie had her suspicions that Cecil might have had something to do with it. "And I know you'd rather she stay with us, but I'm still not over her walking in on us the last visit. We need space."

Evan let out the cutest giggle. Just bringing it up had them blushing. "To be fair, it was in the living room."

"Exactly." Frankie smiled, wrapping her arms around Evan's waist. She rested her forehead against theirs, adding softly. "I clearly can't control myself when it comes to you if I forgot your mother was asleep in the apartment."

"It's okay. I'm just glad she's close by this Christmas." Evan tilted their face up, catching Frankie's lips in a soft kiss. Then, almost as an afterthought, they pulled away to frown. "You think she'll be fine walking home?"

"Are you kidding? Did you see that knife?" Frankie rubbed Evan's back in a soothing gesture. "If Leah is anything like you, then I have no doubt."

Now that they were in each other's lives again, Frankie knew Evan spent a good amount of time worrying about their mother. Funny how that happened. It was the same for Frankie and her uncle. She'd rarely thought of her family in the last few years. Work had often taken precedence in her mind. Now that she was speaking and visiting with them on a regular basis again, Eamon's condition was often on her mind.

Evan disappeared to take a shower, muttering that they still smelled like the deep fryer from their shift at the pub earlier. While Frankie liked to keep it open over the holidays, she shortened the hours and reduced the menu by half to better accommodate her staff. Now that Evan was in her life, she'd made a point to schedule enough people so that she wouldn't need to make an appearance at all tomorrow.

As Evan showered, Frankie busied herself with tidying up the dishes and straightening up the living room. There was something about the original brick walls on display, and the classic, uneven, wooden flooring of the apartment that always gave Frankie a sense of peace. Or maybe it was the constant ticking of Uncle Eamon's antique grandfather clock that, after all these years, still held the power to lull her to sleep. Since Evan moved in, almost a year to the date, Frankie had a feeling they had a lot to do with the serene space.

Several of Evan's art supplies were in a scattered mess on the workspace Frankie had provided for them months ago. Cups with water and brushes sat on the windowsill of the bay window overlooking Davie St. A contented smile graced Frankie's lips as she carried the used supplies to the kitchen sink. She could appreciate a good distraction when she was met with one. Cleaning helped ease the anxiety over her plans for intimacy that night. If her therapist believed she was ready, then getting vulnerable with Evan was something she was prepared to do. Her thirty-ninth birthday had come and gone already, and she still didn't know what it was like to be touched by a lover. Not the skin-on-skin vulnerability that McCoy had occasionally pushed for when they were together. Frankie had never loved or trusted the former playgirl enough to try, she knew that now. But with Evan ...

The bathroom door clicked open, steam from Evan's shower billowing out around them as they stepped into the hallway in just a towel. Frankie forgot what she was doing, her gaze heating as she tracked their movements to the bedroom. Desire tightened low in her belly. Desire and *concern*.

"I have a surprise for you," she said the moment Evan returned, now dressed in an insulated long-sleeve shirt and pajama pants.

Evan came into the living room, their nose wrinkling with a dour expression. "I thought we were waiting for Christmas morning to open gifts. I only got you one."

"It's a surprise, not a gift," Frankie corrected, but then heaved a sigh, winking through her uneasiness. "Though I suppose if you're a good boi you can unwrap it like one."

"Oh, I can be a very good boi," her little thief bragged, excitement making them rock back and forth on their heels.

"Okay, great. Would you like a drink first? A beer, glass of bourbon?" she asked Evan, moving past them to make a beeline for the kitchen. Her fingers trembled as she retrieved glasses from the cupboard.

They trailed slowly behind her, the silence loud in the small space. For several long seconds, the only noise came from the two tumblers being set on the counter and the sound of ice clinking into the bottom of each one.

"You're nervous," Evan said finally, wonder in their voice. "Why didn't I see it before?"

"I am *not* nervous." Frankie didn't *get* nervous. No way, not about sex and never about Evan. Now fear, that was a whole other beast that bested her from time to time. Tonight, she feared she'd accidentally hurt Evan, either physically or emotionally. She feared that even if Evan was able to bury any part of themself safely between her thighs, that she'd realize she was too fucked up from the past to orgasm. What if she could only come on her terms and not from a partner pleasuring her?

Evan approached carefully, watching her like she was a skittish rabbit. They reached for the tumbler in her hand, setting it back down on the counter. Tears pricked Frankie's eyes as Evan murmured, "If it's okay with you, Daddy, I'd rather receive this surprise with a clear head. Alcohol and deep conversations don't mix, remember? I'll assume that whatever you plan to give me, the same rules apply. Can I make you tea instead?"

"No. Thank you, baby, but no." *No more waiting*. Evan had waited long enough. Frankie rested her forehead against theirs, closing her eyes and inhaling their fresh shower scent. "I want ... I want you, little thief. In every way. All the ways. Tonight, I want to feel you against me, your lips on my skin, your fingers and tongue inside me. Do ... do you still want that?"

Unadulterated shock came over Evan for maybe five excruciating seconds, and then their face split into the widest grin Frankie had ever seen on her lover. "Fuck yes, so long as it means you're still my Domme. But are you sure?"

Frankie gave them a tentative nod. "I'll allow you to top me, but I'm still in charge."

Evan nodded enthusiastically. "I wouldn't want it any other way."

"Good then." Frankie took their hand, leading them to the bedroom. This wasn't something she wanted to happen in their playroom. She paused just before reaching the bed. "You can start by undressing me."

"Okay, umm … I hate to jinx this, but like, why now? And will this be a scene like we always do?" Evan peered up at her, looking unsure as well now. "I just don't really know—"

"Not a scene, no." Slowly, Frankie shook her head. "I want to be with you like two vanilla people coming together for the first time. I never have."

If anything, Evan seemed even more unsure at her comment. They lifted her hand in theirs, kissing the back softly before placing her palm against their cheek. "Okay, but … we aren't two vanilla people. *You* aren't."

She was damaged, that was what they weren't saying. Frankie took a deep, ragged breath, pulling out of Evan's grasp to slump down onto the end of her bed. She wiped at her eyes, unable to look at them. "You're right. It was a stupid idea. I just want to be normal for you, little thief."

"You *are* normal. And you're a rape survivor, Frankie. Give yourself some fucking grace."

"But …" Frankie bit her lip, trying hard not to linger on that godawful word. She hated it being out in the open like that. It was much easier to refer to what happened as an assault, or the "incident". "B-being with me comes with so many rules, all the time. You must be sick of it."

"I happen to love your rules," Evan said quietly. Their small hands landed on hers, prying them away from her eyes. "And I love you just the way you are, whether you're paddling my ass and restraining me to the bondage frame as Daddy, or if you're sharing a meal with me and entertaining my mom as Frankie."

"What are ... what're you doing?" Frankie's lower lip trembled as Evan lowered themself to the floor. They didn't reply, just gave her a small smile and lifted one of her feet onto their thigh. She watched with rapt attention as each of her socks was removed, and then Evan pressed loving kisses along the arch of both soles. Their touch always felt comforting on her feet, and tonight was no exception. Contented tingles danced along the sensitive skin.

"I'm going to undress you, just like you wanted," Evan explained, getting off the floor to give Frankie a kiss. Their eyes met. "But you're still in charge, Daddy. I'm still yours to use as you wish, and tonight, you want me to pleasure you."

"Yes, that's right." Frankie swallowed. "And ... and the color system, safe words in general, are practiced between both Domme and sub, so it's completely normal if I use one from time to time."

"Exactly." Evan twirled a lock of her hair around their finger. The other hand, the one with the previously broken arm, began clumsily working on her blazer buttons. "One of the first rules you taught me was the importance of safe words. And consent. Do you still consent to this?"

"Yes. Undress me, little thief."

"It'd be my honor." Evan held her gaze as they removed her blazer. Frankie's mouth felt dry. A lump lodged halfway up her throat, but still, she didn't look away. There was something hypnotic with the way Evan watched her watching them, as if they were counting her shaky exhales with each blouse button. Frankie's stomach tightened as the sleeves were slowly pulled down her arms. One got caught on the bracelet around her wrist, and a tense chuckle escaped her.

"You're gorgeous," Evan said, their gaze on the quick rise and fall of her heavy breasts. "What do you want me to take off next?"

"My pants, my good boi." Frankie's teeth sank into her bottom lip as Evan dropped to their knees once more. Ugh, that might have been her favorite position to see them in. She was acutely aware of the small tufts of air passing through her lips the closer Evan got, but she forced herself to lean back on her elbows and remain still as they undid her belt buckle, waist clasp, and lowered the zipper. There was absolutely nothing about what Evan was doing that was in any way familiar to her assault. They were painstakingly gentle, for one. She was clearheaded and not drugged, for two. And Evan loved her. She wanted this. Hell, she was the one who initiated it! She was safe in the haven she called home and with her favorite person.

"I can hear you breathing from here, Daddy. What color are you in right now?"

Frankie blinked, Evan's blonde hair coming into focus. Behind their glasses, soft mismatched eyes watched her, waiting, and Frankie swallowed hard. "S-still green, baby." She could do this. She didn't survive all these years to now fold under the pressure. Gritting her teeth, she lifted her hips for Evan.

"I love you," they murmured, shimmying Frankie's slacks past her wide hips and down her legs. Upon her nod, they removed her underwear next, never rushing the process. When all that remained was her bra, Evan sat on their knees before her, hands folded in their lap, and waited.

Frankie cleared her throat. "You aren't rushing to touch me. Why?"

"I'm waiting for the next step, Daddy. You're in charge here. I'll sit until you decide how you want to use me."

Fuck me, was what Frankie was dying to say to them. For the first time ever, she wanted to be fucked by someone else's fingers. "Take my bra off and kiss me."

The edges of Evan's mouth curled up, and they purred out a seductive, "Yes, Daddy." Then her bra was off, tossed aside with the rest of her clothes, and Evan's lips covered hers. Frankie breathed into the kiss, aware of Evan's hands on either side of her on the bed, close but not touching. The usual addicting scent of their after-shower skin smelled off tonight, more robust somehow. Aggressive, even.

Frankie broke the kiss just before she gagged, guiding Evan's face to her naked breasts instead. "I want your lips," she panted out, "here. Tease and suckle my nipples like I know you've been dying to."

"Thank you, Daddy."

A soft, involuntary gasp left Frankie when Evan's nose made contact first. She held her breath as they nuzzled each breast before burying their face between them. Hot air and short blonde bristles tickled the over-sensitive flesh, causing goosebumps to pop up all over her arms. Speaking of arms, both Frankie's and Evan's kept firmly on the mattress.

Shouldn't we be touching or something?

When Evan looked up at her, the thought quickly fled again. "Can I lift them up to kiss them?"

Lightheaded, Frankie nodded mutely. She tilted her face up to the ceiling, breathing in and out through her nose while locking in on the faint crack lines in the plaster. Her breasts were pushed together higher on her chest, cupped by Evan's careful hands, and then Frankie was gasping as the slick sensation of their tongue coated one nipple.

Evan stilled. "Want me to stop?"

"No," Frankie heaved. "It ... it feels good." And it did. Evan's tongue making slow patterns in and out of her hoop piercing and around her nipple felt fucking amazing. Even their hands, squeezing and kneading her breasts, felt nice. She found herself studying them again, her pleasure emerging with each lick and flick. When Evan sucked her nipple into their mouth, Frankie actually moaned aloud. Desire raced along her nerve endings, shooting arousal straight to her core. Her pussy pulsed and twitched for Evan's attention.

"Baby. Ugh." Frankie's breath hitched as Evan began kissing other parts of her. The sides of her breasts, and then upwards, to her sternum and directly over the knife scar.

"I love everything about you," Evan proclaimed between kisses. Their mouth found her shoulder, and as their lips and tongue teased her, their hands left her breasts as well. Frankie's breathing increased as those hands moved up to her shoulders. Evan kissed her again, and Frankie was temporarily distracted by their teasing tongue against hers that she didn't immediately notice they'd pushed her backwards on the bed. Mismatched eyes bore into her brown ones. She saw Evan's lips move. "What's your color, Daddy?"

"Green," she ground out, blinking at the bright spots clouding her vision.

"Are you sure?"

No, no, she wasn't. The only thing she was sure of at that moment was how suffocating Evan's presence was on top of her. Pain stabbed in her chest. The air seized in her lungs, and perspiration dotted her forehead. *Panic*, she realized. She was beginning to panic. "R-red," she amended with a croak, but she had to yank the truth from her lips. Tears pricked her eyes.

Evan climbed off her immediately, and a sob left Frankie. She squeezed her eyes shut; her breaths ragged even to her own ears. "I'm sorry, I'm okay. Just ... just give me a minute. Your weight on me was a surprise."

The mattress shifted as Evan got off the bed. Their absence made the tears break free, and Frankie threw her arm over her eyes. She was better than this ... this sobbing mess. No fear, not anymore. Hadn't that been her mantra since Emily was alive?

No fear is a joke. Face it, you're a broken mess. Broken ...

The mattress dipped under Frankie again, and Evan's warm hand landed on her stiff shoulder. "You aren't broken. And if you were, I happen to love all the broken parts."

Frankie sniffled. "I figured you'd left."

"Never. Now, will you look at me? I wanna try something."

"I wouldn't blame you. You deserve a better Domme." When her bloodshot gaze fell on Evan sitting next to her, Frankie's lips parted in shock.

"I'm not interested in another Domme. I'm proud to call you Daddy Frankie." Evan gave her a shy smile, holding their hand out for her to take. It was a moment before she could peel her attention away from the completely naked body. Everything, even the binder, was gone.

"W-what're you doing?"

"Will you just lie with me? No sex, no touching parts, no pressure. Just Frankie and Evan, Daddy and her little thief, falling asleep naked beside each other. No expectations, just love."

"I've ..." Frankie swallowed and tried again. "I've never—"

"I know. Do you want to?"

Frankie gave a slow nod, her heart cracking open a little more. The intimacy she'd begun to crave was being handed to her on a silver platter. The question was, did she have the courage to take it? "Yes," she whispered. A wobbly smile appeared, and together they crawled up on the bed and pulled back the sheets. She let Evan lie down first, getting comfortable, before taking her usual place beside them. Her satin sheets felt strange against her bare skin.

"It's been a long time since I slept naked," she blurted, and cringed at how unlike her it sounded. She rolled onto her side to face Evan.

"And you don't have to tonight. It was just an idea." They smiled, reaching out to tuck a loose strand of hair behind her ear. "You're in charge, don't forget. I'll do anything you want. I just don't want you to force it, force being with me because you think it's what I want. You told me from the beginning that you were a stone top, and I was okay with that. Who cares what your aunt says? Unless it's you who's changed your mind, then why—"

"I did," Frankie interrupted, tracing her fingers along the contours of Evan's cheekbone. She shrugged, smiling a little. "I changed my mind. *You* changed me. Sometimes I crave your touch so much that I think I'll go mad without it. It's never happened with any other partner, but I want this, Evan."

"Well, okay then." Evan laughed softly, their shoulders sagging in what must have been relief. "Then we keep trying. And you keep going to therapy."

Frankie was silent for a long time, her fingers languidly trailing up and down Evan's arm. Goosebumps broke out in their wake. She scooted closer, her breath catching as their bodies pressed flushed together. Chest to breast, their tummies touching. "Is this okay?"

She watched Evan swallow. "Yes."

Frankie studied them, looking for any sign of doubt. "What's your color?"

A soft sigh left them. "All the way green, Daddy."

"Good." Grasping their hand gently in hers, Frankie placed it carefully on her hip. Her skin melted under the warmth of their touch. "I'm green too. And I want you to touch me."

Under the dim glow of the bedside lamp, Evan's gaze sparkled. They closed the small gap between them, lips meeting Frankie's in a sweet kiss. Being with Evan like this, it was easier to set aside her earlier fear. Simpler to focus on the increasing pressure of her mouth on theirs, parting for the sensuous glide of Evan's tongue along hers. She breathed them in, shoulders relaxing when the typical woodsy scent of their body wash engulfed her and not the illusion from earlier. Intertwining Evan's fingers, her free hand slid theirs above them on the pillow so it was out of the way. And then she was touching them too, skimming her hand up and down Evan's thigh and over their tight ass. She palmed the skin there, giving it a gentle squeeze and relishing Evan's muffled moan. They followed Frankie's silent direction, their smaller hand inching bravely to her backside. They gripped one of her cheeks, and Frankie broke the kiss, a soft gasp escaping. Her back arched instinctually, her breasts pushing into Evan, and her nipple piercings jutting against their chest.

"Little thief," she said, breathless. Frankie kissed them again before placing her hand on the back of Evan's head and guiding them lower, toward her breasts. Her body felt like it was alight with flames, heat scorching everywhere Evan touched her. Her breasts were heavy with need, and the arousal trickling down her thighs was something Frankie thought impossible without being accompanied by pain.

"I love you." She bit her lip, watching with hooded eyes as Evan tongued her nipples. Pleasure shot through her, making them tighten further with the attention. She'd known her breasts were sensitive, but nothing like— "Mmm, fuck baby. That's it, suck them, bite them."

It was safer positioned on their sides like this. The only thing Evan was in control of was her pleasure, and even then, it was because Frankie allowed it. She still had one hand locked in hers above the pillow, so she could succumb to the sensation without losing track of where her sub was putting what. When their hand stopped squeezing her ass and began kneading her breast instead, Frankie moaned her appreciation. Desire pooled low in her belly. Her clit throbbed for Evan's tongue, and when one of her feet slid up the bed to prop her legs open, she grabbed Evan's wrist.

Their lust-filled gaze met hers. "Color?"

Frankie took a deep breath, let it out, and slowly guided their hand toward her pussy. "Green, my good boi."

Evan touched her with reverence, as if they were afraid she'd break, their careful fingers grazing her trimmed mound first, like they were gathering courage to go further. Frankie dipped her face to theirs, finding their lips and kissing them long and sweet. She nipped their bottom lip, her hand pressing their fingers closer to her soaked center. "Touch me, please."

Evan's eyes fluttered shut, their forehead resting against Frankie's chin. "I-I'm afraid to hurt you."

"You won't; just ... just don't try to change our positions."

Their eyes blinked open, acceptance settled in their gaze. As their lips met once more, Evan deepened the kiss, their fingers swiping upwards through Frankie's slick folds. It was a startling, intrusive sensation at first, but then Evan's fingers found her clit. Frankie moaned, illicit pleasure skirting along her nerve endings.

"More," she demanded, guiding Evan's face back to her breasts. As they swirled their tongue around the hoop piercings and suckled her nipples, Evan's fingers drew lazy circles over Frankie's clit. Her need swelled with each stroke and wet glide of her thief's tongue, but so did her apprehension. The longer it took to build her climax, the more out of her head she became. It was too quiet in the room, her thoughts too loud.

"Tell me again who you belong to," she panted, grinding her pelvis against Evan's fingers.

Evan's swollen lips popped off her nipple. "You, Daddy. I belong to you, always."

"That's right, my good boi. Now fuck me with those talented fingers."

Frankie sucked in a sharp breath when Evan finally penetrated her. She stilled, half expecting her panic to resurface, but the delicious feel of their fingers pumping into her slick pussy was it. God, Evan inside her was euphoric. Frankie grabbed their chin, scattering kisses along their jaw before dropping her forehead against Evan's shoulder. A ragged sigh left her. The precipice was close, she could feel it. "Faster. Fuck me *harder*."

Evan adding another finger pulled a guttural whine from Frankie's lips. Their thrusts quickened, pumping hard in and out of her pussy with their thumb scraping her clit each time.

"Yes, that's it. I'm coming, baby ... oooh ... oooh, fuuuck." Frankie threw her head back, crying out as an orgasm overcame her. Waves and waves of mindless pleasure rippled through her core, stealing her breath. She moaned, quaking with aftershocks as Evan wrung out every last bit of orgasm.

"That was fucking beautiful," Evan said, scattering kisses along Frankie's damp throat and chin, their fingers still locked inside her. "Thank you, Frankie."

She nodded, her breath still deep and unsteady. Frankie swallowed, her movements jerky as she pulled Evan into a lingering kiss. Her lips left theirs to wander, stopping just at the pulse point along their throat. It was comforting to know Evan's pulse was as erratic as hers was right then. She nuzzled them, whispering, "I'm yours too, you know that, right? I belong to you, just like you belong to me."

She felt Evan gulp, felt their fingers ease out of her. "I-I know, but hearing it out loud makes it so much more special."

"I love you, Evan."

Evan's palm cupped Frankie's cheeks, guiding her face up to theirs. Happy tears clung to their long eyelashes. The sheer amount of love in that captivating, mismatched gaze was almost overwhelming to Frankie. They pressed a salty, wet kiss to her lips. "I love you, more than I ever thought possible. Merry Christmas, Daddy."

Thank you for reading *For The Price*! If you loved Frankie and Evan's story, please consider leaving a rating and/or review. Reviews are the lifeblood of indie authors, and leaving one can really boost ones chances of getting their books in front of other readers. Even a single sentence is a significant help.

Want more Frankie and Evan? Get a free bonus chapter when you sign up for my newsletter . I send my newsletters out once a month, and, when not sharing updates about my own book, I often share what books I'm reading or my current DIY project.

Again, thank you for supporting an indie author like me!

Acknowledgements

This book took so much planning and research (I joke to my wife that the research gets more challenging with each story). This time around, it included a very enlightening tour of a microbrewery, Google, and a few very patient men on the other end of an IM or phone call who helped me dodge a few bullets along the way. I'd like to give a shout out to Adrian, Jeffery, and Eric for being so awesome in answering my never-ending questions about "hypothetical sabotage and other crimes". Hehe.

Early in the WIP, when Evan informed me of their They/Them pronouns, I think I might have had a mini panic attack. I've never come across a sapphic BDSM romance with a non-binary submissive butch lesbian before. My imposter syndrome beckons me often, and I worried there were a hundred other authors who could write Evan better than I could. So, I did what I do best. Research. And more research. And I asked A LOT of questions in our sapphic community, put feelers out, and found a few incredible sensitivity readers to help make sure I wrote respectfully. So, a special thanks goes to Emily, Vesper, and Chloe. I couldn't possibly thank you enough.

A special thanks also goes to Katie! Thank you for shedding light on your personal experience with dyslexia. It really helped in understanding Evan's character.

And to my regular crew of beta readers, thank you for sticking with this story and with me, even when I disappeared at times. Sarah, Amber, Dianna, Lisa, Rebecca, you guys are the best!

I'd also like to thank my wife and kids. Thank you for hanging in and hanging on. I love you all more than words can say.

Finally, thank YOU, the reader. I appreciate you picking this book up, and taking a chance on Frankie and Evan. I hope you loved them as much as I do!

Until next time,

Jen-Lea

About the Author

Hiya, nice to meet you!

One thing you should know about me is I'm a huge, socially awkward book nerd who needs to ship characters or I get bored. I'm a lover of all types of sapphic romance and have a weakness for dominating ice queens and slightly unhinged fictional women. Buuut I also have a sweet, romantic side and can swoon over small-town gals, so long as in whatever I'm reading the spice is medium to red-hot!

Interests that don't include reading, writing, or daydreaming about future WIPs include: plenty of coffee, mood-music listening on Spotify, binge-watching episodes of my favorite shows (currently it's *The Rookie* and *Arcane)*, and home renos.

I live in Eastern Canada with my wife and kids but hold an unfathomable adoration for Vancouver.

As the maid of honor, all Tess Moore wants is to give her sister the wedding of her dreams. Even if it means stepping out of her comfort zone and organizing a pre-wedding bridal party adventure. To make matters worse, the woman whose heart she shattered years ago will be participating. A woman she's never been able to forget.

After what happened between them, two weeks in proximity to Tess should be hell for Abi. Instead, she deems it one last chance to show Tess the woman she's become.

Will Tess be able to relax her role as the responsible sister long enough to notice? Or will Abi forever be seen as the kid with a silly crush?

HOW ABOUT COY AND SAWYER'S STORY?

**Aloof ice queen with secrets? Check. Legendary playgirl?
Check. When it comes to love, all bets are off.**
Recently widowed, the last thing Sawyer Lavoie wants is to be
dragged out for a night of dancing. And she especially doesn't
want to be hit on by a twentysomething, cocky lesbian over-
achiever. Not because she's mourning her late husband, but
because Sawyer has zero interest in entertaining women her
daughter's age.

McCoy 'Coy' Miller can charm her way into almost any
woman's bed. As a certified playgirl, she's convinced the chase is
sweeter than the capture. When she first meets the smokey-eyed
beauty and her foolproof pickup lines crash and burn, Sawyer
quickly becomes Coy's biggest chase yet.

When a flat tire brings them together again, Sawyer can't decide if it's luck or misfortune, but learns that McCoy's mechanical skills are—reluctantly—exactly what she's been looking for.
As they become closer, Coy's ready smile and kind eyes threaten to destroy every defense Sawyer has built. Can she thaw long enough to let McCoy in, or will they forever be at an impasse?

COMING SOON

<u>For The Win</u> (Sloane's story)
Featuring:
Forced Proximity
Opposites Attract
Mental Health Rep
Second Chance
Friends to Rivals to Lovers

PLAYLIST

You can find the full playlist on my Spotify

Little Girl Gone – CHINCHILLA
FERAL – Xana
Destiny – NF
See You Bleed – Ramsey
What If I Told You – Daya
Not For Me – Sarah Proctor
CHIHIRO – Billie Eilish
Mansion – NF, Fleurie
greedy – Tate McRae
you should see me in a crown – Billie Eilish
why me – SkyDxddy
Forbidden Fruit – Tommee Profitt, Sam Tinnesz, brooke
In the End – Linkin Park
Where the Dark Things Are – Kerli
I Am Here – P!nk
Manipulate – mxze, Clarei
eyes don't lie – Isabel LaRosa
Beautiful Pain – Eminem, Sia
Fall in Love – 76th Street

Desire – MEG MYERS
Oxytocin – Billie Eilish
Beautiful Things – Brynn Elliott
The Summoning – Sleep Token
Not All Men – Morgan St. Jean
Daddy – Ramsey
The Lipstick Lounge – 76th Street
Power Over Me – Dermot Kennedy
A Heart Is A House For Love – The 5 Heartbeats
Give You What You Like – Avril Lavigne
Woman – Emmit Fenn
The Heart Wants What It Wants – Selena Gomez
Kill for You – Zolita
Like You Do – Ramsey
Focus – Elvis Drew
If I Try to Find You – KiNG MALA
hostage – Billie Eilish
Ghost – Noah Cyrus
I Found – Amber Run
Heavy – POWERS
Alibi – Sevdaliza, Pabllo Vittar, Yseult
Free – Rumi, Jinu, EJAE, Andrew Choi
Playmate – Olive B
Tattoo – Loreen
Love Me Like You Do – Ellie Goulding
Drive – Melissa Ferrick
she calls me daddy – KiNG MALA
She's My Religion – Pale Waves
Dangerously In Love – Destiny's Child
Wicked Game – Daisy Gray

Only Love Can Hurt Like This – Paloma Faith
Holy – King Princess
PILLOWTALK – ZAYN
Hey Daddy – USHER
Cut You Off – CHINCHILLA
Oil & Water – PVRIS
I Would Die For You – Jann Arden
Chosen Family – Rina Sawayama, Elton John
Close – Nick Jonas, Tove Lo
My Forever Love – Faye Peraya, Yoko Apasra